Death in Sight

SR GARRAE

This is a work of fiction. All the characters and events described in this book are fictional, and any resemblance to real events or persons living or dead is entirely coincidental.

DEDICATION

To my family and everyone who has supported my writing.

CONTENTS

ACKNOWLEDGEMENTS

Dani, for her total support since the very beginning of the first Casey & Carval novel, and for reading and commenting, Joan for reading, commenting and correcting my English to American. The writers' group, for encouragement and help, cheering up and endless support.
And finally, although the cover photo is my own, the art and retouching were done by Alana Dill, for which I thank her.

CHAPTER ONE

Morningside Park glistened with fresh snow, the sun shone, and frost sparkled on the bare tree branches, reflecting in the small pond. Jamie Carval, celebrated reality photographer, wealthy darling of the cultural elite and sometime playboy, admired the New York winter, and took more shots.

Except for the corpse centred in his viewfinder, it was a beautiful morning.

Carval didn't go in for the beauties of nature. His interest was the team of mismatched cops surrounding the body: the heart of his next blockbuster exhibition, eclipsing his previous sensational success: *New York's Ugly Underbelly*. He'd stumbled on them by accident while looking for inspiration, five months earlier, and worked his way into following them around.

He focused his next shot on the four cops, capturing their depth of purpose, united by death. His detectives, his current obsession: each as driven by murder as he was by photography. Their latest case lay at their feet: dressed in winter running gear, lean, African-American, medium height. He was the epitome of a fit, healthy young man – if he hadn't been shot and died on a pile of bloodstained crystalline snow in Morningside Park, far too early for Carval's comfort. He picked up his go-cup and swallowed a slug of mercifully hot coffee, then wandered up to them, shooting one-handed all the way. In the middle, always at the heart of the team, stood their leader, his lover: small, dark, intense Casey Clement. Around her were her team of misfits: the massive bulk of her gigantic partner, O'Leary; burly, fit Tyler; slim, delicate Andy; but Casey was the darling of his camera: his centrepiece, his focal point.

"I'm cold," Andy complained, muffled up in scarf, hat and gloves.

"Not as cold as he is," O'Leary pointed out: cop black humour on full display.

"A little respect for the victim?" Casey shivered, wrapped in a heavy winter coat, toes in flat boots which left her even shorter than usual against O'Leary's bulk. Carval shot her cool face: brown eyes chilly, tendrils of dark curly hair escaping from her clip. She didn't look up as he approached: she never did when a murder had to be solved.

"That would be appreciated." Medical Examiner McDonald's snippy tones were almost as biting as the thin January wind. "Your victim was shot from behind, from a distance, and, although the shot may have killed him, I cannot confirm that. Nor can I confirm the calibre of the bullet until I can extract it. If he did not die instantly, the shot would have incapacitated him, in which case he may have suffocated in the snow. I cannot confirm that until the autopsy is completed." His stork-like form exuded irritation, which was McDonald's natural state of being. He disliked the whole of humanity, and those who had met him disliked him right back. Corpses suited him just fine; living people, not so much.

"Time of death?"

"I cannot be precise, as you well know, Detective Clement" – Casey winced – "until I have returned to the morgue. However, my initial estimate is between four and seven this morning."

"Who found him?"

"Woman there, with the uniforms," Andy said.

"I'll go talk to her," Casey decided.

Carval snapped her looking the long way up to O'Leary's six-ten of massive muscle, topped with a buzz cut that was even more intimidating than his size. It took a while for anyone to notice that his light blue eyes were down-home friendly, and longer to realise that his yokel drawl was deliberately designed to hide a sharp mind.

"She looks scared enough, Bigfoot. Andy, you don't frighten people. C'mon."

She and Andy picked their way over the snow to the officer and a flustered, upset, elderly woman. "Hello. I'm Detective Clement, and this is Detective Chee. I understand you discovered the body?" The woman nodded. "Could you tell us how?"

"I walk here every morning to calm down before I start work. I was walking past the lake and saw a heap, and I was annoyed because I thought someone had just dumped some trash. But when I got closer I saw it was a man...."

"What did you do?" Andy asked.

"He wasn't moving and I knelt down right next to him and his face was in the snow so I dialled 9-1-1 because he couldn't have been alive and I knew you shouldn't move a body..."

"You were absolutely right," Casey reassured. The woman relaxed

2

slightly. "Was anyone else around?"

"Well, there were a few other people walking across the park, but I don't remember anyone near to me or to...to him." Her voice trembled.

"Anyone standing still, or near the body?" Casey knew that was a long shot.

"I don't remember. I don't think so."

"Okay, thank you. Is there anything else you can think of?"

"No."

"Could you leave us your details, please? If you remember anything else, here's my card. Just call me. It doesn't matter how small it is, or if you think it's irrelevant. Anything can be important, so tell us."

"Sure."

Casey left the woman with the officer, and returned to the group. McDonald was still prodding at the corpse, with Carval – of course – taking photos, a large go-cup in his other hand. She surveyed him from under dark lashes. Tall – taller than everyone except O'Leary – broad, blue eyes, tousled brown hair. Darling of the cultural elite; reality photographer par excellence. It was the one thing she'd change, if only she could: but he was as obsessed by photos as she was by murder; the main reason that she still held him at a distance. Photographs were not her favourite thing, ever since her experience at the Academy.

"Do we have an ID?" she asked.

"Waiting for McDonald to finish," Tyler said tersely.

"Okay. You're the gym nut, anything from his clothes?" she queried.

"Good stuff. Serious runner – or a wannabe pretending, but he's fit. High end shoes. Serious," he repeated.

If Tyler said that the corpse had been serious about running, Casey could take that to the bank. Tyler didn't have religion: he had the gym. His burly black form was sculpted, which was one reason he was – they thought – still dating Allie, the music major and model from their previous, nasty, modelling case. The attraction of complete opposites.

"Iffen he was out here runnin' when it was below thirty degrees," O'Leary rumbled, "then he's crazy, not serious."

"How'd you know? Bigfoots don't run."

"Naw. We lift weights, an' spar. An' I beat you ev'ry time, so I guess it works."

"Don't."

O'Leary merely grinned. He won nine times out of ten. The tenth time he'd probably been sick.

"If you two are done squabbling?" Casey recalled them to the job. "What have we got?"

"Proper shoes, proper gear. No logos, no club name, but CSU'll look for the brands. Might be on a t-shirt underneath."

"I have finished for now, until he thaws," McDonald intervened. "I assume you will search the victim before I convey him to the morgue?"

"Yes. Thank you," Casey said.

Andy had already pulled on his nitrile gloves. "Let's see," he murmured.

Unnoticed, Carval moved in, taking close-ups of the slim, small hands; delicately searching the cold-weather gear: as precise as McDonald had been. Some of those shots would go into his smaller exhibition: *Hands*; others into the main show: *Murder on Manhattan*.

"Ah," Andy breathed, unzipping a discreet pocket. "Driver's licence and keys. Asher Washington. West 126th. Age twenty-nine."

"Good. We can run him without waiting for prints. Phone?"

"No phone. Fitbit™ on his wrist," Andy answered her.

Casey made a face. Phones were always good to have. However, with a driver's licence, they had an ID and an address, for which they also had keys.

"Okay. McDonald can take him away to work his voodoo, and we'll get back to the bullpen and run him. Tyler, is that Fitbit™ good for anything?"

"Could sync to a laptop."

"What about searching his apartment?" O'Leary asked. "'Specially if we wanna find a laptop so Tyler can check if this guy was fitter than him." Tyler scowled. O'Leary smiled angelically. Casey and Andy ignored them both.

"We'll go over there this afternoon – sooner if we can start everything. I'll call CSU when we know when we'll be there."

"Why'd he carry his licence?" Carval asked. "I mean, I get why he needed keys, but…"

The cops swapped cynical glances. Tyler answered. "ID."

"But…" Carval began.

"He was running in public while black," Tyler gritted out. "Cops shouldn't ask if there's no reason to suspect him. But they do." He bared his teeth. "Ask me, sometimes. Then they see the badge."

"Oooooppppppsssss," stretched out Andy.

"An' then they see their Captain," O'Leary said heavily. "Because we don't do that racist bullshit, an' any cop who does deserves what they get. Kent's a hardass, but he backs us every time."

"He carries ID so he doesn't get arrested. Or shot. Maybe not by a cop, but by a passing security type. Or a trigger-happy idiot. Or someone who didn't like him running faster than them, or not moving over, or just being there. Or maybe some macho asshole blocked his way and then shot him for not stopping." Casey ran down.

Carval looked sick. White, male, educated – none of that had occurred to him. "Oh," he stuttered.

"He got shot anyway, but we'll be able to rule out any cops."

"Not cops," Andy said. "Dispatch wouldn't call if it was."

"Yeah," Tyler agreed.

"Okay." Casey shivered again. "Can we get back to somewhere warm? I'm freezing." Shivering at a Manhattan murder scene wasn't Casey's first pick for things to do on a cold and frosty morning, especially not before her second cup of scalding espresso. At least she'd had her first cup before the call came in.

She turned to the CSU tech and ME McDonald. "Dr McDonald, he's all yours. Guys – give us anything you find. I'll call you when we're on our way to his apartment."

"Thanks for the job in the scorching sunshine, Casey," the tech said sardonically. "I'll give you a snowball if you don't lose the smirk."

"We'd win a snowball fight," she said. "Mobile barrier" – O'Leary squawked – "a dead-eye shot" – Tyler preened – "and a tactics master," she added, waving at Andy.

"What's your job?"

"Hiding. Preferably in a nice warm bullpen, like the one we're aiming for now."

"Not me."

"Huh?" Casey stared at Tyler.

"Sightlines. Now, before someone screws up the place."

"Okay," she agreed.

"Wanna keep Carval here."

"Me?"

"Sightlines," Tyler said again. "CSU'll process the whole area, but they won't get sightlines like I can."

"Care to explain?" Carval asked.

"McDonald said it wasn't close range. Need a clear sightline. Dark. Difficult shot. Lots of trees."

"Could you do it?" Carval prodded.

"Sure. Not many like me, though." Tyler had earned his arrogance out on the sand, back in the day.

"No. Hm. Gun clubs?" Casey thought aloud.

"Not till after I've checked the sightlines."

"I'm gone, then. I'm an icicle."

"Me too," Andy agreed.

"I'm an iceberg," O'Leary grinned as they left.

Tyler turned to the CSU techs. "Need to work it out. Tell you where to process after that."

"Okay."

Tyler beckoned Carval's well-wrapped up form towards him.

"You got here early," Tyler said.

"Coffee." Carval downed another third of the go-cup's Americano, to force a non-camera-related neuron or two to function.

"Same as Casey. Can't move without caffeine."

"It's too early."

"Same as she says."

"She does? I thought she started the day before it's even begun?" Tyler looked as if he wished he hadn't opened the subject. "Is this another thing you don't talk about because it's her business to talk when – if – she wants to?"

"Yep. Team don't chatter."

Carval knew that: he just didn't like it. "Sightlines," he said, rather than start a pointless argument. "I guess you want to work out where the shooter was standing."

"Yep. Victim here. Face down, shot in the back of the head, medium range."

The two men looked back along the route that the shot might have taken, and then looked speculatively at each other.

"If I wanted a medium range shot," Carval said, "I'd stand over there." He gestured to a clump of bare trees a hundred yards or so away, icicles dripping from the twiggy branches.

Tyler's sniper's gaze approved. "Yep. Let's go look. Not too close. Be really careful. Don't go past me."

"How good's a hundred yards?"

"Poor – with good light and a stationary target. Runner before dawn – pretty good."

"But you could have done it."

"Yep. Ten times the range, ten times over" –

There was a sharp bang as a vehicle backfired in the distance. Tyler froze, and for an instant his eyes saw a different scene. He shook himself, and recovered.

"Are" – Carval stopped. No chatter, no stories, and especially no questions. He put two and two together and clamped his mouth shut. Sniper, Iraq, momentary stillness – it equalled flashback, and Tyler wouldn't say a word unless he wanted to.

"Ten times over?" he said instead. "What could you do in good conditions?"

"Thousand yards, in combat conditions. More on a range."

"Wow. Telephoto lens time."

"Much the same." Tyler started towards the trees. "Beer later. 'Cause you're not asking."

Carval followed, camera up, shooting Tyler's straight spine against the bare bones of the icy trees. He stopped a few feet short of the trunks. Beneath them, the snow was untouched, except for some footprints and a dent.

6

"Smallish. Could be a man or a woman. CSU can work out the size, height, all that." He held out an arm, and sighted along it.

"How about I shoot?" Carval said. "It'll be easier to use the shots than your memory."

"'Kay. Straight line to where the victim fell."

"Don't insult me," Carval said easily. "I didn't suggest you'd miss, did I?"

"Guess not. Shots, then clear CSU."

"Can we go somewhere warm? My feet have frostbite."

"Precinct."

Carval took his shots, and they left CSU to freeze their toes in scientific solitude.

***

Back in the bullpen, after she had defrosted, assisted by scalding coffee, Casey had stopped shivering and Tyler and Carval had rejoined the party.

"Okay. Andy and Tyler, you run him. O'Leary and I'll search his apartment."

"If McDonald won't let me shoot the autopsy, can I come too?" Carval asked. "I haven't shot a search of an apartment yet."

"Uh…I guess so, but you can't make it identifiable. Like witnesses."

"Okay," Carval said reluctantly. "I'll come, and call McDonald on the way." He scooted after them to O'Leary's massive SUV and tucked himself into the back seat. Casey had pinched shotgun without giving him a chance to think about it.

"CSU," she said to the air, called them, and briskly gave them Asher's address.

"If he could afford a Manhattan apartment, he had a good job," Carval suggested.

"Sure did."

Casey didn't comment. Her cosy apartment had come from the horror of her mother's death: the brain cancer that had resulted in a road traffic accident. She liked to believe it had been an accident. The life insurance company had agreed, and paid out.

"Or a trust fund baby," she said sceptically. In the back, she could hear Carval muttering to the morgue staff: not getting the answers he wanted. Growls of *not for two days?* floated forwards.

"Why does it take so long?" he complained. "I wanna shoot this autopsy so I've got a story line. McDonald says I can." Casey squeaked with surprise. "Told you he liked me," Carval added smugly. "But they won't even start till Thursday."

"Welcome to Manhattan," O'Leary boomed cheerfully, "where there's as many murders as taxis."

"There's a queue," Casey noted. "First dead, first chopped. Just get them to call you when they're nearly at Asher."

O'Leary pulled up. "Got the keys?"

"Yep." Casey clinked them.

"Let's go search."

*****

"Only one flight up? Wow."

"Yeah, but I bet it's noisy."

"We should tell Andy 'bout this one. Or your Allan guy. On-tap culture from the theatre around the corner," O'Leary said to Carval.

"Allan's got his own place. God knows I pay him enough to live at the Ritz if he wanted."

"Allan? Your manager?" Casey asked.

Carval and O'Leary exhibited equivalent stunned-ox faces at her ignorance.

"Yeah, my manager," Carval said. "He keeps my life organised."

"I guess you'd need to pay him a fortune," Casey teased. Carval scowled. "He's probably gone grey and gotten wrinkles keeping you in order."

"Not exactly," Carval said, thinking of Allan's neat attire, unsilvered hair and lack of noticeable wrinkles.

"How've you not met him iffen you've been hanging around with Carval all this time?"

Casey coloured slightly, and O'Leary grinned knowingly. "Like that, huh? I guess other folks weren't wanted."

"Are we searching, or are you going to quit the force and go be a gossip columnist?"

O'Leary laughed as Carval smirked over Casey's irritated head. "Open up, then. You got the keys."

Carval stayed back, already shooting as Casey and O'Leary knocked, identified themselves in regulation fashion, and then opened up with Asher's keys, guns drawn: the contrast of their relative sizes set in counterpoint to their almost-identical expressions and attitude. Not here the prowling menace of hunting down a suspect, but a cooler, wary, focus. Stalking.

O'Leary entered first, as nothing short of a machine gun would hurt the mobile mountain; Casey was more fragile – physically. Mentally, she was tougher than any of the men.

"Clear," Casey said.

"Clear," O'Leary confirmed, checking out the single bedroom. "It don't look like he's livin' in the lap of luxury."

"What, no caves? No hay and furs to sleep in?"

"'Zackly so," Bigfoot drawled. "Iffen it don't have no hay an' furs, it ain't luxurious for Bigfoots."

"It's still really nice for a twenty-nine-year-old. How'd he afford this? I want his financials," Casey grumbled.

Carval entered, and began to shoot the plain furnishings, the few ornaments and pictures; the neat bedroom with a suit, shirt and tie waiting on the monochrome bedcover. Casey and O'Leary had started at opposite ends of the small kitchen/living room.

"Phone!" Casey said triumphantly, pulling it from between the couch cushions and slipping it into an evidence bag.

"Ain't you gonna open it?" O'Leary wheedled. "It's a neat trick you pull with the standard passcode."

"No. I'm leaving this one for CSU. Looking at that suit and tie, I'm guessing he was a lawyer, or finance" –

"Reachin', ain't you? We don't know nuthin' yet."

"Most likely, but if he is, the phone'll be locked down, and if I mess with it, we'll never get anything."

"Guess so. Anythin' in particular we're lookin' for?"

"No, just getting a feel for the guy. Pretty neat and tidy – look, he's even got his breakfast ready to go."

"Nearly as neat as you. Not quite, though. He's left two pieces of paper on his table, an' his cushions ain't squared off."

"Says the man who's finding coal in the strata of his desk."

"Need it for my Bigfoot cave."

"Your desk needs to be cleared with a flamethrower. How you find anything…"

"Speakin' of findin' thin's – an' not about my desk – here's his laptop." O'Leary's sausage fingers flickered. "An' my oh my, it's not screen locked – holy shit, Casey! Come'n look at *this*."

"What?"

"Our boy Asher had a feed from some body camera thin' to his Instagram. Neat. But look, the last transmission was at 5.35 a.m., January 31, 2017. The man musta been crazy. That'll be time of death, near enough."

"Wow." She smiled nastily. "Wait till we tell McDonald that – hang on a moment. There wasn't a camera anywhere near the body." Carval snapped their assessing gazes.

"Murderer coulda took it."

"Hmmm. Why bother?"

"Mebbe not the killer. Good for a few dollars for a hit. Any druggie lookin' for easy cash."

"Yeah."

"Anything else int'restin'?"

Rapping at the door announced CSU, bedecked with all their gear.

Carval's eyes lit up at the sight – another new facet of police work for his exhibition. As they set up their equipment, he began to set up his shots.

"Who's this?" the techs asked.

"I'm Jamie Carval."

They looked blankly at Casey. "He's shooting us – and nearly everyone else in the Thirty-Sixth – for an exhibition. If you don't want to be photographed, tell him now, otherwise you'll be in hundreds of shots."

"I'm gonna be famous," O'Leary said comfortably. "You could be, too."

The techs' eyes lit up. "Recognition?" one said. "We *never* get recognised. I'm in."

"Me too," agreed the other. "The guys back at base will be sick they missed this one."

"And I'll be sick if you guys don't get started," Casey pointed out, "so how about it, hm? We tagged and bagged his phone – here – for you guys to open, too."

"Okay, okay. Slave-driver."

CSU began their work. Carval prowled around behind them, never getting in the way, but shooting everything.

"We're done," Casey said, a little later. He didn't react. "Carval!" she rapped. "We're done. We're going back to the bullpen."

"'Kay," he said absently. "I'm staying till I've got enough shots of CSU." He didn't look around, lost in the angles and lighting, the careful movements, the powdery dust revealing a mass of fingerprints, the UV light shining around the walls and floor in case there were bloodstains. It was fascinating. He missed Casey's farewell and O'Leary's rumble. He didn't stop shooting until CSU were done, hours later, and then he went straight home to download, consumed by these new aspects of murder.

CHAPTER TWO

"He's a bit obsessed, ain't he? Didn't even say bye-bye. Don't he love us no more?" O'Leary lamented, as they departed from Asher's apartment.

Casey shrugged. "Camera. That's his world."

"That okay with you?"

"Yep." She didn't invite further conversation, especially with O'Leary, the world's largest Cupid.

"Anyways, I didn't want to talk about your boyfriend. How's your dad doin'?"

She thought back to her father's desk appearance, scant weeks ago. Presciently, she'd taken leave for the whole day: trying not to wince at the pity on Captain Kent's face as she haltingly requested permission. Thankfully, his approval had been given as tersely as ever.

She'd collected her father from his small apartment in Brooklyn, more relieved than she should have been that he'd been sober, or able to pretend sufficiently well that she couldn't tell otherwise.

"Dad, are you ready?" she'd fretted.

"Yes, Catkin. You've asked me that twice already."

She had. Even though he'd been in rehab for a month by then, attending AA every second day, and, she thought and hoped, still sober now, her nerves had been getting the better of her. She had supposed, bitterly, that it wasn't every day that a cop took her dad to the courthouse.

"Carla Jankel will meet us there. You won't need to say anything. She'll say it all. You're pleading not guilty, aren't you?"

"I didn't do anything. I don't remember anything." No, he didn't. He'd drunk so much he'd lost his memory – again.

Casey had been sure that he wouldn't plead guilty, even though she had known that he was. Save it for the trial, she'd thought, and save the inevitable argument and desolation for after that. At least he was attending rehab, she'd mused; and allowed herself to hope. Still, she hadn't asked to see his sobriety tokens, and he hadn't shown her them. Surely by then he should have had a thirty-day chip? She had tried not to think about the implications, and attended the desk appearance with him. Always supporting him: after all, he was trying, and how could she not support his efforts? She'd felt – still did feel – guilty for her acid, angry words, even if they'd goaded him into rehab. She simply hoped that her support now would make up for her bitterness then.

Her father had been visibly shocked at the process: one small, frightened, somehow old man in a mass of lowlifes and criminals. *Other* criminals. In his smart, professional suit and tie, he stood out; his confusion written large on his face. Casey had found Jankel, and together they'd steered him into the courtroom. The judge had barely looked at him: blunt, brusque, unsympathetic. His professional appearance had counted for nothing. Plea entered; he'd been dismissed. The judge was starting on the next man before they'd left the room. It had taken less than five minutes, and her father had been left reeling.

She hadn't left her dad alone afterwards. She had told herself it was support, and ignored the voice reminding her that it had been because she was terrified that if she didn't stay, he'd keep company with the whiskey bottle.

Now, the next hearing was approaching.

"Still going to rehab," she said. "Meetings three times a week. He's trying." If only she really trusted him; if only she really believed in his redemption.

O'Leary cast her a piercing glance, and asked nothing further. The team never pried. "Okay," he offered, and she understood that he'd be there if she needed him.

***

"What do we have?" Casey asked, as soon as she entered the bullpen.

"More than usual," Andy said happily. "We ran him, but nothing popped. Doesn't even own a car."

"So how've you got more than usual?"

"The joys of social media and the power of the internet."

"Technogeek," she teased affectionately.

"Yep. And look how it paid off."

"Wow." She turned smugly to O'Leary. "Told you so."

There in front of Casey was Asher's employer – Schickoff & Schultz, a mid-to-large law firm in Midtown – his running habits, his friends, his girlfriend – "A passive-aggressive comment about being ghosted?"

"Guess it's a really recent break-up."

His hobbies were there – all related to fitness and running – and a series of complaints about his ankles and knees and how he'd have to see a physical therapist.

"Who's next of kin?" Casey asked.

"Aunt and uncle."

"No parents?"

"Little Orphan Asher," Andy flipped, and then turned serious at Casey's glare. "No. His parents died fourteen years back – accident on the freeway."

"Have we got financials?"

"Give me a chance. It's been less than eight hours. No. And we don't have phone records yet either, before you ask for the next impossible item."

Casey grimaced. She knew they couldn't possibly have any of that yet. She wanted the autopsy results too, but she wouldn't have those for a day or two. A humph joined the grimace.

"What was that, Clement?"

Ooops. Captain Kent had been passing by at precisely the wrong moment, and his heavy, square-faced form was, as usual, stern. He ran his precinct with iron discipline, and the team tried never to come to his attention. Too frequently for their taste, they failed.

"Our new case, sir – we were called this morning."

"Yes?"

"A runner. Asher Washington. Shot from medium range."

Kent flicked an unobtrusive glance at Tyler. The bald description sounded like a case which might push the buttons of his ex-sniper – not that Tyler knew that Kent knew his history. Kent had made a point of investigating the histories of each of his top team, and consequently knew far more about them than would have made them comfortable. Tyler, although he had passed psychological clearance, had a tendency to react badly to sudden, sharp bangs. Kent resolved to keep a watchful eye on the team, without impeding their exceptional solve rate.

"And? Surely you're proceeding in your normal efficient fashion?"

"Yes, sir." His face demanded a better explanation. "I wish we had more information."

"We all wish that, Clement. However, it's unlikely to be achieved in" – he consulted his watch – "less than eight hours. Moderate your expectations, and work with what you already have, rather than whining that you don't have more."

Casey squirmed. "Yes, sir."

Kent departed, to general relief.

"Okay, that's us told," she said, and shook off the rebuke. "Let's see. We've got club, physical therapist, next of kin – oh, I forgot!"

"You? Forgot something? Casey-the-far-too-organised?" Andy faked a swoon, and was restored to vertical by O'Leary's ham-hand.

"Asher had a laptop, and it wasn't screen-locked."

13

"Wow. Not good security."

"No, but it was open to his Instagram and something had been transmitting running data and a photo every few minutes."

"I got that too, from the social media," Andy said. "We've got a much better time of death – or time of falling flat on his face – than McDonald can give us."

"Not that the photos were much use, seein' as it was dark," O'Leary added.

"There was enough to tell the difference between when he was running and when he fell, though," Casey noted.

"Yeah," Andy agreed. "Transmission stopped at 5.35 a.m."

"Runnin' at 5.35 a.m.," O'Leary marvelled again. "He was crazy. Even Tyler don't do gym then."

"Fitbit™?" Tyler said, ignoring O'Leary, probably because Tyler *did* do gym then. "Sync up. Had one."

"Or some kind of camera."

Tyler considered the options. "GoPro™. Ask Carval, but GoPro™'s my bet, with time lapse shots."

"Casey's boy," O'Leary said mischievously, receiving a scorching glare, "stayed to shoot CSU processin' Asher's apartment. Hope they like it."

"Will he come back?" Tyler asked.

"Guess not. CSU'll take time. Why?"

"Wanted to see the sightline shots. It'll wait." Tyler shrugged.

"Let's get a plan together," Casey suggested. "Andy, sounds like you've already requested phone and financial records?"

"Yep," he confirmed.

"Okay. Employer, next of kin, and physical therapist. O'Leary and I'll take next of kin and employer, this afternoon and first thing tomorrow. Tyler, you and Andy take the PT." She grinned. "All that tai-chi at six a.m. is bad for your joints, Andy, and Tyler's never out of the gym so he could use one too."

Both men muttered at her. She smiled sweetly back at them.

"The autopsy won't be ready for at least two days – three for the report, records won't be here before late tomorrow at best. Okay. What about CSU's report on the scene and apartment – and have they cracked his phone yet?"

"They can't report till they're finished," Andy pointed out. "They'll still be on scene. Let's go start these interviews."

"Okay."

Andy and Tyler disappeared in one direction, and Casey and O'Leary took his massive SUV out to Garden City to break the news to Asher's aunt and uncle.

***

In his workmanlike office, Captain Kent groaned as his phone rang again. His in-tray was as high as Mt. Washington, and all he wanted was peace and solitude to deal with it. He scowled at the phone, but answered.

"Kent."

"Captain Kent. It's Captain Travers, from Narcotics in Queens."

Travers – he was Marcol's captain. Young, thrusting, and self-important. Good, but not half as good as he thought he was, which went for his teams too. Tyler's commentary on Marcol and his behaviour on the model case slipped back into Kent's acute mind.

"What can I do for you?"

"That case you had back in October, with the serial killer and the drugs link."

"Yes?"

"I'd like to dig a bit deeper. I guess you were only interested in the homicides, but I'd like to follow up anything more for Narcotics."

"Mm?" Kent's stomach curdled. He'd hoped that this discussion would never happen.

"Yeah. Can I send one of my guys over to talk it through – Marcol? He'd be happy to liaise with your Detective Clement, and he was involved with the original case, so he's further up the curve than anyone else."

"Look," Kent temporised, "this is a pretty sudden request. The team's tied up on live cases, and those come first. You know how it is with 1PP and homicides. They just got called out on a fresh one, and that's them out of the game for the next forty-eight."

"Sure," said Travers. "Okay, give me a call in a day or two."

"Thanks."

Kent put down the phone, and rapidly dialled Captain Garrett at the Third, his long-time friend. He needed to get a second opinion on his troublesome team and the even more troublesome Narcotics interference. He'd put this conversation off, thinking he'd gotten away without needing to probe any further, but Travers had nixed that.

"Garrett."

"Garrett, it's Kent. D'you remember I wanted to have a chat about Clement's history? Can we make it soon?"

"Sure." Papers rustled and Kent heard tapping on a keyboard. "I could do it tonight. I'll need a beer after the latest set of reports."

"Okay. O'Lunneys?"

"Sure. Seven. Bye."

Kent dropped the phone into its cradle and his head into his hands. He knew Narcotics' request would lead to an absolute shit storm; he just couldn't see how.

**

"Nice house," O'Leary remarked, as they pulled up at a bay-windowed, detached home in Garden City, set in a sizeable lot and sporting clean paint and an impressively columned porch.

"Yeah. Family home. I wonder if Asher lived there – and why he moved out?"

"Mebbe he wanted his own life. This looks pretty stiflin' to me."

"Says the man who wants a big house with a white picket fence and three huge dogs."

"I'd go out to New Jersey. One of them nice suburbs with room to roam." O'Leary smiled.

"I thought you'd go back above the snowline."

"Pete don't like it."

"Well, if Pete doesn't like it, you won't be going, will you?"

"Nup. Anyways, let's go see this Aunt and Uncle Washin'ton."

Casey rang the bell to the side of the blue-grey door, which was shortly opened by a grizzled older man.

"Mr Washington?" she asked, showing her badge. "I'm Detective Clement and this is my partner, Detective O'Leary." Uncle Washington blinked in shock at O'Leary's mountainous form, and then whipped his attention back to Casey as her words sank in.

"D...detectives?" he stuttered. "Uh...what...why – what's wrong?"

"I'm very sorry to tell you, sir, that your nephew, Asher, was found dead this morning. May we come in?"

"Dead? No, no! You've got it wrong. He can't be dead. He's only twenty-nine, and really healthy. He can't possibly be dead." His hands shook as he gestured them forward with, "You'd better come in," ushering them into a beautiful family room, tastefully decorated with taupe furnishings.

"Who is it, dear?" A tall, coiffured woman, a little younger than her husband, arrived.

"Sella, they say Asher's dead," he cried.

The woman regarded them, appalled. "I...no!" she gasped. Her eyes dampened. "You're wrong."

"I'm sorry, but we have positively ID'd him."

"I guess.... Really Asher? Are you sure?" Her voice broke. "I don't...it's not possible."

"I'm very sorry for your loss," Casey said.

"Please," Aunt Washington choked, "what happened to our nephew?" She sniffed, and wiped at her brimming eyes.

"He was shot, while out running."

They both stared. "Shot?" his aunt gasped.

"Someone *shot* him? Have you checked the park security? Or local cops? You hear so many tales of people claiming just because we're black we're

16

doing something wrong by existing and just shooting and never being brought to justice for it," Uncle Washington fired out.

"If it was security, or another cop, or *whoever* it is, we will do our very best to find them and make sure that they answer for it." Both Washingtons looked sceptical, but refrained from further comment.

"Could you tell us a bit about Asher," O'Leary took over, his slow drawl calming the atmosphere, "and your proper names?"

"I'm Sella Washington." She sniffed again, damply.

"And I'm Marlon." O'Leary blinked. "My mom was a big fan of Brando." O'Leary preserved a commendably straight face.

"Asher is our nephew," Marlon repeated. "His parents...their car was sideswiped by a truck on the freeway. My brother was killed instantly. His wife passed a few hours later. Asher was only fifteen. God be thanked, we were close enough to take him in and bring him up as they would have wished."

"He was lucky to have you," Casey said.

"God always provides. Sometimes it's hard, though."

The cops nodded. They usually found that God's provision was substantially misinterpreted by humans, who, far too often, took their misinterpretations too far. Casey thought bitterly of the snake-oil salesmen who'd come out of the woodwork to bother her about genetic susceptibility after her mom passed, claiming that faith and their potions would be better than a good healthcare plan. She'd been short and to the point – the point of her Glock, for preference, though she'd never *actually* drawn it.

Sella gripped Marlon's hand, eyes damp and mouth creased; he gripped back, Adam's apple bobbing, swallowing back his upset.

"His parents left him money, so we made sure Asher went to college, as they would have wanted, and then he aced his LSAT – Law School Admission Test," she clarified, as if the cops were too stupid to understand. Casey knew that: she'd once thought she might go that route, until she found she wanted to investigate crimes, not push paper – "went to law school, passed the Bar exam and got a really good job at Schickoff & Schultz. We were sad he moved out, but I guess kids grow up, don't they? He wanted to be independent."

"He didn't want to rely on us – didn't want to be a burden." Marlon gulped.

"He wasn't a burden. He was the child we never had. We did so much for him, and we were so happy to do it. Paying it forward."

"Do you know who his friends were? Or did he have a partner?"

"He had a girlfriend. Kayla, Karly...something like that. I don't think they were serious. He hardly ever brought her here." She sniffed again. "Now he never will..." Her voice broke.

"Do you remember her last name?"

"Um...Berman? Turton? Sorry," she apologised. "Asher didn't talk about her much. She just didn't seem important."

Casey made a note. "I understand," she said. "So since he moved out, he didn't tell you about his friends?"

"Not much. We didn't pry, and of course he couldn't talk about his job. Confidentiality was key, and he took it seriously."

"Of course. Was there anyone who didn't like him, or arguments at work?"

"He didn't say anything about work, but I thought he was busier than usual — he hadn't come for dinner for the last few weeks, and he complained he'd had to miss church."

Casey didn't remember Asher's social media mentioning church.

"He was renting a pretty nice apartment," she tried.

"He was so lucky to have a job with good pay and benefits."

"Hard work is rewarded," Marlon pontificated, and then his face twisted as he remembered. "He deserved better. He had all his life ahead of him and now it's gone."

"Is there anything else you can tell us?"

"No. But...I know from the TV shows there has to be an autopsy, but when can we see him? We want to lay him to rest." Sella sniffled yet more, and wiped her eyes again. Marlon patted her hand, and then twisted his fingers. "We shouldn't have to..." Tears sprang in both sets of eyes.

"We'll let you know as soon as possible," O'Leary rumbled sympathetically.

"Thank you for your time. If we need to check anything, can we come back to you?"

"Of course. We'll help however we can. Anything at all." She covered her face with a Kleenex, and blotted her eyes again.

"Thank you." Casey left them with her card.

They didn't speak until O'Leary had pulled away from the house.

"What did you think?" she asked.

O'Leary's massive form wriggled. "Nuthin' wrong — came off really upset, but...my gut's not comfy."

"Sure that wasn't your lunch? I told you not to get the food truck salmonella sandwich."

O'Leary harrumphed.

"I didn't get any weird vibe from them. Okay, family's always top of our list, but there wasn't anything off that I could see. We'll run them anyway while we go see everyone else."

"Yeah. I can't put my finger on anythin' wrong. Mebbe it's 'cause that li'l rat from the models case was such a good actor, I'm thinkin' everyone's bad. They were good Christian folks."

"Yeah. So were the Crusaders."

O'Leary guffawed. "Don't see them two pickin' up lances and chargin' on horses."

"No. Let's try to look up their church, and check on any church Asher might have gone to, too. See what their pastor thinks of them."

"Wouldn't be the first guy to move out an' stop churchgoin' as soon as his folks couldn't see."

"No. I don't think anyone's likely to murder someone for not worshipping every Sunday, though. If they did, half of New York would be dead."

"Startin' with us."

"Nope. We'd be attending every church to find the killers."

***

"Who's this PT?" Andy asked.

"Delaine Roberts. Looked up the link. Specialises in runners."

"Mm."

Tyler pulled up at an apartment block in Yonkers.

"Why're we here?"

"Her office hours stop at three."

"Weird." Andy frowned.

"Yeah." Tyler knocked. "Delaine Roberts?" A small blonde opened the door a crack and peeked around. "Detective Tyler, NYPD."

"Detective Chee, NYPD."

They displayed their badges, which she scrutinised closely. "You'd better come in."

Close up, she would have been pretty: big blue eyes, blonde bob, cute snub nose – but the black circles below her eyes and slumped exhaustion in her posture negated all of it. A loud wail suddenly rose from a crib, and Delaine Roberts winced. "Sorry. She just won't sleep."

The cops swapped panicked glances. Crying babies were totally outside their skill sets. Delaine shuffled to the crib and removed a small pink-clad lump of ear-shattering misery. How something that tiny could make that much noise was beyond the men.

"There, there. Mommy's here. Shhhh, honey. Shhhh." Delaine looked like she was about to cry herself.

Andy found a shred of non-panicked mind. "Um...I'll take it if you need a minute."

Delaine stared at him. "You will? Oh, *thank you*. I can't even go to the bathroom without her." Tyler's face said *TMI*. Delaine plopped the baby into Andy's hesitant arms and dashed out of the room. The two men regarded the screaming, red-faced infant and each other. Tyler tried an embarrassed wiggle of fingers. The baby screamed louder. Andy tucked it – the pink onesie hadn't clued him in – much closer, and to their joint

19

astonishment the screams diminished.

"Likes you. Andy the baby whisperer."

"No way."

"Quieter."

The baby was, though she could hardly be described as quiet. Andy's face resembled that of a man handed a live grenade. Tyler's had the expression of a man who'd dodged that grenade.

"Liked being held tight."

"If I hold it tighter it'll break."

"She. Not it. She," Tyler corrected.

Andy muttered, but kept the baby firmly tucked in. Gradually the screams softened into crying, and then to whimpers, and then the baby's eyes drooped and closed.

"Let's get this done fast, before she wakes up again."

A fraction of a second later, Delaine came rushing back out. "What's happened?" she gasped. "Why's she quiet? What's wrong?"

"Shh! She's fallen asleep."

Delaine fell on to the couch. "Sleeping? Oh, thank God."

"We'll talk while she's asleep," Andy said briskly. "Ms Roberts, you were treating Asher Washington."

Thought flickered. "Asher – oh, yes. Runner. Knees and ankles. Ligament issues in his ankles." Intelligence woke in her tired eyes. "Why are you here?"

"I'm sorry to tell you Asher was found dead this morning."

"Dead?" Terror painted her face. "Dead? Murdered? Bill" – she stopped.

"Mm?" Andy said. The baby was clutching his finger in her sleep, which didn't obviously please him. "Why do you say that, Ms Roberts?"

She paled further. "Uh…nothing…uh…you're here and why else would you be? I didn't mean anything. He was so angry but he'd never *hurt* anyone. I don't believe he'd do anything. He wouldn't."

Andy and Tyler exchanged interested glances over the baby's head. "Just tell us about it. If there's nothing to it, then nothing will happen. But we need to know so we can rule it out."

Delaine slumped further. "Bill…. Bill's my husband. He's in construction. He works so hard to pay for everything we need. But since little Anne arrived, it's…it's been so difficult. She cries so much and he can't get any rest and he's got to be on his game for work so he expects me to keep her quiet but she just cries and I can't settle her. I'm just such a bad mom." She took her baby from Andy as the child whimpered, and cuddled her.

"I'm sure that's not true," Andy tried. Delaine sniffed, and Andy rapidly retreated from his attempt at sympathy before she started to cry. "But what's being a bad mom got to do with Asher Washington?"

"Anne wouldn't settle a few nights ago and I asked Bill to take her just for an hour or two so I could get some sleep because I had to work, and Bill said I should be able to settle her and why couldn't I sleep in the morning? But I was treating Asher early because he had to get to work early and then Bill was really mad and said he'd have it out with Asher.... But he took Anne anyway so I could sleep and then he woke me. I don't remember when. But Asher rescheduled the next appointment, for yesterday morning, to tomorrow lunchtime, so I think Bill spoke to him."

"Mm." Andy hummed. "Do you have a gun?"

"Gun? We don't have a gun here with a baby." The baby started to scream again. Delaine looked about to join her. "I have to change her."

"We'll need to talk to Bill," Tyler said. "Where's he working?"

"We won't mention you. Don't tell him we were here. Asher used social media a lot and he's said enough that we could've found Bill from there," Andy added.

Delaine soggily provided the details. "He would never hurt anyone," she snuffled. "Never."

The cops took their leave.

"Think she's kidding herself," Tyler commented.

"Let's talk to this Bill."

"Tomorrow. Let's go catch up with Casey and Bigfoot."

CHAPTER THREE

"What've we got?" Casey was scrawling a sparse timeline on the murder board, next to a photo of Asher. "Look, it's empty."

"We got our two good Christian relatives," O'Leary began.

"Yeah. What about you two?" Casey asked Tyler and Andy.

"Andy got a baby," Tyler smirked. "Cuddled her like a pro."

"Awwwww," O'Leary cooed. "I love babies."

"Roasted, baked or boiled?" Casey snipped. "Since I don't think a baby could've shot Asher, we can rule it out. How about the parents?"

"Okay, okay. You're no fun. Mother was Asher's PT. Said he had bad ankles. Surprised she could remember that: looked like she hadn't slept for a month. Baby screamed non-stop – except when Andy had her."

"You backed off faster than lightning."

"Not my thing. PT's Delaine Roberts." Casey wrote it up on her whiteboard. "Don't think she could focus right now, but she went straight to 'it couldn't be my husband'."

"Oh?"

"He's a construction worker on site in the Bronx. First thing tomorrow, we'll go see him."

"What's his motive?"

"Sounded like he didn't like having to look after the baby so his wife could get some sleep," Andy said grimly. "She needed sleep to treat Asher early, and he was going to – quote – 'have it out' with Asher."

"Let's see if that's anywhere in his social media, first."

"Yeah. She was terrified he'd think it was her."

"D'you leave her any contacts?"

"Not yet. We'll take another swing by in a day or two, though. Following up, hm?"

Casey nodded. Andy knew what to look for, and Tyler would back him up.

"We got the next of kin. Everything was in order," Casey said, and scribbled up the names. "Beautiful house, perfect yard, churchgoing, took Asher in and they were pretty proud of him. Absolutely no reason at all to be suspicious."

"But we are."

"You are," Casey replied to O'Leary. "Whether they're good folks or not, I wanna go much deeper into their backgrounds. They must have had pretty good jobs themselves to afford that place. And, well…nobody fights worse than families."

"So we got a construction worker with anger issues an' a good Christian family. What else?" O'Leary asked.

"Financials, phone, autopsy and CSU all to come. Employer – Schickoff & Schultz – we'll take them tomorrow while Andy and Tyler take Roberts."

"Friends and girlfriend – or ex?"

"After the employer and Roberts."

"Running club first," Tyler said.

"Okay, why?"

"Gets competitive."

Three cops stared at him. Tyler's definition of *competitive* would easily apply to the Olympic men's hundred-metre final.

"How d'you mean?"

"Everyone pretending to be supportive till they get beat. Then it all goes downhill. Don't get that in my gym."

"Just in the precinct," Andy said sourly. "Not that you two would notice, since no-one dares to go near you."

"Iffen you're gettin' hassle, Tyler here c'n make you look good a time or two. Or I'll come take 'em on. No need to put up with that crap."

"I don't. Just because I'm not tall doesn't mean that they don't fall."

"Ooohhh, poetry," O'Leary gibed gently. "So why're you bitchin' if you come out on top?"

"General disposition," Casey said briskly. "Can we get back to something relevant? Tyler, how about explaining?"

"Likely the club was keen on times, improvements, competitions and suchlike. We all know guys who take getting beat hard, huh?"

The other three nodded. They surely did. One such guy, Mark Marcol, had tried to undermine Casey with one of Carval's early photos, at the Academy, and he had come back to haunt them in the modelling case. Casey hoped they'd seen him off.

"So you're thinking that one of them might take it more personally? Wow. That's taking competitive to a whole new level."

"Remember those ice-skaters? Harding and Kerrigan?"

"That was her husband," Casey said.

"Same idea. Over-competitive."

"Okay. You and O'Leary for that one. Andy and I'll find something else to do." She grinned. "Gentlemen, we have a plan."

"Who gets Carval? He'll be buzzin' around lookin' for some more shots."

Casey shrugged. "He'll decide. Maybe none of them. He can't shoot witnesses directly anyway."

"Think that'll stop him?" Tyler pointed out. "He'll promise to blur the faces and leave it at that."

"So talk about the sightlines, like you said you would."

"Okay. Sightlines first, then Roberts. Carval can tag along."

"Okay," Casey said as Tyler finished. "So *now* do we have a plan?" Everyone nodded. "Then let's make sure everything's taken as far as we can tonight, and then get some sleep."

O'Leary smirked knowingly. Casey glared, and, to her relief, he thought better of his commentary. Yes, she would call Carval. Yes, she might end up at his, or he at hers. No, it was none of Cupid-O'Leary's business. He could shove his knowing smiles up his ass.

***

Two hours later, Casey rapped on Carval's door. He hadn't expected her any earlier, and since he'd been sorting, choosing and arranging the CSU shots, forgetting Tyler's suggestion of beer, he was quite happy with her timing. He let her in, took a glance at her face, and hugged her.

"You've got that 'I want information and I want it yesterday' look," he said.

"Yeah. Why can't it be instant, like on TV?"

"They cut out all the boring bits."

"Yeah."

"C'mere, and forget it."

He knew she wouldn't. Casey never let a case go until it was done. On the other hand, since her dad had gone to rehab before Christmas, she'd opened up a little; let him in, a little; indicated that this might be more like a relationship, not just a casual friends-with-benefits arrangement. Sometimes, she even mentioned her father, though never much or for long.

She wriggled in a getting-comfortable fashion when he put his arm around her, and leaned into his wide shoulder, barely reaching it, yawning.

"Tired?" A negating hum came back. "Sure you're not. That's why you're as limp as a wet noodle and your eyes are closed. I could pick you up and you wouldn't even notice." He tugged at her hair clip, and released the riot of dark curls.

"Pick me up and I'll shoot you."

"Can't aim with your eyes closed." He grinned. "Did you get dinner?"

24

he added.

"Grabbed a sandwich. Got any coffee?"

"I always have coffee if you're coming over." He smiled at the top of her head, pushed her towards the couch, and went to make it.

"That's better," she said, after half the coffee had gone in one scalding slug. "Did you have fun with CSU?"

"They loved me," Carval said. "They let me shoot everything they did, from all angles." His expression was changing as he spoke, from smug satisfaction to focused interest. "I got some really nice effects from the fingerprint powder, and really interesting ones from the UV light scans. It'll be great. A real contrast to the interrogation rooms and you guys at the scene or on the chase. They're so placid and smooth: no urgency, even though they work really fast. You're always tense and wound tight, all of you. On the hunt. They're…well, not. They're gatherers, you're hunters." He bounced up. "That's it! That's the title for that sequence. *The Gatherers.* I already got an *On the Hunt* – when you went into the lab after Merowin the first time, with O'Leary." He found a scrap of paper and scrawled. "Back in a sec," he called, and went tumbling out down the stairs to leave it in his studio, then tumbled back and planted a smacking kiss on her lips. "I've been trying to think of a title since I got back."

"So glad I could help," Casey snipped.

"Mean."

"I don't think you'll suffer."

"Definitely mean." Carval ran a hand through her curls. "You shouldn't tease me. It's unkind."

Casey smirked at him in a way that simply invited trouble – so he provided it.

"*Stop it you miserable rat!*" she screeched. Carval laughed, and tickled her again. "That's not *fair*. I hate you," she sulked.

"No, you don't."

"Wanna bet?"

"If you hated me, you'd shoot me. And you haven't."

"Yet." But she softened, allowing him to bring her in close and smooth her hair back from her face, stroking down her cheek.

"You won't, 'cause then I couldn't do this." He dipped his head and kissed her, still not accustomed to the flare of instant desire each time he met her lips, her fiery responses. When he kissed her, nothing else mattered; when she responded, he forgot that they still rarely talked about anything other than her work. He shoved away the niggle, and kissed her harder: feeling her small hands slide to his neck; her mouth raiding. His Casey didn't react; she acted.

Here, alone, was the only time he remembered how small she was; when she dropped her work shields and with them the presence that made her seem so much bigger than the reality. Alone with him, she liked to snuggle, and be cosseted – among other things. Right now, other things were firmly on their minds, and she was ahead of the game. He smiled, swooped her into his arms, stood up, and carried her to his plain bedroom, where they could play in comfort.

"I could walk," she grumbled.

"Sure. But I like picking you up."

"Caveman."

"Yep." He stopped any more complaints by kissing her again, and again; and then she pushed him down and laughed at his surprised face. He pulled her over him, slipping hands under her navy top, and found that as he raised it his shirt had mysteriously become unbuttoned. He didn't mind. He also didn't mind her avid mouth on his, nor the swift removal of all other clothes, though he was always happy to help with that if given the chance.

Tonight, he wasn't being given the chance. Casey was in the mood to take charge. Carval simply lay back and enjoyed the experience, reciprocating when she allowed it, and finally holding her hips as she sank down on to him and took him in. After that, he didn't bother thinking until they were cleaned up and she was sprawled limply across his chest, where she really ought to be a lot more often.

"Dad's still okay," she said into his pectoral.

Since, despite appearances and general inclination, Carval was capable of picking up subtle meanings without the use of his viewfinder, he hummed encouragingly.

"If he can just stay dry..." She curled in. He petted, and tried not to think that she was hiding; that the tension in her spine was merely his imagination. "The hearing's in a few days. If he can get through that..." She slid off to one side, and tried to turn into the pillows.

Carval turned her back around. He didn't like her turning away from him. It felt second-best. *He* felt second-best, and didn't like it. If she wouldn't confide, then she could at least accept comfort. He wrapped her in, and wished he could be as casual about her as he used to be with any other woman.

"Tyler wants you with him tomorrow," she said.

Second-best flash-fried and vanished. "Me? Tyler wants *me*? Why?"

"To talk about sightlines. He says your shots'll be helpful. He wants to start early, so come to the precinct by seven-thirty. After that, you can go to an interview with him and Andy – construction worker, on site. Usual rules – blur the faces of anyone except us."

Carval winced. Mornings were for coffee and slow surfacing. On the other hand...another step into the lives of his cops. He could put up with early mornings for the shots he'd get. "Not with you?" he wheedled.

"Nope. Lawyers' office. You wouldn't be allowed in."

"Too early," Carval grumbled.

"Welcome to cop work," Casey teased, with a giggle.

He stopped the teasing by pulling her back to him for a kiss, after which there were plenty of pleased noises and no more giggles.

***

Kent strode into O'Lunneys and found Garrett already there, meditatively contemplating his beer and the basketball game on the screen. Garrett smiled.

"So, what's this all about? You sounded pretty keen to talk. Get a beer, and we'll have a chat."

Kent requested a bottle of Becks, and sat down. "Like I said earlier, I need a bit of background on Clement and O'Leary. Something's up, and I want a handle on it before anything happens that needs to get official."

"Yeah?"

"You know we had that serial killer porn case?"

"Couldn't miss it. All over the news." Garrett grinned. "Nice to have some good PR for a change, even if you did have to put up with the FBI."

"Yeah. Their profiler is a real stickler." Kent grinned back. "He didn't get much change out of my team. Anyway, it's not the FBI I need to worry about. Along the way, we turned up a link to Narcotics, and Travers sent along one of his guys – Marcol. Son of Bob Marcol – remember him?"

"Sure do. One of the good guys. Must be coming up for retirement pretty soon, if he's still around."

"Yeah. And one of *those* Marcols. Lots of them around, and all of them good cops, as far as I know." Kent's meaty hands closed around the bottle, and he took a long pull of the beer. "Anyway, this Marcol turned up, and something was wrong between him and the team right from the get-go. So I looked him up, and it turns out he and Clement were in the same class at the Academy."

"Ah," Garrett said, noncommittally. Kent gave him an *I-know-you-know-something* look.

"Yeah. Now, my team can be hard work, but they don't take against someone right off the bat." Kent grinned again. "It usually takes them a bit longer – or it takes the other guys less than five minutes to hate them first." His face turned serious. "So there's gotta be a reason, and I don't think I'll like it. I would've gotten to you sooner, but you know how it is. 1PP doesn't wait for anything."

"Sure doesn't."

"So, what d'you know?" Kent wanted confirmation of Tyler's information.

"Okay. So, you know Clement came out top of that class. Well, Marcol was second. Didn't like it much – you know, cop family, lot to live up to, all that stuff. I guess he wanted to graduate top, like his dad did, and Clement spoiled his party." Kent nodded. So far, same as Tyler had told him.

"A bit petty."

Garrett shrugged. "Yeah. Anyway, a little later I needed a new officer. There was the usual politicking and shuffling" – Kent made a sympathetic grimace – "and I got Clement. Now, I should've been pretty happy to get the top one, but…"

"But? When she transferred – with that mountain on legs" – Garrett snorted – "you told me she was shit-hot."

"She was. But there were rumours."

"Yeah, you said. You didn't tell me much, though."

"Okay, so the details weren't relevant when her work was so good. But when she came in, there was talk that she'd taken a few shortcuts to the top of the class – like by way of someone's bed."

Kent choked on his beer. "Say *what?*" he coughed, red-faced. Tyler hadn't made *that* clear. "Clement? She's never outside the team. She'd half live in the bullpen if I let her."

"Yeah. Well. It wasn't what I expected. So I had a chat with Sergeant Carter at the Academy, and when he stopped cussing at the thought of it – he was pretty loud: you'd never think he knew all those words from that clean-cut face" – Kent laughed: Carter looked like the poster boy for clean living and swore like a sailor – "he told me that was nonsense, and she'd never been pals, let alone close pals, with anyone. Fact was, he said, she was doing pretty well right from the start – and then she came top one time, then Marcol, then Clement – you get it. Competition. But about two months in, Clement suddenly switched it up and it was all over. No-one got close to her scores after that. Carter said she pulled down the shutters, too. She stopped pretending to be friends with any of 'em and just worked. Played the team role when she needed to, and froze 'em all out after."

"You think something happened."

"No, I *know* something happened. I did a bit of digging – I couldn't have someone in my shop who didn't make it on merit – and it turned out someone had tried to do a hatchet job on her, using an old photo to prove she was easy. It wasn't so much the photo: pretty girl in a short skirt, low cut top – nothing you wouldn't see on any girl – but what they said about how she flaunted it and with who. It was all smoke, but, you know, pretty uptown girl, beating out a lot of competitive guys – and Marcol was popular, and they all knew he had connections, and she didn't, and, well, usual story. Pretty girl can't do it on her own, she's gotta be cheating, and then there's a photo showing how she could look…they all wanted to believe it 'cause they couldn't believe she was better than them."

"Yeah. Right."

"You mean you knew already? It's good to catch up, but…" Garrett frowned.

"I wanted an independent view. That team...they don't talk to anyone, and I had to drag the story out of one of them. I couldn't be sure it was accurate. They stick together like glue."

"I couldn't prove anything. But the scuttlebutt I dug up said it was that weasel Birkett who spread the photo and the rumours, and Birkett sticks to Marcol like a leech."

"Marcol had something to do with it, and Clement's team knew it...and Clement knew it..." Kent thought furiously for a moment. "Hell. They *claimed* they didn't care if it was Marcol or not, and they didn't accuse him, but apparently he hit on Clement when he should've been talking about the drugs, and none of them took that well." He scowled. "I hate frigging photographs. All over the place."

"The Academy photo was a long time ago."

"Yeah. It's the rest of them."

"Huh?" Garrett asked.

"There's this photographer. Carval. Takes snaps of lowlife and exhibits them. Famous for it." Garrett looked entirely blank. "It's culture. My wife made me go." Garrett's blankness turned to a grin. "Yeah. They were okay, but I'd rather watch the game."

"So what?"

"This Carval is shooting Clement and the team for his next exhibition – what?"

Garrett could barely stay on his seat for laughing. "You're gonna be famous?"

"Hell, no. He hasn't come sniffing around me...yet. He's trailing after the team."

"Bet they don't like that."

"Clement didn't. Puts up with it, though. The other three get along with him and his camera just fine. Weird. I'd have thought they'd have done everything they could to get rid of him, but they seem to like him."

"So what's your problem?"

"Photographs. And Clement knew Carval from way back, and she sure wasn't happy about seeing him again. So I'm wondering about all these goddamn photographs and coincidences and I don't like it." Kent forcibly stopped his rant.

"But they let this Carval hang around?"

"Yeah. I said it was weird." Kent sank the rest of his beer. "Hell. Travers wanted me to let Marcol *liaise* with them – he means, spend some time to chase down the drug connections from the serial killer case – but unless he wants his boy to end up in a shallow grave that won't be a good plan. I need to come up with something better than 'no', though."

The two captains considered the problem, with the help of another bottle or two of beer.

"Did you say the FBI was in on that case?" Garrett eventually said.

"Yeah – oh, that's an idea." Kent smiled. "I'll set Travers on them instead. Thanks." His smile turned sour. "And then I'll haul that team in and choke the whole truth out of them. I'm not having these undercurrents in my bullpen. Sounds ridiculous, but I'm sure there's something more behind it."

"Trust your gut. And if you don't want that team, pass 'em over. I'll take them."

"You keep your paws off my best team." But Kent smiled. "You shouldn't have given them to me."

"Couldn't afford the breakages bill every time O'Leary sat down."

CHAPTER FOUR

"Morning," Carval yawned at the team. Greetings floated back. He managed to focus on Tyler. "You wanted to talk sightlines?"

"Yep. Got the photos?"

"Yeah."

They hooked up Carval's flashdrive to Tyler's computer.

"Okay, here we are," Carval said, opening the photo gallery. "What are you looking for?"

"Not sure. Something."

Tyler's statement wasn't informative. Carval, easily bored, wandered around the bullpen, took some shots of Tyler hunched over the laptop, his brow furrowed in thought, and then some of his hands and muscular wrists against the laptop and mouse. Finally, Tyler now staring into a distant horizon, Carval shot his unfocused gaze and sat down again, thoroughly satisfied.

"Here," Tyler said, stabbing a finger at a picture showing a dent in the snow.

"Er...yeah?"

"A rest – see the mark? Saw it there."

Carval looked more closely. He supposed that it could be.

"CSU'll have close ups. Okay. Means planning, and likely a rifle, though McDonald'll confirm." Tyler stood up. "That'll do for now. Fits the distance. Never thought it was a hand gun – too far. Service Glocks are good at maybe 50 yards max. Closer is better."

"Can you get me in to take shots of you guys – or anyone else – practising at the range?" Carval asked, totally out of the blue.

Tyler blinked at him. "Guess so. Ask the team, later. We got to go interview now. You're coming with me and Andy, yeah?"

"Yep. Construction site and workers. I don't have nearly as many shots of you and Andy as I've got of Casey and O'Leary. I need to balance it up."

"Shown her that centrepiece yet?"

Carval squirmed. Absolutely not. He knew she wouldn't be happy at being front and centre: not after that sonofabitch Marcol had misused his photo to try to bring her down at the Academy – but he'd taken a perfect shot and he wasn't leaving it out.

"Your funeral," Tyler noted.

No doubt. But Carval would worry about burning that bridge sometime after he'd crossed it. Casey would forgive him. Possibly after she'd ventilated him with a full magazine's worth of Glock bullet holes, but she'd forgive him.

***

"So," Casey said to the team, "We'll go to Schickoff & Schultz, and you'll go to Roberts' construction site?"

"Yeah."

"Did you find anything in Asher's social media about Roberts harassing him?" she asked.

"I've been checking again," Andy said, "while Tyler was learning about photography. There's a couple of references to harassment, and a whine on Twitter about how he'd need to find another PT because he'd been told not to see Mrs Roberts any more."

"When was that?"

"Four days ago. He complained about people's over-protective add-ons and how it was weird it was always people of colour who got given shit. He didn't name Roberts, and they were in different Tweets, but it's enough for us to claim it wasn't Mrs Roberts who put us on to Bill."

***

Casey and O'Leary made their way to Midtown and the offices of Schickoff & Schultz, Attorneys-at-Law. The entrance contained enough marble to resurface Times Square; the security guards were practically polished; and the reception staff flawlessly attractive, both men and women. Neither cop was intimidated.

"We'd like to speak to Asher Washington's boss, please," Casey said, discreetly showing her badge.

"Can I tell him what it's about?"

"I'm afraid that's confidential."

Confidentiality didn't seem to surprise the meticulously groomed receptionist. "That's fine. Your names, please?" They gave them, without adding *Detective*. A minor element of surprise was always helpful. "Take a seat, and I'll see if he's available."

Both cops noticed that she hadn't named Asher's boss. Both cops *also* noticed that her discussion with whoever was on the other end of the phone was inaudible five feet away. Discretion was obviously a major feature. How unhelpful. Totally professionally appropriate, Casey knew, but unhelpful.

After only a few moments, the receptionist escorted them into a smart conference room. O'Leary went straight for the cookies. He always did. Casey poured herself coffee, and sat at ease until the door opened.

"Police officers Clement and O'Leary?" queried a sharp-suited man with an eye-catching tie. "I'm Norman Dennison. I understand you want to talk about Asher Washington? Is something wrong?"

"Detectives Clement and O'Leary," Casey corrected.

Dennison's face dropped. "Detectives?" he gasped. "What...why — where's Asher? He's not been arrested, has he? Will said he wasn't in yesterday or today but he thought he was ill."

Point on the good side. He was shocked — or an Oscar-worthy actor, which they'd seen before.

"What's *happened?*" Dennison demanded. After the initial shock, he was recovering composure. "Asher is one of our best colleagues. He has a great future here. Where is he? I'm sure whatever's happened is easily fixed."

Casey took point. "I'm sorry to tell you that Asher was found dead early yesterday morning."

Dennison sat down hard. "Dead?" He fixed them with a cold stare. "So, you're Homicide detectives."

"Yes."

"What happened?" His tone had shifted to that of a man who intended to get answers.

"Asher Washington was found shot dead, early yesterday morning," Casey repeated. "Can you tell us about his work and colleagues?"

"Shot? Asher? Why?" Dennison had paled, shaken.

"That's what we're trying to find out."

"Tell us a bit about Asher."

"Uh..."

"Like his work record with you, far's you can."

"We appreciate that there will be commercial and legal confidentiality," Casey expanded. "If we need to go deeper, we'll do it by the book. We won't ask you to breach confidentiality."

Dennison relaxed. "Thanks," he said. "Asher. We hired him right after he passed the Bar exam. He'd done a couple of internships — not with us, but they went in his favour. And...well, we had a lot of good candidates that time but, well, we're making a big push on diversity — though it wouldn't have mattered if he hadn't been good enough," he added hurriedly, at Casey's raised eyebrow. "He had to be up to what we expected. He was." He eased a little. "He was twenty-seven when he joined us. Right from the get-go he worked his ass off. I think he was trying to prove something – anyway, he worked hard, he was polite, the clients liked him, and he didn't try to come off like he knew everything when he'd been a lawyer for five minutes."

"An all-around good guy, then?"

"Yeah. I mean, he was a bit reserved till he knew the others, but I don't remember anything I had to take notice of."

"Nobody harassing him?"

"Not in this firm."

Casey wasn't quite as sure of that as Dennison seemed to be, though that might be natural cynicism and her own experience of ambitious co-workers.

"Can you tell us anything about his work that might have led to arguments with people inside or outside the firm?"

Dennison sat back in his chair, considering carefully. The cops didn't hurry him: patience and understanding now (however much they'd like to know everything by an hour ago) would reap rewards if there were difficult conversations later.

"Okay," he finally said. "You'll want to talk to his peer group. I'll give you their names and tell them to co-operate." Confidence in that co-operation oozed from him. "Cases...that's harder. Asher was working on a big case, but I can only tell you what's already in the public domain."

"Okay."

"So, we do a lot of intellectual property work – copyright, trademarks, people stealing other people's ideas, patent trolls...basically," he noted, seeing O'Leary's glazing eyes, "if you have an original idea and someone rips it off, we help you go after them. Sometimes we're on the side of the big guys, sometimes the little guys."

"I get it. So there's a lot of money at stake?"

"Sure is. Millions. This time we're on the side of the little guy."

"How c'n they afford you?" O'Leary produced entirely faked naivety.

"We have a pro bono requirement. This case will more than cover it."

"And Asher was working on the case?" Casey asked.

"Yeah." Dennison closed his mouth, and then reopened it. "Our client claims that their design for completely plastic-free eating ware and utensils for babies and small children – made from bamboo – was copied by Varen & Dart. When we win, they'll be on the hook for all profits, and damages."

"I see. So this is a high-profile case, and Asher worked on it. I guess a lot of people wanted in – successes rub off, don't they?"

"Yes."

"Would he have come into contact with the other side?"

"He's – he was – pretty junior. He was working on discovery, supervised, of course."

O'Leary looked entirely blank.

"Searching through records to find anything that might prove or disprove our case, and demanding the other side produce information for the same reason," Dennison explained. Casey knew that to be a gross oversimplification, but since she understood the process and she also knew that O'Leary had studied criminal justice in college, she didn't interfere in O'Leary's dumb-as-an-ox act. She almost expected him to chew some cud.

Dennison couldn't resist the urge to fill the silence. "It's vital to any civil lawsuit. It can blow a case – or a defence – out of the water."

"So someone might want this discovery to go a partic'lar way?" O'Leary queried.

Dennison suddenly saw the pit opening at his feet. "Anyone breaching professional ethics like that would be fired."

"But it *could* happen?"

"It wouldn't."

"Hypothetically," Casey said coolly, "someone could have leaned on Asher not to notice an important piece of information – from either side of the case."

"Hypothetically, yes. In reality – absolutely not. We don't employ anyone who'd behave like that. I'd have them disbarred myself."

"They'd deserve it," Casey agreed. Dennison's ruffled feathers smoothed down. "From our point of view – cops, you know – we wanna be sure that lawyers are ethical, even if we only see them in criminal cases."

"We feel the same about cops," Dennison noted. They smiled at each other.

"So, hypothetically," Casey continued, "someone could have tried to pressure Asher, but" –

"But he would have gone to the supervising lawyer, and if that didn't work, he should have come to me, and if *that* hadn't worked – though it would have – he could have whistleblown to the New York Bar. But if he'd been pressured, I'd have known about it, because it would be something we'd take to the judge immediately."

"I get it. Was he working on anything else?"

"No. This was full on."

"Okay," Casey said. "Could we have the name of the supervising lawyer too, please? We won't ask them about the case, but I'd like their views on Asher."

"Sure. That's Will, Will Cornwall. Can I have your e-mail, and I'll get the rest of the names sent over? If you want to talk to people, my PA will set it up."

"Okay. Thank you." Casey handed over her card, as did O'Leary. Dennison reciprocated. "We'll be in touch if we need to ask you anything more."

"Of course."

The cops took their leave.

"Waaallll, I never would'a guessed that lawyers do good thin's," O'Leary said on the way back.

"Every day's a school day, Bigfoot. I knew," she added smugly.

"Just 'cause you wanted to be a lawyer, till you saw the light."

"Aren't you glad I did?" she smirked. "Who else would put up with you?"

"Mean." The ice shelf of O'Leary's lower lip protruded. "Who else would put up with a teeny li'l tyrant like you?"

"Oh, I don't know. Tyler? Andy? I know – Feggetter!"

O'Leary laughed so hard that he nearly swerved the SUV. "Feggetter? Like hell."

"He likes us. We solved his cold case, remember?"

"Yeah, I remember. An' he watches you like you're a live bomb. You scare him."

"A teeny little thing like me? Scares him?"

"Sure you do. You scare ev'ryone but us 'n' Kent."

"Good." Her satisfaction slid away. "Wish I'd scared the hell out of Marcol a lot sooner."

"He was pretty scared when he last saw you."

"Good," she said again. "I don't want him buzzing around us."

"Aw, really? I mean, why'd you want your photographer when you could have an ordinary cop?"

Casey growled, glared, and blatantly considered bashing O'Leary with a two-by-four. Sadly, not only was there no two-by-four, there was also no chance that hitting him with it would have any effect. She humphed instead, which didn't provide any satisfaction.

"I think we'll get someone to look into this Varen & Dart lawsuit," she diverted. "Let's see what Andy can dig up. If there's that much money sloshing around, well, big business might have wanted a shortcut to success."

"Ain't that the truth."

***

The construction site entrance in the Bronx demanded that everyone wear hard hats and protective clothing. Tyler and Andy looked at their badges; Carval at his coat.

"These won't stop a beam landing on our heads."

"No. Site office that way. Start there."

"You'll look cute in a hard hat and hi-vis jacket," Andy teased.

"You looked cute holding the baby."

"Point made. Just as well it wasn't Bigfoot."

"He'd've eaten her."

"Ugh."

They knocked on the site office door, Carval a step behind them.

"Yeah?"

"Detectives Tyler and Chee, NYPD. We're here to talk to Bill Roberts." Andy showed his badge.

"Bill? Why d'you want him?"

"We think he's got some useful information on a case."

"You'll have to wait."

"Why?"

"'Cause he's up there." The site supervisor pointed to the top of the structure, where a gang of men were directing a crane as it placed huge steel beams.

"Okay. So when'll he be down?"

"Maybe half an hour?"

"Okay. Keep him here, and we'll be back then."

"I wanna stay," Carval said.

"Who's he?"

"He's a photographer," Andy said. "He's taking shots for a city exhibition."

"I shouldn't…"

"Great PR," Carval said. The site manager acquired a calculating expression. "Soaring steels – the structures are amazing in this light." He smiled hopefully.

"You need a hard hat and protective gear, and don't go near anything that might flatten you. Our insurance is high enough already." He regarded Carval's feet. "At least you got boots on."

"I won't go far."

"Don't."

Carval, lost in the possibilities of the thin morning light on the steel skeleton of a rising building, didn't notice Andy and Tyler depart, nor did he object to a hi-vis jacket and hard hat. He sploshed through the slush and mud of the site, focused his camera, and began to shoot: the towering criss-cross of the scarlet crane mast; the massive bulk of the shining steel beams dangling precariously from the jib on dark chains; the gleam of sparse, wintry sunlight and the bright dots of workers, high above the ground. The sheer functionality of the site was beautiful in itself, and he captured it all. He'd never liked architectural photography, but this wasn't a still, dead form: this was a living, moving, growing project; changing and developing even in the short time he had.

"Carval!"

"Uh?"

"Time to interview, if you can put your camera down for two minutes?"

Andy and Tyler had returned to find a broad, red-faced worker in protective clothing in the site office. He wasn't happy.

"You looking for me?" the worker growled.

"Yeah. Detectives Tyler and Chee, NYPD. You Bill Roberts?"

"Yeah." He scowled at Carval. "Who's he?"

"Our photographer." Roberts turned his broad back on Carval, who took advantage of the gesture to shoot his hunched bulk and aggression, now directed at Tyler.

"I don't know nothing."

"We're homicide detectives," Tyler continued, unfazed by the angry interruption. Roberts didn't seem to register why that might worry him. "Asher Washington was killed early yesterday morning. Where were you between four and seven a.m.?"

"Who? I don't know an Asher Washington."

"Really?" Andy began. "You don't remember the guy you reamed out for wanting an early morning appointment for physical therapy with Delaine Roberts – who just happens to be your wife?"

"Della shoulda been home with Anne – our baby. He had no right makin' her get up, go out early. She had to rest, and Anne should be with her mom. Babies should be with their moms."

"Thought your wife had a job?" Tyler queried.

"Yeah. So? No reason for that little prick to mess her around. She oughta rest and look after Anne. Della's working and Anne's in day care long enough without some asshole making it longer."

Tyler and Andy didn't comment. On meeting their *keep-your-fat-mouth-shut* gazes, Carval didn't either.

"Washington put the argument on his Twitter feed. Said you were harassing him. Said he had to change therapists."

"Damn right he did. Not having him keeping Della from Anne when she needs her."

"Had he?"

"How the hell should I know? Told him to see Della in normal hours or find someone else." For an instant, the tough-guy shell broke. "She's exhausted." And re-closed. "She's gotta find a way to get that baby to sleep."

"You could help," Andy observed.

"I work all day. She's home by three, picks Anne up from day care on the way."

"Where were you between four and seven yesterday morning?" Tyler knew there was no point in taking pot-shots at him for not helping his wife. Bill Roberts was straight from the un-modernised man's handbook.

"Home where I oughta be, till quarter of six. Then I left for work. You can check with Tom here" – he jabbed a finger at the site manager – "if you don't believe me."

"He was on site by six-thirty," Tom confirmed.

"Can anyone confirm that you were home till then?"

"Della, of course. Go ask her. She'll tell you."

"We will. What's your address?" Andy provided a little misdirection, so Roberts didn't suspect that his wife had already been interviewed.

Roberts gave them the address. "And don't you disturb my baby," he added. "You upset her or Della and I'll have your asses."

"Like you did with Asher?"

"I told you. That arrogant little asshole was screwing up my wife and my baby just 'cause he's got some smart professional job. Well, his job doesn't come before my wife and I said so. Asshole," he repeated. "I hate those Wall Street types."

"Do you own a gun?"

"Naw."

"Thank you for your time," Tyler said, when it became clear that Roberts wouldn't say more. "If we've got more questions, we'll come back."

They left on an undercurrent of aggressive muttering.

"That was great," Carval said happily.

"Maybe for you. We got nothing useful at all. Hated Asher, no real alibi. Next, we *will* find he owned a gun, like, oh, I don't know, half of New York? I don't believe a guy like that didn't have a gun. He's just the type." Andy's face twisted.

"Ten percent," Tyler corrected. "Officially."

"Yeah, right. Whatever."

"Search the permit register."

"That's fine in the city. They live outside it. Yonkers, remember? There's no register in the rest of the state for long guns. The best we'll get is that he's on the handgun register."

"Fuckit," Tyler said, which seemed to Carval to sum the situation up perfectly. "Background checks'll be our only hope."

"That's what uniforms are for," Andy pointed out.

"Yeah. Takes time, though. Maybe we'll get a warrant if we find he lied."

Carval's cheer at his shots didn't improve the dispirited mood of the other two. They drooped into the precinct to swap information with Casey and O'Leary.

CHAPTER FIVE

"Hey, what've you got?" Casey greeted Tyler and Andy, with a brisk nod at Carval.

"Nothing useful," Tyler replied.

"Bill Roberts is totally Neanderthal, and he didn't like Asher, but he claims not to own a gun," Andy expanded.

"Claims, hmm? I didn't ask the Washingtons – I'm leaving that for another day. I want them to cooperate, and asking about guns right now wouldn't have helped." She grinned evilly. "Let's set someone searching through the state records. Tyler, wanna scare some uniforms into looking for all the names?"

"Sure." Tyler wandered off to exercise his inner intimidator for a few moments, and returned exuding deep satisfaction.

"Okay, Tyler, you've got sightlines." Casey displayed a beautiful map of the site. "How about you draw some pretty coloured lines so we can all see what you saw?"

"We even found you some pink Sharpies," O'Leary teased.

"Those your lipsticks?" Tyler jabbed.

"Naw. I like blue. Goes with my fur tips – costs a fortune down at the salon – and my claw polish."

Laughter filled the bullpen, causing the other teams to look warily around. Casey's misfits laughing generally meant trouble for someone, and it might just be them.

Carval took a few quick, instinctive shots of the team: joyfully in tune with each other: O'Leary's huge grin and belly laugh; Casey giggling; Tyler with a reluctant, rueful smile and even Andy's inscrutability broken by a chuckle. For an instant, their total unity shone through, until O'Leary dropped the Sharpies on Tyler's desk and retreated before Tyler could stab him with them.

"Now I need to find someone who'll search for all the information on Varen & Dart so that Andy doesn't get square eyes doing all the grunt work," Casey pointed out. Andy produced a sigh of relief almost strong enough to reach O'Leary's buzz cut.

"Fremont," O'Leary suggested. "He was pretty useful on the models."

"Yeah. Okay." Casey swung off to request Fremont, and came back smiling. "Got him. Andy, do you want to brief him? Asher's employer said he was only working on this one case." She filled Andy in, and then left him to tell Fremont the searches, databases, and other tricks of his technogeek trade. She'd never do it as well as Andy could, so why waste time?

"That, right there, is why you lead this team, isn't it?" Carval said from behind her, lowering the camera.

"Huh?" She startled.

"You organise. You don't try to do things yourself when others do them better – I bet you want to go to the running club with O'Leary, but you know that Tyler's the expert so you're sending him. Andy's better at technology."

"Screens make my eyes hurt," Casey deflected. Carval regarded her sceptically. "O-_kay_. I like catching the killer. Whatever it takes. We work it out so we all play to our own strengths. It's why I don't tidy O'Leary's desk," she smirked. "He can't think without chaos."

"No fair, Casey!" the mountain pouted at her. "Just 'cause you polish yours ev'ry mornin' an' threaten death if we leave a fingerprint on it."

"Yep. I don't need to grow my own subcultures."

"Need special nutrients to be a proper Bigfoot."

"Yeah, and most of them aren't yet known to science. I should get McDonald to swab your desk and grow the results in Petri dishes."

"Don't you threaten me with McDonald. What did I do to you to deserve that?"

Casey grinned. "As I recall, Bigfoot, you arrested me."

Carval had shot the whole of their bantering, but he choked at that. "He what?"

O'Leary laughed. "Story for another time. Tyler 'n' me are headin' out to the runnin' club. Wanna come, or are you gonna stick around here?"

"Neither. I need to go back to the studio and download. I've taken a lot of shots already today and I have to sort them out." He looked a little wistful.

"Tell you what. Here's the address. You go download, an' meet us there." O'Leary gave Carval a little push. "Scoot, or you'll be late." Carval scooted.

Casey regarded O'Leary. "Huh?"

"He wants to see. No harm in givin' him a treat, an' we'll make sure he don't do nothing naughty. An' it's diff'rent. Me an' Tyler's not like you an' me."

"Thankfully."

"Anyways, we should get goin'. Seeya later."

"Okay." Casey turned to Andy. "Let's work out what we're searching for. I want a deeper dive on the Washingtons and Asher. Have we got his financials yet?"

"No."

"Dammit. Okay, we'll just see what our good Washingtons are about. And a good look into Roberts – both Robertses. He might have a history."

"Domestics or some fighting wouldn't surprise me," Andy said bitterly. "He was just the type."

"How'd he take you and Tyler?"

"Didn't get a racist vibe, if that's what you mean. Just general aggression. Angry at the world, if you ask me."

"Okay. No financials, no phone, no autopsy. Ugh. I guess we'll both have square eyes, bleeding from the screens, by the time the others get back. Let's start."

***

Captain Kent contemplated his overflowing in-tray and his best homicide team with almost equal disfavour. The team won the annoyance prize by a short head. Garrett's information hadn't improved the situation one little bit – except for the suggestion about the FBI. Okay. That, he could do something about. If he could fob off Travers on that profiler and his team, the whole issue might go away without muss or fuss. He felt sure that Renfrew, whose patronising attitude had grated on Kent from the get-go, would be able to squash Travers and Marcol, and Marcol's family had no pull with the FBI.

He picked up the phone, and dialled. "Captain Kent, NYPD. Could I speak to Dr Julian Renfrew, please?" The line clicked.

"Dr Renfrew," the patrician tones announced.

"Dr Renfrew, it's Captain Kent from the NYPD's Thirty-Sixth precinct."

"Ah, yes," Renfrew said without hesitation. "The murdered models. Is there an issue with which you require assistance?"

"Not precisely," Kent admitted. "However, Narcotics wants to follow up the drugs, and since my team deals with homicide, and the drug issues cross state lines, likely they're best talking to you."

"What do they wish to do?"

Renfrew, Kent thought acidly, was a damn sight too perceptive for anyone's good.

"They want to 'liaise'." The quotation marks were audible. "They didn't say how."

"Who would be the liaison officer?"

"Detective Marcol. He briefed my team about the Narcotics aspects."

Dr Renfrew applied his excellent mind to the situation. Detective Marcol had produced a most interesting response from the team, and had left in disarray. Renfrew entirely comprehended Captain Kent's motives for refusing to have Detective Marcol involved with his team, but he was surprised that the point had arisen. He had not thought that Marcol would wish to join a team who so obviously did not want him there. How interesting.

"I shall be happy to assist," he said smoothly. "Please let the relevant Captain have my details. I will brief Agent Bergen – you may remember him?"

"Yes. Good guy."

Renfrew found himself pleased at the compliment.

"I shall brief him after the arrangements are made."

"Thank you."

"Before you go, Captain" – Renfrew was sure that he heard a sigh – "you may be aware that, in addition to profiling, I study the psychology of team dynamics." Captain Kent emitted a most peculiar noise. "I should like to study your team. Have you any objection?"

The response Captain Kent gave could only be described as a squawk, swiftly smothered. "No problem," he choked out, and then – how peculiar – sniggered. "Good luck. If you manage to learn anything, I'd love to know."

"I am sure I will. Actions often speak much louder than words."

"Good luck," Captain Kent repeated. "Thank you. I'll pass your details on to Travers."

"Good bye."

Dr Renfrew smiled in satisfaction, and reached for the file he had begun while working with Detective Clement's team. His review of their dynamics would be a seminal work.

***

"Waalllll," O'Leary drawled, longer than the Mississippi river, "we found it."

"Finally."

"An' there's Casey's boy. He musta scooted."

"Yeah. How'd he find it so fast?"

"Mebbe he asked directions."

"Real men never ask for directions." Tyler grinned.

"I don't like quiche. That count?"

"You're not a man, but a Bigfoot."

As Carval hurried towards them, both men were laughing. He snapped off a sequence in the fading light of afternoon. He'd print them in black and white, and in colour, and maybe in sepia: work out which would be most effective. Maybe more than one of them...

"Carval!" cut through his musings.

"Yeah?"

"Get your head out of your lens and c'mon. We're goin' in. Focus. An' not through that camera." O'Leary turned his head. "Tyler, you're the fitness freak. You take point on the questions, after I've introduced us."

"Sure. You do the looming."

"Yeah. Think there'll be a weightlifter or two?" O'Leary gazed hopefully at the gym.

"No showing off."

"Would I?" O'Leary said indignantly, flexing a tree-sized bicep.

"Yep."

"Waaaallll...maybe just a li'l bit. C'mon. I gotta have some fun. You get to do all the nasty bad cop stuff an' I only get to loom. 'S not fair."

"Suck it up," Tyler said briefly, and they grinned at each other.

The athletics club had dingy walls, poor natural light, and smelled of many years of male working out. There were no women present. There were a lot of bulked-up men, and an equally large number of string-bean runners, without any middle ground. Carval, not asking permission and not expecting forgiveness, took as many shots of the surroundings as possible, and hoped that they wouldn't look like an imitation of Raging Bull or Rocky. There wasn't a boxing ring, though there were heavy bags and speed bags, which he shot too.

Tyler strode in, met by assessing glances: *how fit is he, how much can he lift, how fast can he run, how hard can he spar?* He met the gazes with his own hard-earned confidence: *fitter than, more than, faster than, harder than you.* But as O'Leary entered, jaws dropped, eyes fell, and every man in the room shrank a fraction. Even when O'Leary wore ordinary clothes, men who knew about working out recognised that they would never be able to compete. O'Leary's six-ten height, fifty-four-inch chest and the muscles on his muscles commanded their instant attention and respect.

"Hello, boys," O'Leary drawled. Carval chuckled, and smothered it. "I'm Detective O'Leary, an' this here is Detective Tyler. Behind him's our photographer."

A nicely anonymous photographer, Carval noted, which suited him just fine. Gym nuts – Tyler excepted – tended to be egotistical, and while Carval had an extremely healthy ego of his own, he didn't want to shoot people preening and posing. Unless it were Casey, of course...who was he kidding? Casey? Preen or pose? Maybe there really was a man in the moon.

He snapped his attention – and camera – back to the roomful of fitness freaks as Tyler stepped forward, ditching his coat on a chair. One of them, and yet not. The men playing at fitness were…playing. Tyler had used it for real, and it showed.

"We're here about Asher Washington. Runner."

"Yeah," said one of the string-beans. He sounded unfriendly.

"He's dead."

"What?" Carval couldn't tell how many people had gasped, but Tyler's words had hit every corner of the room.

"Who knew him?" As if in a classroom, hands rose. "Okay. All of you who knew him, we wanna talk to you. Rest of you can go back to your workouts."

"Why us?" The same string bean spoke, still unfriendly.

"He got murdered when he was runnin'," O'Leary chipped in.

"Want to know how good he was. I'm no runner, prefer working out, and O'Leary here's too big to run, but I can do a mile in around six forty-five."

The whole room stared at him, visibly shocked.

"*How* old are you?"

"Thirty-eight."

They exploded.

"How do you train?"

"What do you eat?"

"What's your carb loading?"

"Do you compete?"

"Do you do weights as well? How much do you lift?"

"What about other cardio?"

"Okay," rumbled O'Leary, intervening. "This ain't a trainin' session. We wanna know about Washington, an' maybe if you all talk to us, Tyler here'll talk to you. So how's about you give us what we want?"

"Tell me about him." Through the strange brotherhood of fitness training, Tyler had already become one of them. They crowded around him.

"He wasn't as good as he thought he was," the previously unfriendly string bean said.

"Better than you, though," another whispered. The string bean glared.

"Start at the beginning," Tyler instructed.

"He joined here a couple of years ago." Another man, not the hostile string bean, spoke. "Decent enough times, and looking to get better. He ran every day. Always the same route, through Morningside Park. He said he liked the peace there."

"Real calm guy," another added. "Did his five miles first thing in the morning, rain, shine or snow. Like meditation, and then he would go off to work with his mind cleared, he said. Sometimes he'd do another run in the evening, but he was a lawyer down in Midtown so he could never guarantee the evenings."

"Lawyers ain't known for their calm," O'Leary threw in.

"Asher never seemed to get uptight. Never saw him mad. I mean, it wasn't like we were close friends – he had his life and we had ours; just the running in common."

"Got real irritating," the hostile man said. "He was as competitive as all get out."

"Just 'cause he beat you."

"What was that about?" Tyler asked.

From the babble, a clear tone emerged. "We all did a 15K together, late fall. Asher came out top. Steve didn't like it much. Asher beat his time by ten seconds" –

"Seven," Steve snapped.

"Whatever. He beat you fair and square, and you said he'd cheated."

"He had. No-one improves that fast without help."

"You saying he was taking something?" Tyler interjected.

Cornered, Steve scowled. "Yeah."

"We'll look for it." O'Leary wandered off to a quiet corner, and placed a call to the morgue. Shortly, he lumbered back. "Iffen he was usin', our ME'll find it."

"He was using. Had to be. That prize was mine and he stole it."

"Prize?" Tyler queried.

"Prize my ass. It was a plastic model of a runner. It wasn't worth squat," the other runner clarified.

"No cash prize?"

"Hell, no. Steve's just mad 'cause no-one ever beat him before." Steve muttered blackly. "And Asher wasn't improving that fast, he was just training more. He said he'd better get his running in while he had the chance, 'cause after Thanksgiving he'd be really slammed at work and likely wouldn't have any time. Didn't say why," the man put in, before Tyler could ask. "He never said anything much about work."

"What else? Did he talk about anyone else – girlfriends, family, anyone he'd argued with, anyone who'd got a beef with him – apart from Steve?" Tyler's quick grin flashed in the murky gym.

"He was having PT – complained about his ankles. Came in maybe three, four days ago complaining that the PT's husband had laid into him for early appointments. He wasn't impressed. Sounded like a real ding-dong."

"Okay." Tyler made a note, more to show approval than anything else.

"He just broke up with his girlfriend," a small, so-far quiet man said. "Only a few days ago, and he was pissed about it. Said she ditched him."

"Do you know her name?"

"No. He didn't say a lot about her. I was surprised he'd admit he'd been ditched, but I guess he was mad about it."

"Didn't say a lot about much, did he?"

"No. But none of us do. We talk about stats and improvements and competitions and fitness. That's why we're here."

An hour later, Tyler had extracted the few relevant pieces of information, along with a slew of names and addresses in case follow ups were required. Carval had caught the quick eye flick between Tyler and O'Leary when Steve opened up, and was pretty sure that String-Bean Steve would be meeting the detectives again, in an interrogation room.

***

"Let's take a run at Asher's friends and girlfriend - or ex," Casey suggested. "Can you find out about them from social media? Not the runners – I guess Tyler and O'Leary have scared them into cooperating."

"Easy," said Andy, and tapped some keys. "Why do people put so much on social media? I could probably hack his bank account, never mind stalk him everywhere he went."

"Heard it before. Not again, please. Let me know when you're done. I'm still running down the Washingtons and Roberts."

Silence fell, for a while. Captain Kent poked his nose from his office, unnoticed, surveyed his domain, and retreated, satisfied with the level of work.

The vibrations of the floor signalled the return of O'Leary and Tyler, trailing Carval. All three exuded smug satisfaction.

"Waaalllll, that was fun."

"Fun to watch," added Carval. "These guys were treated like rock stars. I haven't seen that much drooling since I took some shots at a day care centre, back in the day."

"Anything useful, before all this fame goes to your heads?" Casey gibed.

"Aw, don't be like that. We gotta get used to fame before Carval's show opens. We'll all be famous then."

Casey said nothing, loudly. No-one commented on her momentary shut down.

"Enjoy it. They'll take you off to the Zoo as soon as they find you." Andy covered the silence.

Everyone rearranged themselves to update the murder board and fill in Casey and Andy on the running club.

"So you like this Steve guy?" Casey asked.

"Dunno if we like him for murder, but we sure ain't rulin' him out," O'Leary confirmed.

Casey scrawled his name up. "Add him in. Andy, what about friends and girlfriends?"

"Girlfriend – ex. Kayla Burton. She's another lawyer – at Parish Steinmacher. It looks like the break up was only a few days ago. He was

47

pretty pissed about it — says she just ghosted him. Friends — several, but there's nothing obvious to pull in any of them. I think we can leave them to the uniforms while we concentrate on the girlfriend."

"Sounds good. Okay, let's put her up too."

Kayla-the-ex added to the murder board, Casey stepped back and handed O'Leary the pen. "Your turn. I started looking into the Washingtons. They attend an Assembly of God church — I've got the details, and we'll go see the pastor tomorrow. They bought that house when Asher came to live with them. They both had okay jobs: she was a teller in a bank, he was a store manager, so I'd love to know how they could lay out a million plus dollars."

"Mebbe it's mortgaged."

"Yeah. I expect so. It still seems a lot of money set against their jobs. Nothing else yet, because I haven't got those searches. If there's so much as a teenaged smudge on them, I wanna know."

"What about Asher's parents?" Tyler said. "They rich?"

"We don't know yet," Casey grumbled. "No financials, but they left Asher some money."

"Won't stop us getting the will."

"Good point. Let's get that." She scrawled again.

"What about Roberts?" O'Leary asked. "You said you'd do a bit of lookin'."

"Our friend Bill has a few issues with anger management," Casey said. "A few citations, though nothing major. Doesn't like people disrespecting him or his wife."

"Any domestics?" Andy queried.

"No. Though maybe have a word with the neighbours, just in case."

"Doesn't always get reported," Tyler noted.

"It doesn't *often* get reported," Andy corrected, with bitterness born of experience.

"Neighbours," Casey reiterated. "Nothing much else. Yet. He's definitely up there."

They all stared at the board, except Carval, who stared through his viewfinder at the team staring at the board.

"Okay. We've got nothing about the case he was working. Fremont's still searching — he'll likely be done tomorrow. No autopsy — I guess nobody called Carval to go shoot it, so it hasn't started — and no financials or phone. Andy, will you put a hurry-up on both of them, and if we don't hear about the autopsy tomorrow, I'll poke McDonald."

"Rather you than me," Andy said. "Sure."

"Okay. Let's finish up — Tyler, can you get some uniforms prepped for talking to Asher's friends?" Tyler nodded. "When we're done, let's get out of here."

CHAPTER SIX

An hour or so later, another batch of uniforms had been firmly instructed in the delicate art of canvassing, using Tyler's patent tactical strategies for information gathering. All known clues and data trails had been pursued as far as they could possibly go, and the team packed up for the night.

"Promised Carval beers yesterday, but he stood me up for CSU," Tyler noted.

"We could do it now," Carval said.

"I'm in," O'Leary agreed.

"You're *always* in when it comes to beer," Casey snipped.

"Sure am. Keeps my fur glossy and my temperament equable. You wouldn't love me iffen I didn't have my reg'lar beers."

Casey smiled sardonically. She knew that, despite his constant suggestions of the Abbey at every opportunity on a hard case, if they were stuck with simple, ordinary cases, O'Leary happily went home every night to domestic bliss with Pete. "Guess it's a team outing, then. Okay. We can't do more tonight. Let's scoot, before Kent chases us out."

They scooted.

Comfortably settled in their usual spot, with Casey tucked into the corner and Carval, by common and unspoken consent, next to her; to everyone's surprise except Carval's, Tyler opened his mouth to talk rather than pour beer into it.

"Carval noticed that I don't like sudden loud noises, yesterday. Seeing as he didn't ask" –

"Gettin' to know the ropes," O'Leary sub-woofed –

"Yeah – I'm telling." He turned toward Carval. "Was a sniper." Carval nodded. He knew that. "Spent time in the sandpit. Came home. Had a problem with sharp bangs. Went to see a guy: said I had PTSD. Guess

49

that's what it's called when you dive for cover if a truck backfires. Medals don't stop the nightmares." Carval's expression invited the answer. "Silver Star. Coupla Bronze Stars." He moved quickly on. "Got past it, mostly, with a bit of work. Passed psych. No need to say anything to anyone."

The team sat quietly, listening to a story they'd heard before; silently supporting. O'Leary's enormous form had bent protectively towards Tyler, Andy motionless, Casey likewise: both of them focused on Tyler; comradeship in their faces. Carval felt the draw of the team.

"Doesn't usually matter. Guns don't worry me. Expect them, most times. Not rifles. This one's a shooter."

"We got your back," O'Leary said. "No frettin'. Kent don't know if this case is botherin' you, an' if it is, he still won't know. It's history. We all got some of that."

"So that's it," Tyler concluded, and downed his beer.

"Thanks," Carval said, and didn't add a single word. Pretending that he could understand would offend, and other words weren't necessary.

Casey mused that Carval was getting the hang of the team: don't intrude, don't interfere, wait for them to open up. Maybe if he understood that, she could allow herself to rely on him a little more, talk a little more…. He hadn't pushed about her father: simply been there if she wanted comfort. Doing it like the team did: there for each other, whatever each other needed, without words.

And, of course, he'd never taken photos in her sanctuary: never suggested that he should meet her father. His photos were strictly confined to work and his apartment, and the latter only if she was thinking or talking about the case. Never in personal moments.

***

"Dad's hearing is coming up," she said, nestled against him, later. "I hope we're done with this by then."

"Mm?"

"The case. Kent'll give me leave for the day, but…"

"Mm?"

"I just wish I'd seen a thirty-day chip," she rushed out. "Or even a seven-day one. Anything to show he's staying off the booze."

Carval stroked down her back. "Have you asked him?"

"No." The word hung there, as bleak as the winter night outside.

Carval considered, rather than blunder straight in, but eventually curiosity – and sympathy for the pain under her cold reply – won out. "Why not?"

During the extended silence that followed, he had ample opportunity to consider that he'd screwed up by raising the point. Casey, while physically in his arms, was mentally in another universe entirely.

"Because if he can't show it to me …there's no hope," she finally mumbled. "I don't want to know that." She sniffed, just once. "If he wasn't drinking, he should have a chip and he should *want* to show me. Prove me wrong, or prove he's trying. But he hasn't." Another sniff, and she turned away into the cushions of the couch. He didn't try to bring her back into him, or to face him. In a time for confidences, anything could break the mood. "I can't bear to ask him; in case he says he is."

Carval filled in *still drinking* at the end of that sentence, but, with unusual tact and self-control, said nothing. He'd watched Casey completely lose it with her father because of his drinking, and then seen her joy when he'd said he was attending rehab. The man had gone, too – or at least, Casey hadn't said he hadn't gone. These few words were the most she'd said about her father in nearly three months. She hadn't mentioned the court hearing, except to say that she wouldn't be around that day: whichever day it was. He didn't know the details. The only reason he knew about any hearing was because, when she'd lost it with her father, she'd mentioned him being arrested, and Carval had put that together with Tyler's early comment that Casey had some shit to deal with. Two and two normally made four, in Carval's experience.

Casey sniffed once more, then blew her nose and dumped the Kleenex in the trash bin by her couch. "Want some dinner?"

It appeared that the time for confidences was over.

"Sure. What ready meal is it tonight?"

Casey wandered to her fridge, and surveyed the contents. "Mixed Asian," she said, almost hiding the strain in her voice. "Gyoza, spring rolls, some sushi, chow mein. Or pizza."

"Take-out's just as easy."

"And five times as expensive."

Carval, who never thought about the cost of daily living, thanks to Allan's careful management of his extensive royalty streams and an extremely good financial adviser to whom he actually listened, clamped his lips shut on an unfortunate comment.

"Mixed Asian sounds good," he said instead. "Can I do something?"

"Plates in the cupboard over there, cutlery in the drawer below. I'll deal with the microwave."

Dinner done, they repaired to the couch again, coffee mugs before them. Carval slid his arm along the back of the couch and around Casey's slim shoulders, gently encouraging her to shift closer. On other nights, he might have been more assertive, but her unusual openness led him to think that she was more in need of cossetting than carnality. Presently, she wasn't indicating anything that wasn't intense attention to her coffee mug, though she wriggled into a comfortable position which conveniently left her dark head on Carval's receptive shoulder.

"Do you think the autopsy'll be tomorrow?" he asked.

"Hope so. I want the results."

"I want to shoot it."

"Thought you already did?"

"Yeah, but this one's your case. It's a better flow for the story."

"Story?" Casey said suspiciously. "What story?"

"Didn't I say? I like the photos to flow in a logical fashion, and that means putting them into a story." He flipped into work mode. "So I've got pictures of you – all of you – questioning witnesses, at the murder scene, CSU, you interrogating suspects, some work with the one-way glass, the other autopsy – but I've also got the bullpen and the Academy" –

"You went to the *Academy*?" Casey squawked. "Why?"

"I wanted to see where you grow New York's Finest," Carval said, which wasn't a lie but was a very partial truth. "It was really interesting, and I got some great shots."

"Carter won't have liked that," Casey muttered.

"Sergeant Carter was great. He said I could shoot everything as long as I blurred the faces, so I did and he was really impressed."

Casey grumbled into her coffee mug, which was mildly annoying.

"He showed me the trophy display, too. Don't you guys ever share?"

"Hell, no – *what*? You were nosing into the trophy cabinet?"

"Yep. Every single one had one of you on it. Greedy." Carval was frantically trying to keep Casey away from asking whether he'd inquired into their pasts. "I think O'Leary should've been handicapped. And Tyler."

"O'Leary *was* handicapped. He couldn't see the floor through the cloud layer." Carval chuckled. "Tyler…well, he had his own stuff to deal with."

"Yeah. So he said." Carval's mind flittered elsewhere. "What about the sightlines?"

"We need the CSU report and photos, and we don't have them yet either," she humphed. "I want information."

"You say that on every case, don't you?"

"Yep. Why can't we get it all right away?"

"Too many murders." Casey humphed again. "You could carry on complaining, or you could think about something else."

"Like my empty coffee mug?" she quipped.

"I was thinking of something a little more tactile. Like this."

He dipped his head and kissed the tip of her nose. She always looked up – and usually glared – when he did that, which conveniently placed her lips perfectly for a second kiss. He didn't resist temptation.

"Forget about murder for a while."

"Like you forget about photos?"

"Touché. Okay. You stop thinking about murder and I'll stop thinking about photos." He ran a hand into her hair, taking out the clip and letting the curls fall loose. She curved into the stroke like a cat being petted, and smiled invitingly. He accepted the invitation, hoisted her into his lap, and gave up thinking in favour of the inferno that blazed, scorching through them, as inevitable as the tide.

"Take me to bed," she murmured, and he simply picked her up and carried her there. She reached up and pulled him down, and then there were no more words.

Afterwards, cleaned up, she lay soft against him, happy to be quiet; content in his arms. In these moments, he felt that he saw a side of her that others didn't: not the focused, in-charge leader, but a cosy, cuddly woman. Not domestic – never, ever domestic – but less terrifyingly intense.

If only she would relax a little more; open up a little further – confide and rely on him.

He reminded himself firmly that she *was* opening up, slowly: that she was professionally sceptical; that they'd barely been together five months and he had no right to demand that she tell him anything, let alone everything. It didn't really help. Reminding himself that he didn't *want* an in-each-other's-pockets relationship – he was perfectly happy with their casual, one stage better than friends-with-benefits arrangement – didn't help either.

Less cheerful than he had been, he spooned around Casey's sleeping form, and slept himself.

***

Carval's phone rang as he was shaving, back in his own apartment. Casey had woken him far too early – though her sour expression had indicated that she didn't much like early mornings either – and rather than follow her to the precinct, where nothing interesting would happen until the team arranged their day, he had gone home, downloaded, scrapped a third of the shots as useless, admired a few, and had a bucketful of coffee to compensate for the early hour.

"Carval," he yawned.

"It's Dalling, at the morgue. We'll be opening up Casey's latest victim in an hour or so. You said you wanted to watch. Better be here to ask McDonald's permission."

"Thanks. I'm on my way."

He grabbed his camera and sped out of the door to the morgue.

"Ah, Mr Carval," McDonald snipped. "I should have guessed that today would bring you here. I will remind you of the rules. You will wear scrubs and a mask. Do not lean over the body. Do not touch the body. Do not breathe on the body. Infraction will result in your instant removal. Do not talk. I am not here to enlighten your ignorance. I have enough to do to enlighten the detectives."

Carval thought that the last sentence was another attempt at humour by

McDonald, although his cadaverous face didn't twitch. "Understood," he said.

"Good. Be ready in five minutes." He gazed stonily at Carval. "Do not wander. This is not a gallery. You are not entitled to peruse or pursue the inhabitants."

Carval whisked himself into scrubs and mask, and returned in less than three minutes. McDonald wasn't grateful for his haste.

"I cannot say I am impressed by your persistence," he said acidly. "A murder victim should not be a subject of prurient public interest, or a mere detail in your story. He should be at the centre."

"He is. He's the reason for everything. The beginning."

"That is the only acceptable answer. You will show the ignorant that a morgue is not a place for necrophiles or those who cannot deal with live patients, but a branch of medicine in its own right: as vital as any other."

"That's the idea."

"Achieve it." McDonald's tone made it an order. Carval shut up, followed McDonald into the autopsy room, and raised his camera.

"I have already examined the exterior of the body," McDonald said, as he selected a scalpel and made his first precise cut: the blade gleaming under the lights. "I shall continue with the matters to be gleaned from the interior. Observe the stomach contents," he said didactically.

Carval would rather not, but he swallowed down his revulsion and observed as directed.

"These will be analysed to identify precisely his last meal, but my hypothesis is that it was dinner, containing substantial quantities of vegetables." McDonald carried on, while Carval rigorously controlled his own stomach and its contents. He was glad he hadn't had breakfast.

"I will now take samples from the heart, eye, bladder, liver and gall bladder for toxicology, which will accompany the investigations of the blood samples. Detective Tyler informs me that it is suspected that this man was using performance-enhancing drugs." Carval emitted a stifled snigger. "I do not mean Viagra," McDonald snapped. "Steroids, or similar."

Duly chastised, Carval concentrated on shooting the needle and syringe: the foetid fluids being drawn up; and after that, the fine cuts revealing the skull and brain. McDonald's accuracy and pathology skills were outstanding, even if his people skills were non-existent.

With McDonald's unenthusiastic cooperation, Carval had almost filled his memory card by the time the autopsy was over and Asher had been delicately stitched back together.

"You may tell Detective Clement" – McDonald sneered – "that the first report will be ready by the end of the day. She need not request my toxicology report, which will be ready as soon as the tests are completed. She is aware that those tests take time. You may tell her, since in that way I need not waste my time in calling her, that her victim did not die from the shot, but had water in his lungs from being held down and suffocated in the snow, which would have melted slightly from the heat of his body. We are done."

"Bye," Carval said, which went unanswered except by the snippy click of the door. He shrugged, and pulled out his phone.

"Casey? It's me. I'm done at the morgue. McDonald says Asher was held down to suffocate in the snow, and he'll have a report for you by the end of the day. I'm going home to download."

***

"We got financials," Andy called.

"Finally!"

"It's only been a day."

Casey shrugged that off. Information *should* be fast. "What do they look like? Do we have the parents' will too?"

"Why?"

"Match up the money – we know he inherited."

"No, but we should have it shortly."

Casey strode over to Andy's desk to read over his shoulder. "Shoo," he flapped at her. "I need to concentrate. Go bother Fremont, or McDonald."

"I wanna know."

"As soon as I know, you'll know. Give me a few minutes."

"Let him be, Casey," O'Leary said. "Go ask Fremont about Varen & Dart."

Casey went. Fremont saw her coming, quivered, and acquired a nervous tic at the corner of his eye. "What've you got?" she asked briskly.

Fremont collected his sizeable self together, ceased to quiver, and began. "I did a press search first," he started. Casey nodded approvingly, and he gained confidence. "Summary is that the plaintiff, Stacy Pellew, says she invented a plastic-free way to make kids' plates, bowls, that sorta thing. She says Varen & Dart stole her idea. They say no way, they invented it independently. Schickoff and Schultz" –

"Asher's firm" –

"were working for Stacy. Pro bono. Varen & Dart were fighting it hard."

"So that's the headline. What else?"

"I got into the court filings, and, stripping out all the procedural crap, seems like it was he-said, she-said. I got all the preliminaries here." He tapped a neat file.

"Good."

"There's one about discovery – looks like Varen & Dart weren't happy, but the judge said they had to do more. Sounded like they were complaining it was too much work."

"I'll look at that one first. Anything else?"

"No. Docket references and filings are all listed at the front of the file, so you can find 'em easy."

"Great. Thanks, Fremont. Good work."

Casey swung back to her desk to consider the contents of the file, and shortly lost herself in the details, scribbling notes and points for follow-up as she went. After half a morning's focused work, she surfaced, desperately in need of more coffee, made herself a mugful and stretched out the kinks in her back. Shortly, Andy joined her.

"Asher was getting a monthly payment from somewhere," he said.

"Where?"

"I'm trying to track that down."

"When did it start?"

"It goes back as far as I've got records – years."

Casey made a face. "I'd hoped it coincided with this case he was working on."

"No-one's that dumb." She quirked her eyebrows. "Well, not if they're a lawyer, anyway. If there's something hinky, he'll have hidden it better."

"Prizes?" Tyler interrupted from behind them.

"Prizes?"

"Could hide money as prizes from running."

"Nice thought," Casey mused.

"I'll look. Or lottery wins, maybe?"

"We got the phone records," Tyler said.

"Anything good?"

"Tell you when I'm done. More calls than AT&T's switchboard. All hours of the day and night."

"Lucky you," Casey said unsympathetically. "Land lines or mobiles?"

"Both."

"Ugh." She looked around. "Where's O'Leary?"

"Running down Kayla-the-ex."

"Okay. I guess we just carry on with that. When he's done, O'Leary and I'll go see the pastor, if you go see the girlfriend. D'you wanna get a uniform canvassing Roberts' neighbours, rather than you doing it?"

"Yeah. Quicker."

"'Kay then. You set it up. Andy, you requested the will, didn't you?"

"Yeah," he said. "It's coming: should be here later today."

"That just leaves the autopsy. I'll give it till after lunch, then I guess I'll have to chase up McDonald." Casey sighed.

"Lucky you," Tyler said, as unsympathetically as she had. "Let's get to it."

Casey's phone rang. "Casey Clement," she rapped. "Oh, hey." There was a slight pause. "Great. Thanks. See you later."

She turned to the rest of the team. "McDonald's report'll be here by the end of the day, but the key thing is that Asher didn't die outright from the shot. He was held down and suffocated in the snow."

"Not quite such a good shot, then."

"That doesn't narrow the field at all," Casey said crossly. "Let's get on with it."

Shortly, all was quiet.

CHAPTER SEVEN

Captain Kent, weary of the everlasting demands on a respectable captain of the NYPD, decided to take a break from personnel reports to dispose of one of his many problems, and called Travers of Narcotics. He'd push him off on to the FBI, and that would serve both Renfrew and Marcol right. They weren't likely to get on. Petty, he knew, but this morning he really didn't care.

"Travers? Kent of the Thirty-Sixth here."

"Hi."

Travers seemed pleased to hear from him, but Kent wondered how long that would last.

"I've thought about your suggestion that your Detective Marcol liaises with my team on the drugs issues from our case" –

"Great."

"Yeah. My guys didn't look into that" –

"So Marcol can really help out there."

"As I was *about* to say," Kent grated, "the FBI team took that up, because the case crossed state lines. So you should liaise with them. They've got all the data and they're chasing down the trails, but I'm sure that Detective Marcol's knowledge and experience" – might as well throw Travers a bone – "would help them."

"Okay, I'll let him know. Who should he call?"

"Agent Bergen – he's in the New York office. If you need to mention any names to get through, use mine."

"Okay, thanks."

Kent put the phone down with relief. He'd tap-danced through that inter-precinct problem successfully, and, he hoped, defused the whole mess between Clement, her team, and Marcol. He *hated* interpersonal politics, and the Clement-Marcol disaster, with the added complication of Marcol's family connections throughout the NYPD, had all the makings of an inter-precinct shit-show.

***

"Okay, O'Leary, let's go see the Washingtons' pastor. Hope your conscience is clear?"

"My conscience is always clear," O'Leary drawled, "but…mebbe we'll not mention bein' gay, huh?"

"Wasn't intending to. You worried?"

"Naw. But I don't want our pastor to be uncomfortable."

Casey blinked. Normally O'Leary, while not blatant, didn't conceal his gayness, and anyone who had an issue with it found – usually when he stood up, and up, and up – that their issue was less important than their continued survival. One or two idiots from other precincts were probably still nursing their wounds.

"Up to you," she said, clambering into his SUV.

"Yep," he replied comfortably, and took them out to Queens.

The Assembly of God church was an almost-white building, larger than they expected, with arched windows and, as they went inside, plenty of light streaming in. The pastor wasn't hard to find. Casey knocked on his office door, and, as they entered, a slim, neat, elderly African-American in a dark suit and plain green tie stood to greet them. He confined evidence of his astonishment at meeting a mobile mountain to a brief widening of eyes.

"You must be Detectives Clement and O'Leary," he said warmly. "I'm Pastor Stephen Jarmyn. Thank you for coming out here. I'm sorry I couldn't come to you, but I have church matters to attend to with my flock, and they can't all be rearranged."

"That's fine," Casey said. "As we said on the phone, we're investigating the murder of Asher Washington, and we understand that the family attended this church."

"God rest his soul," Pastor Jarmyn grieved. "It's hard for us to have someone taken so young, though."

"Yes," Casey agreed. Her own mother had passed far too soon.

The pastor focused. "Mr and Mrs Washington – Asher's uncle and aunt – have attended worship here for many years. They're good folks. After they took Asher in, he joined them. He couldn't have stayed with his parents' church: it was too far away." He paused. "Asher was very lucky to have them. God will provide – but human hands have to make it happen. We are His instruments."

"Manna doesn't fall, these days," Casey said, to an approving look from Pastor Jarmyn.

"No, but we can all do our share to make sure we help people in need."

"Yes." Casey paused. "Are his aunt and uncle very active in your

59

church?"

"Yes. Sella organises our social events – I don't know what we'd do without her. They always go so well and they raise a lot of money for charity. Marlon helps our Men's Mission. He's a real draw, because he can show the young men who might be tempted by sin that it's possible to resist."

"What do you mean?" O'Leary asked.

"Marlon overcame many temptations and challenges. Before he met Sella, he was tempted by violence and gangs, but God showed him a better path. He bypassed the easy route, went back to high school and then graduated from college, and along the way he met Sella. You know what the Bible says: a good wife is worth more than rubies. That was certainly the case for Marlon. She supports him in so many ways. Truly he was blessed when he met her. She shared his healthy interests, and throughout their life they've helped each other."

"You said Asher attended here too?"

"Oh, yes, right through till he finished law school. He was active in the youth group – so good with the smaller children. I was disappointed when he had to leave, but he needed to live much closer to his work. I hope he found somewhere else to worship, but when he was visiting his aunt and uncle he would come to worship here. Of course, he had been rebellious: questioning God's will and his faith because of his parents' death, but he returned to the fold."

"When was that?"

"When he first came. The first few months, he was angry – part of his grief. He didn't want to attend here, or indeed at all, but gradually he became more receptive, and I think he found support in our faith and our community." The pastor frowned slightly. "I did wonder if maybe it might have happened quicker if he hadn't been pushed so hard to become involved and to attend worship, but it all worked out for the best." The smile returned. "God's will can't be thwarted."

Both cops nodded.

"Was Asher involved in any trouble?"

"No, no. He was very hard working. It was a way of honouring his parents."

"Did he share the Washingtons' interests – apart from church, of course? He was a runner. Did that come from them?"

"Not really. Sella keeps fit, but they're more outdoors people – they spent vacations hiking, walking trails, camping. Less so now, but they used to be really keen. Asher came to camps, but I never thought he really enjoyed it."

"Did you know Asher's parents?"

"No. They lived in Ardsley, and worshipped there. If there hadn't been the tragedy…" he trailed off, but it was clear that the only reason Asher had joined this church was that the Washingtons had taken him in.

"Is there anything else you can tell us about Asher, or the Washingtons?"

"No. I hope you find whoever did it, though. Vengeance may be the Lord's, but justice should still be done on earth."

"Amen," O'Leary's bass chimed in.

"Thank you for your time," Casey said.

"God be with you."

The two cops exited.

"Waaallll, he sure didn't see any bad in the Washin'tons," O'Leary opened, once they were rolling back towards the city.

"No. But…. I haven't got those runs on Sella and Marlon yet. Searches are taking forever, and it sounds like Marlon might have had a bit of a past."

"Yeah. An' you know what else? Outdoorsy types c'n often shoot straight. Livin' off the land an' suchlike."

"The way this is shaping up, we'll find that Bill Roberts is a skeet shooter and the ex is a target shooter. I want something solid on one of them. Any of them. And that other runner. He's probably a biathlete, just to make my life harder." She sighed.

"You want to have a coffee," O'Leary said comfortably. "An' I do too, so let's get one on the way back."

***

"Kayla Burton?"

"Yes?" A tall, pretty African-American woman answered, looking as if she'd just woken up. Strange, for mid-afternoon.

"Detectives Tyler and Chee, NYPD."

"Uh? What do you want?" She peered around the door, which remained firmly on the chain. Tyler held up his badge, which she inspected carefully. "It's not my mom siccing you on me 'cause I haven't called home in three weeks, is it? Not again."

Tyler and Andy exchanged baffled glances. "No," Andy said, extending his badge. "We need to talk to you about Asher Washington."

"We broke up. Can we do this another time? I only just got home. I was working all night, and I need to get some rest before I go back in."

"Ms Burton, could we come in, please?"

Kayla took another slow perusal of both badges before she removed the chain from the door.

"What's this about? Why's it urgent?" Worry began to bloom in her face. "What's happened to Asher?"

"I'm sorry to tell you that Asher was found dead early on Tuesday

61

morning."

"Dead?" She turned white. "He can't be dead. How did he die?"

"He was shot." Andy didn't mention the snow in his lungs.

"*Shot?* He doesn't even own a gun. He isn't into gangs – he's a lawyer!"

"I'm afraid so. Can you tell us about your relationship?"

"We don't have a relationship. We broke up."

"When was that?"

"A few days ago. Sonofabitch ditched me by text."

"Callous," Andy sympathised.

"Damn right. Didn't even give me a good reason. Just: 'it's not you, it's me. Sorry.'" She looked like she wanted to spit. "So I blocked his skinny ass everywhere and went out with my girlfriends and I haven't thought about him since." But she sniffed.

"Sounds like it was a shock."

"It was." Her eyes glistened. "We'd been – well, I thought we were serious. He'd been making noises about moving in together – I even thought he was hinting at getting engaged" – a tiny bell rang in Andy's head. Had there been a jewellery payment in the financials? – "and then the rat bastard *asshole* just ditched me. Couldn't even tell me face to face." She sniffed soggily. "Impersonal wasn't the word."

Tyler and Andy exchanged interested glances. Asher's social media indicated that *she'd* done the breaking-up.

"Kayla, what if I told you Asher's social media says that *you* ghosted *him?*"

"What? No. I have the text right here – see?" She tapped at her phone and produced the evidence.

The cops read it. *Kayla, I can't do this anymore. It's me, not you, but it's over. Asher.*

"Does that sound like Asher?" Andy asked. Tyler left all interpersonal questions and especially questions about dating to Andy, who was much better at the touchy-feely stuff. Tyler didn't do feelings or emotions.

"How would I know? He didn't ditch me before."

Andy waited.

"No, not really. He always used K and A for the names. But I guess it's different when you're breaking up with someone." She sniffed again, and blew her nose.

Andy moved on. "Did you know anything about Asher's work?"

"No. I knew the people he worked with but we couldn't talk about his work or mine – I'm a lawyer too. Mine's just as confidential." She listed his closest colleagues, and Tyler noted them down.

"Anyone who didn't like him?"

"Apart from me?"

"Apart from you."

"My friends — after he ditched me. They got along fine with him before that."

"Anyone else?"

"This guy at the running club — Asher was a runner. He ran five miles every morning. He said it cleared his head — I'd rather do Pilates, personally," she added irrelevantly, "and he went to a club near his apartment — anyway, this guy got pretty pissy that Asher was better than him."

"What was his name?"

"Steve something. I don't know. I met him once and he was a bit sleazy, you know? Tried to come on to me and I wasn't having it. He said he was a better runner and Asher was using something, but he wasn't, I know he wasn't. Sure, he did all the protein shakes and health drinks and things, but he wasn't doing drugs. He'd have been fired if his firm even thought that."

"I see. Anyone else who didn't like his running abilities?"

"Nope."

"What about work?"

"Everyone I met seemed to like him. I didn't notice anyone with a problem."

"No prejudice?"

"No. If there had been, I'd have noticed — because I'd have gotten the vibe too. I've had that often enough," she added bitterly. "There wasn't anything."

"Did he ever mention any problems about the case he was working on?"

"No. He was stressed about it, but it was a real big case and if he did well it would seriously boost his career, you know? He thought it would. That's why we were talking about moving in together. He was really — actually, you know, just before he broke up with me, he was totally buzzed with something, so I figured he was really doing well on the case."

"Mm," Andy hummed. "Anything else you can tell us?"

"No."

"We have to ask: where were you between four a.m. and eight a.m. on Tuesday?"

"I get up at six — when I'm not pulling all-nighters — Tuesday I'd've been asleep, then I got to work around seven-thirty. You can check that." She gave them the contact details. "Is that when he died? But he'd be out running between five and six-thirty. It must have been some stand-your-ground type asshole. Nobody would have shot him." She sniffed again and wiped at her eyes.

"Yeah," Tyler said, non-committally. "Did Asher have any other hobbies apart from running?"

"No. His folks liked hiking and camping, but he wasn't really into that."

"Could he shoot?"

"I guess. He didn't have a gun, though. He once said it just invited trouble – if he ever got stopped it wouldn't help. He worried about being stopped."

"Last question," Andy said, to Kayla's visible relief, "can you shoot?"

"Yeah." She paled. "But I didn't shoot Asher! Why would I? You don't shoot someone just 'cause you broke up!"

"Can we see your gun, please?"

She went over to a small safe, unlocked it, and brought out a handgun, which Tyler instantly identified as a Smith & Wesson 9mm. She checked that the safety was on before handing it over.

"Do you have any other guns?"

"No, only this one."

"When did you last fire it?"

"I went to a range, a week or so back." She gave the range address. "They'll remember me."

"Why?"

"I shoot there every week or so. Keep in practice."

"Okay. We won't need to take this."

"Good. I'd feel unsafe without it."

"Thank you for your time. If you think of anything else, let us know. We'll come back to you if we have more questions."

"Okay. He's a yellow-bellied sonofabitch, but he didn't deserve to be shot." She yawned, eyelids drooping. Tyler and Andy departed.

"Wrong gun," Tyler said. "Need to check she doesn't have another."

"We should go see that range, too. Maybe she's shooting rifles there."

"Yeah. What about the break-up?"

"That was weird. She thinks he dumped her. He obviously thought she dumped him. Something doesn't add up."

"Phone was locked."

"Yeah, but…we all know you can get around that."

"You thinking someone did it for him?"

"It's possible. It's a bit high-school for grown adults, though."

"Yeah."

"Range first or bullpen?"

"Range. Not far. Get it done."

"Okay."

***

Kent's phone rang again. He cursed it liberally, but answered.

"Captain Kent."

"What the hell did your team do to Marcol?" Travers snapped.

Kent's irascible temper fired. "You will speak to me with respect. I don't answer to you and I have no idea what you're talking about. I'm far more senior than you, so stand your temper down and start again with proper courtesy."

"Your team" –

"You will address me as *Captain*" –

Travers didn't. "– treated Marcol like he was a dog with fleas and now I find out that they sent him a legal letter threatening him with a lawsuit for stealing a photograph and misusing it."

"If my team treated him that badly, why, less than two days ago, did you call so he could liaise with my team? Surely, if he was badly treated, he wouldn't want to liaise? If he was interested in his investigation, he would have been happy to call the FBI, rather than complaining about the team. And if there *are* issues between them, it was completely inappropriate for him to ask you, and you to ask me, to be in a position of liaison without *full* disclosure of those issues to you and to me, so that I could interview *my* detectives and get their side of the story."

Kent had pulled on full authority, which he didn't often need to do with other captains, and didn't mention that he had already heard at least two sides of the story, from Tyler and from Garrett. Travers made some indeterminately incoherent noises. Kent deduced that he wasn't challenged often, but Kent had been a Captain for far longer than Travers and he, Kent, wouldn't be bullied by a jumped-up Narcotics Captain who didn't find out the full facts before wading in. Marcol's family might have pull, but Kent wouldn't be intimidated by a rude junior captain, no sirree.

"Your detective used a professional meeting, where he was present to provide information relevant to a homicide investigation, to ask one of my detectives for a date, which was entirely uninvited and unwanted. I can only assume that your lack of professional courtesy is reflected in your team."

Travers squawked. Kent concluded that Travers hadn't known that Marcol had hit on Clement.

"If any of my detectives acted that inappropriately, I wouldn't be assisting them to *liaise*" – he put a deeply sceptical and disbelieving emphasis on the word – "with their target, I would be reprimanding them. I have to ask myself – as I'm sure that you will – why they were seeking further *liaison*, as I can't think of a single valid reason to do so." Kent's formality was terrifying. "I can only conclude that he was attempting to harass my detectives. Perhaps you know better? Or do you support harassment?"

Travers stayed silent, which was the first wise move he'd made.

"As regards *photographs*" – though Kent already knew that there was only one candidate – "my team are not photographers. Therefore they had nothing to do with any such letter, and I have no idea why your detective thinks they have. Have you?"

"The photograph was of your Detective Clement."

"That explains nothing. Was it a photograph of her on duty?" Kent rapped.

"Er…"

"Explain the relevance of this *photograph*. I fail to see what it has to do with my precinct."

"The photo was spread around the Academy, and this legal letter blames Marcol."

"Spread around?" Kent said coldly. "Do you mean that a recruit misused a photo of another recruit?"

"It was a photo taken before they were at the Academy."

"Let me get this straight," Kent said, dangerously icy. "A photo of Detective Clement, taken by an unknown person, before she joined the Academy, was, as you put it, *spread around* by another, equally unknown, recruit. I guess you mean the photo that was used to start the unpleasant rumours about her. There is not one single word of truth in those rumours, and I concluded that they were started out of spite and jealousy of her exceptional performance in the Academy. I have no idea who started them, and I don't care. However, I *do* care that Detective Marcol didn't tell you the whole truth, and when he failed in his attempts to weasel his way into a position where he could harass my detective, has used a partial story to try to smear the good name of my team. I suggest, Travers, that you consider very carefully the whole story, before you take any further action."

Kent clacked his phone down sharply, thoroughly irritated. He was even more irritated to notice that not one of the infuriatingly difficult misfit team was in the bullpen, so he would have to wait to haul them in and uncover the latest in their exasperating series of secrets. And just to put the cyanide icing on that strychnine cake, he had meetings at 1PP now and all of the next morning.

CHAPTER EIGHT

"Allan, Allan!" Jamie bounced into Allan's office, full of loud enthusiasm.

"Turn it down," Allan pleaded. "We don't need the whole block to hear your happiness."

"Don't be mean. Anyway, come look at this sequence. I went to the autopsy and they're great. Even better than the last set. Come and see!"

Allan went. There was no point in not going, because Jamie would just keep pestering him until he went. He sometimes wondered if this was what having a toddler was like: listening to a constant stream of *Mommy Mommy Mommy* until one's head exploded.

"See?" Jamie said proudly. "Aren't they great?"

Allan stared at the sequence. Somehow, Jamie had found beauty in the glass vials and steel scalpels; in the detritus of death that an autopsy produced. He'd given it…well, *reverence*.

"I guess so," he said temperately. "Where does it fit?"

"It's better than *I guess so!*" Jamie said indignantly. "It's great. Use your eyes!"

"My job is to get this exhibition housed and running. You do the artistic implementation. Yes, they're good. Now, where does it fit? You have to start storyboarding, Jamie."

"I have. Stop micromanaging me. I always get the story straight eventually."

"How about getting the big picture straight now? What's your progression?"

Jamie coloured. "I don't know yet. I don't know whether to go chronological or to do it like flashbacks. I don't know if I want to do the story of the cases with flashbacks to – say – the Academy or if I want to show how cops grow from the training to the real job. It's not clear." He drooped a little. "I just don't know yet."

"Okay. I get it. Why don't you mess around" –

"I don't *mess around*."

Allan ignored that obvious lie. "– with the corkboard for a while and see if that helps? Anyway, you need to take a lot more shots. You're doing pretty well, but you need to keep the momentum up till you've got enough."

"They're doing interviews with witnesses. I have plenty of those, and since they won't let me show anyone's faces," Jamie sulked, "it's not really interesting. I can't do more till they start interrogating and even then I won't get faces."

"Treat it as a challenge – how to bring out the emotion without a face."

"I guess."

"If anyone can do it, you can," Allan said briskly.

"Yep."

"So make it work."

Jamie grumped and grumbled and probably groaned, all of which Allan ignored.

"While we're talking, when will you show your Casey that centrepiece?"

"When I'm ready," Jamie snapped. "Stop nagging about it."

Allan merely shook his head. "Don't blame me when it backfires, then."

"Anyway, I got something else. Another, different one. Look!"

"More? You've got the main exhibition, and this *Hands* one – are you telling me there's something more? You have to focus."

"Just look, and stop *fussing*. I was on a building site, and I got some really interesting shots of the structure and cranes...."

Allan looked, and resolutely did not whistle. "Yes, they're good. But what will we *do* with them? They don't fit anywhere, and you keep telling me you hate architectural shots."

"I don't know, but...if there's nothing interesting with the cops, could you find me a list of construction sites in the city? I don't like *built* buildings, but when they're in progress it's a lot more fun. Please, Allan?"

"Okay. But you have to focus on *Murder on Manhattan* first."

"Yeah, yeah. Nag, nag, nag. I am. It's just that all these other interesting things keep popping up too."

As Allan went back to his office, he could hear Jamie rustling prints and muttering at the board. Allan supposed that that meant progress. He merely wished that Jamie would put all his cards on the table with his Casey-cop, because he just *knew* that it wouldn't go well when she found out, and it would go much worse the longer Jamie didn't tell her about that photo – or about Marcol. And then guess who'd be picking up the pieces? Yes, Allan Penrith. Manager, psychologist, and babysitter.

Oh, God. Why him?

***

Tyler and Andy dropped in at the range on their way back to the precinct. It wasn't exactly helpful. Yes, Kayla Burton practised there most weeks. No, she'd never so much as picked up a rifle – or anything bigger than a 9mm, not at that range. Yes, she was pretty accurate with a handgun – never outside the eight and nine rings, with enough ten scores to be happy about her shooting.

"That didn't help us any, did it?"

"No," Tyler said. "Search the registry. She's Manhattan, so if she has another gun legally, it'll be there."

"I guess that's something," Andy replied. "The rest's all hope and square eyes from searching."

"What uniforms are for."

"Yep. Aren't you glad it's not us any more?"

"Yeah."

"Let's go back and relieve their misery with our happy smiles."

Tyler groaned.

Back in the precinct, Casey and O'Leary were jointly scrawling on the murder board: one high, one low.

"I c'n lift you up iffen you wanna write those chicken-scratchin's up here," O'Leary said, as the other two joined them.

"You should join my calligraphy class," Andy suggested. "Maybe then we'd be able to read them."

Tyler and O'Leary snorted. Casey growled.

"What did you guys get?" she asked, when her growls proved ineffective at suppressing grins.

"Kayla can shoot. Claims never to have used anything except a handgun. Range says the same. She's just about good enough to've tried that shot if she can use a rifle, but if she made it, it was luck not skill."

"More interestingly," Andy said, eyes bright, "she said Asher ditched her."

"What?" said Casey and O'Leary in imperfect harmony. "But his social media looks like she ditched him."

"Yeah. And String-Bean Steve came on to her, and she brushed him off."

"Funny how he never mentioned that," O'Leary rumbled.

"Isn't it?" Casey said. "Guess who'll be visiting Interrogation sometime soon?"

"For Tyler to take another crack at him?" Andy mused.

"Naw," O'Leary said. "I'm thinkin' that our string bean deserves a proper boilin', an' that's Casey."

"I'm not a kettle!" Casey complained.

"Boil suspects like one." Tyler grinned.

"It's about time you got yourself a nickname," Andy added, mischief dancing in his eyes. "Casey-the-Kettle sounds pretty good to me."

"I like Ice-Cold-Casey," she snipped back.

"You like ice cream better than coffee? Call 9-1-1."

"Can we do some work?" she asked. "Or are you going to continue playing around?"

"Aww, can't we do both? All work an' no play makes us dull boys 'n' a girl."

"Going back to our victim," Casey said firmly, "what else about Kayla?"

"Nothing till we check the gun permits," Tyler said.

"What did the pastor say?" Andy asked.

"Wished us luck. The Washin'tons are good churchgoin' people."

"Marlon's got smudges in his past, and they're outdoor types, so they might be able to shoot, but he didn't know."

"Respected 'em, I'd say."

"So we don't know anything more about anyone than we did yesterday?" Casey summarised.

"We know about String-Bean," Andy reminded her.

"Yeah. Okay. We've a little more. Who's looking at gun records?"

"Larson. Fremont's busy."

Casey made a disgruntled face at Tyler. She'd wanted Fremont, who was fast and accurate, not Larson, who was decidedly slow, but at least methodical.

"What about that case? C'n we go see Varen & Dart yet?" O'Leary suggested.

"With what? An unsupported accusation that one of them might have been bribing or taking out Asher so that he would falsify discovery and the case would go their client's way? We'd be thrown out in half a second flat. We need more."

"Okay, let's look at that, then," O'Leary offered. "An' Andy can carry on with the financials, an' Tyler can" –

"Phone records," Tyler said.

They put their heads down.

Casey buried herself in the minutiae of the legal case, which should have, but didn't, stop her worrying about her father. Somehow telling Carval her fears had magnified them, not reduced them. A problem shared...was a problem doubled. While she worked through the case filings and publicly available information, she couldn't stop thinking about her father.

When he'd called her, before Thanksgiving, he'd said he was going back to residential rehab. He hadn't contacted her for a month, and then she'd had a call from him, to say that he'd completed his residential stint, and was now going back to outpatient help through a Brooklyn community centre and AA. She'd been so happy in December: spent Christmas with him and not minded a bit that they could only drink sodas: but she'd seen him for their regular weekly dinners ever since and he hadn't mentioned the length of his sobriety once. If he'd stayed dry, he'd be at two and a half months, but he hadn't said a word. Horribly, she'd considered searching his apartment; or checking his small dishwasher to see if there were glasses with traces of liquor, and had barely stopped herself. Every time she went to see him, the urge to force answers from him, to interrogate until he *confessed*, grew stronger. She found herself wishing for reasons to cancel their dinners, but made herself go, and pretended that everything was fine. He hadn't noticed any difference, but she didn't know if that was because of her excellent acting or because he didn't care enough to notice.

Or whether he had drunk enough not to notice, of course. There was always that possibility.

She sighed, and returned to the case, trying to squash down her worries in work.

Now, here was something interesting, just like Fremont had noticed. In the procedural filings, there was a complaint that discovery requests were far too detailed and oppressive, and both teams had been ordered to meet in front of the judge to sort it out. There was an opportunity for someone to lean on Asher. Where was that list of colleagues? She'd definitely want to talk to them about that hearing.

Her train of thought was interrupted by a muffled whoop from Andy. "Got the will!" he announced.

"Amazing," Casey said dryly.

"We only asked yesterday. Wow, they were *loaded*."

"Loaded? Like billionaire loaded?"

"Compared to us poor cops, they were loaded."

"Oh. So not super-rich then?" Casey said.

"No. But they left – when you add in all the life insurance and their apartment and so on – over eleven million dollars."

"What the *hell*?" Casey choked on her coffee. "How did they have that much?"

"That's super-rich," O'Leary added.

"Uh," Andy hesitated, "let's see now…. Okay. Two life insurance policies at two million each. House in Brooklyn, probate value one-and-a-half million. That's five and a half. Savings, investments, between them – Dad Washington was on Wall Street, Mom was a corporate financier – all the rest. They were older, so I guess they'd been pulling down real big bucks for several years. Most of it – nearly ten million – into a trust fund for Asher, a million to charity, and a bequest to Marlon – a hundred thousand."

"Interesting balance," Casey noted.

Andy continued. "The trust fund would vest" –

"Ooohhhh, proper attorney-type words," O'Leary gibed.

"Would vest," Andy repeated, with weary emphasis, "when he was thirty, or if he got married after he was twenty-five."

"We could use a copy of the trust deed," Casey said. "Can we get it? Andy, can you look into that?"

"Seems to me that our live Washin'tons might've used some of that trust for that pretty house they're livin' in," O'Leary added.

"Yeah, but that doesn't mean they were doing anything wrong. Buying a nice house so Asher could live there could be just fine, especially if it was close to a good high school," Andy said. "Trust funds often pay for living costs and college. We'll check when we get it."

"The Washin'tons said his parents left money, and Asher used it for college."

"Mm," Casey hummed. "They didn't mention a trust, or the amount, though. Anyway, let's not get too hung up on the money till we see the trust deed. They might not be trustees. If they're not, the trustee's another suspect."

"Likely those unexplained deposits into Asher's account came from the trust fund," Andy theorised. "It explains how he could afford that apartment."

"Yeah, though he'd be pretty well paid by the law firm too."

"Lot of money sloshing around Asher," Tyler said.

"Ten million? You betcha that's a lot. If I had ten million dollars" –

"Save it for the bar," Casey snipped. "We can swap what-would-you-dos later."

"Anyway, it's a lot of money, and that's always a motive," Andy pointed out.

"Yes…but we got angry-caveman Roberts – Asher was a good lookin' guy, an' Roberts sounds like the sorta man who'd get mad with that – an' we got possible work problems, an' we got the ex, an' we got the string-bean too." O'Leary sighed.

"We got far too much," Casey complained, "and we don't have enough. Tyler?"

"Yeah?"

"How's Larson going with the gun permit searches? What about the phone records? We have to start narrowing this down. What about the Roberts' neighbours? What about the rest of Asher's friends?"

"What about the sun, moon and stars?" Tyler grinned. "Want it all, don't you?"

"Yep. Right now."

"Okay. Uniforms are still canvassing friends. Narrowing down phone records – identifying callers." He scowled. "Hate 'number withheld'."

"Most likely that's other attorneys."

"Maybe. No guarantee. Take a while yet. Got another couple of uniforms helping out, but it's slow. Calls all the fucking time – practically twenty-four/seven."

"Okay."

"Go see the neighbours tomorrow – after Caveman Bill's out."

"Smart thinking. What about Larson?"

"Slow but thorough."

"Emphasis on slow." Casey scowled.

"Rather have it right."

"Yeah, but I'd rather have it," Casey stated.

"Yeah, yeah, yeah. Have to wait. Go pull in Steve. Cure your temper."

"I don't have a temper," Casey argued. The other three laughed at her.

"Su-ure you don't. An' that cross face ain't your temper talkin'? Iffen so, better tell your face to stop tellin' lies."

"Telling fibs is naughty," Andy added.

"Turn that frown upside down," Tyler improved the shining moment.

Casey's jaw dropped. "Say *what*?" she exclaimed, directed at Tyler. "Who are you and *what* have you done with Tyler?"

"'S his girlfriend," O'Leary grinned. "He's gone all soft an' squishy."

"Come sparring and I'll show you *soft*," Tyler threatened.

"Sure. An' what about that Allie of yourn?"

Tyler shrugged, though a tiny quirk touched his lips.

"Don't share, then," O'Leary pouted.

"Won't."

"O'Leary, leave him. He doesn't need you playing Dear Abby. We need cops, not Cupids."

"Can't you see my teeny-weeny wings?"

Everyone groaned.

"C'mon. Let's finish all this up and then tomorrow morning we'll haul Steve in."

She yipped happily as an e-mail from McDonald flashed up. "Autopsy! Hallelujah!" She whisked through the summary. McDonald might have had the world's biggest stick up his skeletal ass, but he invariably produced a well-structured report. "Shot to the back of the head. Twenty-two calibre. He's passed the bullet to Ballistics for testing so we can match it, but he won't speculate on rifle or handgun."

"Gotta be a rifle," Tyler reminded everyone. "Too far for a handgun."

Casey continued. "Held down – though the shot would have left him unconscious and would have killed him anyway – and drowned from inhaling the snow. Ugh, but we knew that. Time of death: between five and six a.m. All the same as he said at the scene." She grinned around at the team. "Who wants to tell him that it's within five minutes either way of five thirty-five a.m.? I really wanna see his face when we do that."

"Draw lots. Only way it'll be fair. We all wanna see that."

"Uh, where was I – oh. No unexplained substances from tox."

"Wasn't using."

"Steve won't like that one."

"Such a shame," Casey said insincerely, and turned back to the report. "Nothing else unusual. Healthy eating – lean meat and lots of vegetables." She leaned back in her chair. "We can get to the detail later."

"If you're gonna grill Steve like a burger, maybe have a better look at that suffocation," Andy suggested. "Didn't he say Asher was held down? Who did that?"

"Yeah. Good catch." She scrolled down to the relevant section. "Okay. Marks on Asher's shoulders indicated he was held down, though McDonald won't commit to whether it was enough force to rule out women. In fact" – she made a disgusted noise – "he says that it could be a fit woman or a man. Well, gee, thanks. That really narrows the field. Width of marks: six and a quarter inches – 15.95 centimetres, to be more exact." She put her hand flat on the desk, and measured with a ruler. "Um. Wider than me."

"Yeah, but you're li'l," O'Leary drawled.

"No point measuring your paws, Bigfoot."

"Aw, g'wan. Please?"

"We'll do everyone. And a few normal sized uniforms."

"It could be a tiny piano-player with a side line in weightlifting," Andy grinned.

"And how likely is that? Can we stick to realistic scenarios?"

"We could wander down to all the music schools and ask there."

"Or we could ask Allie," O'Leary teased.

Tyler scowled.

"Or we could stop wasting time on ridiculous hypotheses and see what we come up with around here," Casey suggested.

Everybody put their hands in pushing-down positions, and O'Leary, complaining mightily at the unfairness of leaving him out, measured. To shut him up, they measured him too, but since his span was nearly three inches wider than everyone else's, it didn't improve matters. They pulled over a few uniforms too, and then looked at their results.

"Well, that sure don't help anyone much," O'Leary said.

"Nope." Casey glared at the measurements.

The results of their ad-hoc experiment proved absolutely nothing except that hands came in all sizes.

"Total washout."

"Could there have been two of them?"

"Shot left him unconscious," Tyler reminded them. "Only a hundred yards. No need. Dark. If the shooter didn't hit clean and Asher got up –

unlikely – they could hide."

"Unlikely?" O'Leary asked.

"Get shot, shock puts you down, even if it's not fatal. No need to have two killers."

"Let's get on with the rest of it, and see if we find anything more useful." Casey was already turning to her papers.

"Decent shot," Tyler mused. "I could do it easy, but even if he was standing still, it's good. If he was running, even better. Don't think Kayla could do it, unless she's using another range." His teeth flashed whitely. "Wouldn't mind shooting against this guy."

"As soon as we get any information on gun permits, we can start looking at ranges." Casey frowned.

"Why wait?" Tyler asked.

"Just in case we manage to rule someone out. Right now we could be searching every range in New York City, and we haven't enough for a warrant to force them to cooperate." She grimaced. "I hate this bit."

"We know," everyone chorused.

"So let's keep searching," Andy said, "until we're too tired to focus."

"Tomorrow, I'll haul Steve in, and grill him till he's charred," Casey said. "Maybe that'll get us somewhere."

***

Hours later, eyes and brain exhausted, Casey arrived in her cosy, warm-toned apartment; changed into soft, comfortable clothes, and put a chicken and vegetable pie into the oven. Comfort food, for a frustrating day. She wanted answers, and a suspect or two to grill, beyond String-Bean Steve. Some hard-edged interrogating would occupy the whole of her brain.

She had just finished her dinner when her phone rang.

"Hi, Dad." She put on a bright voice. "What's up?"

"I just wanted to make sure you'd come with me to the hearing," he faltered. "I know you said you would but I wanted to check."

"Yes, of course." Didn't he remember her saying she would? Her gut twisted. "I booked the day off. I'll be there."

"I just…"

"Dad," Casey cut him off, "I said I'd be there. Kent won't stop that."

"Your boss knows?"

"I told him it was a family thing."

She didn't mention that Kent knew the truth. Her father was humiliated enough already, and so was she. The memory of telling Kent about the situation still made her cringe, months later. No point in upsetting her father. No point in doing or telling him anything that might have…unfortunate consequences.

"Oh. Uh, good. That's good. So you'll definitely be there?"

"Yes. Promise, Dad. I'll be there."

"Okay. Bye, Catkin – oh, I almost forgot. Will you come for dinner Sunday?"

"Yes, sure. See you then."

When she swiped the phone off, she blinked hard, and then hunted down her best chocolate-coffee ice cream. It wouldn't help, but it was something. Maybe she'd forget his lack of faith in her.

It didn't help. And after eating far more ice cream than was healthy, even the dessert hadn't been enjoyable. She thought about calling Carval, and then thought that she couldn't bear to explain why. She'd simply drown it out in work, just as she always had.

CHAPTER NINE

Casey arrived the next morning, fresh from an hour spent in the precinct gym: running and then thumping the speed bag, to find the rest of the team harassing the uniformed officers to work faster and scowling at the lack of database results.

"Is someone bringing in Steve?" she asked, before she'd even reached her desk.

"Yep. Already gone. Should be back soon."

Forty minutes of impatient finger-tapping and fidgeting punctuating her work later, a uniform whisked up to Tyler, who grinned widely. "He's here."

"Good."

"He's not a happy bunny. Didn't like being picked up."

"Good," Casey said again, with a feral smile. "Okay. Who wants to play?"

The men exchanged looks. O'Leary swept a theatrical bow. "You go, Tyler. I wanna watch the show. I love it when it's bad cop and really bad cop."

"Don't think he'll like a woman questioning him," Tyler noted.

"Ain't that a shame?" O'Leary said.

Casey bared her teeth. "Let's go." She looked around.

"Your boy's already on the way to Observation. We'll make sure he blurs the faces."

O'Leary and Andy hurried off to join Carval, while Casey and Tyler smiled nastily at each other.

"Ready?" she asked.

"Born ready."

The door to Interrogation swung open, and a stone-faced Casey preceded a grim Tyler inside, where Steve stewed.

"Stephen Marthen."

"I've been sitting here for twenty minutes!"

"Five," Tyler said.

Steve ignored the facts in favour of his anger. "What the hell is this?"

"Before we begin," Casey said coldly, "I will read you your rights."

"What?" Steve's colour drained almost as fast as his rage. "What's this about? I haven't done anything. You can't do this."

Casey read out the Miranda rights with precise, cold enunciation. "Do you understand your rights?"

"Yes, but I didn't *do* anything! You got this all wrong." he babbled, already flustered and frightened. "What's this about?"

"Stephen Marthen," she repeated. "You knew Asher Washington. You accused him of substance misuse in order to win a race, and exhibited considerable jealousy."

"That's no crime. He was on something."

"So you said. The autopsy shows that he never had been. Did you have *any* evidence for that statement other than that he beat you in a race?"

Casey's cold tones matched Tyler's contemptuous face.

"He *had* to be cheating. He wasn't nearly as good as me. He could never have beaten me without something extra."

"Training, most likely." Tyler's contempt didn't lessen. Steve's temper rose again.

"No way! How could some desk jockey *lawyer*" – rabid dog would have carried less hatred – "run like that? At least you're a cop. He sat hunched over a desk all day and I don't believe he was running five miles every morning, whatever Ted said." It took both cops a moment to remember that Ted was another of the runners.

"Actually, his girlfriend confirmed it too," Casey corrected. "So Asher's got two witnesses and all you've got is lies. Jealousy's not attractive, Steve, but it's a good motive for murder, and you're looking good to me. What else were you jealous of? Kayla Burton said you hit on her. Jealous of his girlfriend too? *Friends* don't hit on their friends' girl."

"That stuck-up bitch? Couldn't take a little banter. She was only with him for the money anyway."

"So you knew Asher was rich? Jealous of that too? Wow. Three for three."

"She got hers," Steve said unpleasantly. "He ditched her. She wouldn't have seen a penny."

"How did you know *he* ditched *her*?" Casey pounced. "Asher said to all you guys that *she* ditched *him*."

Steve gaped. A desperate silence stretched out.

"How did you know?" she repeated.

His gaze slithered away from her, frantically dodging from corner to corner, hunting for escape.

"Answer the question." Casey rapped, ice-cold. Steve's mouth opened and closed, wordless. "You did it, didn't you?"

He gasped. "How" – and realised his error, crumpling.

"You did it. How?" She was implacable. Tyler sat, silent and intimidating, beside her. "Asher's phone was locked. How did you open it – or did you clone it?"

He winced. "It was only a *prank*," he whimpered. "He left it open. It was his own fault."

"Did you clone it? Phone cloning is illegal under the Wireless Telephone Protection Act" – her formality was deliberate – "and the penalty is up to fifteen years inside."

Steve resembled a week-old corpse. "I…. It was open and I sent the text and then I downloaded an app so I could see her reaction. It was a *joke*."

"Really." It wasn't a question. "Doesn't sound like a joke. I don't see anyone here laughing. I didn't see Kayla laughing. Or Asher. It sounds to me like you were deliberately screwing up his life. Wonder what your pals at the running club will think of that?" Her words fell like stones. "I think they'll wonder who else you've done it to."

Steve huddled into his chair.

"Do you own a gun?" Casey fired.

He paled further, and gulped. "What…what's that got to do with anything?"

"Do you?"

Another intimidating silence stretched out: tension so taut, a breath would snap it.

"I wouldn't have *killed* him!"

"Why should we believe that? You were jealous enough to ruin his relationship. It's not much of a step to ruining his life – or taking it away." Steve quailed. "How much did you really hate him?" Still silence. "Answer the questions. Do you own a gun?"

He stared, a trapped rat.

"Do. You. Own. A. Gun?"

With every ominous space between her words, Steve shrank further away from her.

"Yes," he choked out.

Casey made a note. The apparent temperature of the room dropped another ten degrees. Steve shivered. "We'll send a uniform to pick it up."

"With me?" he blurted, hoping for a glimmer of light.

"No. You give us your keys – and the code to any gun safe – or we'll get a warrant and break your door down."

"But I have to be there."

"The only place you're going is a cell. You've admitted putting spyware on Asher's phone. That's a crime. Criminals belong in cells. I can hold you while we search your apartment, and I will."

Steve crumbled. "I didn't! I didn't kill him! I hated him but I promise I didn't kill him!"

"Start writing. A full statement, and then – unless you want us to break them open – every code to every safe or lockbox in your apartment. Phone passcode – for every phone you have."

By the time Casey was done, Steve would have handed over the code to his best friend's mother-in-law's sister's phone if only it would satisfy Casey and get him out of there. When he was taken to a cell, he almost looked relieved that he was out of her sight.

"Sleazy, nasty, spiteful little ratbag," Casey spat, as he was removed.

"Should tell Kayla."

"Mm. Yeah. But...I think we should use it. It might surprise an admission out of her. And before that, I'd like to know if Asher left a will, and if it says anything about her."

"Thinkin' she might've known 'bout his money?" O'Leary ambled up.

"If they really were on the point of moving in, it's possible, tending to likely. I might take another look through the CSU search of Asher's apartment – if that wasn't just wishful thinking from Kayla, there might be something about moving, or moving her in, or even engagement rings."

"If he didn't dump it all in the trash when he thought she'd ghosted him," Andy said cynically. "I'll take another look at the financials."

"Before that, better search Steve's apartment. Cool how you got consent. No need for all those borin' warrant things."

Casey grinned, utterly delighted with O'Leary's compliment. "It's only ten o'clock," she said. "What shall we play now?"

"Cards?" quipped Andy.

"I got a better idea," O'Leary drawled. "Let's play annoy McDonald. We still gotta draw straws" –

"You pulling them out of your hair, haystack?" Andy snickered.

O'Leary ruffled his buzz cut. "Iffen you c'n find any, sure." Everyone laughed. "As I was sayin'," he continued with massive dignity, "we gotta draw straws for who gets to call an' tell him the accurate time of death."

"Sure it's a good plan?" Tyler restored common sense. "Need him. Won't get results if we rile him." He received three identical pouts.

"I guess," Casey conceded. "Okay, then, spoilsport, you can send him the details so he'll have the accurate time."

Tyler strode off, briefly tapped on his computer, and returned. "Done."

"Okay. I'm sure he won't appreciate it. Now, how about Kayla? Who wants to talk to her?"

Tyler and Andy looked at each other. "We had her first time – do you want continuity or fresh eyes?"

Casey considered.

"An' you're a girl," O'Leary said.

"Woman. Not girl," she chided.

"Okay. Female."

"What's that got to do with anything?"

"Mebbe you'll see somethin' the boys" –

"Men," Tyler stated –

"di'n't. Woman to woman, like."

Casey regarded O'Leary as if he'd developed blue spots with green stripes. "Me?" she squeaked. "You've got to be kidding. When am I around normal women enough to know how they react? All I ever meet are cops, criminals or hookers."

"An' Allie."

"Yeah, like she has anything in common with normal, if she's seeing Tyler."

Tyler preserved a bland face and silence. Another attempt to find out his dating status died.

"Fresh eyes, Casey," O'Leary rumbled. "Prob'ly best."

"Okay, then. Where does she work?"

"Parish Steinmacher. Midtown."

"Who's coming with me?" Silence, since they all knew that Casey would decide as she thought best whatever they said. She looked quizzically at their non-replies. "Andy, you're best, for continuity."

"Okay," he said cheerfully. "Let's go."

"While we're out, why don't you pair go canvass the neighbours about Caveman Bill, instead of the uniforms?"

"Okay, iffen we must. Why us?"

Casey shrugged. "Nothing else you can do right now."

Tyler merely nodded. Everybody dispersed again.

***

"It's just as fancy as Asher's place," Casey said, discreetly sizing up Parish Steinmacher's reception. She moved to the desk. "Kayla Burton, please."

"Who shall I say is here?"

"Casey Clement and Andy Chee."

They waited. After a few minutes, the receptionist came over to them. "I'm afraid she's in a meeting. She won't be free till twelve. Can you come back then?"

Casey flicked a glance at her watch, and found it said eleven-thirty. It wasn't worth going back to the precinct. "That's fine," she decided. "Could you arrange for us to meet her then?"

"Sure. I'll get the time blocked. Will she know what it's about?"

"Yes," Casey said, which wasn't entirely true. "We won't need more than an hour."

"Great."

"See you later," Casey said.

Five minutes later, Casey and Andy lodged themselves in one of Midtown's profusion of coffee bars, supplied with espresso and green tea, to consider the other leads to be pursued. No point in wasting time.

Precisely at twelve, they reappeared; the receptionist ushered them into a meeting room; and shortly Kayla joined them. The confusion on her face fell away on seeing Andy, replaced by nervousness.

"You again?" she directed at Andy. "Why? I answered everything. There's nothing more to say."

"Ms Burton, I'm Detective Clement. We've discovered something you should know."

"What?"

"Asher didn't ditch you."

"What? Yes, he did. I have the text right here."

"Asher didn't send that. His phone was used – but it wasn't him."

Kayla's face crumpled. "What? He didn't send it? Oh my God. I blocked him…" She dissolved in a swirl of sniffs and tears, choking out bitter remorse. "He must have hated me. I didn't even wait for him to try and explain. I was so mad that he dumped me by fucking *text* and didn't even have the balls to do it in person and it wasn't even him…" Her head fell into her hands, sobs and regrets mixed in incoherent misery. "I can't even put it right…"

Finally she stopped crying, and her face changed as the implications sliced through her overwhelming agony.

"Someone did it *deliberately*?" It wasn't really a question. "Who was it? I'll see them *dead*," she bit. Her tears dried; her fury blazed. "I'll *kill* them." She cursed her way down a grief-fuelled, vengeful path for several sentences. "Who *was* it?"

"I'm afraid we can't tell you," Casey said.

Kayla swore liberally – Casey took note of the more sulphurous phrases for her own use – again.

"However," Andy added, when she'd run out of words, "they will be prosecuted. They're currently sitting in a cell and they're staying there till we find out if they murdered Asher too."

"Don't take it into your own hands," Casey added. "We'll find Asher's killer." She watched Kayla carefully, and didn't see a single flinch or twitch.

"I'll be there in court to see him put away."

"That's fine. Right now, we'd like to ask you a few more questions."

"Okay." She checked her watch. "I've got till one. Is that long enough?"

"I think so, but if not, we'll come back, or you can come to the precinct after work."

Kayla emitted a damply cynical snicker. "I'm an attorney. After work is usually ten p.m., when it's not all night."

"Let's get on with it, then." Casey swiped a pad and pen from the pile on the table. "Did Asher have a will?"

"Oh, yes. He was very organised about things like that, and he got a discount for doing it through his own firm, so he just got on with it." She managed a rather soggy smile. "If...if we'd gotten serious, he said he'd update it, and I'd have needed to make one. Not that either of us had that much."

Casey blinked. "Asher didn't have much?"

"No...I mean, he was making good money, but Manhattan rent, you know, and it was nice to go out every so often, and we were both trying to save – 401K's, that sort of thing." She looked between the cops. "He was just normal."

Casey tapped Andy's foot, and made a tiny negating gesture below the table top. Telling Kayla that Asher had been worth millions would be interesting. She started down a different line, to create some distance and shock a true reaction out of her when they did tell her.

"Did you ever meet his aunt and uncle?"

"Yes, but not often. He...we...well, we were both so busy and we wanted to spend time together. He loved them, but they could be a bit full-on about church, tithing, and what he should be doing, and how he was too young to settle down. He found them a bit stifling sometimes, but he did love them really."

Casey and Andy exchanged a glance that added *from a safe distance* to the last sentence, and changed tack.

"Who would have the will?"

"If it's like here, the firm would have kept a copy – or offered. I guess now he's..." she sniffed, "anyway, they'd tell you if they had it, and they won't have confidentiality obligations any more."

"Okay. We'll ask them," Andy soothed.

"Kayla," Casey said. Her head came up, sensing an issue. "Asher was rich."

She laughed. "Asher? You must be kidding. He wasn't rich. He had his salary and nothing else."

"He had a trust fund worth over ten million dollars."

"Who told you that? It's nonsense. He was just ordinary, like me."

"Kayla," Andy said, "we know it's true. His parents were very well off, and he inherited most of it."

Her face paled as she realised they weren't joking. "But...but.... I guess he was never who I thought he was," she said flatly.

"You didn't know." Casey wasn't asking a question. Kayla's reaction was further evidence that she had had nothing to do with Asher's death.

"No. I had no idea." She shuddered. "That *asshole*. He was testing me. Making sure I wasn't after his money. I didn't need his damn money; I got my own salary and my own apartment. That rat-assed" – she released another string of curses and epithets at which even the cops, accustomed to foul-mouthed criminals, blinked. "He didn't trust me." She swallowed. "What a *shithead*."

"He didn't have access to most of it," Andy pointed out.

Kayla stopped swearing. "Is that supposed to make it better?" she asked bitterly. "He never mentioned it. He never trusted me. I'm *glad* I never replied now." She swallowed. "But he still didn't deserve to die." Her head dropped. "Just go away," she said. "Go away."

They went.

"Ouch," Andy said. "She's not happy."

"I'm not surprised. I wouldn't be happy if I'd found out that my boyfriend was lying to me about something that important. It's not like they'd only been together five minutes."

Andy nodded, and was profoundly grateful that Casey couldn't see his face.

***

Back at the precinct, over their sandwiches, the four cops discussed Kayla and then the Roberts' neighbours.

"They all said they could hear the baby cryin'," O'Leary noted, "but none of 'em mentioned fightin' or shoutin' or Delaine bein' upset when Bill was there."

"I don't remember any bruising, either," Andy added.

"Fact is, one of 'em said that Bill took the baby out most evenin's, to give her a break. Cooed over it an' cuddled it an' tried to soothe it."

"Her," Andy said.

"Whatever. Don't matter when they're that li'l."

"Father of the year," Tyler said cynically. "Spending an hour a day looking after his own child."

"Well, yeah. But they all said he was pretty protective of Delaine, makin' sure she was gettin' some rest, not happy if she was doin' extra hours."

"Any police reports?" Casey asked.

"Only the ones we knew about," Andy replied. "Nothing about domestics – just the anger management issues."

"So...if there is anything domestic, it's going completely unnoticed."

"Yeah."

"Total washout," Casey grumped.

"Yep." O'Leary shrugged.

"It doesn't mean he didn't shoot Asher," she said. "It just means there's no evidence that he's a domestic abuser. Has Larson got those gun records yet?"

Tyler strode off, and shortly strode back. "Bill had a handgun licence. Larson had a bright idea. Running down gun purchase background checks on all our persons of interest."

"Good work. Let's make sure he gets the credit for that one."

They scrawled the various data points up on to the murder board, and ticked off some more items on their to-do lists.

"Okay. So Kayla's dropped way down the list. Bill's still up there. Steve's in a cell, and the Washingtons are still high up too. At least we've more or less gotten rid of one possibility."

"Good," Tyler noted.

"Okay. O'Leary, you wanna give CSU a call and ask them to meet us at Steve's place?"

"Sure will," the giant agreed. "Why?"

"Well," she drawled out, "seems to me that our Steve was very quick to accuse Asher of taking drugs..."

"You think he might have been using?" O'Leary queried.

"Worth a proper look. We can always hand it over to Narcotics if we find anything – our Narcotics. Not the boys in Queens," she added acidly. "We don't need to get them involved."

"Naw. We don't need foreigners involved this time."

"Let's get going."

As Casey scrambled into O'Leary's massive SUV, he glanced at her.

"Where's your boy?"

"Uh...I guess he's working with the shots." Casey rallied. "Where's Pete?"

"Work, where he oughta be. Why's Carval not buzzin' around? You have a fight?"

"No, but if we did it wouldn't be your problem. I don't own him. He'll show up when he wants to." She frowned. "Why're you asking, anyway?"

"Just keepin' tabs." She glared fearsomely. "C'mon. You got your dad an' all, an' I wanna make sure you won't come cryin' all over me." The subsequent glare would level mountains. "I'd melt."

"We're good," she said, and offered up nothing more.

"Waaalllll," he stretched out, "try'n keep it thataway."

"Why're you fussing at me?"

"You're my pal." O'Leary turned serious, losing his hayseed persona. "I don't care if Carval gets upset. You're dealin' with a lot of stuff, an' you gotta have someone that's not us if it all gets too much. Sure we'll pour the beers down you if that's the right thin' to do, but...better to have someone who'll hug you."

By the time he'd finished, his ears were scarlet, matching his wide face.

Casey meditated a sharp reply on the subject of not interfering, but, seeing O'Leary's violent embarrassment at breaking the team code of not talking, scrapped it in favour of remembering that he was her best and oldest friend in the NYPD.

"I hear you," she said instead. "But…"

"Naw. No buts. Let the man be nice to you." He grinned enormously as he turned the SUV. "Ain't nobody else gonna be."

"Meanie," Casey complained.

"Yup. That's my middle name."

CHAPTER TEN

Over two hours later, Casey and O'Leary returned from Steve's apartment, smiling smugly at the depressed forms of Andy and Tyler, who had clearly had a much less productive afternoon.

"I guess you found something," Andy said sourly. "We didn't. If I see one more phone number that doesn't mean anything, I'll go blow up AT&T, Verizon, and anyone else who carries calls."

"We found a whole lotta pills, an' I don't mean Advil," O'Leary said cheerfully. "We left CSU singin' happy songs."

"We didn't find any rifles, though," Casey added. "I really wanted to find a rifle. Found a Glock, but we left that for CSU and Ballistics. Did Larson get anywhere yet?"

"Still hunting," Tyler said.

"Carval showed up," Andy smirked. "Sulked 'cause you weren't here, sulked more when we said you'd gone searching another apartment, and then sulked off, likely to mess with the one-way glass. I think that's a love-hate relationship right there."

"I guess. He's been trying to make it work since day one. I think" – but they didn't find out what Casey thought, as Captain Kent's icily angry tones cut through the bullpen.

"Clement, O'Leary, Chee, Tyler – my office, now."

They stared at each other. That wasn't good. In fact, that was disastrous. And then it got even worse.

"And get Carval in here too."

They frantically tried to think of any reason for the furious summons, and the inclusion of Carval, who Kent ignored with aplomb at every opportunity.

"Where is he?"

"Prob'ly still at the one-way glass, since he ain't here. Tyler, you go see."

A moment or two later, Tyler returned, trailing an irritable Carval.

"I'd just about got it," he griped. "It's taken me months to work out the one-way glass, and you're dragging me away? You don't have anything new on the case, so what's up?"

"Didn't you tell him?" Casey asked.

"Left it to you."

"What?" Carval bit.

"Kent wants to see us all," Casey said flatly. "Now."

"Why me?" Carval asked.

"Why any of us?" Andy said gloomily. "We haven't done anything."

"Case report?"

"Doesn't need all of us." Tyler was even gloomier.

"We better go," O'Leary muttered. "He won't like it if we're late."

They hurried to the portal of doom, also known as the door to Kent's office, and filed in, not quite shuffling to see who could hide at the back. O'Leary lost. He usually did.

"You wanted to see us, sir?" Casey, as their leader, had the unhappy privilege of speaking.

Kent looked up, worryingly slowly, and surveyed the five people in front of him in an icy silence which boded ill.

"Close the door."

Andy, who had managed to enter last, did so, with extreme care. Kent's tone had gone past glacial towards absolute zero.

"I want to discuss photographs," he said bleakly. They stared at him. "Specifically, the provenance of the photograph which was allegedly used against Clement at the Academy." He waited.

"We don't know who used it, sir," she said.

"Who took that photograph?" said Kent, with heavy emphasis on *took*. Silence fell.

"I did," Carval eventually said. "I was shooting out in Palo Alto years ago and I took a whole series of shots for a college application poster. That was one of them. Um…why?"

"We will get to that. Later." That didn't reassure anyone. "This photograph, Clement."

"Sir?" she said blankly.

"Was it used against you at the Academy?"

Faced with the direct question, she couldn't lie. Kent would spot it in an instant. "Yes, sir."

"Who else in this room knew that it had been so misused?"

All four men nodded. The cops all knew that Kent was perfectly well aware that they knew.

"I see. Which of you threatened Detective Marcol for using it?"

Casey's jaw hit the floor. "What, sir?" The colour had drained from her face.

"Clearly, Clement, it was not you."

Her exculpation was no consolation. "Someone threatened Marcol about that photo?" She spun around to look at the others. "One of you?" Her voice broke on the last word.

"Clement, dismissed."

Her team and Carval watched her shattered exit, closing the door behind her. Kent coughed, and their attention snapped back to him.

"Which of you threatened Marcol?"

Carval spoke again. "That photo was stolen from me. I can enforce my copyright in it, and I will. If Detective Marcol sees me enforcing my legal rights as a threat, that's his problem."

"How, *exactly*, did you decide that it was Marcol who had used it?"

"That's my business," Carval said coldly. "But before you ask, none of the team were involved."

Kent's attention switched to the others. "Marcol was here to provide information about links with Narcotics in the models case. Detective Tyler!" Tyler came to full attention. "Did you discuss that photo with him?"

Tyler hesitated, which wasn't his normal style.

"Truth would be appreciated," Kent bit out.

"He tried to hit on Casey instead of giving us the information we needed."

"I know that."

"She said no. Warned him off." It wasn't quite the truth, but close enough. "Accused us of sending some lawyer's letter. Said we hadn't. Told him we knew he'd spread the photo around, but we didn't care. We don't. Not relevant. He couldn't take being beaten. Second-rater," Tyler finished contemptuously.

"Did you know about the letter before Marcol arrived?"

"No, sir." O'Leary and Andy shook their heads in violent agreement with Tyler.

"So why are you not surprised that Carval had sent it?" Kent scowled blackly. "I dislike coincidences. I dislike your evasions even more. Explain. Now!"

The team looked dubiously at each other and Carval. They had no idea why Kent should care about the situation. Finally, O'Leary spoke up, leaving his bucolic drawl behind. No sense in irritating Kent further.

"Sir, why does this matter? Marcol won't be comin' here again."

Kent's face reddened. "If I think something matters, O'Leary, it matters."

O'Leary stood stolidly.

"However, I'll explain. Captain Travers recently requested permission for Detective Marcol to liaise with you about the Narcotics aspects of the modelling case. I sent him to the FBI" – an unattributable sigh of relief rose – "but Marcol complained to Captain Travers that you – that means, detectives from *my* precinct – have engaged in conduct unbecoming to a fellow detective. So, it *is* now my business."

The bombshell Kent had just thrown exploded.

"That weaselling sonofabitch!"

"Tyler!"

"Sir." Notably absent was any word of an apology.

Carval, who had stood silent for some moments, and (amazingly) hadn't even considered whipping out his camera, finally intervened again.

"They had nothing to do with the letter," he repeated, "and they didn't know about it till long after I had it sent." Kent's furious face turned to him.

"You had better provide a full, complete, and truthful explanation. I can and will remove you from my precinct if I'm not satisfied with it."

Carval gulped.

"When I stumbled over the team originally, I took a series of shots, and I thought that" – he looked around to make sure Casey was nowhere near Kent's office – "the central shot of Casey was familiar. So I searched my archives and found I'd shot her before – way back at college, like I said a minute ago." He drew in a breath. "When I came to show Casey the crime scene photos, I brought it, and she was mad at me. But I didn't know why." He swung an anguished gaze at the team. O'Leary nodded once, reassuring him to continue. "So the team met me later to tell me I could shoot them" – he omitted the finer details of Casey's commentary – "and she left, and we, um, had a discussion and we worked out that *my photo*" – his voice rose in still-raw anger – "had been stolen and misused to slut-shame Casey."

He stopped, and forcibly calmed himself. "I don't let *anyone* use my photos without permission. We – me and Allan – take that really seriously. We don't let anything pass," he added with conscious arrogance. "I'm that good, and if we let one person steal my work, we're giving the whole world a free pass."

"Fascinating," Kent growled. "None of that tale explains how you knew it was Marcol."

Carval gulped again.

"We investigated. Legally," he added. "It has to stand up in court if we take a copyright case. It had to be someone in Casey's Academy class, and when we went looking, we found Marcol. So we wrote. Legally. And when there was no answer – not even a denial or a *what are you talking about* – we wrote again. And if we don't get an answer this time, we'll go to a process server."

Kent's face turned purple. "You'll do *what?*"

Carval faced him down. "We'll do what I *always* do" – well, what Allan did – "enforce my rights. That's got nothing to do with the NYPD, you, or anyone in your precinct."

Kent spluttered and gobbled, as red-faced as a turkeycock. Carval stood impassively in front of him. The other three watched with well-concealed admiration.

"Told you he had balls," O'Leary whispered.

"Till Casey cuts 'em off."

"We'll get her out to the bar tonight. Fix it."

Andy looked as if he disagreed, but Kent's glare had landed on the muttering men.

"Do you have something to add, Detectives?"

"No, sir." O'Leary's moon-face coloured.

"Then be quiet." Kent turned back to Carval. "You intend to pursue this?"

"Yes. That's nothing to do with the NYPD and you can't stop me."

"Even if I ban you?"

"Yes. I don't lie down for blackmail. I'll just find another team from a different precinct." He was bluffing, but Kent didn't need to know that. "It might work better. Start with what I got here, and then contrast it to different precincts."

Kent was stymied. He didn't like photographs, and right now he loathed the infuriating photographer, but he wasn't prepared to give up good PR for his precinct. And, of course, he'd promised his wife a personal showing, which was keeping him in domestic bliss, which would disappear if he – which he would love to do – kicked Carval to the kerb.

"I have dealt with Captain Travers. Don't come to my attention again. Dismissed."

They fled.

***

Only fear of Kent's iron discipline took Casey out of his office, rigid-spined and as pale as death. She went straight to the coffee machine, made herself an espresso and threw the scalding liquid down her throat; repeated that until her hands were almost shaking.

How could they? How could Carval? She was sure that he'd instigated the mess. The others had known for years, and done nothing. It must have been him, but he'd dragged *her team* along with him.

Her team, on his side, *not telling* her something that important. How would she endure the remains of the day until she could leave, knowing that?

She looked at her slim watch and discovered that shift was, thankfully, almost done. For once, she'd be leaving on the dot. She badly wanted to be at home, alone. For now, she returned to her pristine desk and buried herself in paperwork, reconstructing the cool, collected shell that had protected her throughout the Academy and the later comments and rumours. Concentrating on work meant that she didn't have to recognise the team's betrayal and her devastating misery. She tapped out an e-mail to Dennison, asking if Schickoff & Schultz had Asher's will, and if so, whether they would be able to release it to her without a warrant.

Not nearly enough minutes later – that was, before shift ended and she could escape – the rest of the team, plus Carval, emerged from Kent's office. Her team seemed relieved. Carval was irritated, which was an unusual outcome of an interview with Kent.

Relief fell off O'Leary's face as soon as he took a good look at Casey. He squared his massive shoulders.

"We're all goin' to the Abbey," he said. "as soon's shift's done."

"I'm going home." Casey's tone cut.

"Naw, you're comin' too. Seems to me we all need to have a bit of a chat an' clear the air."

Casey didn't answer.

"C'mon, don't be like that. It's just a beer."

It was easier to stay silent than argue. She concentrated on her papers, and said nothing more. O'Leary looked down worriedly at the dark curls spilling out of the clip, but went to his own work, exchanging glances with Tyler and Andy.

Casey could sense Carval behind her, but the last thing she wanted to do was speak to him. If she did, it would rapidly turn bad. She hoped, hopelessly, that he wouldn't come to the Abbey.

"Time to go," O'Leary rumbled, exactly on shift end. Carval shrugged on his coat. Three men packed up their desks and shut down their computers. One woman didn't. "C'mon, Casey. You too. We got things to talk about."

"*You* have things to talk about. I have nothing to say to any of you."

O'Leary's forcedly cheerful smile slid away. "You're comin'. I ain't havin' trouble an' fuss."

"Really? Seems like you've got it. Not my problem."

Tyler strode up. "We're going. Team."

Casey looked from one big man flanking her to the other, and then to Andy, joining them. "I guess I don't have a choice," she said bitterly. She pulled numbness around her, and went with them: surrounded, but completely apart.

O'Leary steered the group to the back of the quiet bar, and, unasked, put beer in front of everyone. Casey had ended up tucked into the corner: back to the wall; silent and unreceptive. Outright anger was barely a breath away. She didn't touch the beer. She didn't look at any of them.

After a moment, Carval spoke.

"It wasn't them. I went after Marcol for stealing *my* photo."

"You did what? This isn't your fight to have! If I didn't care, why'd *you* get involved?"

"It was my photo. *Nobody* steals my photos. I don't care if it was yesterday or last week or nine years ago, *nobody* gets to steal my photos and misuse them."

"So? Now you've dragged up a whole bunch of problems that should've stayed dead. Does Marcol know you're shooting us? Not that it matters, because it'll take about ten seconds for him to find out, and then we'll be in the shit. My team. Marcol's got pals everywhere, and he's from an old cop family. How d'you think they'll take this? Popular guy, against the misfit team? We're fucked."

Nobody said a word.

"And you all knew." Casey's words fell heavily, weighing down the team. "Didn't you think I would have an opinion?" They squirmed uneasily. They had known she would. "That photo was used against *me*. Not any of you." Her words excluded Carval. "You had no right to make that decision for me. You should have told me."

She stood up; beer still untouched. "Since you've already made all the decisions about my affairs, I don't think I'm needed here. I guess you won't bother telling me what you decide. Nice to know how much my opinions count."

"Casey" – Andy began, but she was already squeezing past them, and not even O'Leary dared to stop her.

She turned away, and then, two steps taken, turned back, face white and tired. "It wasn't your fight to have," she said to Carval. "You didn't know there *was* a fight to have until you met me." Her eyes pierced his soul. "You did it because it was me. You were trying to be a hero. I didn't need a hero. I dealt with it myself, long ago."

He sat and watched her walk away, back straight, shoulders stiff, head high.

"She's not happy. Shit," Tyler commented.

"Yeah. I've never seen her so mad with us." Andy's head dropped.

"Mebbe we should've told her?" O'Leary suggested.

"What would that have changed? You'd been and gone and done it long before we found out," Andy directed at Carval. "And now we're all deep in it."

"Tell me something I don't know," Carval snapped.

"Got one thing wrong, though. Marcol doesn't have the support."

"How'd you know?" Andy asked Tyler.

"We got the rep. He doesn't. Sure, he's popular, but his record's good, not great. Talks big, doing fine, but we do it better. Those who matter, know." Tyler took a long slug of his beer. "Not your fault," he said to

Carval's hunched, defensive form. "Drink your beer. One of us now. Bigfoot'll fix it."

O'Leary made a face. "Might be a bit difficult," he said. "Casey's mad. She don't get mad often. Not with us."

"You could explain it was all about the copyright," Andy suggested. "She'll get that."

Tyler nodded decisively. "Good plan."

"Yeah. It would be."

"But?" Andy asked Carval.

"But it's not exactly true," Carval said heavily. "Casey'd spot the evasion in half a second. She already worked it out."

"What d'you mean it's not true? All you said was that he stole your photo."

"Ten times over," O'Leary added.

"Oh, fuckit," Tyler said. "Only cared 'cause it was Casey."

"You mean you wouldn't have done any of it if it wasn't?" Andy added.

"I would." Carval was still hunched. "Probably."

"So no lie."

"It's not the whole truth either."

"Mebbe not," O'Leary chimed in. "But I don't guess she's too keen on you right now, so spillin' your guts ain't gonna help. Mebbe you should've said earlier – an' Tyler there suggested it – but we didn't say nothin' either, so now we're all swimmin' in the shit together." He sighed, and a few napkins blew away. "Tomorrow ain't gonna be fun."

"She'll sulk?" Carval queried.

"Naw. She'll just work. An' work. An' work some more, an' all she'll talk about or think about is work."

"In two days she'll act like it never happened."

"It's happened before?"

"Not with us," Andy said. "Never with us. Even when she's buried herself in work, she's been one of us. Now?"

"'Nother beer?" O'Leary suggested into the silence that Andy's words created.

"No. I need to go see her," Carval said. "Explain. Get you guys out of the mess."

Scepticism painted three faces. "Not a good plan," Tyler noted.

"You got a better one?"

"Sure. Let sleeping Caseys lie. Give it a day or two, then talk."

"She won't talk. If I leave it, she'll think I don't care."

"Waaalllll," O'Leary drawled, "it's your life to lose. But I ain't tryin' to talk to her till tomorrow, 'cause I like my skin exactly as whole as it is right now."

"I'm going." Carval stared at the table.

"You got some balls, man."

"Better hope you've still got them tomorrow," Andy quipped.

Carval drained his beer and stood. "Death or glory," he said mordantly.

"We'll send lilies to the funeral."

CHAPTER ELEVEN

When the door sounded, Casey knew that it was Carval. She didn't want to see him. She didn't want to see anyone. She needed time on her own: thinking time; time to deal with her own emotions; time to cram down the shocked hurt that *her team* had hidden something that important from her. If only it hadn't been so cold, she could have gone running, beating out her pain in the rhythm of the strides, lacquering on her shell before work tomorrow. Sunday, they would all be off shift, and she could…what? Deal? She couldn't deal with this. But at least she would have time to think, and to process Carval's actions.

How could he? she thought. How could he drag up old, dead quarrels? She'd left Marcol behind, and now here he was again, trouble that she didn't need, just because Jamie Carval had decided to play the hero.

She hadn't needed a hero the first time, and she damn sure didn't need one now. She was her own hero.

"What do you want?" she snapped, blocking the doorway.

"To talk."

"No."

She started to shut the door, but Carval stopped it. "Look, I just wanna" —

"What? Screw up my life some more? No thanks."

"Apologise, okay?" He stepped forward. "Let me in."

For an instant, she didn't move, until sense kicked in and told her that an argument in the hallway would rouse the neighbours. She stepped back. Carval shut the door behind him, by which time she was some way out of reach.

"Say what you want to."

"I'm sorry, okay? I didn't think it would come back on you or the team. I just wanted to go after him for stealing the photo."

She stared coldly at him. "So if you hadn't been trying to follow me around you'd have done it anyway?"

"Yes…"

"Really?" she challenged.

"Yes."

"You're lying. You went after him because it was me. Because I wouldn't give you the time of day after I knew it was you who took the photo." She took a leap of logic. "If he'd admitted it, you'd have handed it to me like a present and hoped I'd be grateful enough to let you in to take your shots."

"You let me in anyway."

"Yeah, and look what a mistake that was."

"What?"

"We're screwed. All because of you and your photos, not that you care. All you want is photos and as long as you get them you don't care what damage you cause. Well, you'll get plenty of that to shoot. Just watch Marcol's friends fuck us over. You'll get some great shots from that."

"That's not true! I don't just care about the photos. I care" –

"Yeah, right. If you'd *cared*, rather than looking for a notch on your bedpost, you'd have asked my opinion before meddling in my life. You wouldn't have hidden it, hoping I wouldn't notice. What else are you hiding?"

He remembered his central shot, and winced.

"So there is something. Don't tell me. I don't wanna know. Just go."

"Casey…" He took a step towards her – and she retreated.

"Go. I can't stop you taking shots but I don't have to have you here. I didn't need a hero then and I don't need one now. Go be a hero somewhere else."

He went, slamming the door behind him. Casey sank on to her couch, furious and utterly miserable. Eventually, she went to bed. Too early, drained from too little sleep, she rose and went to work. Work had never let her down; never disappointed her.

***

Parking under the grimy light of sodium streetlamps, hours before shift formally began, Casey stared at the unlovely shell of the precinct and wondered why she'd allowed Carval into her life. All he'd ever done was fuck it up for her: first at the Academy; now, not just a rerun of that disaster, but destroying her team as well. When it came down to it, the team had trusted his judgement, not hers; let him carry on in a course that was bound to screw with her reputation, and, worse, she had now worked out, would inevitably uncover her father's weakness. Marcol would use her father against her. She just didn't know how, yet.

She stepped out into the freezing air, and shrugged. She'd done it without a team at the Academy, and for the time until she paired up with O'Leary, and she could do it again. As long as they could work together, they didn't have to have more. Cold distance settled on to her shoulders just like the frost clutched at the branches of the bare trees. Shortly, her mind was icily serene; her demeanour perfectly, frigidly calm.

In the empty bullpen, she made herself an espresso, settled at her pristine desk, and pulled paper and pen towards her. Silence surrounded her; a small puddle of brightness from her computer screen, a single fluorescent tube dribbling out light above her. She didn't need or want more. Her attention focused on her case, and nothing more was permitted to enter her mind.

Some two hours later, O'Leary, the last member of the team to arrive, entered the bullpen, took note of Casey's bent head and Tyler and Andy's look of relief as he lumbered in, and concluded with total accuracy that the team weather forecast was set firmly to forty below.

"Mornin'," he tried.

"Hey." It was perfectly normal, and carried all the interest, depth and warmth of a sheet of black ice. To O'Leary's heightened senses, it covered as much danger. He went to his own desk, worried.

***

Kent, arriving from another frustrating meeting, which had taken up precious time that could have been better used, cast an apparently casual glance around the bullpen and noticed the fracture in his team of misfits. He passed on. Interfering would simply produce more issues, and that team fixed themselves. He'd step in only if he absolutely had to, and that was emphatically not now. Kent, with considerable justification, was a great advocate of the philosophy that interfering too early was far worse than giving adults a chance to mend their own differences.

At that point, his phone rang. Couldn't he have *five minutes* to organise his thoughts and priorities? He cursed liberally, but answered.

"Kent."

"Good morning, Captain."

Oh, *hell*. The last thing he needed was that prissy, pedantic, stick-up-the-ass profiler.

"Dr Renfrew."

"Agent Bergen and I have spoken to Captain Travers and Detective Marcol, and have provided them with the required information." Dr Renfrew coughed. "I shall be in Manhattan on Monday, as I am lecturing at Columbia. I should like to visit the precinct, and observe your team, should they be present."

"If they're here, you can observe. I'm sure you won't distract them."

"Of course not. I would appreciate it if you would advise them of my visit. If they wish to employ my profiling experience, I would be happy to assist. I expect they will not need it, but I enjoyed working with them and would be happy to do so again."

Kent thought that Renfrew might have enjoyed it, but he was damn sure that his team hadn't. Still, telling Clement about it, and instructing her to tell the others, might help their problem.

"I'll tell them." He had a sudden thought. "When you're here, I'd like to know how our murder case fitted in with this Narcotics issue."

"Certainly. Thank you. Good bye."

"Bye."

Kent put the phone down, more thoughtful than aggravated. Maybe, he mused, Renfrew's visit would be helpful. Clement's reaction to telling the others would be informative, and Renfrew might provide some insight into the whole situation. He hadn't missed Clement's utter horror that everyone except her had known what was going on with Marcol, and he *also* hadn't missed that the three other members of the team were regarding her as if she were a hand grenade with the pin pulled out. Being an expert manager, Kent concluded that there had been an unpleasant discussion, likely the previous night. Since he also hadn't seen the annoying photographer, he concluded that he'd been given the bum's rush too, though, unfortunately, that probably wouldn't prevent him turning up again.

He poked his head out. "Clement," he ordered. "My office."

"Sir?" Clement queried, already on her feet.

"Close the door." She did so, standing at formal parade rest. "Dr Renfrew, the FBI profiler from the models case" – she didn't speak, but it was clear from her suddenly-tight mouth that she remembered – "wants to observe your team. He'll be here on Monday and, after meeting me, he'll stay in the bullpen. If you want his advice, he'll be happy to help, but only if you ask him. He won't butt in."

"Yes, sir," Clement said, completely unemotional.

"Please advise the others."

"Yes, sir." She turned to the door.

"Clement?"

"Yes, sir?"

"Detective Marcol won't be involved in any case of yours. I will not allow harassment of my detectives."

She stared at him, then shut down again. "Thank you, sir."

"Dismissed."

On balance, Kent felt, that had gone just about okay. The team clearly had some issues. Equally clearly, they wouldn't mention them. No change there from the previous four-plus years. He'd leave them to fix themselves, for now.

***

Casey walked back out to her desk, gathered herself together, pulled on cool, bland, disinterested normality, and summoned her team together. They looked hopeful, for all of five seconds, until they focused on her face.

"Dr Renfrew will be returning on Monday to observe the team," she said flatly. "Kent told me. He'll help if you want him to, but that's it. He's not here to participate."

The three men gaped at her. "He *what?*"

"Ah, shit," Tyler emitted.

"Do we hafta?" wailed O'Leary, who had least reason of all to be worried, sounding like a three-year-old presented with Brussels sprouts.

"Yes," she said flatly. "Deal with it on your own time. Right now, I want to go through what we're all doing today." She would have said the same, in the same brisk tone, on any other day, about any other case, but, mysteriously, each man heard it as a shut-down.

"Sure," they said. Casey went to get her pad and list, missing the exchange of worried glances behind her. She was perfectly, utterly normal, and it was terrifying. They clustered around the murder board, ran through everything, and didn't say one single solitary word about when she might have done all this work.

Half an hour later, there had been a distinct lack of banter and a distinct preponderance of terse laying out of the various paths to be followed. Tyler strode off to encourage Larson. Andy went back to financials and the will, following up on the trust arrangements.

O'Leary stayed put, gazing down at Casey. "You okay?" he tried.

"Fine. I'm going back to that discovery hearing. You look at the rest of Varen & Dart. See if Fremont can help."

For an instant, it looked like O'Leary might say something, but then he thought better of it, and trudged off to find Fremont.

Casey buried herself in the minutiae of the hearing, and then sent Dennison a further e-mail, asking to interview the team present at that hearing – as a group. An hour or so later, during which she hadn't spoken to a single other person in the bullpen about anything other than the case, she received a reply, suggesting a time later that afternoon. Apparently, the time limits on the case meant that they were all working over the weekend.

Dennison's agreement left Casey with a dilemma. She didn't want to spend time with any of the team unless it was directly concerned with the case. Specifically, she didn't want to spend time with O'Leary, who would have another go at her. She wasn't ready to deal with him, or the others, but she had to take one of them.

Tyler. Tyler was the least likely to talk, *and* she'd get to see if there was any conscious or unconscious bias within Asher's team. Cynically, she thought that Dennison – white, male, forty-something and at the top –

wouldn't notice or understand the finer points of prejudice. Tyler certainly would.

"Tyler?" she called over. He glanced up, as did Andy and O'Leary. "I'm visiting Schickoff & Schultz this afternoon to talk about the discovery hearing. If someone was pressuring Asher to falsify discovery, that's where he'd come in direct contact with the opposing side. No-one's dumb enough to do that on the phone. I want you to come with me. They were a bit casual about *of-course-we-aren't-biased*, but I'm not sure I believe them."

"Stereotyping?" he teased.

Casey, rather than accepting the open invitation to banter, simply stared straight back at Tyler's burly form. "Not from my side." Tyler made a marginally apologetic gesture. "They might, and that's what we're checking." She half-turned. "Andy, I'll ask them if we can get Asher's will while I'm there, so tell me if it comes through before then, so I don't duplicate."

"Okay." Any further words dissolved under her unreceptive expression.

Casey went back to her work, and the men went back to theirs. The pile of coffee cups on Casey's desk grew higher. At lunchtime, she went out alone, and then took herself and her sandwich to Sakura Park, despite the freezing air. She huddled into her thick coat and scarf, tugged her hat down over her ears, and tried to think.

Every time she thought of the previous day's disaster, furious pain ripped through her. The one thing she'd thought she could rely on: their team bond; more than four years of unwavering support and understanding; the connection that made the four misfits one tight team; their separate, painful histories, disclosed in occasional words and half-sentences...had failed her. She hadn't understood how comforting their unity had become: the bone-deep confidence that it had given her that the disaster of the Academy simply *didn't matter*. But now it did. There was no way Marcol would let this lie. He'd be digging for any dirt he could find – and he'd find her father, and his court hearing: a whole mountain of dirt once Marcol and his weasels had finished spinning stories.

She sniffed, and then shook herself. So she was upset that they hadn't even *thought* that she would want to know, to be prepared. Well, she'd just have to deal with knowing that the team wasn't as tight as she'd thought. All she needed was a work relationship. She would protect her dad by herself. That was all. She hadn't been able to rely on anyone else at the Academy and didn't have anyone to rely on now. Come to think of it, it was pretty much the same problem. Some asshole with photos, ruining her life. She could deal with that just plain *fine*.

She painted on another thick layer of unemotional lacquer, and stalked back to the precinct.

***

Allan tip-tapped up the stairs, surprised to have heard movement in the studio.

"Aren't you going to the precinct today?" he asked Jamie's back.

"No." Jamie didn't turn around.

"No? I thought you were following this new case?" His heart sank. Jamie was sulking, which was never a good start.

"No."

"What's happened?" Allan said in resigned tones.

Jamie hunched defensively.

"You've fought with your Casey-cop, haven't you?" Allan sighed. "What happened to the easy-come, easy go attitude? You used to boast about getting lucky with a different girl every few days."

Jamie hunched some more. "She's different."

Allan's face said *cliché*. His mouth said, "Well, you still need to keep shooting. You've only got about half of what you usually have, and you said you wanted to show in six months from the last one closing."

"You said that. I didn't. I'll show when I'm ready. Go away and stop fussing. I don't need a mom."

"No, you need a keeper. When you've finished sulking, go shoot something. If your Casey won't play, shoot the others. Or that ME – the autopsy shots were a good sequence. Or the Captain – Kent, isn't it? You've hardly got any of him, and it's a hole in your story."

Jamie grunted.

"I thought he was happy with you?"

"Not right now, okay?"

Allan didn't have to think for long. "Marcol complained about the letter, didn't he?" It was the only matter which would involve Captain Kent. Casey being mad with Jamie was pretty understandable – Jamie had never learned the value of restraint when it came to photography, or indeed anything else that he wanted – but if Kent was mad too, it had to be wider.

"Yeah. Weaselling tattling sonofabitch hit on Casey and then, when he got knocked back, tried to weasel in another way, and when *that* didn't work, he went running to his Captain to bitch. That got back to Kent and he roasted us all."

"Oh. And that was the first she'd heard about your letter. I guess she didn't like it?"

"No."

"Oh, Jamie. I told you it wasn't a good idea."

"I told *you* that nobody steals my shots! And *you* agreed. You were the one agitating to protect all my rights. Well, we will. You get an answer to that letter or you start a lawsuit. I want him to *hurt*. I'll turn that rat bastard into pulp." Jamie trailed off into an ominous dark mutter which contained no distinguishable words but a great deal of anger.

Allan left him to fester. Trying to talk sense into Jamie was a losing game at the best of times, and this wasn't the best of times. He'd known — and said — that this was one of Jamie's crusades, and those rarely ended well.

He had a thought. Maybe he'd give Jamie's Andy-cop a call. He'd been a good guy, and they'd shared some interests. He might get a better understanding of the whole mess that way. He wandered downstairs to his neat office, and extracted Andy's card, then left it for Monday.

**

Casey summoned Tyler in good time to reach Schickoff & Schultz for their interview with Asher's team. Conversation on the way, directed by Casey, stuck strictly to the tactics of the meeting.

When the cops were shown into another boardroom, walls adorned with chiaroscuro sketches of buildings, six people had already assembled. Not one of them was African-American. Two — the youngest — were female. Casey sensed Tyler going on alert, precisely as planned.

"Good afternoon," Casey said. "I'm Detective Clement, of the Thirty-Sixth Precinct, and this is my colleague, Detective Tyler. We're investigating the murder of Asher Washington, and you may have relevant information." She paused. Nobody spoke. "First, we're interested in Asher's role in your team. Second, we're interested in the discovery hearing on January 27. We don't need to know the legal details, but we need to know who was there, and as much as you can remember about the opposition and their movements." She didn't want to say explicitly that she was searching for a time where Asher could have been approached, in case any of this team had been involved. "Another pause, unfilled. "Could you start by introducing yourselves, please." She gazed meaningfully at the first person to her right.

"I'm Will Cornwall."

"Terry Venmar."

"Marla Darter."

"Rick Morris."

"Vanna Wells."

"Simon Palliser."

Casey wrote them neatly on her pad to keep them straight. "Okay. Tell me about Asher." She smiled encouragingly. "What was he like to work with?" As she held the group's attention, Tyler faded into the background, sitting away from the table. Nobody had really noticed him, as planned.

"He worked hard," Vanna offered.

"We all work hard. He was efficient. Good at what he did."

"A bit eager," Rick said. "Always making sure he was present."

"What makes you think he was too eager?" Casey asked.

"He was just like the rest of us," Marla snipped. "He didn't do anything

Terry didn't, or me."

Rick subsided. Will stepped in. "I was in charge of the team. Asher was as strong as anyone. He was in early, left late, took care. He didn't need any more guidance than anyone else."

Casey noted a slight hesitation in Will's description, and decided to ask him to stay back for a private discussion.

"Okay," she said. "About this discovery hearing, then. Will, could you give me a general overview, and everyone else can add to it?"

Will outlined the hearing, with Simon adding detail. Casey scribbled down a messy timeline and then the movements, and looked up. "Okay," she said. "Can I use this whiteboard?"

"Sure."

Casey drew the courtroom in one corner, and then listed out in order what had happened.

"This is what you've told me. Could each of you think back and make sure that this covers everything?"

Rick stood up. "Here," he said, taking the pen and scribbling. "Asher wasn't there then – the judge had called recess. He'd gone to the restroom." He marked it on. "Quite a few people did – it was likely the only chance."

"Thanks. Anything else?"

"No." Rick sat down. Casey noted that he'd paid no attention to Tyler and that he hadn't hesitated to write on the whiteboard, rather than simply telling her. Interesting. Rick's unconscious bias was showing. He was assuming he was more important than she or Tyler, but…Will was the team leader here. Mm. Nothing like ambitious co-workers to add a little venom to a mix. A solo chat with Will was definitely indicated.

"Can anyone else add anything? It doesn't matter if you think it's irrelevant, we might not. I'll give you all a card, just in case you remember anything later. We're always happy to hear from people."

There was a brief silence. Nobody added anything.

"Are we done?" Rick asked, flicking a glance at his watch.

"Yes. Thank you."

Casey took advantage of the general shuffling for the door to tap Will on the shoulder and draw him discreetly aside. "Can you stay on for a few minutes?"

"Sure," he said, "but why?" His forehead creased.

"I want your candid impressions, without the rest of them hearing."

He relaxed. "Give me a moment, and I'll be back."

CHAPTER TWELVE

Will slipped back into the conference room, smiling. "I guessed you'd want a chat," he said. "Norman said I should co-operate as much as possible, and you've agreed to respect client confidentiality, so if we get into anything tricky I'll tell you and you can decide whether you'll need to get a warrant or try to subpoena it."

Casey grinned back, consciously establishing ease between them. "Thanks. So, let's talk about the team and how Asher fitted in. I got the impression you didn't totally agree with Rick."

Before answering, Will looked hard at Tyler, still slightly back from the table. "Does your partner wanna come join us? Or is he deliberately keeping out of the picture so I forget he's there?"

Casey accorded Will a look of respect. "He was. I think we're done with that tactic."

"Sure." Tyler sat beside Casey. "I'm Tyler."

"About the team?" Casey recalled them all to the discussion.

"Sure. Asher was eager to be on this case, but they all were. It's huge, and when we win, there'll be plenty of kudos to share out. Still, he was more than pulling his weight. He felt he had to work harder, prove himself."

"Rick didn't seem to like him," Tyler said.

"Yeah, well. Rick's gunning for the top, and Asher was competition." Will shifted on his chair. "And, well, Rick's not great when he's challenged, and he'd missed a couple of things – that's normal," he added quickly, "that's why we have a team. It's set up so more than one person goes over the same files. Anyway, Asher was the second eye and Rick was a bit embarrassed by that."

"The others didn't say much."

"They all got along fine. There was no bitching that I heard, except Rick occasionally."

"Okay. What about the hearing?"

Will's expression turned serious. "The other side was playing hardball. It's not like big litigation is ever nice, but they were pulling every trick in the legal book to try and run up our costs – we swallow them, you know: this is all pro bono. So they complained to the judge that we were oppressing them, but he wasn't having any of it" – he smiled broadly. "It was all a bit tense," he digressed, "and then they complained that he wasn't listening to their arguments" –

"Bad idea."

"Sure was – and he glared over his glasses and said, 'I'm listening, I just don't agree with anything you've said'."

Casey laughed. "Ouch. Guess that was a good moment?"

"Oh, yes." Will smiled again. "Anyway, not long after that he called recess to see if we could get an agreement without needing a ruling, so that's when everyone took a restroom break." He leaned forward. "Asher came back, and he looked worried, so I took him aside and asked if everything was okay. He said that two of the guys from Dorland & Andrews – they're Varen & Dart's lawyers – had asked him to go get coffee with them, and he didn't think that was appropriate. He was right, and I said so. Even if they'd only discussed the ball game, it wouldn't be appropriate."

"I see. Can we have the names of both of them, please?"

"Michael Farman – the junior – and Dermot O'Hagan." Tyler made a note. "I told Asher to come straight to me if anyone else approached him, but as far as I know nobody did." He glanced at his watch. "I need to get back to it. Monday's the deadline for them to produce the response to our first batch of supplementaries, and for us to send ours across, so it's all go. They're due by five p.m."

"Thanks. If you think of anything more, or if any of the team says anything, give one of us a call."

***

"What did you think?" Casey asked, before Tyler could open any discussion.

Tyler shrugged. "Nothing open. Didn't get the vibe there was. Unconscious, yeah. Don't think there's a likely issue in there."

"Okay. You'd know."

"Same as you would for women."

"Yeah. Remember Sackson?"

"Sure do." Tyler shifted in his seat, which was as good as a squirm from anyone else. "Like Marcol."

"There are plenty of them about," Casey shut him down. "No need to give them airtime." Tyler took the hint. "I don't think we got much from that. I hoped there'd be something more from the discovery hearing, but Asher closed it down right away."

"So Will said," Tyler pointed out.

"Yeah. You're right," she mused, even though Tyler hadn't drawn a conclusion. "We should talk to those two." She pulled out her phone and called Fremont: asking him to find contact details. "Okay," she said. "That's for Monday. We're all off shift tomorrow."

"Not too long till off shift now," Tyler muttered.

"Finish up, then an end of day round-up, and then we can all go home."

Tyler didn't comment, though he expected that Bigfoot would have views on the end-of-day activities.

***

Casey looked up as O'Leary's mountainous shadow fell across her desk, a mere few minutes after she'd briefed the team on the results of the meeting. The mug of coffee that followed it didn't change her closed expression.

"You get anything more on Varen & Dart?" she asked neutrally.

O'Leary's caterpillar eyebrows drew together. "I don't wanna talk about the case, an' you know it. You ain't said more'n three words in a row that ain't about the case all day, an' I've seen thunderstorms with less black clouds than're floatin' around your head right now."

"There's nothing to say. Let's talk about the case." Her face was utterly bland, her words unemphasised. O'Leary felt like she'd slapped him.

"I ain't seen your boy today, either," he tried.

"I don't own him. Call him, if you're worried. You've got his number." She looked up; eyes shuttered. "Now, about Varen & Dart. Did Fremont turn up anything more?"

"Not yet."

"Then get Larson to add these two guys – O'Hagan and Farman – to his gun checking, as well as the discovery team at Schickoff & Schultz."

O'Leary gave up, but the next time Casey took a break, he exchanged a few words with Tyler, who, not long after that, made a call. When he looked up after that, Casey had gone, without farewell.

***

Carval had spent the day in sour solitude. He'd heard Allan making calls and managing matters, but hadn't cared enough to go and find out if anything interesting was happening. He'd messed with the photos and filters, but hadn't managed any enthusiasm for that either. He'd picked up his phone a dozen times, and put it down again. He wouldn't apologise for defending his own interests. Casey should have understood. She should

107

have let him explain. He heard again *what a mistake that was*, which bit just as hard as the first time she'd said it. *I didn't need a hero* echoed through his head. He hadn't been acting the hero. He *hadn't*. Why would he bother acting the hero? It wasn't that sort of a relationship – and that was her fault too. She wouldn't let him in more than an inch.

It never occurred to him that Casey had hit the nail on the head. He'd done it all in the subconscious hope that she'd open up.

His morass of misery was interrupted by the phone, which he forced himself to answer.

"Carval?"

"Yeah?"

"Tyler. Didn't see you today."

"No." Carval was as brusque as Tyler.

"Want to spar?"

Suddenly, mindless violence seemed like an excellent plan. "Yeah."

"Precinct gym. Soon as you like."

Shortly, Carval arrived at the precinct gym. Tyler, ready for action, was waiting there for him. "Best of three?"

"Whatever," Carval said. He'd be happy to hit things till either they broke or his hands did.

"Okay. Till it's out of your system. Go change."

When Carval came back out, O'Leary and Andy had turned up. He nodded at them.

"We came to see the circus," O'Leary drawled. "I always liked the elephants."

"Yeah, because they were your best friends in the Zoo," Andy quipped.

Carval regarded the men. O'Leary's light eyes were wholly sympathetic. Even Andy, whose history had left him wary of Carval, was indefinably aligned to him.

"An' when you've dropped Tyler on the mat a coupla times, we'll all go for a beer."

"Like hell," Tyler said. "If he does, you're up, Bigfoot."

"Sure. I love an easy workout."

Carval got on to the mat, tried to grapple – and hit the mat hard.

"That the best you got?" Tyler taunted. Carval growled, and made the next attempt with more guile: eyes open for the main chance, guard up. Hitting Tyler became his only focus: he only just missed a kick to the side, defending against Tyler's shots; moving in – and then his feet were taken out from under him and he hit the mat again. At that point, he lost his temper. He didn't remember much about the next ten minutes: going down, but hitting Tyler *hard* with a solid punch and then sweep-kicking his legs out while he was trying to recover breath; Tyler getting up and taking him down again.

"Okay, enough," O'Leary rumbled. "You c'n fight, when you like. Now come sit down an' take a breather."

Tyler grinned. "Better?"

"Not really," Carval admitted.

"Go clean up, an' then me 'n' Tyler'll show you how it's done. An' if you like, you c'n take some shots of it." In O'Leary's tones, Carval had a sudden memory from very early in their acquaintance: O'Leary telling Casey *we'll go by that li'l coffee shop you like so much*, trying to cheer her up.

"Throwing me a bone?" he asked acidly.

"Naw. Tyler said it: you're one of us now. Cheerin' you up. You 'n' that camera are never apart, an' you won't get a better chance to take shots of sparrin'. You won't get better sparrin', neither. So do somethin' you like doin', an' iffen it don't make you happier, leastways you won't get any more miserable. Then we'll all go get some beer an' if you're still miserable you c'n drown it."

"I guess."

Carval cleaned up, picked up his camera, and came back out to find that O'Leary in sparring gear was even more intimidatingly huge than O'Leary in everyday clothes. The man had muscles on his muscles, and it was clear that, haystack imitations notwithstanding, he was in top condition.

"Watch carefully," Andy said quietly. "We don't go in for compliments" – he flashed a quick grin at Carval – "but you won't see anything better. They take the inter-precinct trophies every time. I'm surprised they're still allowed to play."

"Guess there's no money if you win?"

"Nope. Just pride, and we've got plenty of that."

"Pub quiz," Carval remembered.

"Yep. We like winning. You might've noticed that we're not the popular team. We don't care. We're the best."

Carval winced. "Unlike Marcol's pals," he said heavily.

"Save it for the bar," Andy advised. "Watch this."

Carval watched, open mouthed, camera clicking non-stop: full views, close-ups of grips and kicks, the hard impacts of feet and fists to bodies, the slap of Tyler hitting the floor: his gasped, lung-filling intakes of breath: the flex and contrast of biceps and distended veins. The men were unbelievably fast, and he had to use the full range of shutter speed, fast focus and aperture to have any hope of capturing the motion. He'd call it *Training*, then set it against his shots of the recruit-officers training at the Academy and show the world the difference.

Finally, he shot O'Leary's massive paws reaching down to Tyler, dumped on to the mat one last time, pulling him up: the contrast of dark skin with light in a handclasp of brotherhood and mutual respect.

"Beer," O'Leary decided. "Abbey."

The others grumbled, for form's sake, and acquiesced.

"So. Guess it didn't go well." O'Leary said, when they'd all sat down with their beer.

"No." Carval's tone didn't invite questions.

"'Kay. We still like you. An' anyone who faces Kent down like you did has got some stones."

Tyler nodded.

"Yep," Andy said. "I'm cool with you. I could even take you to some culture." He made a dismissive gesture at the others. "It's not like they're interested."

"Naw."

"I think you'd do better with Allan," Carval said, insensibly eased by the camaraderie. "I take photos. I go to art exhibitions – you never know what you'll learn – but if you want theatre or opera or ballet, don't look at me. The only dancing I wanna see is the Giants' wide receivers dancing around the opposition defence."

Andy grimaced. Tyler and O'Leary grinned.

"Told you he was a good guy."

"Philistines," Andy muttered.

Nobody mentioned the elephant in the room again, until Andy called time on his sodas and O'Leary claimed he needed to get home to Pete's cooking.

Tyler didn't move. "Another?" he asked.

"Might as well."

"Don't do talking about things. But…all in this shit together. Going after that sonofabitch wasn't wrong. Coulda told her earlier, but it's done. No blame on you."

"Who'll help her with her dad?" Carval asked.

"Huh? Us, same as always."

"You think she'll let you?"

Tyler shrugged. "Bigfoot'll interfere. Get that you're upset. Nothing you can do about it now."

Tyler put another beer down, and Carval drank it, and the next, and the next. And then he went home and sat, empty, in his soulless apartment, until the late evening faded to night and the night to morning. His camera lay on the table, untouched from the moment he'd downloaded it. He hadn't even looked at the shots of sparring.

***

Casey woke on Sunday morning, far too early for comfort, looked out of her window at the frosty city, and went back to bed, hoping to find that the last two days had magically been erased. Her soft décor didn't soothe her, the plump pillows couldn't pet her, the warmth of the quilt had no heartbeat, nor did it wrap arms around her. She refused to acknowledge the unsatisfactory performance of her bedlinen, rose, dressed, and, sipping at an excellent espresso, considered the day ahead. Not only was there rather too much day for her taste, dread crept over her as she remembered that she had to have dinner with her father that evening.

She stared sightlessly out over the streets, thick, grey clouds matching her grey mood. She'd have liked to go out for a long run, but it was too cold and the streets too slippery. Besides, she didn't want to think about the case, and running would push it to the front of her mind. Breaking an ankle wouldn't help anything, and being unable to work would leave her going crazy inside two days: especially since she wouldn't be able to escape O'Leary's attempts to play Big Brother.

She needed, she decided, something to take her mind of the whole lot of infuriating, oversized, overbearing, unhelpful...*men*! If she could simply find a distraction, she could put it all behind her and be normal again. No arguments, no discussions, no hurt.

No heroes.

She brewed another cup of coffee, and pondered. She didn't like the look of any of the current exhibitions, and the only way she'd pass the doors of MOMA was as a Haagen exhibit: dead as a doornail. She could read, but nothing appealed; she didn't do crafts. Daytime TV was dreadful. She needed to exercise: the stretch and burn of exertion until she was too exhausted to think, remember, or care. There were, she remembered, treadmills in the precinct gym.

She collected her gym gear and left immediately, parking around the corner from the precinct and sneaking past her floor to avoid unwanted questions. She squashed the impulse to work: Kent would have her guts for garters if he caught her, and the way her luck was running, he'd be at his desk. Less than ten minutes later, she was on a treadmill in a mercifully vacant gym, turning up the velocity and adding a slight incline. She sank into the motion of her muscles and her hard-beat playlist, and let her mind empty while her body stretched and strained. After the first mile, she turned the incline up again, after the third, she brought it back to flat, and kept on running.

When she physically couldn't run any more, she showered, slipped out, and went home, where the whole mess of her life was still looming, elephantine, in her apartment. All that she'd achieved was an aching body to join her aching heart, and she still had to face her father and pretend that everything was fine; everything was just as it used to be: he'd never been arrested at JFK while drunk, never been given a desk appearance ticket, never promised he'd attend rehab and AA. At least then she wouldn't have hoped.

At least then she wouldn't have been disappointed.

She changed into a dark green wool skirt and co-ordinating sweater; drove to Brooklyn, obeying every traffic regulation; parked precisely – it occupied an extra few seconds – and walked up to her father's apartment.

"Catkin," he said happily. He didn't sound drunk. Of course, that didn't mean he hadn't been drinking. She used the excuse of hanging up her coat to glance around, as if his apartment were a fresh crime scene. The room was tidy; table set for dinner, a jug of water and glasses already out. She could smell cooking, and noted an apple pie on the counter. It all screamed 'family dinner on a Sunday evening'.

It all screamed *fake*, but she had no proof. Feelings weren't evidence, and preconceptions were dangerous.

Casey wandered over to the kitchenette. "What's for dinner?"

"I got some of those Southern chicken tenderloins."

"Sounds good. What are we having with them?"

Panic skittered over her father's face. "Peas," he managed. "I'll put them on in a minute." Panic was overtaken by relief that he had a solution.

"Mm," Casey soothed, covering up the void that had opened in her gut at his failure. "Apple pie for dessert?"

"Yes. With ice cream," he added, as if that proved his ability to make dinner.

"Great. I love apple pie. Can I do anything?"

"No, it's all fine. Go sit down – do you want a soda?"

"Yes, please." She'd rather have had whiskey, straight up, but that wouldn't help anything. If her father *was* dry, it would be cruel. If he wasn't...she couldn't bear to be the one who started him off tonight.

He poured her a Coke, and then poured himself a different drink.

"What's that?" she asked.

"Dr Pepper. You know I never really liked Coke, or Pepsi."

True. But a separate bottle could hide so many things. She suspected him, and hated herself for it; unconsciously resenting him more for dragging her down to that level. She should have faith in him.

Her father put the peas in a pan of water, and turned the ring on. It was all normal. All fine.

Up until the third time he put a pinch of salt in.

"Dad, you already salted the water."

"No, no. I didn't." But his eyes flickered, as if he couldn't remember.

Casey put the salt away, rather than argue further, and then sat down to sip her Coke.

"Dinner's ready," came a few moments later. Casey helped to set it out, and served them both some chicken and peas.

She almost spat it out, but choked her mouthful down. He was eating as if it were a gourmet meal.

The chicken was atrociously overcooked, the peas indeed over-salted.

Had she cooked this, she'd have thrown it in the trash. Since her father had, she couldn't. He'd used to be able to cook the basics. Even eight months ago, he'd been able...or had he? They'd had a lot of ready-made meals – but then, that was mostly what she ate. And yet, eight months, six months, even four months ago – he could read the timing instructions. Today, he'd failed that test.

CHAPTER THIRTEEN

She chewed and swallowed, washed down each mouthful with copious gulps of water or Coke, and tried to talk about banal cases, pretending that everything was normal, everything was fine. Her father pretended he was following the stories, but that was as unconvincing as she felt she was. By dessert, she'd almost given up. She tried one last time: a story she couldn't remember telling him before, from way back in her uniformed days with O'Leary at the Third Precinct, before they'd both made detective and moved to the Thirty-Sixth. Before her mom had died.

"Did I ever tell you about the time we got called to a domestic dispute?" she asked, oh-so-painfully-bright and cheerful.

"No, I don't think so. Is that recent?"

"No. It was before I made detective."

She swallowed. She hadn't told him about anything that wasn't a murder case for years, though she didn't tax him with the gorier details. He'd loved them, till it was his wife on the slab; but he still – he *had* – liked the stories of who did it, and how they found them. Before…he'd have known it couldn't be recent. Then again, until he'd been arrested, drunk – she'd thought he'd been proud of her, so maybe he'd just hidden his lack of interest. Even so, even though she'd far rather leave now: go home and *not* cry for the dad she didn't have; even so, she had to try.

"Well, we – O'Leary and me" –

"O'Leary's the big guy?"

Her gut twisted again. Her father had met O'Leary. O'Leary was unforgettable.

"Yeah. So we were told to go deal with a domestic dispute in one of the parks. We could hear the yelling long before we saw them, but the funny thing was that it didn't sound like usual. Anyway, we came around the corner and guess what we found?" She waited hopefully, while her father

114

caught up.

"A park warden?" he tried.

"Nope." She consciously forced a wide grin. "There were these two dog walkers, and one had the weirdest dog you've ever seen. It looked like a rag rug – all black, too. O'Leary stared at it till he nearly tripped over a bench, and just said" – she tried to match his bucolic speech – "'I ain't *never* seen a dog with dreadlocks'."

Her father blinked. "A dog with dreadlocks? I don't think I've ever seen one of those either." Life sparked in his eyes. "We had a dog when I was a boy. A spaniel – mostly. I think there was a good chunk of something else. So what about this dog?"

"Well, the other guy had a bunch of little teacup rats, all nipping at the black dog. So O'Leary loomed up behind them and asked what the problem was, and suddenly they shut up – funny, that." She waited expectantly, and her father managed a slightly confused smile. "Whenever they see someone who's six-ten, they tend to calm down in a hurry."

"Six-ten? I thought O'Leary was the other big guy?"

"Tyler."

"Yeah, him."

"No, it's O'Leary." A year ago, her father could have picked each of them out of a line-up. "Anyway, turned out that the two walkers had history, and then a really pretty girl turned up with a pure-bred retriever. We found out that she was with the rag rug's owner, and the other guy was jealous. So we wrote him up, and threatened to have the rats given to the local pound if we had to deal with him again."

"No corpse? I thought you only did murders."

"This was before I was a detective." She'd said that already. "I guess we've seen murder for sillier things."

"I'd forgotten how much I loved that dog," her father digressed. "He was great. Dumb as a rock, but I used to take him out most days." Memory clouded his eyes. "Brown and white. Soft ears. He loved me playing with them." He drifted off.

"Do you want a coffee?" Casey asked.

"No, that wasn't his name."

"No, a cup of coffee." Her tone was sharper.

"No need to snap, Catkin. Just because I can't remember his name, forty years on."

"Dad, I asked if you wanted a *drink* of coffee. Twice."

"No, thanks. I won't sleep if I have coffee now."

"Okay. I'd better get home. Early start tomorrow. I'll see you on Thursday."

"Thursday?"

"For the hearing, Dad."

"Oh. Yes. Sure."

She forced herself to hug him, shrugged her coat on, and left.

She didn't allow herself to think about the faint scent of breath mints until she was in her own apartment. She didn't allow herself to cry at all. There was no point. It wouldn't change anything.

Nothing would change anything now.

***

O'Leary ambled into the bullpen around an hour earlier than he normally arrived, hoping to beat Casey to the punch. He had some idea of walking her out to that pet coffee place of hers, and trying to pound sense through her concrete head, though he also knew that he needed to start with an apology. He couldn't leave his pal to deal with all the shit with her father without telling her that the team was just as much there for her as it had been four days ago – whatever she thought.

His hopeful plan was derailed as soon as he saw Casey, already at her desk, and collapsed entirely when she lifted her head at his cheerful "Mornin'."

"Hey," she said, and dropped her gaze again. Even that short glance showed O'Leary that far more was wrong than there had been on Saturday. From the unusual untidiness of her desk – three loose pieces of paper on which she wasn't writing – he concluded that she was deep in thought. From her pale face and the circles beneath her eyes, he concluded that Sunday hadn't gone well, and further that it most likely concerned her father. He also knew that Casey would have hated that he'd reached his conclusions in less time than it took him to amble to the break room, where he started his own barrel-sized mug of coffee and assessed his options. None of them seemed good. He contented himself by making Casey one of those tiny little espressos she tossed back like water, which he carried cautiously to her desk. Tiny little cups tended to end up in tiny little pieces, O'Leary found, which was irritating. He didn't do a thing to them, and they shattered. It wasn't fair.

"Thanks," she said automatically.

O'Leary returned to his desk, casting an eye over the murder board, which was more extensively decorated than on Saturday, and conferred with Fremont over Varen & Dart. At an appropriate moment, as early as he could hide it from Casey, he beckoned Tyler.

"I reckon Casey's gotten another problem with her dad," he started. Tyler nodded. "An' it seems to me that there ain't nobody she wants around." Another nod. "So I think you oughta keep Carval close to us, 'cause she's gonna need him whether she admits it or not, an' you an' Andy stay outta the way at lunchtime an' I'll take her for a little chat, old-pals-like."

"Won't listen," Tyler said.

"She don't hafta. She just needs to come with me. Team's there for her, just like it's there for all of us, whether anyone wants it or not. Even iffen she don't believe it right now, it's true."

"She can't shoot you," Tyler said mordantly. "Okay. Take Carval. You got Casey. Dumbasses," which accurately summed up the situation.

***

Casey contacted Dorland & Andrews early in the day, and assembled her existing evidence until they called back. They could, they begrudgingly admitted, see her that afternoon. Their tone flicked her on the raw.

"You can arrange for the two people to be available in your office, or I'll have them brought in right now," she snapped. "This is a murder inquiry, and if your firm obstructs me, I'll make sure it's known to every lawyer in Manhattan. How will that look?"

Suddenly, they couldn't do enough to help. Farman and O'Hagan would be available as soon as Detective Clement could reach Dorland & Andrews, for as long as necessary. Whatever she needed.

"Tyler?" she called. "Let's go see Dorland & Andrews." She everted her lips in an expression which bore no resemblance to a happy smile.

"I wanna go," O'Leary pouted. "You don't take me anywhere any more. 'S not fair. You don't love me no more."

"Nope," Casey said, which, a week ago, would have been more of a joke. "Tyler saw the first lot. He's coming with me to see the others. Same reasons."

"Same shit," Tyler added. "Biases."

"Or they were worried that Asher would get them into more trouble," Casey said. "I'm sure that's unethical, and even if Will didn't escalate it, it didn't look good."

"If it went down like that. Only got Will's word for it."

"That's why we're going to see them now."

Casey had put her coat on and started down the stairs before Tyler caught up.

"Bit quick," he commented.

"I want this solved. It's been almost a week and we don't have a clear suspect; we don't know who owned rifles; we don't know who was calling him. We don't freaking know *anything*," she bit.

Wisely, Tyler said nothing. Since that was his usual mode of operation, Casey didn't notice his caution.

"I want something solid. What's Larson been doing? Can't he read? I've seen blind frogs who can cross-match faster than he can. There must be something in the background checks."

Tyler could see doom heading for Larson, which wasn't wholly justified.

Sure, the man was slow. But Casey at Force Twelve intimidation wouldn't speed him up. He had a thought.

"Least we're missing Renfrew."

"He'll be there all day. Poking his interfering nose in and getting in our way."

Tyler decided to stay quiet. Uncomfortable silence didn't stop his brain working, however. He thought that Casey could do with a good hard sparring session, which thought was parked for later discussion with Bigfoot.

As they pulled up at Dorland & Andrews, Casey donned cold professionalism, only thinly covering her frustrated anger. She announced them to the receptionist with frigid courtesy, and, to Tyler's private horror, didn't pour herself coffee when ushered into the boardroom. She sat down at the head of the table. The two lawyers arrived mere seconds later.

"Mr Farman. Mr O'Hagan. I'm Detective Clement, Homicide. I'm investigating the murder of Asher Washington. You are persons of interest."

The two lawyers thumped down in shock. Tyler sat back to watch the show. Both men were already rattled.

"You were in attendance at the discovery hearing for the Varen & Dart case on January 27. Asher was also present. During a break in proceedings, you approached Asher. Describe that meeting, please." It wasn't a question. Skittering glances bounced between the two lawyers.

"Need I remind you that you are obliged to co-operate with a murder investigation?" Casey enquired coldly after thirty seconds of silence. "Or should I inform your superiors that you are refusing to talk – and why? I take it that they are unaware of your actions?"

"We didn't do anything wrong!" O'Hagan broke first. "We only asked him if he wanted a coffee."

"Is that normal practice for opposing sides of a major case?"

Silence.

"So it isn't."

More silence.

"Who asked you to approach Asher?"

"It was my idea," Farman said sulkily. "There's nothing wrong with being pals with other lawyers."

"So you decided to make friends with someone from the firm with which you were directly engaged in litigation, when you knew that Asher was intimately involved in the case? Interesting. Most people go to a bar to make friends, not the men's restroom in the district court." She dripped disbelieving contempt.

"So what? What's that got to do with you?"

"Asher Washington was murdered. So everything to do with Asher is relevant to my investigation. Start talking." They didn't. Her fingers tapped on the table, short nails clacking down. "I'm waiting."

"He was clearly the low man on the team."

"Had to be."

Tyler's knuckles tightened. *Why* was written across his features.

"So we thought maybe he'd be so green that he'd say something if we were nice to him."

Farman picked up the story. "We got a chance in the restroom. We only said if he wanted a coffee, we were getting one, and he could come along with us, have a break. He said no."

"Was that all you said to him?"

O'Hagan coloured.

"Every word. Truthfully." The snap of command made him blink. Farman cringed. Under the weight of intimidation emanating from Casey, any defiance disintegrated faster than wet Kleenex in a wind tunnel.

"We said that we were hiring, and if he did us a favour, we'd make sure that we said we knew him and he was a good guy."

"Like a recommendation," O'Hagan added.

"And he said no. Then he went off and we never heard from him."

"Tell me," Casey said coldly, "are either of you familiar with the New York State Bar Rules of Professional Conduct?"

"Of course we are!"

"Don't lie to me. You are not. Because if you *were*, you would know that you were asking Asher to reveal confidential information and giving him a financial reason not to act in the client's best interests. You weren't taking care — as a lawyer is required to do — to prevent the disclosure of confidential information, *and* you were trying to employ a lawyer who was working for the opposition. You do realise that if Asher had been employed, your firm would have had to recuse themselves from acting for Varen & Dart?" Casey wasn't entirely sure about that, but she was certain that the sorry pair in front of her didn't know either. "So your firm would have lost a major client. Well done."

They stared at her. "How" –

"That doesn't matter. What *matters* is that you were prepared to violate every ethical principle the Bar tried to instil in you. If you'll break those rules, you'll break others. Right now, you're my best suspects. Both of you had motive. Asher Washington could have reported one or both of you for unethical conduct. That's your jobs gone – and no chance of ever getting another one. You'd be flipping burgers till you were ninety to pay off your student loans. Do either of you own a gun?" she rapped out.

"Uh?"

"We're already checking."

"No," Farman said.

"Yes," O'Hagan admitted.

"We'll need to check ballistics. Bring your gun to the Thirty-Sixth precinct within twenty-four hours." Casey knew she was pushing her luck, but they were scared stiff.

"Okay," he faltered. "This evening."

"Tell the duty officer what it's about. They'll ensure I get it. You'll be given a receipt."

"Okay."

"Now. Exactly what happened at the court?"

"I didn't kill him!" O'Hagan cried, suddenly catching up with the implications of Casey's demands. For a supposedly intelligent professional, he wasn't showing himself in a good light.

"Really? Start talking. Both of you. Just because only one of you had a gun doesn't mean you weren't both in on it."

Tyler scrawled on a piece of paper and pushed it under Casey's nose. She whipped a glance over it. *One phone call, one shot.* In Tyler-speak, that meant that he thought that they had planned that one man could call Asher so the other had a clean shot. She tapped her finger on the paper, thumb very slightly upward, which told Tyler that she'd both gotten it and complimented his insight, and conveniently also conveyed impatience to the two terrified lawyers.

"We couldn't have shot him. We're here twenty hours a day. Work, go home for four hours, back here."

"I'll need your exact whereabouts and timing for the seven days starting January 28. If I so much as think *once* that you're shading the truth, I'll request the security system records for you swiping in and out of these offices." She'd do that anyway. "How will that look to your bosses? They already know I'm interviewing you in connection with a homicide."

Her brown eyes were hard as she pushed two blocks of paper at them. "Start writing. Everything. We'll wait. Oh – and just move apart several spaces."

They gulped and moved. Fast.

They wrote as quickly as their fingers could fly, and handed over their sheets.

"Now. Write down all of your telephone and cell phone numbers. Home, work, pagers, every single one." More sheets were passed over. "Is there anything else at all that you should tell me, bearing in mind your professional duties not to obstruct a criminal investigation?"

They shook their heads in frantic harmony.

"Here's my card. Anything you think of, you tell me right away."

"Are we done?" one quavered, eyeing the exit.

"For now," she said ominously. "Thank you for your co-operation." She stood. Tyler, who hadn't needed to say a single word throughout the interview, followed her out. She didn't look back.

"Now what?" Tyler asked.

"Cross-check numbers to Asher's phone. Warn Ballistics. Scare Larson into working faster. Check their alibis, if any."

"Gonna report them?"

"Might ask Will Cornwall why he didn't."

Conversation lapsed until they got back to the precinct and relayed the information, after which Casey buried herself in cross-matching and refused to lift her head for a moment. She didn't like cross-matching, but it required her full concentration and meant that nobody would disturb her. She noticed with relief that Renfrew hadn't appeared, and got on with her work. She'd talk to Larson later.

Not long later, O'Leary ambled up to her. "Lunchtime, Casey."

"I'm not hungry. I'm trying to get this done."

O'Leary peered down at the papers. "'Kay. I'll give you the half hour you need to finish, an' then we'll go get lunch."

O'Leary had no business knowing how long she'd need, Casey thought bitterly. It was clear that he wouldn't leave her alone. She knew his game: playing Big Brother and trying to convince her to forgive the team and Carval. Especially Carval. Well, she wasn't ready for that. And Carval could go sit on a sharp stick and swivel, and she'd press down on his head as he did. With a sledgehammer.

Half an hour later, during which Casey's vengeful thoughts had reached truly frightening heights of viciousness, correlating precisely with the lack of any useful cross-matching results, O'Leary returned, coat and a violently scarlet scarf already on, and loomed meaningfully over her.

"Lunch," he said. "An' iffen you were plannin' to object, that profiler's due in any time now, an' iffen he sees that scowl you're sportin', he'll be all over you wantin' to talk about the team."

Casey's expression would have ignited rock, but she stood up and pulled on coat, scarf and hat. O'Leary was – marginally – a better option than Renfrew, and more importantly, O'Leary would continue the argument until Renfrew turned up and *observed*.

CHAPTER FOURTEEN

Over sandwiches and soda, Casey resolutely didn't rise to a single bait that O'Leary dangled, until his normal equable state began to crack.

"You can't just pretend everythin's okay. It's not, an' you know it's not."

"I'm not the one who's making all the fuss and wanting cosy chats. Just leave it."

"You're part of the team."

"The team that decided what was best for me without asking?" she hissed. "Tell me where that's in the rulebook? Anyway, it doesn't matter. We can work cases just the same as ever, and as long as work's good, it doesn't matter once shift's over."

"That ain't true," O'Leary said sternly, "an' you know it."

"I don't need anything else."

"That ain't true, either. Anyways, it don't matter what you think. You're a part of the team whether you like it or not an' we ain't lettin' you drop out. You got us, like *that* or not."

"I thought we were a team but when it came to choosing you went with *him*."

"Don't be dumb" –

"You could have told me," she said flatly. "You could have warned me."

"We screwed up. We know that. All of us've screwed up before an' we've fixed it. C'mon." His light eyes watched her from under short, sandy lashes. "'T ain't like you to walk away like this."

"I don't have *time* for this," she spat, temper snapping. "I don't have headspace to deal with you whimpering about something *you* got yourselves into. It doesn't need to be fixed because it doesn't affect work and if it doesn't mess up work, I don't care. Go play with your new pal and stop interfering, and when we're on shift, concentrate on solving the case and leave the amateur psychology to Dear Abby. This conversation is *done*."

O'Leary reached a ham-hand over the table and patted Casey's slumped shoulder, leaving his paw there so that she couldn't escape. "We're not done," he said. "'Cause this ain't just about us screwin' up. It's your pa, ain't it? He ain't dry." She shrugged. "Aw, Casey. Why didn't you say?" He drained his soda and ate the remains of his sandwich in two bites. "'Kay. We got time. Let's take a walk."

"We need to get back. There's nothing to talk about."

"Naw. We're not goin' back yet. Now you come along with me, so's the cold c'n clear your head a bit. Get your lunch to go, an' you c'n eat it later."

"I don't want it."

"Iffen you don't, I'll have it. That li'l bitty thin' they called a sandwich wouldn't feed a mouse."

Casey's pale, pinched face looked back at him, and she shoved the sandwich in his direction. O'Leary, who would eat anything that wouldn't eat him first, disposed of it in two more bites, and lumbered to his immense feet.

"C'mon. Ten minutes, an' then we'll go back. We c'n get you some more coffee on the way."

Casey acquiesced. It was easier than arguing, and she had no strength to argue with O'Leary's mass on a mission.

O'Leary led them up the steps into Sakura Park and over Riverside Drive to the Grant Memorial, consciously moderating his pace to Casey's. In other circumstances, he'd have hugged her, but today he didn't dare. She'd either shoot him or cry, and neither would be helpful at lunchtime on a work day. He simply padded along beside her, waiting.

When she turned towards the precinct, she still hadn't said anything.

"Coffee," O'Leary said. "Here's that shop you like."

"Whatever." She showed no enthusiasm whatsoever, and stopped before they reached the door. "It won't fix anything. You can't buy forgiveness, because there's nothing to forgive. Stick to work."

"Naw. An' bought forgiveness ain't no forgiveness at all, so we're not goin' down that rabbit hole. Coffee tastes good, though, an' it's hot. I'm cold, even if you're not." Casey simply shrugged, and didn't ask for anything.

O'Leary guided Casey inside the coffee bar, not allowing her the opportunity to shake him off. He ordered for them both, because whatever she might say, Casey with coffee was a better bet than Casey without coffee. She took it, with muttered thanks which conveyed no appreciation or gratitude, and marched back to the precinct without a further word.

Her mood darkened further when she spotted Renfrew in Kent's office, looking totally at home. Still, she could take the results of the final cross-matching forward, and then light a rocket under Larson's ass. There was plenty of work to be done, and nothing and no-one to distract her from doing it.

She put her head down, and went back to Tyler's idea. If someone had called Asher in order to stop him running…. "Tyler," she called.

"Yeah?" He came over to her desk.

"Your idea." Whatever she thought of the past three days' events, solving the crime was far more important than her feelings. Case, first to last. "You meant someone might've called Asher, so that he would stop to take the call?"

"Yeah. Easier to hit a stationary target."

"Okay. So if we look at the calls to his phone between five and, say, five forty-five – I know he was dead by five thirty-five, but if there were two of them one would have kept calling till the shooter told them that Asher was dead – maybe something'll ping. It's not those two from Dorland & Andrews – at least, it's not any of the numbers they gave us, and it doesn't look like it's any other number we know about." She tapped at the list of calls. "Look here." Tyler peered at the page. "There were calls up till one a.m., then a pause, then a constant stream starting again at five, near enough." She thought. "Did we get into his voicemail?"

"I'll call CSU."

"Anything to do with work would leave a message. We can wipe that out fast, and then see what's left."

"Never stopped working."

"No."

"Like someone else."

"Leave it." Her tone could cut rock. At his desk, O'Leary's massive head lifted. Andy looked up, and blinked.

"CSU," Tyler said tersely, and turned on his heel.

Casey stalked across the bullpen to Larson, who saw her coming but couldn't hide without it being obvious.

"How are you doing with the background check data and the permits?"

Larson squirmed. "Almost finished, Detective."

"Anything come up?"

"Uh," he stammered, "uh…nothing more on Kayla Burton, Mrs Washington, Steve Marthen or any of the Schickoff & Schultz lawyers. But Bill Roberts and Mr Washington both came up on the background checks for rifles" –

"When did you find them?"

"Early this morning."

Casey gasped. "And you didn't tell one of us *then*?"

"I was still checking for Farman and O'Hagan."

Casey clamped down on a deep desire to tear Larson's head from his neck and drink the blood. "Next time," she said, terrifyingly calmly, "as soon as you find something, tell one of us. That way, there's no delay in following up on it." She walked away, went straight to an interrogation room, and spent five minutes regulating her breathing and *not* throwing a tantrum of which any self-respecting two-year old would be proud. Larson must have had his brain surgically removed. How could he not know that they'd want to know that right away?

She returned to the bullpen, scrawled *Rifle* on the board next to both Caveman Bill and Uncle Washington, and left square brackets with question marks next to the Dorland & Andrews lawyers. Bill and the Washingtons would be meeting her again very soon. Now, a warrant for Bill's rifle wouldn't be an issue, since he'd lied to them. But the Washingtons might be a lot harder, because she had absolutely no evidence to tie them to the shooting and, she remembered with annoyance, she hadn't directly asked them about guns. Maybe Andy had that trust arrangement. Or Asher's will. Or *something*.

Anything that meant she could drown herself in work and not go home until her eyes closed.

***

Dr Renfrew had arrived at the Thirty-Sixth from a satisfying lecture given to an interested, interactive class of would-be psychologists. He first attended Captain Kent's office, both from courtesy and to inform the Captain about the Narcotics connections. Walking through the bullpen, he noticed that Detectives Clement and O'Leary were absent, but on recalling that they partnered each other, supposed that they were conducting an interview or pursuing another lead. He greatly anticipated observing their team dynamic, which had presented as extremely strong, despite the considerable differences between its members.

As he advised Captain Kent of the complex relationships traced by Agent Bergen, he became aware of tension at each reference to Detective Marcol. Dr Renfrew had not warmed to Detective Marcol, although he had attributed his feelings to his high regard for Detective Clement's team and had thus taken great care not to allow any taint to mar his interactions with the Narcotics detective. Detective Marcol had been perfectly adequate, if overly self-assured, and had provided useful assistance. Dr Renfrew's relief at his departure had, therefore, been unreasonable.

"Was there a further issue with Detective Marcol?" he inquired.

"I'm sorry?"

"When you contacted me, the initial approach had been to have Detective Marcol liaise with your team, but you considered that this would be ineffective. Your tone, however, suggests that there have been further developments."

Dr Renfrew's attention was momentarily distracted by the return of Detectives Clement and O'Leary, unusually out of charity with each other.

How strange. He refocused on Captain Kent.

"I was," Dr Renfrew continued, "surprised to hear that Detective Marcol wished to liaise with your team, given that they are not a Narcotics team and that he had not appeared to be a 'good fit' with them."

Captain Kent turned a worrying shade of purple, and emitted a most peculiar noise. Dr Renfrew hoped that a physician would not be required. Fortunately, the captain calmed himself.

"Since you clearly knew something that I didn't, why don't you tell me what you think was going on?" Captain Kent snapped.

"I believe, without firm evidence, that Detective Marcol expressed a personal interest in Detective Clement, which was not reciprocated. I further believe that Detective Tyler informed Detective Marcol that any attempts to approach Detective Clement would be unwelcome."

"Didn't you think I'd want to know that?"

"The issue had been resolved at the time. There was no point in troubling you with an irrelevant matter."

"And do you *believe* anything else?"

Dr Renfrew, glancing into the bullpen, noted Detective Clement's team coming to sharp attention, and almost missed Captain Kent's question.

"Not presently," he said. "I have some suppositions, but none are worthy of airing."

Captain Kent harrumphed.

"Please enlighten me?" Dr Renfrew requested.

"You remember the photographer – Carval."

"Indeed. He is difficult to ignore, however much one might wish to do so."

"Yeah," Captain Kent agreed. "He took a shot of Clement some years ago, which was used to try to discredit her at the Academy."

Dr Renfrew raised his eyebrows.

"No, I didn't believe it. Clement's work is top class, and I checked. Somehow Carval found out about it and went after the theft of his photo."

"Mr Carval informed me that, when they first met, he showed Detective Clement the photo and the team allowed him to 'tag along'."

Captain Kent spluttered. "Something like that," he choked out. After a significant pause to recover his breath, he resumed. "The team believed it was Marcol who misused the photo, but they didn't care and simply ignored it. Carval did care. As soon as he found out about it, he started investigating, and that turned up Marcol."

"So when Detective Marcol arrived here, the team already suspected that he had committed misconduct, and he still endeavoured to pursue Detective Clement, who, presumably, was quite sure of it?" Dr Renfrew was utterly astonished. "Is the man insane?"

Captain Kent cast him an appreciative glance. "Obviously. However, that's not the problem. The problem is that he was trying to use the liaison role to pursue Clement further, and when I passed him on to you, he complained to his captain that someone from my team had threatened him."

"I see."

"His captain now knows that Marcol didn't tell the whole story," Captain Kent said. "I hauled in the team to find out the truth, and it turned out that everyone but Clement knew about Carval going after Marcol."

"How interesting," Dr Renfrew said, with masterly understatement. "I take it Detective Clement was not pleased with the revelation?"

"No."

"I see," he said again. "Should I endeavour to assist?"

Captain Kent shrugged. "That team fixes itself, but it's up to you. You want to study the dynamics." He paused. "Let's find you a desk – I guess you want to be near the four of them?"

"If you would be so kind."

***

Casey ignored the fuss and bustle surrounding Renfrew's installation at a bullpen desk. "Andy," she called instead.

"Yeah?"

"Roberts and Uncle Washington both have rifles. Still waiting on the lawyers."

"That's new."

"Yeah. I can haul in Roberts, but do we have anything from the financials that justifies hauling in the Washingtons?"

"No."

"Where's the will?"

"I asked Schickoff & Schultz, but I didn't get an answer Friday or today."

"Chase them. We need Asher's will." Andy's face said *this isn't my first rodeo*, but his mouth stayed shut. "What about the trust arrangements?"

"I've tried to go around the back, but we either need the will or we need to ask the Washingtons outright."

Casey's face twisted. "I guess. Get the will and then we'll ask the Washingtons. Nicely. And we'll ask them about rifles too, just casually."

"Okay."

Andy returned to his desk, ready to call Schickoff & Schultz, when his phone interrupted him.

"Chee."

"Andy, it's Allan Penrith."

"Oh. Hello." Andy wasn't inviting.

"I know Jamie's messed up. But...have you got time to talk?"

"I guess."

"Thanks. There's a wine bar – Barawine" –

"I know it."

"I'll meet you there. It's not too far for either of us."

"Seven o'clock?"

"Sure. Thanks."

Andy didn't bother putting the phone down before dialling Schickoff & Schultz, and, a few threatening moments later, had ensured that Asher's will would be provided within the hour. Since he had time to kill, he wandered off to the break room to brew a green tea.

O'Leary and Tyler joined him there: O'Leary concocting a mug of coffee, Tyler retrieving a lurid blue sports drink from the small fridge.

"Not going well," Tyler said.

"No."

"Naw."

"Carval should have another go-around on the mats."

"Andy oughta have a go with Casey. That'll shake the fidgets outta her." O'Leary smiled.

"Thanks," Andy said sourly. "I thought you liked me."

"Huh?"

"The mood she's in, she won't hold back. How about one of you two do it instead? She can't break you. I'm more fragile, like fine porcelain." The others laughed.

"Still a good plan. Not tonight, if I take Carval," Tyler said.

"I can't anyway. That manager of his, Allan, wants to have a chat. You're not invited."

O'Leary faked disappointment. Tyler didn't bother.

"I can't see why he's calling me, but I'll see what he says."

"Sure. We all want this fixed." O'Leary stopped, and restarted. "Her dad's hearin' – that's Thursday. An' he ain't dry no more, if he ever was." His ears coloured. "Tol' her we weren't lettin' her drop outta the team. Anyways, we'll be around her. Won't we?"

The others nodded.

"If she lets us," Andy warned.

"Can't stop us. Won't stop us." Tyler's tone was firm.

"Yeah."

When Andy returned to his desk, he found an apologetic e-mail containing Asher's will. He settled down to read it. After he'd reached the end, he sat back, astounded, and tried to get his head around the revelations.

"Casey, guys. I got the will. You've got to see this."

"What?"

"He'd changed it, three weeks ago. In contemplation of marriage to

Kayla Burton. He must have been planning to propose – and she didn't even know it."

"CSU didn't find a ring, did they?" Casey asked.

"Naw."

"Hm," she hummed.

"What'cha thinkin'?"

"He might not have got it yet – if you wanted to propose, wouldn't you do it pretty soon after you got the diamond?" she thought aloud.

"Dunno," O'Leary said. "I never got Pete an engagement ring. Just the weddin' ring."

Tyler looked entirely blank.

"What did the will say?"

"Left everything to Kayla."

"Dear God," Casey said. "She'll freak out."

"That'll be interestin'," O'Leary added.

"Fucking hell," Tyler emitted, which summed up everything pretty well.

Casey frowned. "Would that trust fund go to Kayla if Asher died before he got his hands on it?" Three blank stares. "We need to talk to someone who knows about this stuff."

"I may be able to assist you with that." They jumped. Renfrew had ghosted up behind them.

"Uh?" Casey managed.

"You will require a probate lawyer. I would be pleased to introduce you to an acquaintance."

"Thank you," Casey recovered. "I'll call Asher's firm, who drafted the will."

"That would undoubtedly be better."

Casey bridled.

"Once you have arranged that, I should like to talk to each of you. I believe that Captain Kent has informed you that I am studying your team dynamics?"

"Yes," Casey confirmed. Her total panic was completely hidden.

"I would be grateful if each of you would spare me a few moments this afternoon, at any point where it would not hinder your investigation."

"Of course," Casey said briskly. "O'Leary, Fremont can carry on without you." O'Leary looked like she'd taken his favourite toy away. "Tyler, you next. Larson'll survive. After that we'll see who's got time."

"I'm going out this evening," Andy said. "I need to be gone at six-thirty. I'll swap with Tyler."

Tyler merely nodded.

"More culture?" O'Leary asked mischievously, knowing Andy's real destination. "Man, you'll be too good for us soon."

"I already am," Andy flipped back.

"Some work, perhaps?" Casey clipped.

"Detective O'Leary, if you would come with me?"

Nobody had missed that Casey hadn't arranged to see Renfrew: commenting, however, would be bad for their health.

"Okay," O'Leary sighed, and followed Renfrew to a conference room.

Casey put a call in to Dennison, and left a message for him to call her back on her cell phone. She kept her mind firmly on Asher's will, and then pulled up CSU's report on Asher's apartment. They hadn't bagged and tagged the papers, and the descriptions weren't sufficiently helpful to tell her whether there had been a receipt for a ring. She called them, but that didn't help either.

"I'm going back to Asher's apartment," she announced, and departed before Andy, who had been checking his notes on the financials, could comment.

Asher's silent apartment was still dusty from CSU's work, and, crucially, entirely unoccupied. Casey began to look around, carefully turning over papers in gloved hands; leafing through drawers and files. Suddenly she paused. If Asher had indeed bought a ring – then it would be on the financials, and Andy had searched those. She grimaced. Financials meant going back to the precinct, whereas Asher's apartment meant solitude and no interfering Bigfoots.

Professionalism won.

CHAPTER FIFTEEN

"Andy!" Casey called before she'd removed her beanie. "Asher's financials. Was there a payment to a jeweller?"

"Yep," he confirmed. "You ran off before I could tell you that."

"And?"

Andy grinned. "Look."

Right under her nose was a payment of $5,000. "That's to a high-end jeweller," Andy said.

"Guess where we're going?"

There was a moment of shared *this-means-no-Renfrew*, which briefly overcame the tension between Casey and the team. An instant later, they were gone, Andy still wrapping his scarf around his neck as they left.

Jenretta & Jones's window was full of beautiful pieces of jewellery, any of which Casey would have killed to wear, never mind own. Unfortunately, a cop's salary didn't pay enough to rent one of the pieces for an hour, and even if she could have afforded anything, she couldn't have worn it to work. The best she managed was small stud earrings, occasionally, which didn't give lowlifes purchase to tear them out: anything else would have been unprofessional.

Inside, there were locked display cases with yet more stunning gems in elegant settings. A dapper little man was fussing with a duster, ensuring that not a single speck of dust nor fingerprint marred the view of the sparkle within.

"Excuse me?" Casey opened. "Are you in charge?"

"Hello," the man chirped. "I'm Theodore Jenretta. Are you looking for something in particular? We have a beautiful selection of rings." Andy choked. Casey squawked, and then recovered herself.

"I'm afraid that's not why we're here." She showed her shield. "I'm Detective Clement, and this is Detective Chee." Jenretta stopped dusting, and stared. "We're investigating the murder of Asher Washington. His records show that he recently made a purchase here." Casey produced a photo of Asher.

"Oh, yes. I remember him. He's *dead*? That's tragic. He was head-over-heels for his girlfriend. He said that he wanted everything to be absolutely perfect for her. He was pretty nervous about proposing, not that that's unusual, but" – Jenretta smiled fondly – "well, nervous would-be fiancés tend to unload on us, and he was especially nervous because he hadn't told her about his finances and he thought she'd be a bit annoyed with him, though he was sure she'd forgive him when he proposed. He really loved her. He spent weeks with us – we design as well as simply sell, you know, and he wanted his own design for her ring."

"Had he picked up the ring?"

"No. He'd paid the last instalment, and he'd arranged to pick it up Tuesday, but he never showed and he hadn't been in touch. Is that…"

"I'm afraid so. Asher was found dead on Tuesday morning."

Jenretta made a soft noise of upset. "Poor man," he said. "And his poor, poor girlfriend."

"They'd broken up." Andy said.

"What? No. That…no. I just can't believe it." His shock couldn't have been counterfeited.

"You'd be right. Someone broke them up, just a couple of days before that. I guess he hadn't had time to speak to you."

"How *wicked*."

"So the ring was paid for. I guess that means it's part of his estate now." Casey indulged her curiosity. "May we see it?"

"Sure. Wait here a second." Jenretta disappeared through a discreetly heavy door, and shortly returned with a small crimson velvet box. "This is it." He opened the box with a flourish.

"Wow!" Casey emitted. Andy simply whistled. It was utterly gorgeous. A deep green emerald, cut teardrop-style, was set diagonally, angled towards the length of the finger, above a diamond, which was cut and set in the reverse orientation. A smaller diamond sparkled at the lower end of the main emerald; a matching emerald at the upper end of the larger diamond. The whole arrangement was set in white gold.

"He said she had long fingers, but slim, so he wanted something that suited those – not a wide band, or the gems looking as if they were too big for her fingers, and…well…he said this would have been perfect."

Casey and Andy considered Kayla. "It would have been," Andy said. "It would have been just right."

"I think it's probably safer here than anywhere else," Casey said. "We'll inform the beneficiaries of his will that it's here. It's up to them to decide what to do with it."

"That's fine," Jenretta said. He looked down at the ring. "Tragic."
They nodded. "Thank you for your time."

***

"Wow," Casey said as they turned back to the precinct. "That…. Kayla'll have a lot to handle."

"Are we going to tell her?"

"Not yet. We've still got a killer to catch." She paused. "We need to re-read the will and get those trust arrangements."

"Yeah," Andy said. "I think we'll have to get them from the Washingtons – the trust arrangements, I mean. I haven't found anything or anyone else that might have them."

"I don't have any reason to suspect them, but, well, there's a lot of money sloshing around here, and now we know they have a rifle, they've shot right up the list again."

"Ouch," Andy teased about the inadvertent pun.

Casey ignored him. "I need to question them. And Bill Roberts. And I need to ask Will Cornwall why he didn't report Farman and O'Hagan."

"Maybe he did."

"Yeah, well, if he did, he didn't tell us, did he?"

"No."

They'd reached the precinct. O'Leary greeted them, humphing.

"You ran out on us," he grumped. "Left me with that there profiler."

"You survived," Andy said callously.

"Tyler's up. He ain't so fond of you neither."

"Irrelevant," Casey said. "Asher had designed and paid for an engagement ring. Together with the revised will, it looks like Kayla was it for him. So why didn't his aunt and uncle know that?"

"Mebbe they did," O'Leary suggested.

"His trustee would have to know." Andy said.

"We need to know who that is" – Casey's cell phone interrupted her.

"Clement."

"It's Norman Dennison."

"Hello, Mr Dennison. Thank you for calling back. I'd like to speak with the lawyer who drafted Asher's will."

"Uh, sure, um, why?"

"We have some questions about the effectiveness of certain provisions given his untimely death."

"Oh, okay. I'll get them to call you as soon as possible."

"Thank you. This number is best."

"Thanks. Bye."

"Bye."

She looked around. "That'll clear up how the trust money goes."

"Ah, Detective Chee. Would you have a few moments?"

Andy's lips pinched where Renfrew couldn't see him. "Yes," he groaned, and followed Renfrew to the conference room.

"You next," Tyler said.

Casey ignored him, and went to her desk to untangle all the strands of her case into a lovely logical list. Unfortunately, that didn't take her long enough to have an excuse to avoid Renfrew, and shift didn't end for another hour.

***

Carval's phone rang, late in the afternoon of a long, frustrating day. He'd cured his hangover and lack of sleep with two Advil and a nap, gone out with his camera, shivered through a variety of shots about which he was totally unenthusiastic, brought them back, and ditched the lot on sight. Allan hadn't found him any construction sites, and nagging Allan would only result in Allan nagging back. Since Allan had a lot more ammunition, Carval didn't feel like starting down a path which would only end in annoyance.

"Yeah?" he snapped into the phone.

"Tyler."

"Oh. Er...sorry."

"Sparring. Sounds like you need it. Six-thirty."

The call ended before Carval got his head together. He knew exactly why nothing felt right: he hadn't been to the precinct because he couldn't bear to see Casey ignore him, and his hurt and anger changed the view he saw through his lens. All the shots he'd taken were disturbingly cynical: none of his usual empathy or tinge of sympathetic humour. He didn't like what that said about him, and he liked still less that Casey could affect him so deeply.

Still, the other men weren't dropping him like a hot coal. He supposed that was something...and then thought to wonder why. Well, maybe he'd get a better answer from them tonight than he had before.

Oh. Surely her father's hearing was due soon? He bristled. He wouldn't be used as a comfort toy or – more likely – a punch bag, and if Tyler or O'Leary thought otherwise, they had a bagful of other thoughts coming.

By the time he left for the precinct, his black mood could have swallowed black holes.

***

Dr Renfrew completed his interview with Detective Chee, but did not immediately request Detective Clement's presence. He wished first to consider the data he had gathered, much of which he had inferred from the silences of the three male detectives as from their speech.

Detective O'Leary had been concise but informative: he had majored in criminal justice, having decided, with unusual good sense and modesty, that he would not succeed as a professional football player. Detective Tyler had not emitted a single sentence exceeding four words, but had conveyed that he had previously served in the Army. Detective Chee had merely said that he had joined the NYPD after college. The unifying theme was a positive decision to enter the NYPD. However, the inciting motivations for those decisions were unclear, and their commentaries unhelpfully limited and partial.

The development of the team bond was still less clear. Detectives O'Leary and Clement had formed the original pair, but Detective O'Leary had merely said that they had been paired up soon after Detective Clement had completed her training, as they had worked well together. Dr Renfrew was sure that considerable information had been omitted. Detective Tyler had simply said that Captain Kent had requested him. Detective Chee had said the same, adding that he had been selected for his technological skills.

Dr Renfrew reviewed his findings, adding his suspicion that Detective Chee had been subjected to abuse. He would review their personnel files later, after receiving permission from Captain Kent.

He hypothesised that the team was presently dysfunctional because the other members had not informed Detective Clement of the legal proceedings which Mr Carval had instigated. It appeared to Dr Renfrew, on the basis of his afternoon's observations, that Detective Clement had received a severe shock, and had reacted by withdrawing. He considered that the men wished to mend matters, but that their attempts so to do had been rebuffed. He had then asked about the absence of Mr Carval. According to the men, Mr Carval had been enthusiastic about a construction site, and might be shooting there. Dr Renfrew had admired the precision of language which had permitted each of them to be entirely truthful while revealing nothing of use.

Of course, that had in itself been an admission of considerable use. He deduced that the men were still in contact with Mr Carval, and that they were, unbeknownst to Detective Clement, ensuring that Mr Carval continued to be an unofficial adjunct to the team.

Dr Renfrew had noted that, whatever the fractures within the team, Detective Clement was aggressively pursuing the case. He considered that it was a displacement activity, to block her feelings of betrayal. He had no cause whatsoever to believe that there was any other reason.

He tidied the papers on the conference room table, and poked his head out to request Detective Clement's presence. His request obviously displeased her; though she complied without audible demur.

"It is very pleasant to see you again, Detective Clement." Her blank face told him that she disagreed. "I have a professional and academic interest in team dynamics, which assists me in both my profiling work and constructing appropriate teams for cases and specialised programs." Detective Clement remained unimpressed. "I was struck by the close bond" – ah. A small crack in Detective Clement's façade – "between the members of your team, and I wish to explore it."

Casey would rather have been anywhere than under the scrutiny of an overly-perceptive profiler. She could be getting on with *something* – she wasn't sure what, since Dennison's colleague hadn't yet called her back – rather than wasting her time here.

"I shall start with your reasons for joining the NYPD. Please would you briefly describe your education and any previous roles before you entered the Academy?"

"I majored in public policy," she began. Her history was a safe subject.

"At which institution?"

"Stanford."

Ah, yes. It had previously been mentioned.

"I thought about law, but I tried a couple of pre-law classes and I wasn't interested. Then I tried a criminal justice class and liked it a lot better, so I looked into it further and found that I really liked the idea of actively going after the criminals, rather than prosecuting them later." She painted on a smile. "Paperwork isn't really my thing." Dr Renfrew nodded. "I entered the Academy, graduated, and ended up at the Third Precinct, with O'Leary. They teamed us up. We moved here" –

"The Thirty-Sixth Precinct?"

"Yes. We moved here five and a half years ago; then Tyler joined us, and then Andy – Detective Chee – came along."

"I see. You are all very different?" he probed.

"We're all cops. That's all that matters." Casey slammed the shutters down. Their differences were none of Renfrew's business. Sure, it was one reason why they'd banded together – they were all totally different from everyone around them – but their idiosyncrasies weren't relevant.

"Of course. You share a common goal."

"Catching killers. That's our goal."

"Your success rate is notably high, which may be linked to your strong team dynamic. Exploring that will assist the NYPD in selecting successful teams." She nodded. She could get on board with that: jailing more criminals was a good thing by her. Renfrew steepled his fingers. "You have different backgrounds and personalities, overridden by a common goal."

This had precisely *what* to do with the price of fish – or in this case, catching killers? All detectives had a clear goal of crime solving, which kept them ticking along nicely.

"However, your team appears to have a deeper personal bond, into which you have admitted Mr Carval, who" – Casey missed the next several words. Say *what*? No, no, *no!* They would not be discussing the now non-existent personal bonds, and they *certainly* wouldn't be discussing that asshole photographer. "Detective Clement?"

"I'm sorry. I didn't hear you."

"Your team has a deep personal bond, going far beyond normal professional relationships. I note that, whilst you maintain courtesy, you appear only to have superficial relationships with other members of the precinct. I am exceedingly interested in the development of your team's bond." Casey waited Renfrew out. He might expect a comment, but she wouldn't provide it. "Owing to the present strain within your team, I shall observe for longer."

"I'm sure that Captain Kent will agree," Casey said politely, while panic hamster-wheeled in her head.

"Perhaps you can provide me" –

Casey's phone rang. "Excuse me," she said. Renfrew gave a *please-proceed* gesture. "Clement – Ms Jankel? Dad? Hang on a moment." She looked at Renfrew. "I have to take this. Excuse me." She left precipitately.

Behind her, Dr Renfrew allowed wild supposition to roam his mind. It seemed to him that, to add to Detective Chee's history, Detective Clement had a pressing personal issue relating to her father. Dr Renfrew was not a man who pried. His next step, reviewing the personnel records, would merely be following a legitimate line of professional inquiry in order to improve the performance of all types of law enforcement teams.

***

Casey reached an empty conference room. "Ms Jankel? Is something wrong?"

"No. I was just calling to make final arrangements for Thursday." Casey heard *because we both know that your father won't remember*, and winced. "It's a violation hearing – he was damn lucky with that – so no jury, just a bench trial. He pleaded not guilty" – Casey remembered, but whatever he'd pleaded, he *was* guilty. He'd been sodden drunk – "but unless we have some evidence to disprove the breathalyser and blood-alcohol levels, that won't stand."

"We don't. He was drunk." Casey's voice was totally flat. "He's got no defence."

"Okay. Worst case: he'll get" –

"Fifteen days inside and a fine."

"Yeah. I'll try to make sure that doesn't happen. It is his first violation, isn't it?" Jankel asked.

"It's the first time he's had a ticket."

"What aren't you telling me?"

"He gets picked up regularly. But so far, they've just put him in the tank and called me. No record." Casey breathed in slowly, holding firm control.

There was a significant pause, then, "Should be okay, unless someone's actually checked up, and I don't think that's likely."

Casey sighed out relief.

"Whatever happens, he won't get a criminal record. Will he be able to pay the fine? Max is a thousand dollars, but for a first offence, likely they'll be lenient. Two-fifty, maybe, plus court fees. Budget for five hundred, is my best guess."

"Okay. If he doesn't pay, I will." Casey had a thought. "He has paid you, hasn't he?"

"Yes."

"Good."

"Okay. So I'll see you at Queens County Criminal Court on Thursday, eight-thirty a.m. Will you bring your father?" In Jankel's unemphasised question, Casey heard *to make sure he turns up.*

"Yes."

"Thanks. I'll do my best for him."

"I know. Thank you."

Casey swiped her phone off, and slumped. She'd have to call her father...but not just yet. She couldn't face it.

***

O'Leary noticed Renfrew's return to his desk, and assumed that Casey would be back shortly. When she wasn't, he became mildly suspicious. When he realised that Renfrew was also looking for Casey, he became worried.

And then the shit really hit the fan, because Carval, who had obviously left his brain in his studio, marched into the bullpen, bold as brass, just as Casey walked out of a conference room looking like she'd cried the Mississippi into flooding, all under Renfrew's far-too-interested gaze.

"What are *you* doing here?" Casey spat.

Please don't say it please don't please don't, O'Leary prayed.

"I was invited."

Fuck. He just had to say it, didn't he?

"I see," Casey said. Glaciers were warmer. She gestured him towards O'Leary with exaggerated courtesy. "I'm sure you and your friends have plans. Goodnight."

She was gone before even O'Leary's stride could have caught her.

"I'm out," Andy said. "Got commitments." He fled.

"Waalll, that was a disaster," O'Leary drawled. "Where's that brain of yourn?"

"I'm not lying to save your ass. Mine's already burned from not telling her about the letter, so if she wants truth she can have it, right down her

138

throat."

O'Leary's squirrel-tail eyebrows elevated. "Someone ain't full of sunshine an' bluebirds," he said, with a hint of warning. "I'm thinkin' that someone needs to work it out on the mats."

"Bring it on," Carval grated. "And then we'll talk about why you three are still talking to me, 'cause I don't think it's got anything to do with my camera, but it looks like it's got a whole lot to do with finding a punch bag for Casey that isn't one of you."

Dr Renfrew watched, utterly fascinated.

"We don't need a new punch bag for Casey," O'Leary snapped. "We've been her team for years and we don't *have* to add some blow-in with a camera. We liked you, but I'm reconsiderin' that in a hurry right now. Iffen she needs us, we'll be there. You got invited in on your own merits, an' I'm reconsiderin' that too. So come spar or don't come spar, but don't you go takin' out your temper on us."

Carval stopped in his tracks, shamefaced. Tyler came up to the pair of men, and stood between them, much to Dr Renfrew's admiration.

"Enough," Tyler said. "Bigfoot, you're hurting. Not Carval's fault any more than yours or mine. Carval, you're pissed and hurting. Not our fault. Come spar, settle your temper, then beer. And you, Bigfoot. Tell your Pete" – Dr Renfrew startled, and reproached himself for unconscious biases when he knew that Detective O'Leary was gay – "we're fixing it. Shouldn't wait up." Despite being the shortest of the three men, Tyler projected more menace than both of them. "Stop screwing around and shake," he rasped. Under his intimidating glare, O'Leary and Carval managed an uncomfortable shake of hands, after which all three men disappeared.

Dr Renfrew made some notes, and left, thoroughly intrigued by the team's revelations.

CHAPTER SIXTEEN

Tyler stayed between O'Leary and Carval all the way to the gym, well aware of their sneaked, embarrassed glances at each other.

"Change," he ordered, borrowing the note of command from a particularly stern sergeant from his past.

When they returned, Tyler gestured to the heavy bag. "Bigfoot, ten minutes here. Carval, speed bag. Get rid of the rage. Expect you to be full on before I'm back." He went to the changing rooms.

Carval and O'Leary stared at the two bags, and then each other, and then shrugged and started to hit their targets, full force and with venom.

"Better," Tyler said, taking in the hard breathing, red faces and harder punches and kicks. Ten minutes up, he spoke again. "Mats."

"What?" Carval ejaculated. "Me against *him*? I like my ribs in one piece. He'll flatten me."

"So fight better," Tyler said unsympathetically. "Your black mood, your party."

"What's that supposed to mean?"

"You riled him. Fix it."

The following few moments were short and decidedly unsweet. Carval had no hope against O'Leary, and O'Leary wasn't shy about proving it. Eventually Tyler called time on the display.

"You'n me, Bigfoot."

O'Leary grinned cheerfully. "Bring it on, little man."

"Okay to take more photos," Tyler said towards Carval, and smiled. "Could use a good one."

"Dating Allie?" Carval said, without letting his brain interfere with his conclusions. Tyler smirked, and said nothing.

Carval snapped off another series of shots to go with Saturday's sequence. Knowing what to expect, he thought that these would be technically better. He'd mess around with them later. Or tomorrow. Whenever. He'd need some shots of Casey and Andy sparring...and just like that his shoulders slumped and unhappiness flooded back. His chances of getting those photos were slim to none.

"We'll get you some," O'Leary rumbled. "Don't you worry none." Carval gaped. "'S obvious you'll need some of the other two."

Why Carval forgot that O'Leary only pretended to be a haystack, with as little brain, he didn't know. "Urgh," he grunted.

"Beers," O'Leary continued. "An' we'll all be pals again."

Carval went for beers. It was easier than trying to stop the O'Leary juggernaut, and besides which, Tyler's nods indicated that it would be two against one. Frogmarched wasn't a good look. He trudged down to the Abbey without a word.

"'Kay," O'Leary said, drinks on the table. "Let's clear this up. You're sore at Casey, sure. But we're not keepin' you around just 'cause she's mad at all of us an' you c'n be point man for us to hide behind."

"Like you can hide behind anything smaller than a skyscraper."

O'Leary flipped Tyler the bird at the comment. "We like you. You don't take shit from anyone an" – he coloured – "you fit in. An' you're good for Casey, whether she admits it or not."

"Not," Carval blurted.

"She don't say any more than Tyler here, most times. Anyways, this ain't her best week. You know her dad got himself arrested, an' the hearin's on Thursday. Kent's given her leave for the day. We'll be there for her, but..." O'Leary regarded Carval hopefully.

"You think I should show up at her door? You just said you liked me. I won't be very likeable when I'm dead." Carval looked down at his camera. "Anyway...well, she still doesn't know about the centrepiece. I was about to tell her...and she said she didn't want to know and threw me out. I couldn't stay when she'd told me to leave."

"Not cool," Tyler noted.

"An' it could get embarrassin'. Imagine if she'd'a called us to get you out?"

"Nasty."

"Might leave that eviction to Andy," O'Leary chortled. Even Carval snickered. "Now, I ain't tellin' you what to do, or when to do it, but likely she'll be interrogatin' Caveman Bill tomorrow, or mebbe the Washin'tons. Good reason for you to drop by, an' we'll make sure she don't shoot you. Guess you're gonna need more interrogation shots."

"Yeah."

"An' more of Kent," O'Leary said mischievously. "An' that stick of a profiler's back, too."

"What?"

"Renfrew's back. Wantin' to study our team dynamics. He's been sitting out in the bullpen all day."

"Wow – oh, *shit*."

"Yep. He was right there watchin' it all go down."

"I am so dead," Carval sighed.

"Naw. *We* are so dead. Or mebbe Renfrew'll be dead. Don't see Casey givin' him much 'cept death stares."

"Got a plan?" Tyler asked.

"I guess so," Carval said. "You tell me when the interrogations start, and I'll show up and shoot. After that – sometime, because I'm not getting in the way of you solving the case – put Casey in a room where I can tell her about the centrepiece and you can stop her killing me. Then we'll see."

"Don't make plans for Thursday," O'Leary warned him.

"I wasn't intending to."

***

Andy briskly betook himself to Barawine, where he found Allan's precise, dapper figure already seated and contemplating the extensive wine list. Though he was intrigued and irritated in roughly equal quantities, he was convinced that Allan was much more civilised company than all or any of Casey, the rest of the team, and Carval (especially given the disaster that he'd just escaped). He also approved of Allan's choice of table, some way out of the general bustle and hubbub.

"Wine?" Allan offered, without greeting or preliminaries. "I sure want a glass or four."

Andy quirked an eyebrow. "Guess you've been taking the worst of the other side of this mess."

"Yes. I *told* Jamie this was a mistake."

"Going after your copyright?" Andy queried.

"No. That's never a mistake. Making it a personal crusade was, though."

"Mm. Let's get that wine, and you can tell me your side. I left your boy fighting with O'Leary, and Tyler trying to talk them down long enough to get to the sparring mats. I guess they'll be bonding over beer."

"Great. Miserable, angry, bruised *and* hungover. Maybe I'll take a day off tomorrow," Allan said. He looked down the wine list. "White? Let's get a Napa Valley Chardonnay." When Andy nodded, Allan flicked a glance at a server and ordered. Nothing more was said until the wine arrived and Allan had pronounced it acceptable.

Both men sipped contemplatively.

"Nice," Andy said. "Especially as it doesn't come with scowling."

"Guess you've had a rough few days."

"You're not wrong. That's our problem, though. You wanted a chat, so what do you want to talk about?"

"Jamie and your Casey."

"I guessed that," Andy said dryly.

Allan smiled equally dryly. "Look, I get that you guys never talk about anything, and I don't want you to spill secrets. But it's my job to get Jamie's exhibitions up and running, and, well, this one will be his best ever."

"Better than the panhandlers?"

"Absolutely. The shots are phenomenal – don't go telling Jamie that: his ego'll be visible from the Space Station and God knows he's bad enough now" –

"Don't worry. We won't."

"– anyway, they are, and it'll be a really popular theme. Cops resonate with everyone, whether it's for good or bad reasons" –

"Yeah" –

"– but Jamie's caught something in you four. Yeah, sure, it's centred around Casey, but it's everything. I guess you haven't seen any more of the shots, but there's a sequence from the morgue that'll eclipse everything ever done on forensics; there's a set of shots from the Academy – and there's you. It'll be *huge*."

Andy gaped. Precise, controlled, cool Allan Penrith was enthusing like a child taken to the zoo for the first time.

"So," Allan finished, "I want this exhibition to come off the way it should." Andy stared. "What?"

"I guess I never thought – why *do* you work for Carval?"

"He pays me *very* well." Andy fixed Allan with a hard stare. "Okay. I enjoy it. I *like* Jamie, though it's a bit like managing a mixed herd of toddlers and cats; and I like making order out of chaos."

"And?"

Allan gestured ruefully. "I can't create like he does. I love culture. But I can't create it and Jamie can."

Realisation spread through Andy. "I get it. Like watching Ibsen write, or Fonteyn dance."

"Or Callas sing. I went to see Manon Lescaut, last year, with Roberto Alagna stepping in. It was…transcendent. But I can't do any of it myself. Jamie is the closest I'll ever get."

Silence fell. Both men drained their glasses, and Allan refilled them. Andy made a snap decision.

"I became a cop to fight back," he said. Allan wordlessly invited further confidences. "O'Leary and Tyler told Carval some of it, but I guess he didn't tell you."

"Never said a word."

Relief flickered through Andy's face. "Okay."

"I won't mention anything to Jamie, either, not that he remembers much that isn't directly relevant to his photos. If I didn't manage him, he wouldn't remember to put his pants on before rushing out with his camera."

A small smile emerged, and died. "So. My parents died when I was small, and my uncle took me in. He believed in physical discipline." Harsh breath scarred the air. "Turned out he was also running a porn business." Andy's voice was cold and hard. "When I was eleven, twelve, he decided I'd be a good participant. I disagreed. Took off. Hid. Managed high school and then college. Joined the Academy, so I could stop it happening to anyone else." He gulped back his wine.

"Seems reasonable," Allan said, without pity or admiration.

"Seeing a play, or opera, or great art — it's everything I couldn't have growing up."

"Yeah."

"So," Andy closed off that line of conversation, "Carval. He's not happy."

"You could say that. You could say that Hurricane Sandy was a bit of a problem." Andy grinned at Allan's understatement. "I want Jamie to be happy, focused and take good photos. I don't want him moping and going off to shoot pretty, vapid girls, like he did last time."

"She's not vapid," Andy pointed out. "She's a music major at NYU."

Allan choked on his wine. "Say what? Jamie shot a girl with *brains*? Did he actually know that?"

"Don't think so. She's paying her way through college by modelling." Andy grinned evilly. "She's dating Tyler — we think. He isn't admitting anything."

"You guys are just full of surprises. Your monster sings, Tyler dates smart, cultured women, you can talk about Ibsen and opera — and lots more, I guess — and your Casey-cop is the only woman I've ever seen totally upend Jamie." He sipped more wine. "It shows in the shots, you know. There's something there: a connection between you. You're all so different, but you're all the same."

"We've been a team for years. Even if Casey's telling herself it's all broken, it's not. I don't think anyone expected us to work out, except maybe the captain. But we did, even if none of them get any closer to culture than passing MOMA on the subway."

Allan laughed. "Jamie'd rather go to a game."

"Philistines." They saluted each other with their wine glasses. "Okay. What do you want to do about Carval?"

"Every other time there's a problem — before he found you guys — he solved it by picking up some pretty girl, shooting her, bedding her for a while till he got bored, and moving on. He won't do that this time, because he's fallen for Casey and he's screwed it up. Even Jamie realises that trying to make her jealous won't work."

"Have you met Casey?"

"No. I've only seen the photos."

Andy shrugged. "Not surprising. Anyway, she can be a bit stubborn." Allan raised his eyebrows. "Okay, a lot stubborn. Like rock. Carval really screwed up with her, and I don't know how he thinks he'll fix it, but we don't have any good ideas on our side. Casey's truly *pissed* that we knew and didn't tell her. If you've got any good ideas, I'd love to hear them. It's no fun when Casey's angry."

"It's not much fun when Jamie's sulking, either."

"He got to shoot Tyler and O'Leary sparring, and he'll probably take more tonight, if he comes out of his sulks long enough to focus."

"Did it make him any happier?" Allan asked.

"It didn't make him more miserable. I left him being sent to the gym to spar, and then I guess he'll have a drink with Tyler. They get along. Carval's got some stones, and Tyler respects that."

Allan grimaced. "Taking shots of sparring didn't cheer him up?"

"Nope. Well, he wasn't quite as miserable." Andy pondered. "If I was Carval, I'd tell Casey about the centrepiece before that screws things up any more, and then leave Casey alone for a day or two. There must be something else he can shoot."

"I threatened to put him in a cell for a night, once. We could do that."

"Up to you, but don't choose our precinct." Allan grinned. "That's all I can think of."

"It's not a bad plan. I'll talk to Jamie in the morning."

"Talking to Casey is a losing game."

"I gathered that. Jamie tried."

"We told him. It's not our fault if he didn't listen."

"It's not one of his skills. How he can be that perceptive through a lens and that *dumb* otherwise…" Allan sighed.

"Let's leave them to it and talk about something civilised. I'm off to see Jitney, at the Friedman, on the 24th."

"I'm seeing that too, but not till mid-March. Celia" – Allan caught Andy's confusion – "my girlfriend – got tickets for my birthday." He acquired a delicate colour. "Jamie doesn't know about her. He'd want to shoot her, and she'd hate it. It's bad enough that I won't let him photograph me. And he'd tease me, and, well…." He trailed off.

"Safe with me." Andy didn't offer up any information in return, and Allan didn't ask. They finished their wine, accompanied by a satisfyingly detailed cultural discussion, and left for their respective homes thoroughly content with each other's good sense and intellect.

***

Allan tip-tapped up the stairs to Jamie's studio on Tuesday morning, hoping to find him there rather than dragging him out of his living space. He wasn't hopeful as he peeked in, but, surprisingly, he could see Jamie at his computer, hunched in concentration.

"Can I see?" Allan asked.

Jamie grunted, which wasn't a *no*. Allan approached the screen, and peered over Jamie's shoulder at the shots he was reviewing. "Where'd you get these?" He knew, but riling Jamie by telling him that he'd been talking to Andy behind Jamie's back wouldn't improve anything.

"They let me shoot them sparring."

"Pretty decent. Nice contrast to the Academy shots."

Jamie grunted again, and scowled at the screen.

"What's next?"

"Dunno. I'm going to the precinct to shoot interrogations later."

Allan glanced around Jamie's desk. "What's this card with *Jail* written on it?"

"Oh. That."

"Yes, that. What is it? Were you arrested and didn't tell me?"

"Don't be dumb."

"Then what does it mean?" Allan could feel a headache gathering. If he wanted to deal with toddlers, he'd work at a day care centre. "Tell me it's about photos."

Jamie hunched more.

"Okay, snap out of it. You screwed up by not telling Casey about going after Marcol when you told the rest of her team. Yes, she'd still have been mad at you, but at least you wouldn't have treated her differently. She's likely angrier because they knew and she didn't. Get your interrogation shots, then give her some space and shoot something else till you've both calmed down. If I were you, I'd tell her about that centrepiece soon, too."

"Easy for you to say."

"Yes, it is. And don't think you can take your foul mood out on me, because I'm not having it. You're sulking, and it's not attractive."

Jamie growled, but subsided. Allan changed tack.

"I guess you wrote *Jail* because you thought you'd get some shots in a jail. What do you want? Local police cells – the others'll get you those, but likely you won't be allowed to shoot there because the prisoners might not be guilty – or something like Rikers?"

A spark of interest lightened Jamie's black gloom. "Rikers. It's the end point of cop work – well, an end point for murderers. It's all about the end of the story: brutality, no hope, an answer for the relatives...." He brightened further. "I could shoot Sackson, and even go out to San Francisco for Yarland – he ended up there, didn't he? You can check. If he's on Death Row that would be even better."

"Okay. Sounds good. Let me make some inquiries." Jamie's mood lightened even more as he planned a new series of shots. "Now, show me those sparring shots properly?"

Jamie shifted his chair so that Allan had a clear view. "Yep. Those are pretty good." Allan had a hard time not telling Jamie that they were magnificent. He'd caught a sense of raw physicality and power in motion that would both contrast with and conclude the shots of training at the Academy; and the handclasp shot could, if Jamie wanted, be used as a solo poster shot of brotherhood. Still, Jamie's ego didn't need to be fed.

"If you can take some that good in prison, we'll be most of the way there. It looks as if we might get the show on the road this side of Christmas 2020 after all."

"Mean," Carval muttered, but his lips had twitched out of their misery.

"Yeah, I am. I'll go see if we can get you into Rikers – and out again afterwards. San Francisco might take longer. Leave it with me."

"'Kay."

Allan hurried back downstairs to his own tidy office, and began to look up numbers and make calls. He could faintly hear Jamie on the phone, and a moment later he dashed past calling farewells.

CHAPTER SEVENTEEN

Casey thumped out her still-flaming anger on the speed bag early in the morning, imagining Carval's stupid smirking face with every blow. It didn't help at all. Deep inside, where she didn't notice, she was miserable as well as angry. He had no right to demand that she open up to him, and then to keep secrets himself. And her team had no right *at all* to help him. Men were a heap of over-testosteroned dumbasses whose hormones had clearly squeezed out the few brain cells they'd been born with. She added their faces to her imaginings, and walloped the bag still harder.

Fortunately, no men (or women, or indeed a solitary living thing) came near her as she pounded the bag and then the treadmill. Finally, she felt calm enough to approach her desk; even now, she was in no mood to deal with anyone who would increase her annoyance level, possibly merely by breathing. She was, however, absolutely in the mood for an interrogation where she knew the suspect was lying. Unconsciously, she bared her teeth and flexed her fingers.

She reviewed her suspects. Roberts' weakness was his wife. If Roberts thought that his wife was at risk, he'd cave – or lose it. Either way, he'd admit everything he knew. Then, after Roberts, the Washingtons – once she had the probate lawyer's answers. Somewhere in between, she'd make a call to Will Cornwall, concerning whether he had reported Farman and O'Hagan.

While she was waiting for some nice burly uniforms to arrive – Fremont and Larson, she thought, and Fremont could do the thinking for both of them – she started tapping out search warrants for the Roberts' apartment, and, though she didn't have any good reasons to start it, the Washingtons' house.

By eight, she'd filled in as much as possible on the forms. Fremont and Larson hadn't arrived, but she could call Cornwall. All those lawyers seemed to work 24/7, but he'd said that the deadline was yesterday, so he should be available. She dialled.

"Will Cornwall," a tired voice answered.

"Mr Cornwall, it's Detective Clement."

"Uh, er, hey? I haven't thought of anything else."

"I have a question."

"Yes?"

Casey could hear his worry. "Why didn't you report the Dorman & Andrews lawyers for unprofessional conduct?"

"I did, to our internal people. They take care of it. Means we don't get involved or distracted."

"Why didn't you tell me?"

"It wasn't top of my mind. We have procedures, so once I followed them, it wasn't my problem any more. It might be theirs, though." He sounded very smug about that, for which Casey couldn't criticise him.

"Okay, thanks. Could I have the name of the internal person?"

"Sure. Sue Tethers. Want me to put you through?"

"No, it's okay. I'll call her later."

Will's rapid offer had closed off another line of enquiry. Cynical she might be, but it was always possible that Dorman & Andrews had tried the same line on Will that they had on Asher – and that Will had gone for it. She'd check with this Sue person, but it was pretty unlikely. She added it to the bottom of her to-do list.

When she looked up again, she spotted Fremont, and then, trying to hide, Larson.

"Fremont, Larson, I need you to go pick up someone."

"Yes," they said, less nervously. "Who?"

"Bill Roberts." She gave them the construction site address. "Thanks." Fremont and Larson despatched, she went to see the sergeant to keep them available, so that they could pick up Delaine Roberts later. Casey didn't believe that Delaine didn't know about Bill's rifle, but, from Tyler and Andy's description, she could believe that Delaine hadn't had enough mental space to remember it if they'd asked.

While she'd been arranging matters, the others had arrived.

"Tyler, Bill Roberts is coming into Interrogation. You're with me."

O'Leary flashed her a look. "Not me?"

"Tyler did the first interview, on site. Continuity."

O'Leary might not believe her, but it was true. And if, subconsciously, she was avoiding pairing with O'Leary because she was angrier with and more hurt by his failure to tell her about Carval's actions than by any of the others, she wasn't admitting it.

"Fremont and Larson went to pick him up. You said he was a big guy. They're pretty big themselves, so there shouldn't be any trouble."

Casey turned back to her papers, missing O'Leary's expression, his subsequent departure for the break room and his call to Carval.

"Detective Clement, we've put Roberts in Interrogation," Fremont said, a while later. "Uh, he's not happy."

"I didn't expect him to be. Maybe he shouldn't have lied about owning a rifle?"

"I guess not."

"He didn't take a swing or try to assault you?"

"No – but I'm pretty sure he thought about it. His boss wasn't happy, but I said it was a murder investigation and he shut up quick."

"Good. Okay. Next thing" – Fremont blinked, and shrank a little – "bring in Roberts' wife, gently – and make sure she brings her baby from day care too."

"Baby?"

"You know what a baby is?" Casey didn't stint her sarcasm. "Small human, usually wailing." Fremont cringed. "They have one. I want Roberts to know that because he lied to us, his wife is sitting in a cop shop, with their baby, being questioned."

Fremont's face was an astounding mixture of admiration and complete horror. "That's…cold."

"Murdering Asher Washington was cold." Casey dismissed Fremont to collect Delaine Roberts and the baby.

When he returned, she was ready. "Tyler, we're up." She marched off towards Interrogation without a backwards glance. Tyler followed.

O'Leary looked around. "Showtime," he announced. "Fremont, Larson, you've been doin' the legwork, so it's only fair you see the fun. C'mon." They trailed like ducklings to Observation, and were joined by Andy and Renfrew. Just as Casey entered Interrogation with Tyler at her shoulder, both blank-faced, intimidation levels at max, Carval dashed into Observation, camera already out.

Bill Roberts radiated aggression and anger, palpable even through the glass. He began yelling as soon as Casey walked in, and didn't drop the shouting as Tyler followed.

"Why the *fuck* am I here? I didn't do anything and if I get fired I'll sue you and the whole fucking NYPD. You got no right to haul me off site. I'll have your jobs for this."

Casey waited out his ranting.

"William Edgar Roberts," she said coldly. "You are a suspect in the murder of Asher Washington." She read him his rights in the same frigid tone. "Do you understand?"

"'Course I do! I never did anything, you dumb bitch! I told him to stop messing my wife around and book his appointments in normal hours!"

"Pretty determined to protect your wife, aren't you? Shame that because you lied to us, she's in here too, with the baby. She's next for interrogation."

"What the fuck? You can't do that! That's my baby and you got no right" –

"I can," Casey said.

"Why're you dragging Della into this? She" –

"You lied to us about owning a rifle," Casey stated. He stopped talking. "What else did you lie about? We'll be asking your wife what time you went out that morning."

Through the door, they heard a baby howling. Roberts paled. "Is that my Anne?"

"Probably," Casey said offhandedly. "You won't be seeing her, though. You lied about owning a rifle."

"I..."

"Asher Washington was shot with a rifle. You own a rifle. You argued with Asher three days before he died – and he died just before he was due at another PT session with your wife. You've got a record, Bill." Casey let that sink in. "It all adds up. You're my best bet for murder." The baby howled again, followed by a surprised squeak and more bawling. "Hear that? Better listen up, because you won't be hearing it in Rikers."

The small room was totally silent. Fremont must have put Delaine in the next room, because Casey – and Roberts – could hear the baby's cries, and Delaine desperately trying to soothe her. Suddenly, a deep bass rumble sounded, the baby's wails diminished, then turned to gurgles as the bass continued to reverberate.

"Guess someone else can keep your Anne happy," Tyler said. "Doing better than you. Shouldn't think Anne'll miss you. Got her mom." He implied that Delaine would have other options, though given that the bass was O'Leary's, it was totally misleading. The door of the next room opened, and O'Leary's heavy tread echoed.

"I didn't do it!" Roberts roared. Anne began to bawl again. "I didn't! He was a selfish arrogant prick who didn't get that Della needed a break."

"Why? Surely she could tell him herself?"

Roberts stopped yelling for a moment, and his red face paled. "She'd been ill. First she'd lost one, and then the birth was really hard. Emergency. She hadda go back to work but I didn't want her to! She wasn't well."

"So why weren't you helping look after Anne?" Casey asked frigidly.

His rage flared again. "I hadda work to pay the healthcare. Just 'cause you cops got good insurance, well, we don't. That sonofabitch prob'ly had full coverage but we gotta pay it off. He didn't get that Della needed to rest and just wanted his own fucking way and Della – we – couldn't afford not to have the money he was paying. So yeah, I wanted to punch his lights out but I didn't shoot him."

"You own a rifle."

"Yeah," he admitted, slumped and defeated.

"Why didn't you tell Detective Tyler?"

"We got a family cabin upstate. I keep it there. I didn't think it mattered 'cause it wasn't here."

"Address?" He gave it. "We'll take it for testing. An officer will collect it."

"But" –

"You can spend the night in the cells. Lying to a cop? Obstructing a homicide investigation? I can hold you on that. I can charge you."

"But Anne – Della" –

"Not my problem."

"What sort of a fucking woman are you, keeping me away from my family?"

"A cop woman."

Casey let that iceberg float between them.

"You should have a family, not be playing at doing a man's job. Women don't belong in this job."

He couldn't have picked better words to tear her apart if he'd tried. Her father had said the same.

"I'm a cop," she said, stone-faced. "And you're a suspect. Detective Tyler, have him taken down to Holding. I'll amend the warrant to include searching this cabin, and the locals can do it for us. While you're doing that, Detective O'Leary and I will be interviewing Delaine Roberts on suspicion of aiding and abetting William Roberts to commit homicide." She stood.

"I want to see my wife!"

"Not seeing anyone," Tyler said. "Not till we check out your rifle."

"What about my child?"

"If your wife is detained, Child Services will be called." Casey provided no sympathy.

"You fucking stone cold bitch!" As Tyler took him away, Roberts' swearing could be heard from one end of the precinct to the other.

In Observation, Andy, Carval and Renfrew looked at each other. O'Leary, who'd sidled back in after his venture into baby-whispering, left precipitately.

"Where's he going?" Carval asked.

"After Casey," Andy answered, leading the way out of Observation.

"Why – oh. It's – oof." Andy's elbow hit his ribs.

"Sorry," Andy said. "I stumbled." His face said *shut the hell up in front of Renfrew*. Carval complied, but he wanted to say *I should go after her. I should be there*. He remembered Casey's fury as she'd ripped her father apart for saying something similar; then her devastated, overwhelming misery. And now this chauvinistic lowlife had punched the open wound, and he *should be there.*

Except she wouldn't take sympathy from him. His own stupidity had locked him out, and now she wouldn't take anything from him.

***

O'Leary had seen Casey's face in the instant between Roberts' words and her response, and understood immediately. While he thought that she should cuddle up to Carval, that wasn't likely to happen this side of a miracle, and even if they were on the outs right now, he wasn't letting his pal be miserable on her own. He caught a glimpse of the stair door swinging, and followed his nose to the floor above. He didn't often go to the wild shores of the Robbery and Narcotics divisions, but since even the greenest rookie knew him, he wandered through with aplomb. He peered through a conference room window, and then entered.

"Go away."

"Nup. Not happenin'." He pulled up a chair, surveyed it for fragility, and then cautiously sat down beside her. "Still pals."

"Go play with your new pal."

"That ain't nice. You're my pal, even iffen you're sulkin'. I heard that dumbass, an' I'm amazed you didn't deck him."

"Don't want the black mark. Anyway, it's not important. He's wrong."

"Waalllll," O'Leary drawled, "I know that, but do you know that? 'Cause you were pretty damn upset when your dad said it, an' I'm thinkin' that you ain't quite as sure as you're sayin'."

"I'm sure."

"Sure you are. That's why you're sittin' here tryin' not to cry when you could be scarin' the shit outta that poor Delaine Roberts an' her cute baby." O'Leary, at some risk to his health, put a tree-sized arm around the unyielding Casey. "C'mon. You know you like terrorisin' suspects."

"She's not a suspect. He is. She's a witness."

"You mean that whole spiel *wasn't true?*" O'Leary gasped with entirely faked amazement. "Waalll, I never did."

"Lose the hayseed. It's not funny." She shrugged away from him. He let her go.

"We'll have a chat later," he said, which sounded suspiciously like a threat. "Now, we need to go terrorise Delaine Roberts. You c'n terrorise an' I'll play with the cute baby. She's darlin'. An' when you're finished terrorisin', mebbe you'll be in a mood to listen an' remember that we're pals whatever."

"Will you just *stop* trying to pretend it's all fine? It's not me who broke it, it's you three."

"An' it's not you tryin' to mend it an' apologise, it's us three. But you don't want to try any more, an' I think it's nothin' to do with us an' plenty

153

to do with Carval." O'Leary stood up and took Casey with him. "What's between you an' him is your business. He messed up. We messed up. But you can't keep carryin' the world on your shoulders on your lonesome." He assessed Casey's frozen face. "Not that you're listenin' to me right now, but I'm goin' to keep tellin' you till you do. We know you've got shit comin' down on Thursday. We'll be there, like it or not."

"I don't want you anywhere near the court. Isn't it bad enough I have a dad who's puking drunk more often than not, being picked up so I'm known by every desk sergeant in Manhattan and Brooklyn, and now he's gotten himself arrested? How's that look, huh? Detective Clement, Academy star – and a criminal father. Thanks to you and Carval, Marcol's got it in for me again and he'll use it. It won't take him five minutes to find out about Dad and then…. It won't matter that it's just a violation, 'cause they'll make it look like he has a record." She thumped down again and hid her face in her hands. O'Leary laid a huge paw across her back.

"Shit," he agreed. "We didn't…nobody thought of that. But Casey, your dad ain't you. You're you. What he does ain't no reflection on you."

"Till Marcol and his weasels start saying that he wasn't arrested before because I pulled strings. Or did *favours* for the cops who picked him up. Some of them'll back it up, 'cause Marcol has pull and I don't."

"Kent won't stand for that."

"Kent won't hear about it. It'll be all rumours and whispers and ghosts. Nothing to see, nothing I can fight. Why'd he have to play the fucking *hero*? I didn't need a hero." Her shoulders convulsed under O'Leary's hand, and then stilled.

O'Leary watched, appalled, as Casey simply shut down; her spine straightening and stiffening, her face perfectly emotionless.

"I'd better interview Delaine Roberts," she said.

Following her downstairs, O'Leary considered the set of her head, and put his own brain to work. He didn't like his conclusions, and he was damn sure Casey wouldn't, but Marcol hadn't hesitated to play dirty before. O'Leary didn't think that rat's ass would've changed, even if Kent had – he made air quotes around the next words – 'dealt with' Marcol's captain. If anything, that would make Marcol worse, and while taking him on to the mats for a little amusement - for O'Leary himself and Tyler – would be satisfying, likely it would make matters worse. Still, it would be fun, and the man wouldn't be making any more trouble from the ICU.

O'Leary's normally cheerful, amiable face wore an expression that left the bullpen shuddering as he passed, and even Renfrew showed surprise as he returned to Observation to watch Delaine Roberts' interview.

***

Both Delaine and the baby were crying, though at least Delaine was quiet about it. Casey exchanged glances with O'Leary, whose expression had altered to disgusting sappiness as soon as he'd seen the little pink bundle of ear-shattering misery. He took the infant from Delaine and cuddled her to his enormous chest. Anne, Casey thought acidly, was so amazed to meet a big friendly giant again that she stopped the howling in favour of surprised squeaks and gurgles, which allowed Casey to speak at a normal volume.

"Delaine Anne Roberts."

"Why am I here? Where's Bill? He didn't do anything. He wouldn't do that to me or Anne."

Casey made not one single move to reassure her, or even pass her a Kleenex. "Your husband had an argument with Asher, and three days later Asher was shot with a rifle. Your husband lied about owning a rifle. He had motive, means – and opportunity."

"He was with me till quarter of six."

"How do you know? You're so tired you couldn't read a clock, and anyway you're his wife. You'd lie for him without a second thought."

Delaine cried harder. Casey, hard and cold, simply waited. O'Leary allowed the baby to cling to his fingers, tickled her round tummy, and wobbled little toes in their pink bootees.

"How do you know?" Casey repeated.

"Bill wouldn't lie to me."

"He lied to the cops. That's an offence. Why wouldn't he lie to you?" More floods of tears from Delaine. O'Leary took the baby over to the window and helped her to wave her hands at it.

"He always goes out at quarter of six. He gets the six twenty-five from Yonkers to Yankee Stadium and he's on site at seven. The site manager can tell you," she wept. "He'll confirm. Bill's a good worker."

"But you wouldn't know if he'd left early."

"He'd wake me for the baby. It wasn't Bill," she cried again. "It *wasn't*."

If Roberts rode the Hudson line, they could check station cameras.

"Does he use the MTA?"

"Oh, yes," Delaine whimpered. "He even has one of those new e-Tix. I don't need one but he does."

Behind her cold face, Casey's brain ran hot. That meant that there would be records, which they'd be on to as soon as she wrapped this up.

"You say" – disbelief dripped from her – "that Bill left at quarter of six. Are you sure? We'll be checking, and if you've lied to us you'll be charged with obstruction. Who'll look after Anne then? It'll be Child Services."

"I'm *not* lying. I'm *not*. I'd never put Anne at risk. Bill didn't do it!"

And there Delaine stuck.

"We'll check. You can go, but don't leave New York."

O'Leary handed over Anne, whose baby face had almost managed a smile, and escorted Delaine, still weeping, out.

CHAPTER EIGHTEEN

In Observation, Carval lowered his camera, as shocked as he'd been after Casey had eviscerated her suspects in the models case. He hadn't seen that concentrated viciousness for the last four months, and the contrast between Casey's aggressive posture and gestures in her questioning of both Bill and Delaine, set against O'Leary's fond soothing of a tiny baby, would rock viewers back on their heels. It had rocked him, and *he'd* been safely on the other side of the glass. He'd forgotten, or ignored, Casey's titanium spine; remembered the curled-up, kittenish lover and failed to recall the diamond-hard investigator with the steel-trap mind.

"That was exceedingly interesting," Renfrew's prissy tones interrupted. "It is always intriguing to see gender expectations – on the part of the suspect or witness, naturally" –

Yeah, Carval thought bitterly. *You wouldn't have a single bias, would you? You're just the perfect profiler.*

"– entirely reversed, confusing the recipient. I am most impressed by the use of the technique. The witness would not expect Detective O'Leary to take a nurturing, feminine role, or Detective Clement to be the aggressor."

Hard on the heels of that statement, Casey walked into Observation, saw Renfrew and Carval, gave them both the cold shoulder, and addressed Tyler and Andy.

"She said Roberts has an MTA e-Tix account. Andy, find out how to get the information out of it – from the MTA or however, and check every detail of his journeys that day. I'll file an amended warrant. Tyler, as soon as I" – a week ago, that would have been *we* – "get it back, you deal with the boys upstate to have it executed." She turned on her heel and left again. The four men avoided each other's gaze.

Amending the warrant didn't take nearly long enough, but the interviews and sending the amended warrant off to the court for approval had taken

Casey well past the witching hour of lunchtime; not that she was hungry. However, O'Leary couldn't force her out when it wasn't a mealtime, and she would ensure that she had plans this evening. She tapped on her phone, and found some movies that wouldn't cause her to throw up her non-existent lunch or raise suspicion any higher than it already was.

"Casey." Andy hesitated. "We can get the travel data, but they require a warrant and then a couple more days after that."

"So get the warrant in."

"I've done that, and the results will come to all of us, just like usual." Andy's irritated snap brought her head up. "It'll still take two full days. You haven't charged Roberts, so we've only got twenty-four hours. We charged String-Bean Steve with installing spyware on Asher's phone, and he hasn't posted bail, but we don't have any evidence to hold Roberts."

Casey said something short, pungent, and unrepeatable.

"Tyler's on the phone to the site manager."

Tyler joined them. "Site manager confirmed Roberts wasn't late any day, just like they said."

Casey swore viciously under her breath. "I don't want to let him go," she bit. "I don't trust him not to run. We need to find something." She looked up, caught a glimpse of Carval taking shots, swore again, and stomped out of view. Nobody dared follow her.

"Good time to go," Tyler said to Carval. "No point putting you two in a room. Casey's out for blood."

"Yeah."

"Before you go," Renfrew's unwelcome prissiness pronounced, "I wish to interview you."

"Say *what?*" yelped three men.

"I believe I was perfectly clear," Renfrew said pedantically. "I wish to interview Mr Carval, since his presence results directly from your team dynamic."

Carval emitted a strangulated noise.

"Your funeral," Tyler said to Carval, and he and Andy skedaddled, leaving Carval pinned to the spot, like a skewered butterfly.

"Excellent," said Renfrew. "Let us have some coffee."

Carval weighed up his options. Leave, as Casey had clearly wanted, and sulk miserably in his studio; stay, and be grilled by Renfrew; or stay, finish photographing, and be shot by Casey. *Would he prefer to die by drowning, the Inquisition, or a bullet*, he wondered bleakly, and decided that he would prefer not to die at all. Sadly, that option wasn't on offer.

He was sure he hadn't agreed to the interview, but in some mysterious fashion he was already holding a large coffee and halfway to the smallest conference room. He decided that he couldn't be in any worse trouble with Casey, so he might as well gain credit from Renfrew. That way his death might be investigated.

"Mr Carval, you are an extremely well-known and successful photographer of New York life," Dr Renfrew began.

"Yeah."

"Your last exhibition was *New York's Ugly Underbelly*, about the panhandlers and street life of Manhattan."

"Yeah."

"It was an outstanding success."

"Yeah."

"It would, therefore, be disappointing if a subsequent exhibition did not match or surpass it."

Mr Carval stared, and then swallowed half of his coffee without pausing.

"I assume that you expect that your next show, featuring Detective Clement and her team, to be as successful." Dr Renfrew smiled kindly. "I saw your previous show. It was most impressive. To bring out the humanity of those unfortunates who live on the streets, cringing from a kick or a curse.... I was glad to have taken the recommendation of Dr McDonald, and visited it."

Mr Carval remained completely wordless. Dr Renfrew steepled his fingers. "What drew you to select this team as your next subjects?"

A prolonged pause occurred, during which Dr Renfrew sipped his excellent coffee and determined that he would purchase a small machine for his own office.

"It was sheer luck," Mr Carval eventually articulated. "We discussed this before."

"We discussed it briefly, paying no attention to your reasons for choosing this team. I wish to explore that in detail."

Mr Carval's mouth twisted. "Fine," he forced out. "I needed to go to the store, and on the way I saw the crime scene tape, so I stopped." His expression expected a rebuke.

"A natural, if morbid, human instinct."

"And there was Casey. It was the perfect shot. So I took it, and then I saw the rest of them. They were all so different, but they had this bond. I could see it..."

Dr Renfrew observed Mr Carval's fingers moving, as if to frame a shot, and then drawing out an invisible thread.

"I can show the world that bond," he said with simple conviction, far beyond arrogance. "That's what I do. Once I saw it, I had to shoot it. Sure, there are other things around it – I took a whole sequence at the Academy, and McDonald let me shoot the autopsies, but they're the core."

"How did the team bond manifest?" Dr Renfrew hoped for artistic insight, but an instant later was sorely disappointed.

Mr Carval stared blankly at him. "It just is. You can see it. It's obvious."

"Can you be specific?"

Another prolonged silence. Dr Renfrew thought, dispiritedly, that Mr Carval was not a man of deep thought, analysis, or introspection. The possession of even one of those qualities would have immeasurably improved the current discussion.

"First it was their focus," Mr Carval began, promptly destroying all of Dr Renfrew's assumptions. "It's in their faces, and when you get closer, it's in their eyes. Not quite an expression, but the quality of how they were looking at the scene: dispassionate passion; unemotional anger. All of them had the same look, no matter which way they were looking: at the corpse, at the surroundings, or talking to the ME or CSU. Nothing else mattered to them. I mean, lots of people have heard of me, and they're desperate to be photographed; they play up to the camera and pose. *They* were annoyed I was getting in their way, even after they knew I wasn't some misery tourist rubbernecking."

Dr Renfrew made a *please-continue* gesture.

"That was it. That was what I needed. And they're each a perfect contrast to the others, but that was just the same. The contrast, and the similarity. I mean, look at them. They've got *nothing* in common. Casey's Stanford and up-town Manhattan all the way; totally uncompromising and never doesn't get her man. O'Leary acts like a haystack and is twice as big – you could put Casey on his shoulder, like a parrot on a pirate, and he wouldn't even notice – and he almost never gets riled. But they've been partners for more than five years and they *work*. And Tyler never uses one word when none'll do, and he's all fitness and sport and spars with O'Leary and sometimes he wins" – Mr Carval's evident amazement was matched by Dr Renfrew's – "and he's ex-Army."

Mr Carval clearly stopped himself from providing extra information.

"Andy's cultured – the rest wouldn't know culture if it bit them and don't care, except O'Leary because he does am-dram and sings" – Dr Renfrew could not prevent his splutter – "he does, but he must have the deepest voice *ever* because his vocal cords have to be a mile long and obviously longer means deeper – and he's – Andy, I mean – smallish and precise and neat. He's always calm. Tyler's brisk. O'Leary's amiable."

"And Detective Clement?" asked Dr Renfrew into the hard silence that followed.

"Driven," Mr Carval eventually said. It did not sound as if it was a compliment. Dr Renfrew moved away from that line of inquiry, having no desire to explore romantic complications. Had he wished to be a couples' counsellor, he would not have joined the FBI.

"When I was previously here," he said instead, "it appeared that the team had bonded partly because of their separate histories. It was, for example, clear that Detective Clement's hatred of photographs arose from an incident in her past, in which a photo of her had been used to compromise her."

Mr Carval's expression was fleeting, and swiftly blanked, but exceedingly illuminating. He evidently knew the full story, and equally evidently did not wish to discuss it.

"It was also clear that Detective Chee had personal experience of abuse." This time, Mr Carval preserved an empty expression which told Dr Renfrew more than any other reaction would have.

"I surmise that Detectives O'Leary and Tyler also have matters in their past of which the team is aware, and that the team bond has strengthened as a result of its members' mutual support of each other."

"Do you?" said Mr Carval blandly. "I wouldn't know. You'd have to ask them. Are we done? I need to get back to my studio and download today's shots."

"For now," agreed Dr Renfrew. Mr Carval stopped, seemed about to say something, then clamped his mouth shut. Dr Renfrew observed that he left the precinct immediately.

***

O'Leary tapped on Captain Kent's door when Casey was safely out of the way.

"Come in – O'Leary?"

"Sir." His immense bulk managed to shrink as it sidled in and closed the door. "Uh, sir, could I see you and Dr Renfrew?" Kent stared, slack-jawed. "Uh…not now, but, um, later."

"By that, I take it you mean when Detective Clement won't notice?" Kent rapped. His immediate surprise had been replaced by ominous conclusions.

"Waal, yessir."

"Yes. We will meet as soon as Clement has left, when you will provide a full, open, and completely honest account of the reasons for requesting this meeting and for the mess that the team is in. I will not put up with any more of your team's partial explanations."

"Yessir." O'Leary drooped.

"Dismissed."

***

The warrant for Roberts' cabin came through only a few seconds before Casey expedited its arrival by calling the court and pulling out the clerk's intestines through the phone wires.

"Tyler, I got the warrant. Get the boys upstate on it." She flicked the e-mail on to Tyler, and dismissed both from her mind. She still had a whole heap of nothing. Most likely Roberts was a washout, and that left her with

161

String-Bean Steve and the Washingtons. She tapped her pen impatiently on her desk. The probate lawyer hadn't called. Well, she could fix that. She dialled Schickoff & Schultz's switchboard.

"Putting you through," said the operator.

"Kellie Dennick," said a smooth voice.

"Ms Dennick, this is Detective Clement of the Thirty-Sixth Precinct. I requested that you call me."

"Yes?" Ms Dennick didn't appear to appreciate the point.

"Ms Dennick, this is a murder investigation and I need your assistance," Casey said sharply.

"Oh! I am sorry, but I've had clients to deal with," she said snottily. Casey's already fragile temper rose, but she managed to restrain it.

"Asher Washington was murdered. His will was held by your firm and Norman Dennison suggested that you would assist in understanding the provisions. Shall I tell Mr Dennison that you didn't return my calls or help in a murder investigation?"

The snottiness vanished in a flash of indrawn breath and a pause, which Casey assumed contained a light-speed re-evaluation of Ms Dennick's options.

"What would you like to know?" she said, in a far more accommodating tone. Sheer fear underlay it, which satisfied Casey's temper.

"Asher was the beneficiary of a trust fund. Would the assets within the trust be part of his estate and pass to the beneficiaries of his will?"

"Yes."

"You're quite sure?"

"Yes. When he revised his will because he intended to get married, we talked about that extensively. We analysed the whole trust, how it was set up, and what would happen."

"Do you have details of the trust?"

"Yes."

"Can you supply them?"

"I'll need to check, but if we need a warrant or court order I'll tell you."

"Why didn't anyone tell us about this when we requested the will?"

"No-one asked me about the trust."

Casey thought many vicious and profane thoughts about lawyers who couldn't see beyond their own noses, and choked back every single one of them. "When can we have it?" she asked instead. "This is urgent. The trust's details are critical."

"I'll check now, and let you know as soon as our compliance people give me an answer. If it's okay, I'll send it straight away. If it's not, I'll tell you what we'll need."

"I'll expect to hear from you within the hour, even if you haven't had an answer," Casey said, and gave her cell number.

"Sure. Thank you for calling." Casey was sure that was an automatic ending, because Kellie-dimwit-Dennick hadn't enjoyed that call one iota.

"Bye."

Casey put the phone down gently, and mentally screamed fit to bring the building down around her ears. She stood up, stretched, and went to see Andy.

"Schickoff & Schultz have the trust deed," she bit off. "I'll have it as soon as they've cleared it, or I'll be told they need a warrant or court order. When I get it, I'll know who the trustees are, and then I'll have a nice long chat with them. You'll be with me."

"Okay." Andy didn't dare say anything else. He could see the previously tight team bond dissolving with every instant, each uncomfortable interaction observed by Renfrew.

Casey made coffee, checked her watch, and wished that the hour till the end of shift would pass, so that she could leave. Regardless of her plan to watch movies that evening, she wanted to go, stuff herself with chocolate, and be left in solitary, miserable peace. Her job had always been her joy and refuge, and now it was neither. Her team had always been her strength and support, and now neither of those were true either. She set her shoulders. She could be neutral, professional, and *do her job* regardless of the others' idiotic actions. All she had to do was straighten up her head and block out all the extraneous items.

If only she didn't have the ominous feeling that Marcol was machinating in the background, ready to fuck up her life all over again.

She took a second espresso back to her desk, and considered String-Bean Steve to the exclusion of all other matters. She could do this.

Unfortunately, since she had no evidence whatsoever that Stephen Marthen had ever owned a rifle, and even less evidence that he had been in Morningside Park to shoot his non-existent rifle, she had nothing on him. On the other hand – she bared her teeth at the file – he hadn't come up with an alibi either. She could haul him up, and grill his spiteful, envious ass until he couldn't sit down.

Perfect.

"Fremont?"

"Yes, Detective?"

"Please get Stephen Marthen into Interrogation. Thanks."

"Yes'm."

"If the Sergeant allows it, you can come in to the interview."

"Yes, *ma'am!*" he enthused, and hurried off.

"You're takin' Fremont in 'stead of me?"

"Yes." Casey's single word stopped all discussion.

"We are goin' to talk."

"*I* am going to interrogate."

163

As soon as Fremont returned, shining with delight at being allowed into a detective's world, Casey left to indulge in some nice interrogating. Nice for her, that was, and maybe for Fremont. It wouldn't be nice for Steve.

Steve sat slumped and cuffed in Interrogation, beaten down and defeated. "I didn't kill him," he wailed. "Please, I don't deserve to be in jail."

"Asher didn't deserve to have his engagement broken up by your lies, either, and he sure didn't deserve to die. You're alive, aren't you? That's a lot better than he is."

Steve stared brokenly at her. Fremont stayed quiet, and the only sound was Steve's harried breathing.

"What do you want?" Steve asked in abject capitulation.

"Where were you between midnight and eight a.m. on Tuesday, January 31?"

"Home," he eventually said. "Co-op City. Asch Loop. I go out to work around seven-thirty."

"Where did" – Steve cringed – "you work?"

"Duane Reed, on West 135th Street."

"That's not that far from Morningside Park, is it, Fremont?"

Fremont nodded. He would have nodded if Casey had said it wasn't far from Mars.

"Ample opportunity to shoot Asher and be at work on time."

"I was at home!"

"Prove it."

Suffocating silence stretched out.

"I can't. I live alone."

"Yeah," Casey said contemptuously, "I'd guessed. You wouldn't have broken up Asher and his girlfriend if you could have gotten one of your own. Well, it's back to jail for you. I can't say I'm sorry."

"You could check street cameras. They'd show I wasn't there. Or on the B28 bus and the Five Line. I get that from Gun Hill Road station every day."

"Can't prove a negative, Steve. Enjoy the cells." She turned to Fremont. "Please take him back, and then come back here."

"Yes'm."

Fremont returned quickly.

"Okay, I want you to get transit information on Stephen Marthen, and see if we can use it to eliminate him properly. If we can find him, then it might be at a time which rules him out. Or in," she added.

"Shouldn't I look both ways, around the time of death? He might've done it, and then gone back, so he was on the train going in the right direction at the right time."

"Good thought. Yes. If you need help, ask the team."

164

"Yes'm." Fremont hurried off, anxious to start. Casey didn't move. She looked at her watch again, and discovered that she could leave. Kellie Dennick would call her cell phone.

CHAPTER NINETEEN

Trudging back to her desk, Casey discovered an intervention posse comprising the other team members.

"Let's go chat," O'Leary said. "I got some stuff to finish up, an' then let's go an' fix this. I'll see you in the Abbey."

"I'm going to the movies." O'Leary looked disbelievingly at her. "Suicide Squad."

"Can't say it'd be my pick. What's wrong with *The Sound of Music*?"

In the background, Andy groaned.

"Just as well you're not going, then," Casey snipped.

O'Leary's exasperated sigh wobbled the chairs. "Mebbe tomorrow you'll've found your missin' temper. An' you're not gettin' out of talkin' to me just by seein' a movie, neither."

"Just watch me." Casey flounced out, trailing toxic anger.

O'Leary looked at the other two cops. "I gotta see Kent. C'n you two go hold a table in the Abbey, 'cause I'll want all the beer they got when I'm done."

"'Kay," Tyler said tersely, recognising that it was no time for questions. "Brief us later."

O'Leary trudged off to Kent's office, finding Renfrew already there, and an irritated Kent. Since irritation was Kent's natural state of being, O'Leary was no more intimidated than usual.

"You wished to see both of us?" Renfrew inquired. Kent's face turned choleric.

"Yessir. Doctor." O'Leary shuffled from foot to foot, trembling the desk.

"You can start by explaining why Clement is on the verge of explosion, the rest of you look like you lost your pet puppies, and that photographer, who was practically living here, has barely been seen for four days. I'm

166

guessing," Kent said with deadly ire, "that Clement wasn't pleased to find out that you all knew about the photo." He fixed O'Leary's quivering mass with a gimlet glare. "You may begin at the beginning, for Dr Renfrew's benefit. I am fully apprised of the circumstances."

O'Leary recognised, resignedly, that he'd been backed into a corner, and that his only option for emerging alive was telling the whole story. He'd admire Kent's acuity, if only it were directed at someone else.

"Sir," he said heavily, and turned to Renfrew. "At the Academy, someone tried to slut-shame Casey – Detective Clement – with a photo that Carval took years ago. We're pretty sure it was Marcol who orchestrated it – the Narcotics detective – because he didn't like comin' second, but we had no proof an' didn't care because he wasn't here. When Carval found us an' started tryin' to get in here to shoot, he showed his original to Casey an', waal, she wasn't too happy. So we had a chat with him, an' he seemed okay to us, an' eventually Casey came around. Then there was the models case, an' Marcol popped up. He hit on Casey, she blew him off, an' Tyler had a word. Somewhere in there, Marcol accused us of sendin' a lawyer's letter about him stealin' that photo. An' since we knew it wasn't us – we don't mix with second-raters an' we don't like assholes," O'Leary said with unconscious arrogance. Kent stifled an inappropriate smile. Renfrew remained impassive – "there was only one candidate. We knew Casey would be a tad upset, so we went to see him, an' told him he oughta tell her. An' that was where we left it. Thanks to that li'l rat, it's all come out an' she's not happy."

"That is one strand. However," Renfrew pontificated, "I do not believe that is all. I observed Detective Clement reacting strongly to the suggestion by Roberts that a woman should not be a detective. Since I cannot imagine that Detective Clement suffers from a lack of professional confidence, and her outstanding record speaks for itself, I infer that there is another matter affecting her."

O'Leary winced. "'T'ain't a professional matter," he evaded.

"No," said Kent, "but it is relevant." He waited, until the silence became unbearable.

"Casey's dad's got a problem with drink. He got drunk an' took a swing at the airport cops, so they wrote him up. Hearin's Thursday. You gave Casey the day, sir."

"Yes."

"Anyways, Casey's dad didn't like it when she went an' got him, an' he told her she shouldn't have been a cop, she should've been a lawyer. It ain't true, but Roberts hit the sore spot. She was hopin' her dad was gettin' dry, but it seems like that ain't happenin' neither."

"And what's the connection between these matters?" Kent jabbed.

O'Leary knew his next words would cause mayhem. "Casey thinks, sir,

167

that since Marcol likely knows that Carval's shootin' us, he'll think that Casey's got somethin' to do with the letter, an'…" he swallowed.

"Continue."

"He'll sniff around – or get his pals to do it – an' find Casey's dad bein' picked up drunk. He'll make it look like Casey's been pullin' strings or" – he turned beet red – "anyways, she thinks he'll use her dad to make her look bad or corrupt." He swallowed. "I don't think she's wrong," he forced out. "He did it before, when she beat him in class an' wouldn't date him, an' now she won't date him again an' he's in a heap of trouble from Carval. Carval don't like his photos stolen an' he really don't like that it was used against Casey."

"I inferred previously that Detective Clement and Mr Carval were involved."

"Not right now, they ain't."

"That would indeed be surprising."

Kent's normally high colour had reached new heights of choler. He tapped a pen sharply on the desk. "In your professional judgement, O'Leary, do you believe that Marcol will try to attack Clement?"

O'Leary gulped again, and then straightened to his full width and height. "Yessir," he said decisively. "I do."

To O'Leary's amazement, Kent's colour receded and his intimidating sternness ebbed. Renfrew acquired a thin smile.

"I'd prefer to be able to disagree with you, O'Leary, but I don't think I can. Marcol's record with Clement is worrying, and while he might have changed, I'm not inclined to chance it. Leave him to us. Try to stop Carval doing anything precipitate, but if he wants to instruct his process server, we can't stop him." O'Leary was fairly sure the word *unfortunately* was lingering on Kent's lips. "Now, your team dynamics."

Shit, thought O'Leary. He'd really hoped to avoid that. "Sir?"

"Fix them."

"Sir?"

"Fix it. Whatever you usually do to fix yourselves, do it. If that means none of you can speak through your hangovers for two days, I'll overlook it as long as you turn up for shift and don't shoot anyone. If it's not fixed by next week, I'll fix it. Tell Clement about this discussion – in full."

O'Leary gaped, and failed to say anything.

"Dismissed."

He fled.

"You will not take immediate steps?" Renfrew asked.

"Not with them. Not yet. They've fixed themselves all the way through and interfering won't help. They'll ignore me, and that's bad for discipline. As long as they keep solving cases, and don't do anything stupid, I can watch from a safe distance. I won't fix them next week, either. I just want them to move their collective asses back to normal."

"I see. So, what shall we do about Detective Marcol?"

"We?"

"I would like to assist. Agent Bergen is an exceedingly talented computer specialist, and would be able to identify any amendments to records that might be made posthumously." Kent raised an eyebrow. "So to speak. In addition, I disapprove of harassment. I would be delighted to remove any person who attempted such misconduct."

Kent smiled evilly at Renfrew, for the first time totally approving. "You know," he said, "I think we have a deal."

***

When O'Leary hit the Abbey, he collapsed into a chair, and downed the first two beers without a breath.

"What went down?" Andy asked. "You look like a truck hit you."

"Nah. Truck would lose," Tyler said. "747."

O'Leary downed a third beer. "Worse," he whimpered.

"Okay, what happened?" Andy asked.

"Need to go back to earlier. Casey's dad's likely drinkin' again, an' she thinks Marcol'll go after her by bringin' up her dad an' sayin' she's got him off charges."

"Aw, *shit*," Tyler said. "That's why she's so mad."

"Yeah. Anyways, I think she's right. So...I reported the whole thin' to Kent an' Renfrew."

Andy spat out his soda. "You did *what*? Are you crazy?"

"Guess he's got reason. Spill, Bigfoot."

"Better be a really good reason, because Casey'll kill him."

"We can't deal with it. Iffen Marcol starts in, we might have the rep but it'll be Casey takin' all the shit from ev'ry half-assed second-rater who's got a burr up his ass about what she's done an' how fast she did it. All that stuff from the Academy's goin' to be dragged up again, an' I ain't havin' that." The last words could have been written on tablets of stone. "So I went to Kent. An' he agrees with me. He an' Renfrew'll deal with it."

"So why're you on your fifth beer in ten minutes, then? That doesn't sound too bad."

"'Cause *one*, I got to tell Casey."

"I'd start on the whiskey now," Andy quipped.

"An' *two*, Kent told us to fix ourselves, quick. Nothin' about how, but he's watchin' us. So now we got a deadline of next week to try an' fix it, an' Casey's gettin' worse by the day."

"Sure is."

"Any ideas?"

"Naw. Kent said he wouldn't notice iffen we all had a two-day hangover, though. I'm havin' mine startin' tomorrow," he added darkly.

"No. Thursday you're looking after Casey."

"I guess so. She can't shoot me, an' she can't hurt me, an' if it gets too much I'll pick her up an' take her away."

"Wouldn't," Tyler said.

"Naw?"

"No. Never forgive you if she's not there for her dad."

"She can't save him," O'Leary pointed out.

"She knows," Andy said bleakly. "But it won't stop her trying. Nothing ever stops you hoping it'll all be okay in the end." Tyler touched his shoulder. "Even when you know it won't be. Ever."

"We've got us," O'Leary said firmly. "Don't need nobody else iffen we need a li'l support. Mebbe we got other people to love" – his moon face pinkened. Interestingly, Tyler coloured slightly as well – "but the team's the team. Ain't nothin' changin' that while I'm here."

"Will you knock that through Casey's concrete skull?"

"Yup," O'Leary said, almost comfortably. "Sure will." But the twitching of his fingers betrayed his doubt, and he swallowed down another beer.

"So," Tyler said. "Thursday. We going?"

"I'm goin'. Can't all go, 'less we've solved the case, an' I don't think we're there yet. Not without Andy's MTA data, an' that's Friday. I'll square it with Kent 'bout Thursday, I guess." He didn't look hopeful.

"'Kay. You know her best."

***

Casey didn't go to the movies. She didn't go home, either. Kellie Dennick had left her a message to say that, in the circumstances, Compliance had cleared the release of the trust deed, but she'd sent that straight on to Andy. She'd read it in the morning. She went up through Washington Heights, past Fort Tryon Park, out of Manhattan to Van Cortland Park, to Lloyds Carrot Cake. Normally, she'd go to their East Harlem store, but O'Leary was well aware of her comfort food preferences, and if he was looking for her, he'd go there as soon as he found she wasn't home.

She couldn't bear to see him – any of them. Morosely, she stirred her coffee, and wondered just when her life had gone to shit. Drunk dad, duplicitous boyfriend, dumbass co-workers. And the hearing coming up on Thursday. She clung to her coffee, stared at her carrot cake, and wished with all her fractured heart that her mother had never died in that car accident, that likely wasn't an accident at all. Nothing had ever gone right since then: since they'd discovered the glioblastoma during the autopsy. Her father had blamed himself for not noticing the symptoms, but how could an *architect* know that the little stumbles and forgetfulnesses weren't just

Mom, but something much, much worse? How could any of them have known?

Except that her Mom had known. Somehow. That accident...before the disease took its inexorable course; before mind and body began to disintegrate; before the pain, the treatments that wouldn't, couldn't, work; before the dragging, dreadful death. The accident had been all too convenient; a lonely road, a concrete abutment. Then only Casey and her father, left behind.

She turned away from her memories. She couldn't bear to remember her father as he had been, or O'Leary's constant, unwavering support. He'd been there...never let her down. Held her up, when otherwise she wouldn't have been able to stand.

But now he had let her down. A tear dripped into the carrot cake, and another, and another. She pressed a napkin to her eyes, and kept her head down. She hadn't felt so abandoned since her mother's funeral; and then, eighteen months later, discovering her father drunk. He'd been sober afterwards, for months at a time, but always he returned to it: shorter gaps between each episode. Now, he was drunk more often than sober, but she couldn't let him drown. She guessed she'd just have to deal with him herself.

Somehow.

Deep inside, she knew it wouldn't work. Deep inside, she knew that he'd already drowned, and he'd take her down with him.

She ate her carrot cake, and drank her coffee, and went home without any further tears. Tears had never helped anything, and they wouldn't help her now. On Thursday, she'd be as hard and cold as she'd ever been in Interrogation.

She didn't need another hero. She just needed herself.

***

Since she hadn't read the trust deed the previous night, Casey went in early. It wasn't difficult to start at dawn, since sleep had eluded her for most of the night. She worked her way through the legalese, and found that the original trustees had been Asher's parents' lawyer and pastor. She read further, and found that the trust would come to an end on Asher's marriage or when he reached thirty, just as his parents' wills had indicated.

She frowned. Asher had been rising thirty, and planning to marry. Either would have terminated the trust. She read faster, skimming the presently irrelevant clauses about using the money for Asher's education and general benefit, and came to the clauses dealing with the trust's termination.

A-ha! On termination, the trustees were required to – quote – *render a full account of all dealings with the finances of the trust, to be certified by* – good God. Certified by a law firm, Marswell & Eglinton, who would choose a firm of accountants to conduct a final audit, who were not to be a firm who had ever audited the fund before. Marswell & Eglinton? She Googled. Oh. They were huge. Really huge. Why on earth would Asher's parents have wanted that? She flipped back. The accounts had to be audited every year, but the trust didn't stipulate who was to do it, or any other requirement for certification.

She frowned harder. The trust deed made no…well, that was wrong. It made plenty of sense, but only if Asher's parents had been totally paranoid about someone defrauding him. Sure, they'd been on Wall Street, and no doubt they'd seen a lot of financial immorality, but this was unusually pointed. Surely they couldn't have suspected their lawyer and pastor? That would be even more paranoid. But Aunt and Uncle Washington weren't trustees, so they wouldn't have direct access to the funds, and anyway why would they spark paranoia?

Casey began to scrawl down questions and thoughts, going back to the uses of the money as well as termination requirements. The Washingtons had been, at best, disingenuous about Asher's inheritance and how much they'd had to do for Asher. By the time the others arrived, her hand hurt, and she'd covered four sheets of paper.

"I read the trust deed. I want to find Benjamin Stanley, who was Asher's parents' lawyer; and Elijah Massapa, who was their pastor. They're the named trustees."

"Hey, Casey," Andy snipped. "How're you this morning?"

"The trust raises more questions than it answers. It should've been audited every year. The trustees should know about that. When it finished, it had to be re-audited and then certified by one of the biggest law firms in America. Someone was totally paranoid. I wanna know why." She brandished her sheets of questions. "Andy, you stick with Bill Roberts – now I've read this, he and Steve are sliding down the suspect list, because this screams that Asher's parents didn't trust their family, but I want Roberts eliminated asap. Tyler, you find these two men. O'Leary, see if you can find a contact at Marswell & Eglinton. Fremont's looking at Steve's travel, and I'll leave that with him."

"What're you going to do?"

"I'll try and find out where the trust financials are held, and then get them. We got Asher's personal financials, and I'll work backwards from the monthly payments." She looked around them. "Let's get started."

"Casey," Andy said tentatively, "I told you yesterday that I wouldn't get the MTA information till Friday. There's nothing I can do with Roberts till then."

"Upstate cops are searching the cabin. They'll tell me soon as they're done," Tyler added.

"Work it out between you, then," she snapped. "You don't need me to

172

do that."

They stared at each other. Casey never lost the thread of who was doing what with a live case. Never.

"'Kay. Casey, iffen you've read all that this mornin', you've been here for hours. We're goin' out to get you some food an' around four pints of that strong coffee you like. While we're gone, Tyler an' Andy'll work it out like you asked."

"I need to do the financials."

"Naw, you need to eat first. You're hungry an' it makes you cranky. Low blood sugar." O'Leary was carefully manoeuvring Casey towards the stairs. "You can't think with low blood sugar. 'S not possible. All the scientists say so."

"I'm not hungry."

"Waal, you oughta be. An' I am, so iffen you don't come help me get some breakfast I might start on the rookies. That li'l one – Adamo – he looks pretty tasty, iffen I roasted him with a little rosemary."

"Don't be ridiculous."

"You're comin'. You c'n walk, or I c'n walk you."

"You" – the words died in Casey's throat as she caught O'Leary's expression. O'Leary would ensure nobody else in the bullpen knew what he was doing, but that wouldn't change the outcome. Walk, or be walked.

She walked.

"We'll go to Kitchenette, an' you c'n have a proper breakfast an' enough coffee to float an elephant." Casey didn't answer, though her stomach did. "See, you're hungry. An' we need to talk."

"We don't."

"Waal, that's where you're wrong, 'cause I need to tell you somethin' before you get another bug up your ass to join the stick up there."

"Whatever. I can't stop you."

"No. But you c'n listen. I ain't lettin' you go on like this. You'll be ill. We've been pals since forever an' just 'cause you're pissed with me don't change that."

"Whatever."

O'Leary dropped it, and steered them into Kitchenette, where he didn't bother asking before ordering himself an enormous plate of three-egg omelette with sausage, extra biscuits, extra bacon, and French toast with fruit; and getting Casey pancakes with bacon and syrup. He added the biggest pot of coffee they'd serve, and then sat back, regarding Casey through pale blue eyes. He said nothing until breakfast had arrived and he'd eaten half of it. He didn't reckon the conversation he was about to have would improve his appetite, and it sure wouldn't improve Casey's.

CHAPTER TWENTY

O'Leary gulped down another basin of coffee, and prayed for a blast shield. "I said I had to talk to you."

Casey ate her pancakes, without looking up.

"I went to see Kent 'bout the chances of Marcol screwin' you over 'bout your dad," he rushed out.

Casey dropped her cutlery. "You did *what?*"

"An' he agrees with me that it's likely he'll try," O'Leary said over her flabbergasted spluttering.

Casey's jaw hit the table.

"So does Renfrew."

Long, cold silence fell about them.

"I can't deal with this right now." Casey exited precipitately, leaving the remains of her breakfast. O'Leary finished that, and his own meal, and the coffee. On balance, that had gone better than expected. He had no bullet holes, though he didn't get to split the check. He paid, ambled back to the precinct, and, as entirely expected, found Casey head down in a pile of papers and not talking to anyone. She hadn't exploded, however, and since Andy and Tyler seemed pretty equable themselves, maybe she'd lost some of her bad temper.

Casey had forced herself not to think about anything except the fastest way of working backwards from the receipts in Asher's bank account. There had to be an easier way than contacting Asher's bank, surely? She could call Aunt or Uncle Washington, but her gut told her that she didn't want to tip them off. She couldn't have said why, but she'd learned to listen to her hunches, and this one was screaming.

Kayla Burton. Nope, she hadn't known anything about Asher's finances. Maybe she should ask Kayla about Asher's relationship with his aunt and uncle. She wrote that down for later. With considerable frustration, she decided she'd have to back-calculate through the bank, and picked up the phone.

***

During O'Leary and Casey's breakfast absence, Andy and Tyler had agreed that one of them would take Elijah Massapa, and the other Benjamin Stanley. When Casey returned, even more reserved than when she'd left, they kept their heads down and their mouths shut. When O'Leary returned, he started on Marswell & Eglinton.

The morning passed in chilly silence, leavened only by frustration. All the information that Andy and Tyler had – which was almost nothing – had been fed into the databases, which hadn't yet designed to spit out any answers. O'Leary had fought his way into the Marswell & Eglinton switchboard and personal assistant network, which had trapped him in a spider-web of circularity. Even his famous amiability had worn thin. Halfway through the morning, he sidled into Kent's office, and sidled out again a few moments later.

At lunchtime, the three men went out, Casey having declined their invitation.

"So?" Tyler asked.

"She didn't shoot me. Just said she couldn't deal with it and hasn't said a word since."

"Buried in the financials. Hasn't asked me anything." Andy managed a grin. "Even Renfrew hasn't gone near her."

"Not stupid," Tyler clipped.

"Prob'ly means he'll be after us again," O'Leary said gloomily. "I got Kent to give me tomorrow, though."

"Yeah? You telling Casey that?"

"Naw. She ain't gonna see me, neither."

"I didn't know the courthouse had floor to ceiling screens," Andy gibed.

"I c'n sneak. I'll go in late, an' leave early. She can't follow me into the restroom."

"And then?"

"Depends," O'Leary said heavily. "Iffen it's all okay, I'll slip off. Iffen it's not...I'll be there."

"Trusting you to fix this, Bigfoot." Tyler met his gaze.

"Eight years. We were uniforms together, before we made detectives. We were tight long before you came along. I got this. We'll fix us, an' then we'll fix Carval. Team first, though. I ain't gonna let this li'l spat break us. We work, an' we're stayin' that way." He devoured his lunch, and left it at that.

***

In the bullpen, Dr Renfrew decided that interviewing Detective Clement would be counter-productive. Instead, he would review the team's personnel records, from which he might gain a measure of enlightenment.

Enlightenment he certainly found. As he had surmised, the history of each detective contained reasons for their bond. Detective Chee had clearly been abused; Detective Tyler, a much-decorated sniper, showed indications of PTSD, although Dr Renfrew considered that those must be minimal; Detective O'Leary was married to another man. The only exception was Detective Clement, whose record indicated that she had been an outstanding recruit, officer, and then detective. Since Dr Renfrew was already aware of her issue, he required nothing further.

Having digested the files, Dr Renfrew discovered that it was close to 1 p.m., and decided that a pleasant luncheon with Captain Kent would further his research. Before that, however, he would instruct Agent Bergen to review all records relating to David Clement, Detective Clement's father.

Captain Kent was not precisely reluctant to join Dr Renfrew for lunch, but he was not enthusiastic. His demeanour improved markedly with Dr Renfrew's opening words.

"I am impressed that you have managed to weld such a disparate collection of individuals into such an excellent team. Your talent for team management must be considerable."

"I had a hunch," Captain Kent said.

"Could you tell me how you built the team up?"

"Sure. I got Clement and O'Leary as a pair. I didn't want to split them – Garrett at the Third recommended them, and it's difficult to pair up a good-looking woman."

"Detective O'Leary, however, would not present problems, since he is gay."

"Exactly. They were already pretty effective together, so why spoil a good thing? Tyler was a different kettle of fish. Great reputation, but because he was ex-Army, plenty of others tried to take him on – and failed. So his Captain wanted a swap, and I thought that he'd fit with my two. It was a gamble," Kent admitted. "Tyler could have been one of those guys who can't work with a woman or a guy who could beat him on the mats. But it came off. They clicked, though I've no idea why. Then they needed a fourth, and Chee was another problem child – brilliant at tech, but not sociable. So I'd had three problems who'd turned into a team, and so I figured – another hunch – that Chee'd fit. And he did. Nearly five years they've been together, and it's worked out well, though I don't let them play with the others."

"Oh?"

"They're the most competitive bunch you'll ever meet. Doesn't matter if it's sparring or shooting or a goddamn quiz night, they're out to win, and they don't like to win small. Their motto seems to be 'No-one likes us, we don't care'."

"I have not noticed any active dislike within the bullpen."

"They're respected, but nobody's friends with them. They keep themselves to themselves."

"I see. However, they have – or had – included Mr Carval?"

"It's *have*. Even with the latest spat, the men are sticking with both of them. They like Carval – God knows why, because his ego's bigger than the Empire State Building and he's pushy as hell about his photos. But he seems to fit in."

"He is as focused on his photography as they are on solving crimes," Dr Renfrew observed. "Like calls to like."

"I guess. He's around a lot more often than I'd like, but it'll be great PR, so I guess I have to put up with it. But if he upsets Clement any more, he'll be gone. I don't need the PR half as much as I need her solve rate."

"The other detectives are managing that situation, so that they do not encounter each other."

Kent harrumphed. "I'm watching."

"So am I. I find that team most interesting."

"I'd better get back," Kent said. "Thanks for lunch."

"I will keep you informed."

Kent strode off. Dr Renfrew finished his coffee in contented solitude, and then returned to the bullpen, where Detective Clement seemed not to have moved in the previous hour.

Now that he understood more of the team's background, he admired Captain Kent's ability to match their personalities. That had clearly been a key factor in the development of the team, assisted by the Captain's ability to stand back from them. He made a note, and then considered the position. He earnestly wished to assist the team to resolve its differences. However, he would not intrude while they were so heavily involved in the case.

***

Hours of tedious work later, Casey had discovered that the payments had come from Cano Bank, chased down an account number, and had served the bank with a warrant for details of the account holders. She didn't expect to see any answers that day. Banks, in her experience, were less than speedy.

She decided she'd go have another chat with Kayla Burton. It beat the silent reproach from the others, and Renfrew's eagle eye. It might even stop her thinking about the hearing the following day. However, this wasn't a witness interview, more of a friendly chat. Therefore, it was perfectly reasonable to call Kayla and suggest that, if she had time, they should talk, at a coffee bar convenient to Kayla's office. Avoiding O'Leary and the rest, who all too obviously wanted to discuss non-case matters, had nothing whatsoever to do with her decisions. Nor did avoiding Renfrew, naturally: she had no need to avoid anyone. And she didn't need to avoid Carval, because he wasn't there.

Amazingly, Kayla had time. Casey didn't bother mentioning her plans or saying farewells, but simply left. Shortly, she sat down in the coffee bar: her points on a small piece of paper in front of her, together with her coffee. She wasn't hungry. She hadn't been hungry since breakfast. She doubted she'd want to eat before tomorrow: her stomach twisting and roiling in time with her bleak thoughts.

What would she do if her father were jailed? He could be. If, somehow, the judge had found out about the multiple pick-ups; if the JFK cops decided to make more of the attempted swing at them; if…

If Marcol had worked fast and already discovered the truth. What would she do then? Her gut clenched.

"Hi," came from behind her, and Kayla, holding a huge cappuccino, sat down. Despite Casey's earlier reassurances, her hand trembled.

"Hey. Thanks for meeting me. I just wanted a bit of background on Asher's aunt and uncle, and anything you knew about the wider family relationships?" Kayla relaxed noticeably. "You're the best source of information I've got. I know you weren't too happy after the last time we met, but I was hoping…" she trailed off, encouragingly. She wouldn't mention the will or the money again. Save that for a better time, when she'd caught Asher's killer.

"Yeah. I'm still mad at him, but he didn't deserve to be shot. So," she gulped, and tears sheened her eyes, "I'll tell you whatever I can. I've got time right now: my deal closed late last night, and today's just endless paperwork. It'll keep for a while, and my boss won't complain about helping the cops."

"Thanks." Casey smiled. In other circumstances, she'd have liked Kayla, but making friends during a case was unprofessional. "Could you tell me what you knew about Asher's parents, first?"

Kayla thought, mindlessly spooning the foam and chocolate (Casey approved) from the top of her coffee. "Uh, he didn't talk much about them, but they died when he was about fifteen. I thought they must've been pretty successful and hard working. Asher was really focused and ambitious, and I got the feeling that he'd learned it from them, you know? Of course," she added acidly, "now I know how much they'd left him, sure they were. But they'd really loved him. He had that kind of confidence, you know? Like whatever happened, the world was a good place, and people were mostly good people. You only get that if your family's been solid. He always started out by liking people. I don't mean he was dumb – he wasn't *credulous*, but he expected people to be friendly."

Casey tried to think of a tactful way to put the next question, and failed. "But, um, didn't he ever get hassle because" –

"Because he was black?"

"Yeah."

"Sure. But if you're wearing a suit and tie and coming out of a big-name law firm, there's less of it, and he always had ID when he was running, just in case. He'd never have done anything dumb, but he'd have called his firm if anyone had arrested him." She blinked damp eyes. "When you first said he'd been shot, I thought maybe someone had – you know, you see it on the news all the time...but it wasn't, was it?"

"No," Casey murmured. "This wasn't that – but if it had been, we'd have investigated just as hard."

"Anyway. Asher's parents. He went to all sorts of extras: sport, music – all the things that well-off parents do. They went to church, but not like his aunt and uncle did – they were, like, every Sunday, no excuses. Well, maybe death, your own," she said dryly. Casey grinned at her. "Everything in his aunt and uncle's house was because God wanted it. Asher was doing well at work – it was God's will. He hurt his ankle – it was God's will."

"So his aunt and uncle were really into their church?"

"Oh, sure. Tithed and everything. I mean, they put the effort in – church groups, socials, outreach to young people – Asher helped with that, and he liked it, although he didn't get much choice about doing it – camping in the summer.... Their church was their whole life. Almost too much, you know?"

Casey didn't know.

"So when Asher moved out, they hassled him about worshipping regularly, suggested he should be tithing, like I said before – okay, so *now* I know he could have afforded it but it was annoying then, when I thought we were saving for a future" – she sniffed – "wanted him to go back to their church and do all the extra stuff. It was – well, it was like they wanted all his free time to be spent with them. I mean, when were we supposed to have *us* time if he was there all the time? It's not like lawyers get much free time."

"No," Casey agreed, thinking of her Stanford friends who'd gone into commercial law and never seen daylight again. "What were your impressions of his aunt and uncle – besides the church bits?"

Kayla's nose wrinkled. "Um..." she equivocated.

"It's just impressions. It won't get back to them," Casey reassured. "I'm trying to build up a picture."

"Asher loved them, but he didn't much *like* them," Kayla blurted out. "If they'd needed help, he'd have been there like a shot" – she winced. "Ugh. I didn't mean that. He'd have done everything to help them, but day to day he didn't have much in common with them. And..."

"Mm?" Casey encouraged.

"Well, I don't think they got along too well with his parents. Marlon was his dad's brother, and, well, his dad made good but Marlon wasn't quite as successful" – *and had a chequered history*, Casey thought to herself, remembering the pastor's commentary – "and I think they made a few comments about Asher's parents. And like I said, they tried to take up all his time, and they could guilt-trip like nobody's business."

Casey nodded. She was enduring more and more guilt-tripping, and struggling not to let it have an effect.

"But Asher just said that they had a nice house, and a great life, and they'd taken him in and tried to do what they thought was best for him as best they could with their jobs."

A lightbulb lit in Casey's head.

"They didn't have any extra money to do it with?"

"If they did," Kayla said cynically, "they didn't tell Asher. They were pretty good at reminding him about the sacrifices they'd made to raise him. Subtly, sure, but it was there."

"Mm," Casey hummed, bells ringing in peals.

"But they were always really proud of his successes – so he said. And the one time we did go to church there" –

"You went to church with them?"

"Only once. It wasn't my scene. I go to the Episcopal church, when I've time. Theirs was more evangelical, and it didn't suit me, though we met his childhood pastor – he was lovely. Old, you know, but not pushy. I liked him."

The Washingtons had said they barely knew Kayla, but that didn't add up if she'd been to church with them.

"Sorry. The one time you went to church?"

"Oh, yes. The pastor and practically everyone knew how well he was doing, and they were showing him off. It was all 'look at our successful nephew'. I stayed well back. It wasn't like they were introducing me."

"Were they trying to match Asher to anyone else?"

"Nope. It was all their friends, not anyone his age."

"How did it feel to you?" Casey asked.

Kayla winced. "Truthfully, it felt like they didn't like me. Like they just wanted Asher all to themselves. They'd have been happy if he'd stayed in their world, even though they were really proud of how well he was doing."

"I see. Okay, that's been very helpful in getting the background. Thank you."

"You're welcome. I'd better get back to my paperwork."

"You and me both," Casey sympathised.

As Kayla left, Casey bought another espresso, to go, and considered her options. It was an hour past shift end, and she should go home. But, if she went home, she'd simply fret about the morning. She wouldn't eat, she wouldn't sleep, and she'd dissolve into a sodden lump of unhappy worry. Instead, she could go back to the precinct, and write up Kayla's commentary, and then spend some quality, solitary time investigating what it might mean.

Work had always been her distraction from her father's problems, and now would be no exception.

CHAPTER TWENTY ONE

The bullpen was empty; Kent's office was dark (if it hadn't been, Casey would have sneaked out again: Kent vocally disapproved of unauthorised overtime); and Renfrew's borrowed desk was as clear as Casey's own. She sipped her coffee, and began.

She finished late in the evening. She surveyed her sheet of questions, and her murder board, more extensively covered. She had to interview the Washingtons again, but before that she needed to know if their beautiful house was mortgaged. If not...how had they afforded it?

She read down her list once more. The Washingtons had a rifle. They had a bigger house than their incomes would support. Marlon had a chequered past. They'd made Kayla unwelcome. They'd suggested to Asher that they'd had to make sacrifices for him, but the trust fund should have provided for all of his costs. They'd been keen for him not to settle down.

Against that, though: they'd been regular and committed churchgoers, described as good people by their pastor, they'd been transparently proud of Asher's achievements, and – outweighing those considerably – they hadn't been trustees of the fund. If she'd found that they'd been trustees, she'd have hauled them in ten seconds later, and grilled them into ash.

She regarded her murder board. Andy and Tyler hadn't found the pastor or lawyer. O'Leary hadn't written anything about Marswell & Eglinton. Well, those would be top of everyone's hit list tomorrow. They all knew how important they were –

Oh. She wouldn't be in tomorrow. She looked at the board through suddenly-blurring eyes, and then slumped back into her chair, the whole mess crashing in on her again. Tomorrow, her father would be found guilty of disorderly conduct, on the record, where anyone could find it.

She desperately wished that there was someone who would simply hold her; tell her she'd be okay – but there was no-one. Carval cared more for his photographs than for her, which only proved that she'd been right about that non-relationship all along. Right not to let him in, right not to let him near her dad, right to be wary – and right to walk away.

Being right didn't make her happy. It wouldn't have mattered if the team had been tight, but the team was broken too. Her face fell into her arms, her shoulders shook, wholly alone.

A long time later, she raised her head, wiped her face, and went to her empty home.

***

Casey's alarm woke her, terror cramping in her stomach and a headache floating, not quite manifest, behind her eyes. She dressed smartly, as if she were the one appearing in court: slate grey pencil skirt, plain white blouse, slate grey jacket, small pearl stud earrings and neat, black, heeled shoes. She couldn't face breakfast, though her fingers shook through lack of food and her usual espresso tasted acid on her tongue. By the time she pulled up at her father's Brooklyn apartment, her tension had balled tightly in her spine and shoulders.

She went up, praying wordlessly that he'd be ready. She'd arrived early, so that there was time to correct any…issues. *Inadequacies*, her mind said, but she shoved the thought away.

"Hey, Dad." Unobtrusively, she ran a cop's gaze over him, checking everything.

"Catkin."

He was wearing a dark suit and tasteful tie, with a handkerchief that didn't match.

"Let's lose the handkerchief," she said brightly, "it makes you look like a realtor, not an architect. You're well-dressed without it."

He smiled, and removed it. "Where's Ms Jankel?"

"She'll meet us there."

"She will?"

"Yes." She'd explained that. "Don't worry, I checked with her." *Well, she checked with me.* "Let's go."

"Don't I need anything?"

"You, your wallet" –

"Wallet?"

"To pay the court fee." *And the inevitable fine.*

"Oh." He patted his pockets, and produced it, just like a child showing their pencil and eraser for grade school. She wanted to cry at the way he looked at her for approval: shrunken and pathetic. "Got it."

"That's great, Dad. We're all set."

Queens County Criminal Court's glass and steel building was as intimidating as it had been in December. Jankel was waiting inside.

"Hello," Casey said, after an uncomfortable instant in which her father failed to greet, or recognise, his lawyer.

"Good morning," Jankel replied. "I'll just go over this again, so we're clear. There won't be a jury. The evidence will be presented to the judge, and you'll have a chance to speak if you want to, Mr Clement. The decision will be made right then."

Casey's father nodded unconvincingly. His eyes skittered around, taking in the tattooed, shaven-headed thugs; the scrawny, shaking addicts; the stained, ill-dressed, odorous street life of both sexes, down and out; the suffocating atmosphere of defeated bravado.

"I didn't do anything," he pleaded.

"Dad," Casey began, "we've been over this. You were" – she balked at the harsh term *drunk* – "you'd had too much to drink. They tested your blood, and you were over the limit. We can't argue with the forensics."

"I don't remember." He sagged. "I don't remember anything."

"Sit down," Jankel suggested. "We'll likely have to wait."

The wait was long, and Casey's dad became more nervous by the minute. Finally, they were called in.

"David Barratt Clement."

The hearing was nasty, brutish, and short. Casey's father had no defence, and *I don't remember* didn't cut it with the brisk, sceptical judge.

"Guilty. Since it's your first offence, a fine of $250. You're lucky. Next time, you'll be in a cell." The gavel fell, and Jankel ushered them out again. Casey's father was shaking.

"Dad, it's okay. You only have to pay a fine."

"I...yes."

Jankel explained the process, and they went to the Clerk's Office to pay, Casey insisting that it would be easier. *This way he can't forget to pay*, the cynical voice in her head hummed.

"We're done, Dad."

"I need...excuse me," he said, and half-staggered towards the restrooms.

Casey sat down again. At last she could breathe. No-one had come forward to introduce new evidence: Marcol hadn't – or hadn't yet – gone digging for dirt. She waited in the emptying lobby of the courthouse, trying to calm her still-racing pulse, already crashing from the adrenaline drop and the release of all her stress. Surely now her father would take it all more seriously: go back to rehab? They could get lunch, be a family again, recover.

Maybe they'd even plan that trip to DC, to see the Museum of African-American History and Culture; create a far better memory than her father, drunk and angry in custody at JFK; make up for that...misunderstanding.

It would all be fine.

Her father returned from his short absence, and managed a weak smile for Jankel. "Thanks," he said.

"Thank you, Carla," Casey added, standing and shaking her hand.

"You're welcome." Jankel swung off.

Casey turned to her father: shell-shocked and haggard, eyes bloodshot and watery, as tired as she felt. "C'mon, Dad. I'll take you home."

"I need a drink," he said.

She gaped. "Dad..."

"I need a drink."

"Please, Dad. Let's just take you home." Even if he had a drink there...

"I don't want you."

He could have punched her and caused less pain. "Dad?" She suddenly realised that there was alcohol on his breath. This lashing out, this attack...it had to be booze behind it. He must have tipped it down in the restroom.

"Don't want cops. I want a drink and I'm having one." He jerked away from her and out of the courthouse, leaving her behind.

She gazed at the space where he'd been, fighting back her emotions, locking the pain away, waiting the extra moments until she could drive safely.

Home was quiet, still, and solitary. Just what she needed, until there was a heavy knock on the door. She didn't open it. Another knock, and then O'Leary's bass.

"Let me in, Casey, or I'll keep knockin' till the neighbours complain."

He'd do it, too. He'd done it before.

O'Leary didn't hesitate. The instant he'd passed the threshold, he'd summed up the situation. He hugged Casey close as he'd never do in public. "Just let it go," he rumbled. "Let it all out."

"He hit the booze as soon as it was done," she sobbed. "He didn't want me there."

O'Leary said nothing, but he already knew: he'd been eavesdropping from behind the courtroom door. He'd made sure Casey hadn't seen him, and she'd been totally focused on her dad for the few moments the hearing had taken. He sat Casey on her couch, and kept a huge arm around her.

"Ain't no shame to cry," he consoled. "Seems like your dad don't deserve you tryin' to save him."

"He's my *dad*," she cried. "I can't leave him."

"You can't save him, neither."

"I have to try. I *have* to. He's all the family I have."

Not much of one, O'Leary thought cynically, and patted Casey's shuddering shoulders.

"I thought.... I wanted to hope he'd stopped but I think I knew..." She bent forward, head in hands, elbows on knees. He patted again. "Now what?"

O'Leary simply sat there: his huge mass quietly supportive. Casey'd forgotten that they were on the outs, in the much larger pain of her father's rejection, and while it wasn't the way he'd wanted to fix it, if it worked, he'd take it. He'd warned Pete he'd be late home, or maybe not at all, and why. Pete was cool with that. Pete was always cool about the team, just like O'Leary was always cool about Pete's business trips. Went with both their jobs. Now, if Casey would just let Carval back in, she'd have someone who'd be cool with her job. If she wasn't so darned stubborn, he'd've called Carval and let him do all this comforting, but the time wasn't right for that yet.

"I'll make you a coffee from that fancy machine you got," he said, after a long, miserable silence.

"'Kay," she sniffed. She barely moved while he made it, being terribly careful not to break the machine. It probably wasn't fragile, but he wasn't sure. Normally Casey never let him touch anything except a specially bought mug, with an extra-large handle that he could fit his finger through. He brought the drinks over, and replaced his arm.

Casey sipped her coffee slowly, utterly defeated. Outright rejection of his only family, for booze, when he'd *just that moment* been fined $250 and told that he was lucky not to be in a cell; that the next time he would be jailed. She couldn't leave her father in jail. He'd never cope.

If he was even conscious, a dark voice whispered. *If he even remembered*. She shuddered. She could see it so clearly: a small, sick little man, no reserves, no understanding of the harsh reality of a cell. He'd be easy prey. And then – *if* he remembered – he'd have another ghastly memory to blot out, and so it would cycle through, until...

Until one day it didn't. Whether it was in a cell or not, one day there would be that final, fatal, knock, and *Miss Clement? I'm sorry....*

Maybe it would be a relief.

Guilt stabbed through her. She couldn't think like that. She had to save him. He was the only family she had. If he were gone...she'd have no-one at all. Even if he had rejected her...he was her father, and she couldn't reject him.

"You got us," O'Leary soothed, following her thoughts.

"It's not the same. It's close, but it's not the same."

Argument would be pointless, he knew. And, well, he couldn't disagree, though he had his own views on the value of family. His...okay, he had Pete and Pete's family, and his sister and her family, and that would do fine.

"You still got us. We hold each other up. You know that. The team's there, always."

"I guess. But I can't let him drown. I just can't. I don't care what it costs me." Her voice dropped almost to nothing. "I just want him to love me," she whispered.

Her phone rang, shattering the stifling misery.

"Clement?" Her body stiffened. "I see. 112th precinct? Okay. I'll come get him."

"You shouldn't" – O'Leary tried.

"I have to. He's my dad." Pain ripped through her voice. "I have to."

She found her coat and scarf. O'Leary walked her down to her car, and hugged her again. "See you tomorrow," he said, and nothing more. Unusually, she allowed his hug, though she was silent.

He watched her tail lights until they were out of sight, and then turned his own steps to the subway. A chat with Carval was indicated.

***

"Hello?" Allan's prissy voice issued from the entry-phone.

"It's O'Leary. Carval around?"

"Yes. He's just back."

The door buzzed, and O'Leary lumbered up the stairs, poking his head into Allan's sanctum and nodding at him, then passing on to the studio. He tapped, and walked straight in.

"Wow," he gasped. Carval had pinned the sparring sequences and the Academy recruits on the corkboard covering the wall, and was staring at the outcome. "That's…"

Carval spun around. "What are you doing – Casey? What happened?"

"He got a fine."

"That's good, isn't it? So why are you here? Is there a problem?"

"Her dad went straight for the booze afterwards. Said he didn't want her."

Carval gaped.

"An' then she got a call to go pick him up. An' she went."

"Oh, *fuck*."

"'Bout what I thought. You got some coffee or somethin'? I've been with Casey since lunchtime an' I've had one coffee all day."

"Sure." Carval handed O'Leary a large glass of water, which disappeared in one long draught, then found a sturdy mug and poured from his always-on pot. That drained, he poured another, and one for himself, and waited.

Somewhat to Carval's surprise, O'Leary didn't start talking at once. Instead, he examined the corkboard: the shots of the team and of sparring. Carval found himself nervous of the big man's reaction.

"That's how it oughta be," O'Leary eventually said, gazing at the team shot: the one Carval had taken as they walked into the Abbey after he'd first asked to shoot them: Casey half a step in front, the three men around her. "Tight."

"Yes."

Another silence fell.

"We've been partners eight years," O'Leary said. "Ain't never been like this before." He looked at the shots again. "I guess she's so mad because we've always been tight."

"But you spent the afternoon with her," Carval said. "So...maybe?"

"I hope so. But her dad's problems ain't enough. She gotta want to be back in the team, not just want to be hidin' from the truth. She can't save him, an' she can't use work to pretend it's all okay." His large face creased unhappily. "One afternoon don't fix it." He returned to gazing at the board.

"I want it fixed too," Carval offered.

"Why?" O'Leary's words weren't quite a challenge.

Carval's face twisted, cheeks heating. "Partly the shots. It'll be amazing. I wanna show the world what it *should* be like. I can't do it if it's not all four of you."

"And?" O'Leary asked after a moment of uncomfortable quiet.

"Casey," he pushed out, and grimaced. He didn't want to admit that out loud: it made it too real. He didn't *get* involved like this.

O'Leary raised a caterpillar eyebrow. "Like that, now?"

Carval shrugged, still uncomfortably red-faced.

"I guess we'd better fix it, then."

"Even though I caused it?"

"We've all made mistakes. No point beatin' yourself up any more. It won't help. I c'n tell you that Casey's miser'ble, but I can't tell you how much is us, you, or her dad. I'm hopin' that I got some way in after this afternoon, but I can't tell you that'll still be true tomorrow, neither."

"Eight years? Doesn't that carry some weight?"

"Should do."

Carval abruptly realised that under his slowpoke facade, O'Leary was almost as upset as Casey by their differences.

"You're really worried," he said.

"We've been pals for a long time. She don't judge on anythin' but ability an' whether you're one of the good guys."

Carval said nothing, loudly.

"Story for another time," O'Leary said. "When everythin's fixed again." His huge shoulders drooped. "If we c'n fix it."

"I could go see her. Explain that it wasn't you."

"She's mad because we didn't tell her, not 'cause of the letter – well, not with us, anyways." Carval winced. "Never mind that now." He glanced at his watch. "I better go. I reckon I'll need to be in early. Casey won't be doin' so well tomorrow. Might be an idea if you weren't too far away."

"I can shoot construction sites. There are plenty of those." O'Leary blinked. "A different exhibition."

"That where you were today?"

"Yeah. I had my phone. If any of you had called, I could have…" he trailed off.

"We know. Mebbe tomorrow, mebbe later. We ain't shuttin' you out."

"Yeah. I…I could try calling her, later? Just…I don't know. Let her know I'm there?"

"Yesterday, I'd've said don't. Today, well, she's so messed up about her dad that you might just have a chance. Can't hurt. Don't go over." He consulted his watch again. "Iffen it were me, I'd give it another coupla hours. If her dad was picked up in Queens" – his face changed. "Shit."

"What?"

"Queens is Marcol's patch. Sure, he's Narcotics, but there ain't no way he'll miss it. Shit. I gotta go. I don't wanna do this already, but I gotta go see Kent."

"Kent?"

"I'll explain later. Seeya in the Abbey."

O'Leary hurried out, shaking the stairs in his haste. Carval stared after him, completely confused, and then sat down with a thud. The only points he'd really gotten were *call Casey later*, and *see you in the Abbey*, at some unspecified time. What had *Marcol* got to do with Casey's dad being picked up drunk?

He decided to wait and see, and tapped out a text to Tyler. *O'Leary said beer in the Abbey, re Casey. Time?*

Some time later, he received back *Now*, and left at once.

CHAPTER TWENTY TWO

Casey struggled to find her composure all the way to the 112th Precinct. How could he? How could he get picked up fresh from a hearing and a fine for being drunk, and immediately go get drunk again?

"Casey Clement," she said to the desk sergeant. "Here about David Clement?"

"The drunk? Yeah. Picked him up outside O'Hanlons."

"Well, well," said an unhappily familiar voice behind her. "If it isn't Casey Clement. Hello, *Detective*. What are you doing here?"

"Personal business, Officer Birkett."

Fuck. Birkett. Marcol's sidekick and total weasel. *Fuck, fuck*. That was all she'd needed to make the day just plain *perfect*.

Birkett coloured. Clearly he didn't like being reminded that he was a uniformed officer. "If there's anything I can do for you…" he sleazed.

"No, thank you."

Birkett slouched off, not nearly far enough, leaving Casey hanging on to the last threads of her professional calm by her fingernails.

"I'll bring him up. You're a cop too?"

"Yes. Thirty-Sixth, under Captain Kent. Homicide."

The desk sergeant regarded her sympathetically. "I see," he said. "In the circumstances" —

"No. Whatever you would normally do, do it. Do what you have to, like you never knew I was a cop."

She was horribly aware of Birkett lurking nearby, and she couldn't allow anything that would give Marcol ammunition. Birkett had been Marcol's technogeek weasel all through the Academy, and he'd run straight back to Marcol with anything he thought might be damaging. Bad enough that now Marcol would know about her father.

"He wasn't aggressive. Normally we'd keep him in overnight to sober up, if there's no-one to collect him, check his record" – her heart sank – "and take it from there. You're here to collect him, so I'll check his record" – *oh, hell* – "and then release him to you."

The sergeant was already tapping as he spoke. His head jerked up. "Arrested at JFK? When was the hearing?"

"Today," Casey said flatly. "Guilty of a violation, fined."

Pity sparked in the desk sergeant's eyes. Casey ignored it. "He's got a problem," the man said.

"I know."

The desk sergeant wrote up another desk appearance ticket, and handed it to Casey.

"You can take him away. It doesn't look good, though."

Casey signed papers and filled in details as they brought her father up from the cells. He stared vacantly at her.

"Catkin? What're you doing here?"

"Taking you home," she said harshly. "Come on. We're going." She took his arm, and marched him out, Birkett lounging in a doorway where he could see everything, spiteful delight on his face.

The ride to her father's home was completely silent. Casey couldn't bear to talk. Her father wasn't capable of coherent speech. She walked him upstairs, opened his door and steered him inside, terrifyingly controlled and careful, helped him to sit down, all in that same silence.

"Catkin?" But it was hopelessly slurred. "I…I di'n't mean" –

"You never do."

She shut the front door horribly softly behind her as she left.

***

"Sir?" O'Leary followed his knock into Kent's office without waiting for permission.

"O'Leary? Why are you here? I thought – Explain what new complication surrounds Clement."

"Sir, Clement's father went straight from the courthouse to a bar, and they called her to pick him up."

"So? While that might be grounds for allowing her an extra day's leave, I'm sure that Clement can ask for that herself."

"Sir, he was picked up in Queens. 112th precinct."

"And – oh. Continue."

"Detective Marcol is based in Queens, sir. Someone'll tell him. Iffen he's lookin' to make mischief, sir, he's got the chance."

"I see. Leave that with me. Does Clement know you're here?"

"Not yet, sir."

"I suggest you let her know at the earliest opportunity."

"Yessir."

"Dismissed."

O'Leary's bulk no longer crowding his office, Kent considered for a moment, and then dialled the number of the Captain of the 112th.

"Captain Wetherly? Kent, at the Thirty-Sixth."

"Captain?"

"You picked up a David Clement today. He's the father of one of my detectives, and I was advised of his detention. I want to make sure you knew that it was reported to me, so you knew that I support your decision to treat him exactly like any other similar case."

Kent didn't *know* that that had been said, but he was pretty sure that Clement wouldn't ask for special consideration. If he had left the impression that the call was a result of an entirely appropriate report to him by Clement, he had told no lies, which should ensure that nobody could claim that Clement had looked for preferential treatment.

"Good to know. The desk sergeant told me that your Detective had said exactly the same, so he wrote up a desk appearance ticket. Gotta feel a bit sorry for her, though. Can't be easy."

Kent had to admit that he was tempted, just for a moment, to try to get Clement's father off. Then he realised that that would be the worst action he could possibly take – leaving himself open to unpleasant commentary as well as Clement.

"No. But she'll deal, just like anyone else would. Thanks for your time."

"You're welcome. Bye now."

Kent made a short note on Clement's file, and added a note of commendation to O'Leary's.

***

In Casey's apartment, her phone rang. She ignored it. She'd taken a long, scalding shower, but it hadn't warmed her chilled bones, or cured her misery. She didn't care if the call was her father, O'Leary, or the Archangel Gabriel: she couldn't answer it. She tried to watch TV, but nothing distracted her from the disaster of the day; she picked up a book, and put it down again: her father's bitter, desperate face between her eyes and the page. Her phone rang again, and she switched it off. Nothing would solve the problem of her father's...

Alcoholism.

Better say the word. She couldn't deny it any longer, if she ever had been able to.

"I'm Casey Clement, and my father is an alcoholic," she said to the empty apartment, and began, once more, to weep.

***

When Carval reached the Abbey, he found the team, minus Casey, arrayed at their usual table. O'Leary had clearly been explaining the events of the day so far, since they all wore unhappily thoughtful faces.

"So Kent knows he was picked up in Queens, an' I c'n leave that to him. He'll make sure that Marcol can't make more trouble outta this one. Even Renfrew's in on the game."

"Marcol can't weasel around the FBI," Andy said with satisfaction.

"Got a plan, Bigfoot?"

"I was hopin' we'd come up with one here."

"You don't," Andy said.

"Nup." O'Leary stared into his beer. "Casey ain't never been like this before. Not with me." His huge hands settled around the bottle. "Not even when we first met."

Tyler snorted, despite the general despond.

"What's the joke?" Carval asked.

"Bigfoot arrested her."

Carval almost dropped his beer.

"No-one told me it was a Vice Op," O'Leary grumped. "Anyways, she'd already downed two other cops, so they sent me in."

"You arrested Casey?"

"Yeah. *I* didn't know she was undercover. She looked just like all the other workin' girls."

"And you still became friends?" Carval grinned.

"Yeah." Gloom descended on O'Leary's buzz cut once more.

"You said she'd been okay this afternoon."

"Too upset about her dad to remember. Don't know iffen it'll last till tomorrow."

Andy hummed thoughtfully. "She's mad that we didn't tell her. She's mad that – she thinks – Carval here only did it because it was a photo of her." He wriggled his nose thoughtfully, and then looked at Carval. "Us not telling her…we can deal with that. When she cools down, she'll get that it wasn't up to us to tattle."

"You told me to tell her," Carval agreed. "It wasn't down to you guys."

"Doesn't solve the second one."

"I have an idea," Andy said.

"What?"

"Nobody told Casey you were actually going to instruct a process server, did they? She thinks it's about her, but you'd have to be batshit crazy to send a process server into a bullpen just to impress your girlfriend."

"You batshit crazy?" asked Tyler.

"Not *that* crazy," Carval said.

"Crazy in love," O'Leary mocked. Carval scowled.

"Finished?" inquired Andy, much as Casey would do when quelling the banter. "We'll close the case, the three of us'll get Casey out and deal with not telling her, and then we'll drop the process server into the mix and let her stew on that for a while."

"An' in the meantime," O'Leary suggested, already much cheerier, "you give her a call just like we talked about, so's she knows you ain't givin' up."

"Okay."

"Be back in the bullpen, too." Tyler chipped in.

"I got one more idea," O'Leary added. "Andy snuck off before he an' Casey got any sparrin' in." Andy squawked, but O'Leary ignored it. "You need to get some shots of them sparrin' to go along with me an' Tyler – though we'll be the stars," he added. "So Andy c'n get Casey into the gym to work off her temper, an' you can shoot."

"Or be shot," Carval pointed out.

"Nah. No guns in the gym," Tyler reminded them.

"No beer, neither," said O'Leary, and promptly got in another round.

***

"We found Elijah Massapa." Andy said on Friday morning.

"And Benjamin Parsons."

"An' I finally managed to get to a sensible type at Marswell an' Eglinton."

"And?" Casey asked.

"We're interviewing Massapa first, Parsons second," Andy confirmed.

"An' you and me'll go see the lawyers," O'Leary added. "An' then we'll all come back here an' see what we got." Casey looked at O'Leary, who was amiably imperturbable. "I'm pretty sure you got a hunch about the Washin'tons."

"I can't see why they'd do it," she growled. "If they'd had access to the money, they'd be in Interrogation right now. But they didn't."

"As far as we know," Andy said. "You can change the trustees."

"You can?"

"Yes. We'll be asking Massapa and Parsons about it."

"Good," Casey said. "Let's get going."

Before anything could spoil the energised mood that progress always brought to the team, they dispersed.

***

"Casey didn't sound quite so mad," Andy observed.

"No."

"Maybe Bigfoot fixed it after all."

"Believe it when I see it."

They made their way out to Ardsley, where Asher's parents had lived, and, some way away from that address, found the church where Pastor Elijah Massapa preached. The plain brick building had a discreet side entrance in addition to its main doors. They easily located the pastor's office.

"May I help you?" the man behind the desk asked, in a sonorous voice perfectly fitted to oratorical preaching. The cops surveyed Pastor Massapa. Despite the voice, he was elderly: white haired and frail. However, the blaze of passion and faith in his eyes belied his age. He stood, and smiled beneficently upon Tyler and Andy.

"We think so, sir," Tyler said. "We're investigating the death of Asher Washington, and we believe that you were his parents' pastor, before they passed."

"I was. Tragic." Tyler's words registered. "*Asher* is dead? Too?" He swallowed. "The Lord moves in mysterious ways. May he rest in peace," he murmured, and then more loudly, "That's awful." The fire in his eyes died down, replaced by grief. "What happened?"

"He was murdered."

Pastor Massapa thumped down into his chair. "Murdered?" he repeated blankly. "Asher? That's ridiculous."

"I'm sorry for your loss," Tyler said, his normal brevity absent.

"What can I do to help?" the pastor said, suddenly old and shaken.

"We understand that when Asher's parents passed" –

"May they rest with God" –

"Amen," Tyler said automatically, and received an approving smile. "When they passed, they left everything to Asher, in a trust. You were named as a trustee. Could you tell us about that?"

"Well, surely, though I'm not a trustee any more."

"You're not?"

"No. I'm" – he gave a gamin smile – "well, God has made me rich in years, but He didn't stop me slowing down, so I didn't feel I could do the best for Asher any more. But let me tell you about it."

Pastor Massapa took a moment or two to gather his thoughts. Although the cops were eager to learn who had replaced him, if they simply let him tell it in his own way, they would – though possibly slowly – find out more.

Their age-related expectations were confounded when the pastor began to speak.

"I'll begin at the beginning," he said. "Gabrielle and Harrison were part of my flock for many years – Gabrielle first, because she grew up close by, and then when she met Harrison, he joined us. They were stalwarts of the congregation, but sometimes their work got in the way."

"What did they do?" Andy asked.

"They were both in busy jobs – Gabrielle was in finance; Harrison was on Wall Street, so they couldn't always attend worship. They were blessed in their work and in their lives. They gave their time and money freely to help others – time was often scarce for them, but they gave what they could spare. When Asher came along, they were overjoyed. It had been a hard road for them, and though we'd all prayed and supported them, and they had many friends who also supported them, it was hard for them to see the children and not have one of their own. Then the Lord gave them Asher." The pastor's dark eyes looked backwards in time. "He was much loved, but not spoilt, and such a happy child. They brought him up well, though. He was taught to work hard and respect his elders: always to be polite and to try his best. As he grew, you could see his parents in him: Gabrielle was smarter, Harrison made the most of the opportunities sent to him." The pastor's tone changed. "But then, just as he was flowering in high school, they both died in an accident."

"A bad time," Tyler said.

"It could have been. However, God provided, and Asher's aunt and uncle took him in."

"He was lucky."

"He was. His parents had provided for him, but in a way that meant that" – the pastor's mouth quirked – "youthful hi-jinks couldn't go too far. They had discussed it with me and with their attorney – Mr Stanley."

"Yes, sir. We're meeting him later today."

"Excellent. A most worthy man, and of course he understood all the detailed legalities." The gamin smile fluttered back. "Gabrielle and Harrison wanted both the spiritual and practical sides covered."

"The trust is very comprehensive," Andy said. "Audited every year, and then there was to be a final reckoning supervised by a huge law firm."

"Oh, yes. They...well, their one failing was an occasional lack of faith in their fellow men. I guess it came from their jobs, but...they were sometimes a little uncharitable about their relatives."

"Yes?"

"Of course I tried to guide them into Christian charity, but..." he trailed off.

"We won't criticise, but it is important that we have the full picture of the relationships."

Pastor Massapa wriggled his frail shoulders. "I guess so. It seems..."

"It's uncomfortable, I know. But we want to do Asher justice." Tyler's sincerity shone through.

"Trust in the Lord," the pastor murmured to himself, "and the truth will set you free." He took a moment. "Harrison's brother, Marlon, had had a troubled youth, and it had...they weren't estranged, but they weren't as close as brothers can be. They had quarrelled, and though they'd patched it up, when Harrison was writing his will and the trust, he was adamant that he didn't want Marlon as a trustee."

"When was that?"

"When Asher was tiny. As time went on, they became closer, but

Harrison never changed it."

"Why didn't he want Marlon – perhaps with you and Mr Stanley?"

"I believe that Harrison had lent Marlon quite a lot of money, but that Marlon hadn't repaid it. This was before he was earning well, and I believe that he and Gabrielle were left...not exactly in difficulties, but it was close. Being in finance, any issues with money could have had serious effects on his job, but later, they made up. And then, after the accident, Marlon took Asher in. He and Sella couldn't do enough for the boy."

"The trust was there to meet the expenses of bringing up Asher, wasn't it?"

"Yes. We had to agree on anything expensive – the house, for example: Sella and Marlon didn't really have any space for a teenage boy, and we all felt that a bigger house, nearer to a good high school, was appropriate and necessary – though Mr Stanley made sure that the extra cost would go back to Asher when the house was sold."

"When it was sold?" Andy asked.

"Because the money to buy it – most of it – came from the trust, when the trust was finished it was to be repaid. So the house would be sold and Sella and Marlon would have plenty to buy somewhere of their own, but the balance would go back to the trust. Mr Stanley would be able to tell you the exact details. It was all very complicated." He sighed. "It all went along fine. Asher could continue his hobbies, he took AP classes: did all the things he needed to do to get into a good college and then law school. The trust covered all of his living costs, and then college and law school. It all worked out really well. Sella and Marlon did everything they could to ensure he grew up as Harrison and Gabrielle would have wanted. I was sad that they changed his church, but Pastor Jarmyn is a good man."

"You said that you stopped being a trustee?"

"As time went on, I found it more difficult to understand the details. Mr Stanley would explain, but I was very slow. I prayed for guidance, and I had many discussions about it with Mr Stanley and with Marlon and Sella. Eventually, I accepted that I could no longer do the best for Asher. By then he was in college and Mr Stanley and I agreed that I should step down as a trustee, and Sella would replace me."

"Sella, not Marlon?"

"Oh, yes. Sella is very organised and careful. I talked to their pastor, and he praised her commitment to the church and to God's will. We felt that it was the best way."

"Thank you." Tyler paused. "I have to ask you this, sir, but – do you own a rifle or handgun?"

The pastor blinked, and shuffled a little in his seat. "I do," he admitted. "Both. It's not very peaceable...but I have both."

"Would you mind if we took them for ballistics testing to rule them out?"

"I know you have to. Yes. Please do." Massapa shuffled again. "It's such an odd feeling," he said. "I know that I didn't do it, but it's very uncomfortable to be asked."

"I'm sorry, sir." Tyler ducked his head.

"Don't apologise for doing your job properly. My discomfort is minor compared to finding the misguided person who took Asher's life. I have faith that you will find him, and justice will be done."

"That's very helpful. Thank you, sir." Tyler had a thought. "When Asher had grown up, did he ever come back to this church?"

"Sometimes. He brought his young lady, once. I liked her. I hoped…"

"They planned to get married," Tyler said.

"Sometimes…it's very hard." The pastor blinked. "God's will be done," he murmured. "May he rest in peace with God."

"Thank you for your time, sir."

"You're welcome." The pastor stood, small against Tyler's six feet of muscle. "Give me a moment to provide the guns to you."

While the pastor fetched his guns, Andy wrote out a neat receipt for him.

"Thank you." Tyler took the elderly rifle carefully, and the equally vintage handgun went to Andy. "We'll bring them back as soon as we can."

"If there is anything more, please come back. Go with God," Pastor Massapa said.

"May He be with you too," Tyler said in automatic response. Andy ducked his head in respect.

CHAPTER TWENTY THREE

"That was interesting," Andy said, "not just because you were a choirboy."

Tyler frowned. "Church. Not choir."

"Marlon's chequered past might have gone a bit further than came up on the runs – there was nothing much there. And that bit about the house, well – the Washingtons had a lot to lose when the trust ended."

"Yeah," Tyler agreed. "Stanley next. Think he's still a trustee?"

Andy shrugged. "I don't know, but...I figure the Washingtons'll be in Interrogation pretty soon anyway. I don't see Casey letting this lie."

"Scare the truth out of them."

"She's pretty scary right now."

"Get her sparring. Needs to punch it out."

"You really don't love me, do you?"

"No." Tyler grinned, and Andy smiled back.

"How's Allie?"

"Who?" Tyler said blandly.

Andy raised an eyebrow. "Well, if you're not interested, I could use a cultured friend, since none of you get closer to culture than a yoghurt pot."

"Not Allie," Tyler whipped back, and then realised what Andy had done. "Leave it, okay."

"Sure," Andy said smugly. "Just looking out for your welfare."

"Casey. Sparring. When you tap out, I'll cheer."

"I don't think we need to worry about these guns," Andy said, before the bickering could continue. "They're almost as old as the pastor."

"Good rifle'll shoot straight as long as you can sight straight," Tyler pointed out, "but I don't think so either."

"Let's drop them into Ballistics on the way back, and then we can give them back quickly."

"Yep."

They made their way out towards New Haven, Connecticut, in search of Benjamin Stanley.

"Stanley," Tyler said.

"Yeah. It sounds like he'll know a lot more about the finances. I think we need to get hold of the yearly audits that have been done."

"Warrant?"

"Depends. If we have twitches about the Washingtons, it's a sure bet that Casey does. She might already have started."

"Call her."

Andy dialled, while Tyler drove.

"Casey, Massapa said that he'd been replaced as trustee by Sella Washington."

Casey's yelp was audible through the car.

"The fund should have been audited every year" –

"Copies," Casey stated.

"That's what we thought. We'll ask Stanley – we're on the way there now – but if he won't play, are you already on a warrant?"

"Not for that, but I'll get one started in case we need it and we can finish it when you get here. I'm liking the Washingtons more and more."

Andy could hear a bass rumble of *Called it* in the background, and grinned. "Okay," he said. "See you later."

"Good work."

Andy swiped the phone off. "That," he said cautiously, "sounded like Bigfoot got through to Casey yesterday."

"Yeah?"

"Mm. She still sounded normal. Like we usually are."

Tyler breathed a long sigh of relief.

"Shame it took her dad screwing up to fix it."

"Progress," Tyler hummed. "Hope it *is* fixed."

"You think it isn't?"

"Not betting yet."

Andy's cheer dropped somewhat, and they went on in silence to New Haven.

***

"C'mon, Casey. Let's go see these bigshot lawyers."

Casey looked up from her incessant fiddling with the papers on her desk. "Okay."

"Are you okay?" O'Leary asked, as they travelled to Midtown.

"I guess." It couldn't have been told from her voice, which dripped misery.

O'Leary reached over and patted her shoulder. "Let's get today done, an' then we'll all go chat. Mebbe we'll find out somethin' useful."

"Birkett was there," she said in total non-sequitur. "Leaning on the door smirking. He'll have called Marcol the moment I got out of the door."

"Yeah. Um…about that. Don't worry about this one. Kent's made sure it can't come back on you."

"He has?"

"Yeah. I went an' told him your dad got picked up in Queens, an' he said to leave it with him." He waited for the explosion.

"It doesn't matter. Birkett'll tell Marcol and they'll make a big deal of it." Strangely, that worried O'Leary more than yelling would have done.

"Don't make trouble out of it now. Kent'll deal with that, so we don't need to worry none. Let's go find out all about this trust, an' then we'll be a step closer to solvin' this case. I already told Chigthorne that Asher was murdered, so we don't need to go through all that again."

"'Kay." She swallowed. "Thanks."

O'Leary heard it covering more than just his last sentence, and rejoiced. "An' here we are. Someone spent a bunch of money on this place, didn't they?"

They surely had. Tinted glass; soaring steels; huge, marbled atrium; a reception desk half the length of Kansas. Even by the standards of world-class law firm offices, Marswell & Eglinton oozed high-class – and higher prices.

"Yeah. Are we intimidated by all this money?" she asked, sounding more like herself.

"Nup. 'S like manure. Only good if it's spread around."

Casey smiled: closer to a real smile than she'd managed for a week. "Hello," she said to the fashion-plate masquerading as a receptionist. "We're here to see Matthew Chigthorne."

"Your names, please?"

Casey gave them. They were photographed, approved, given security passes, and finally escorted to a waiting area in which, it being mid-morning, there were elegantly arranged plates of miniature pastries. Coffee orders were taken by a neatly uniformed waitress, and shortly an excellent espresso arrived for Casey and a cappuccino was set down in front of O'Leary, who regarded the delicate china cup beside his sausage-sized fingers with some desperation.

Matthew Chigthorne turned out to be a patrician man of fifty-odd, silver-haired and bespectacled. He bore a certain resemblance in demeanour and colouring to Dr Renfrew, which didn't endear him to Casey, but redeemed himself with a cheerfully bright tie sporting colourful parrots. "Come through," he said, and led them to yet another corporate boardroom.

"Now," he said amiably, "Detective O'Leary has told me that you want to talk about the arrangements for closing the Washingtons' trust, following Asher Washington's untimely death?"

"That's part of it," Casey agreed, "but also, I was a bit surprised at how high-powered those arrangements were. Was there any reason for them to be so formal?"

"You mean," Chigthorne smiled, "why on earth use a firm this size – and this expensive – for a comparatively tiny affair?"

"Yes." Casey waited.

"Harrison Washington had worked with us – me, specifically – since we both started out. We were friends, as well as business contacts. I was an usher at his wedding, and he was one at mine. So when he was setting up the trust, he couldn't make me a trustee – ethics rules, you know? It would have been far too close of a relationship – but he could make sure that the trustees knew that, when it ended, there would be a really thorough final accounting. I didn't have any concerns about the trustees – one from his church: Pastor Elijah Massapa, and Benjamin Stanley, his personal attorney, whom I'd known for years too. He'd started off in one of the global firms, and downsized for personal reasons – poor guy, he lost his wife too early. Cancer. He moved out to New Haven shortly after, to get away from the memories."

Casey winced. Chigthorne didn't notice, thankfully.

"But I digress. So we took it on, and when the trust came to an end, we would have ensured that the whole thing was properly wound up. Of course, there were the yearly audits, but the final one would be with a different firm, totally independent of everyone who'd ever been involved."

"I see," Casey said. "Why were they so determined to make sure everyone knew about the arrangements?"

"Oh, I don't think anyone else did, just the trustees."

"Were you told about any changes to the trustees?"

Chigthorne stopped. "We probably should have been, if there had been any. But...I must say, I don't remember any clauses making that explicit, though I haven't looked at the deed for a while. We'd have been told if Asher had gotten married, certainly, because that would terminate the trust."

"Mm. What did you think about Sella and Marlon Washington?"

Chigthorne shifted in his leather chair. "They really stepped up to take in Asher," he temporised. "Harrison didn't like Marlon too much – Marlon had borrowed money and not repaid him, and it put Harrison in a bit of a fix for a few months. But they patched it up, and Harrison thought that if anything ever happened – not that they expected it: you don't, do you? – then Asher would be better with family than Child Services."

"For sure," O'Leary rumbled.

"Sella kept Marlon in line, I thought. She's a far stronger character, and very upright. A good Christian woman."

"I see," Casey said again. "Did you know that Asher had made a will?"

"No, but it doesn't surprise me. I guess the trust'll need to be audited and terminated, so the assets can be passed to the beneficiaries."

"It's a lot of money. Ten million" –

"Oh, it'll be a lot more than that now," Chigthorne said casually.

"What?" Casey squawked.

"Well, investment growth, you know. It was well invested, so it should be close to double."

Casey and O'Leary emitted astonished noises, at each end of the audible scale.

"It should have grown at – on average – 5% per year. It would have been more, but what with the crash and everything…but nearly 14 years, compounded, well, you know."

They didn't know. Casey had been left some money from her mother – enough to put down a decent deposit on her apartment, but nothing like these amounts. She had some savings, and her retirement fund, but – like most people – she was paying off her student loans and mortgage. Chigthorne was talking about sums she couldn't imagine. From O'Leary's expression, he couldn't comprehend it either.

"I guess they'll be pretty well off."

"Who?" O'Leary asked.

"Sella and Marlon – hang on. Aren't they his next of kin?" Chigthorne looked from Casey to O'Leary and back again. "They're *not*?"

"We don't want to release the details right now," Casey said.

Chigthorne regarded them piercingly. "I see." Casey was pretty damned sure that he saw more than she'd like. "I guess I'd better start arranging the final audit?"

"I don't think that would be a bad idea. Thank you for your time. We'll come back to you if we need more information."

"Will you let me know if the trustees have changed?"

"Yes, okay."

"Thanks."

***

"Kayla'll be super-super rich." O'Leary looked momentarily wistful. "Iffen I had that sort of money, I'd give Pete the best house money could buy, with a kitchen stocked with everythin' he wanted."

"I want to know if the Washingtons thought they'd get everything."

"Why'd they think Asher would go before them?"

"I don't know. But my gut tells me there's a lot more to find out about them."

"That your gut catchin' up with my gut? 'Cause I thought somethin' was off right from the get-go."

"With no evidence. Even you admitted that."

"Waalll, yes, but I still called it first."

"Yeah, *okay*. Let's get back. I wanna know what the others got from the pastor and attorney."

"They've got two, an' all the way out to Connecticut. We only had one. We'll be back first."

"Can we get there already?" Casey snipped. "We're finally getting somewhere and you won't even start the car so we can get on with it."

O'Leary turned the key with massive and insincere dignity, and drove back to the precinct.

Casey had barely taken her coat off – she was still unwinding her scarf – when Fremont hurried over. "Detective, I got all the travel information around Marthen, but I can't spot anything except his one journey to work, at the time he said he went. I checked both ways, like you wanted, but there's nothing there."

"Okay. Good work, even if we couldn't get him. We can likely eliminate him, and that's always helpful." She paused. "You up for something else?"

"If the Sergeant lets me."

"Go ask. We've got some more travel to chase down."

Fremont practically ran, and ran back. "I'm good."

"Okay. Wait while I see if we've had travel data for Bill Roberts." She switched on her computer, and, not willing to wait for it to chug into life, checked her phone. Not five minutes earlier, the MTA data had come through. "Got it. Right. This is Bill Roberts' MTA e-Tix data – it should cover all his travel. Go through it and see if there's anything that would mean he could've shot Asher."

"Yes'm," Fremont said.

"I've forwarded it to you." He left immediately, and could shortly be seen hunched over his desk.

"What about the warrant for Roberts' rifle?" Casey turned to O'Leary. "Upstate should've searched Wednesday."

O'Leary tapped a scrawl near the top of her murder board. "Can't your teeny li'l toes take you up high enough to read the top of your board? Here's Tyler scribblin' that they sent it off for ballistics testin'."

"Good. Right. Everything's moving along. Steve Marthen's pretty much out of it. Roberts – we'll see, but I'm not hopeful. Finances from Cano Bank should show up today" – her phone rang.

"Andy?"

After a brief conversation, Casey swiped her phone off and grinned widely at O'Leary. "Sella was one of the trustees. I'll start on a warrant for the audits of the fund in case Stanley can't or won't hand them over, and I'll beef up that one I'd got going on the Washingtons generally. Uncle Washington owns a rifle, too. I'm really starting to like them."

"I'm guessin' they'll see the inside of Interrogation soon-like?"

"Sure will. Not today, though. When I bring them in I'll have all my ducks lined up in a neat row."

"An' then you'll shoot 'em all down." O'Leary smiled beatifically. "Nothin' like some good terrorisin' to make us happy."

"Yep."

"I know what else'll make you happy," he added. "Bit of sparrin' to work out the creaks."

"I don't creak!" she said indignantly. "I'm not sparring with you either. I'd be flattened."

"Naw. Anyways, I c'n squish you with one finger. Andy needs the exercise. He's been slackin' lately." Casey gave O'Leary a cynically knowing look. "An' you'll feel better. C'mon. We'll fix the last bits an' pieces an' be all pals again."

She turned away without commenting, but O'Leary was sure that the team would be okay. Casey's dad…not so much.

***

Benjamin Stanley inhabited a neat, unpretentious office, announced only by a small plate with his name. The cops were admitted, and taken to a small room, where four chairs and a table just about fitted. Tyler's shoulders attempted to shrink, and failed. When Stanley arrived, the room shrank further. He was big. Not O'Leary's size, to be sure, but then, unless you were a pro linebacker, nobody was. Still, he was easily six-three, and broader than Tyler's muscular frame. Andy looked from one big man to the other, and sighed.

"Mr Stanley" –

"Call me Ben." He smiled, exposing perfect teeth.

"Ben. We're here because you're a trustee of Asher Washington's trust fund."

"I *was*," he said. "Where's Asher? Shouldn't he have told you that I stepped down four years ago?"

"Ben, Asher was found dead" –

"You mean murdered." His voice rose. "The only reason there would be two cops in here would be if he'd been murdered. What happened?"

"I'm afraid Asher was shot, last Tuesday."

Stanley sagged. "That's terrible. Why would anyone want to shoot Asher?"

"That's what we're trying to find out."

"We met with Pastor Massapa earlier, and he was very helpful," Tyler said. "It sounded like you dealt with the finances, though."

"Oh, sure, I did, but like I said, I stepped down four years ago."

"At that point, all the audits had been done?"

"Yes, indeed. I wanted to hand over to Pastor Jarmyn in a clean state."

"Could we have them?"

"I don't see why not," Stanley said. "Asher was sent copies – once he was twenty-one, we sent a copy for him as well, and of course that meant that he had copies. I could make you pick them out of his records, but it would be unnecessarily obstructive to refuse to give you my copies without seeing a warrant, when you already have them – somewhere. Might as well speed it up."

"Thank you. Now, you said you'd stepped down and Pastor Jarmyn replaced you, out in Queens." Stanley nodded at Andy's words. "How did that happen?"

Stanley thought. And thought. And wrinkled his brow, and thought again. "You know, I don't quite know. I guess it seemed like a good idea at the time. Asher was grown, and could deal with his own finances, and coming all the way out here seemed silly when he could just talk to his aunt and pastor together any time without having to go anywhere except home."

"I guess," Andy agreed. "We'll need the exact date."

"Sure. I'll need to check. Now?"

"If you can."

Stanley tapped at his computer. "Okay. March 15th, 2013."

"Thanks. Now, Pastor Massapa said that you had approved all the arrangements for the Washingtons' house." Stanley nodded. "Could you tell us how that worked?"

Fifteen minutes later Tyler's eyes had long glazed over, but Andy understood perfectly. "I see. Were there any other similar arrangements?"

"No. Just the house. Everything else was paid directly from the trust, until Asher moved out and we simply gave him an allowance to supplement his pay-check."

"And all of that is covered by the audits?"

"Yes. The accounts are here – up till I stepped down, anyway. Sella should have copies of the later ones."

"Could we have access, if we need it?"

"Sure. Now?"

"No. I'll ask Sella Washington for the most recent ones – just in case there's something in there that might help. I'll get back to you if I need the older ones."

Tyler, detecting the end of financial matters, roused himself. "Do you have a gun?" he asked.

Stanley stared. "Gun?" he repeated, as if he hadn't understood.

"Yes. Do you own, or have access to, a gun?"

"Uh…I used to. I guess I still have it. I used to go shooting upstate with my wife, in hunting season. Since she passed" – he took a breath – "I haven't wanted to. She was always better than me, and boy, did she let me know. It was a joke between us."

"I'm sorry for your loss," Andy put in.

"Could you locate it?"

"It'll be at home, I guess."

"We'd like to take it, test the ballistics."

"What?" Stanley flexed out to his full width again. "Why do you want to do that?" The cops paused for a few seconds, to let realisation dawn. "I'm a *suspect?*"

"No, a witness. If we don't test your gun, you might become a person of interest." Tyler squared his shoulders.

Stanley's brief flare of temper subsided. "Okay. Uh…I don't have any clients this afternoon. We could go find it now." Sadness skated over his face. "It'll take the three of us to find it."

"Okay," Andy said. "I just need to call our boss, to tell her we'll be a while longer."

"Sure. I'll go shut up shop."

"Not getting out of sparring," Tyler said, as Stanley closed up his office.

"Wasn't trying. I notice you aren't offering to spar with Casey. The mood she's been in, it should be you."

"Happy to. She isn't." Tyler smirked. Everyone knew that Casey wasn't stupid enough to try sparring with him – or with O'Leary.

Andy swiped his phone on with decided vigour.

CHAPTER TWENTY FOUR

Much to her surprise, Casey's phone showed Andy calling again.

"Casey? Casey, I got the audits up till Stanley stepped down" –

"He stepped down too?"

"Yeah. Replaced by the Washingtons' pastor – Jarmyn."

"Wow. I'm *really* liking the Washingtons now. Okay. I'll put together a warrant for everything later, in case we need it. Text me the dates."

"And we'll take Stanley's rifle in for testing, to check that off. We have to go find it first."

"Okay."

Casey cut the call. "Bigfoot, both trustees got replaced. It's looking pretty interesting around the Washingtons." She thought. "Why didn't Jarmyn tell us he was a trustee?"

"Dunno. But I called it," O'Leary said again, disgustingly smugly.

"Oh, shut up."

***

From his borrowed desk, Dr Renfrew watched with considerable interest. On Wednesday, the team, and in particular the relationship between Detectives Clement and O'Leary, had been fractured to the point of collapse. On Thursday, neither detective had been present, until Detective O'Leary had come thundering in, late in the afternoon, and gone straight to Captain Kent's office, with an expression presaging trouble for some unfortunate recipient. He had emerged much more calmly, and then left with the other two detectives. This morning, Detectives Clement and O'Leary were on almost normal terms, and the team appeared to be functioning at close to its previous level, although its banter was still missing.

Dr Renfrew hypothesised, based only on Detective O'Leary's behaviour, that the malign shadow of Detective Marcol had re-emerged, and concluded that a discussion with Captain Kent was indicated. Following that, he would interview both detectives again.

He recalled Detective Clement's hasty exit from their interview, and Detective O'Leary's admission that her father had a problem with alcohol. Immediately, Dr Renfrew understood. Detective Clement had attended her father's hearing yesterday, and Detective O'Leary had gone to support her. In so doing, he had overcome her anger and resentment.

Detective O'Leary's success intrigued Dr Renfrew, who did not imagine that even he would have been proof against Detective Clement's rancour. He consulted Captain Kent, and received information, but not full understanding.

When the detectives had reached a standstill, evident from their frustrated scowls at their computers and the tapping of their fingers in unsuspected synchronisation, Dr Renfrew decided that the time was ripe to complete his interview with Detective Clement.

"Detective Clement," he said politely, "I observe that you have reached a point where you are waiting for information before you can continue. Could we complete our interrupted interview?"

Detective Clement did not appreciate the intervention. "I guess so," she begrudged.

"Let us find a private room." Dr Renfrew intended to delve into matters which should remain confidential from the general populace.

The door closed behind them, blocking out the interested looks of the bullpen and O'Leary's worried glance.

"I shall begin at the point where we were cut off." Detective Clement acquired an entirely unemotional expression, with obvious effort. Dr Renfrew continued. "At that time, and on the following two days, the team bonds were substantially strained, and you and Mr Carval appear no longer to be involved."

Detective Clement preserved utter blandness.

"You were absent on Thursday, as was Detective O'Leary." Ah. A reaction. Detective Clement had not been aware of Detective O'Leary's absence. "Today, the team bonds are almost entirely repaired." He waited in vain for any comment. "Please explain the events of Thursday."

"No. That is my personal business, not yours."

Dr Renfrew blinked at the sharp response. Such a tone had not been directed at him for many years. He was unpleasantly reminded of a particularly strict fifth-grade teacher, of whom he had been terrified. He recovered himself.

"It is affecting your team. In any event," he replied equally sharply, "I am aware of the issues surrounding both Detective Marcol and your father's alcohol dependency. You attended a court hearing with your father yesterday, and later collected him from police custody, both related to drunkenness, in Queens, which is Detective Marcol's area of operations. I deduce that you believe that Detective Marcol may use your father's weakness against you."

Detective Clement's colour had drained to the point where Dr Renfrew considered that she might faint.

She did not. "None of that is relevant to you," she pronounced in Boadicean tones, though her fingers contorted where they were linked.

"I disagree. Yesterday, Detective O'Leary resolved your differences, which, I believe, were caused by Mr Carval's pursuit of Detective Marcol. The conflict caused by Mr Carval's action, and that conflict's resolution, are both relevant to the team's dynamics."

Dr Renfrew steepled his fingers. "However, I am more concerned by another matter. You are under severe strain, caused by your father's illness." His tone became sympathetic and conciliatory. "Separately from my study of the team's dynamics, I wish to offer you counselling. I do not imagine that you have any desire to consult an NYPD-approved practitioner."

Detective Clement gaped, wordless.

"I am a qualified psychiatrist," he added. "While two out of the three issues have been manageable, the addition of Detective Marcol's possible behaviour is, as the adage has it, the straw which broke the camel's back."

"*You* are suggesting I need *therapy*?" Detective Clement made it sound as if bubonic plague were preferable.

Dr Renfrew allowed silence to stretch out.

"I don't need therapy and I certainly don't need help from *you*. I might have to put up with your 'study of team dynamics' but I don't have to put up with you prying into my personal business."

"Are you suggesting that if Detective Marcol tarnishes your reputation that is *not* a professional matter?"

"I dealt just fine with Marcol the first time and I'll deal with him now. I don't need anyone trying to fight my battles for me."

"That has already been taken out of your hands. Both Captain Kent and I are aware of the issue, and we will ensure that any attempts by Detective Marcol to smear you are dealt with appropriately."

"If Carval hadn't tried to play the hero, none of this would be necessary. He opened up the can of worms but I'm the one who'll have to deal with it. It doesn't matter what you or the captain do, because mud sticks, and it's even stickier if it's founded on facts. My dad is an alcoholic who's getting himself arrested and you can't get around that *issue*."

Detective Clement blew her nose; face set and cold. "This has nothing to do with the team. I've wasted enough time in here. I intend to find Asher Washington's killer."

"Even if you are called to rescue your father again?"

She stopped in her tracks, and turned, dark eyes cold in her white face. "I can do both," she bit. "After all, *you* think that you can take care of Marcol. Prove it."

The door slammed shut behind her.

Dr Renfrew reflected that the interview had not gone as planned.

***

"That patronising, pompous *prick*," Casey hissed at O'Leary's wondering face.

"What's he done to make you so mad?"

Casey swore sulphurously before adding, "He offered me *therapy*."

"What?" O'Leary's eyebrows hit the ceiling. "You're kiddin' me."

"I freaking well am not *kidding* you."

"Waal, I think some good coffee's a startin' point, an' you c'n tell me all about it. That kinda suggestion don't come out of the blue."

Casey consented to be guided to the break room, though she maintained a stream of under-the-breath furious profanity and suggestions for Renfrew's slow and painful demise, all the way.

O'Leary made the coffee, noticing – but definitely not mentioning – that Casey's hands were shaking. She took a few mouthfuls, then drained the cup. He'd already made another, and pushed it at her. "Drink. Oughta be a whiskey, but we're on duty. An' when that one's gone down, tell me the tale."

Casey related Renfrew's commentary, after which O'Leary could barely keep from choking. "Wow," he eventually managed. "Waal, you gotta say he's brave."

"Stupid. I don't need *therapy*. I've got the team and we fix ourselves. If my dad falls apart" – she gulped – "you'll all be there, same as ever."

"That's as mebbe, but Renfrew's still brave." O'Leary studiously didn't react to Casey's commentary, though inwardly he cheered fit to fill Yankee Stadium.

"Are you *agreeing* with him?"

"Not exactly. But I ain't disagreein', neither. Not yet." O'Leary looked down at Casey's small, angry form. "I don't think you should be runnin' after your dad every time, but that's up to you. I wouldn't be doin' it, 'cause he ain't never goin' to stop an' you an' me both know it. But I ain't you."

"Thank God."

O'Leary grinned. "I'd'a thought you'd've wanted my good looks."

Casey snorted. "If I wanted fur and claws I'd join a Furries Club."

O'Leary choked on his mouthful of coffee. "Casey!" He widened his eyes and acquired an insincere look of outrage. "That's *speciesist!*"

She almost dropped her coffee laughing.

***

211

Carval regarded the shots on his corkboard with satisfaction, swiftly followed by irritated frustration at the space where there ought to be photos of Casey and Andy sparring. He'd woken far too early, and, in default of tossing, turning, and missing Casey, had come down to rearrange his shots. Since her face was right there in the centre of his board, it hadn't helped. Still, the shape of the exhibition had begun to emerge, and his shots were brilliant: even better than his panhandlers. This show would consolidate him as the best: better than Eisenstaedt, better than Cartier-Bresson or Salgado.

"Jamie?"

"Allan? What are you doing here?"

"I thought I'd have to roust you out of bed. I guess following your cops around is improving your wake-up time to something that an adult might achieve."

"What is it?" Carval scowled.

"Don't sulk at me. I've gotten you a visit to Rikers, and I had to do a *lot* of sweet-talking for permission for you to shoot."

Carval flipped around. "You did it? Allan, I love you."

"I've also received consent forms for images from a lot of the inmates, and you'll" – Carval scowled – "okay, I'll – have to check them off and you'll have to blur anyone else."

"When?"

"Now. As soon as you can get there."

"Who do I ask for? Where do I go? What's the quickest way?"

Allan provided all the details – on a sheet of paper: Jamie on a photographic mission didn't pay attention to small details such as putting on his pants or the need for care crossing the street, so he'd never remember any of the entry details – and Jamie dashed off, completely consumed by a new subject to shoot.

In the cab – Allan had carefully specified that public transit would take over an hour, but a cab was only around half that – Carval considered what, and how, he wanted to shoot. Normally he relied on instinct and immediate impressions, but he wouldn't get another chance, so he took the unusual route of thinking and planning. Of course, that wouldn't prevent him taking the instinctive shots that were always the most striking.

As the taxi crossed the bridge, Carval began to shoot the approach. He wasn't sure he'd use those pictures, but they would give him a baseline. He paid the driver, consulted Allan's notes, and asked for the correct person, fingers twitching to shoot every inch of the way, just about keeping himself under control. Being evicted before he could take photos would not be helpful.

His liaison officer – minder – was a burly man in pristine uniform, not matched by his cauliflower ears, previously broken nose, and harsh buzz cut.

"You the photographer?" He wasn't *quite* hostile. "I'm Correction Officer Barlinn."

"Yep." Carval sized him up. "Can I shoot you?"

Barlinn stopped in his tracks. "What" – he obviously bit off 'the fuck'. "Me? Why?"

"The show's called *Murder on Manhattan*. A correctional facility is the end point for murder, and I'm showing the professionalism and training of the police and other officers involved, set against the killers." Carval had chosen his words extremely carefully to imply that all the officers were professional and highly trained, though this man appeared to be one step up from a thug. Appearances, of course, could be deeply deceiving, though the PR around Rikers was unsettling.

Barlinn preened. "Okay, then. What do I do?"

"The best shots come when you behave naturally – poses look faked, and your work is too important" – more flattery, but he needed this to be *right* – "to spoil it with that. So what I'll do is take a few shots now, before we get into the prison, and then I'll just take more as I go."

"Okay," Barlinn said. "This here's where I usually start."

Carval took a few sighting shots, which he knew would be useless, but they relaxed Barlinn enough for him to move more freely through the halls and gates. The cell spaces were much more interesting than the halls: gleams on the steel bars, the pared-back solitude and lack of comfort; light through narrow slits jarringly bright on whitewash. The faces of the inmates contrasted: some angry or brutish, some resigned, some miserable. The walkways and spaces echoed: the heavy tread of officers, the coughs of smokers, occasional cursing or cries. Somewhere, Carval thought, one man might be sobbing. Nobody smiled; body language measured out beaten-down hopelessness; set against the bulk and purpose of the officers, their freedom to walk and move as they pleased.

He took more shots of the officers, capturing a sense of readiness, an almost-aggressive tension, as if they were expecting trouble at any moment. He'd check his shots later, but unlike the inmates, who ranged from bruisers to shifty, rat-like men, the correctional officers fell into a particular type: bulky, authoritarian. He supposed that it was necessary to control the facility, and thought that it would be another excellent contrast to the spark and flair of his cops.

Some three hours later, Carval left, memory card close to full, wholly satisfied with the morning. He was rather less satisfied that he had to wait to leave the island, but once over the bridge he hopped off the bus and got a taxi back to his studio, anxious to upload and review the shots; then to fit them into his story.

As he came in, he had a sudden, and unusual, thought, and popped into

Allan's office.

"It was great," he enthused. "Thanks for setting it up."

Allan almost knocked over his tea. "Who are you and *what* have you done with Jamie Carval?" he gasped.

"Huh?"

"You never say thank you, Jamie. You certainly don't stop on the way to your downloading to thank me, or even say hello."

"I do!" he said indignantly.

"You don't. You're like a five-year old who's spotted free cake. You get back and run up the stairs to your studio – which is about the only exercise you get all year – without so much as a hello."

"I get exercise!"

"Out of bed?" sniped Allan.

"That's mean."

"And true."

"It's not true! I go to the gym regularly" –

"You haven't been since you and your Casey-cop had a fight."

"I've been sparring with the others. Anyway, that's not relevant. Why did I bother saying *hi* if all you do is nag at me?"

"I'm making sure you haven't been replaced by a clone. Now I know you're the real Jamie." He grinned. "How did it go?"

"Great. I got a full memory card and it's so different from the cops it'll be wonderful. This'll make me even bigger. Nobody'll come close."

"Is that the Space Station calling?"

"Huh?"

"I think your ego just blocked out the sun."

"Mean," Carval repeated. "It'll be brilliant, just you wait and see. I have to go download." He had a thought, and paused. "What about Death Row in California?"

"Still trying. Shooting on Death Row is hardly new, though."

"Nor is Rikers – but in *my* context it'll be new."

Carval could hear Allan's disgruntled muttering at his (justified) arrogance all the way upstairs and into his studio. Allan always tried to bring him back down to earth, but Carval was far happier to soar. Allan could look after mundane concerns such as bills and organisation.

Download completed, he started to filter. As ever, a quarter were hopeless: slightly off-centre; fractionally out of focus where he'd wanted sharpness; a tiny amount under- or over-exposed. Technically flawed shots discarded, he turned to artistic selection. The initial shots of Barlinn were just as useless as he'd expected: stiff, posed, bland; but, after that, he could barely pick between them.

"Allan," he hollered down the stairs, "come look!"

Allan's light steps sounded. "Yes?"

"Look," Carval instructed, and moved out of the way so Allan could look at the screens. "Aren't they great?"

"Sure, they're good," Allan said temperately.

"Come *on*, they're better than *good*. They're superb."

"Don't you ever get embarrassed about begging for compliments?" Allan quirked an eyebrow. "I mean, I can stick some of them on the fridge if you want, like moms do for their kids' artwork in grade school."

Carval growled.

"Look," Allan said, "you know how good they are, so why ask me?"

"I like hearing it."

"Get your cops, then. They might tell you."

Carval muttered inaudibly, good mood suddenly shattered.

"What's up – that wasn't wrong already?" Allan asked.

"I need to show Casey that centrepiece." Carval winced. "She won't like it."

Allan merely shrugged. "It won't get better for waiting," he said callously. "Better get on with it. If she shoots you, though, you've got enough here to have a good posthumous exhibition."

Carval ignored that helpful commentary. "Since she's not talking to me, I don't have much choice about waiting."

"I" –

"*Don't* say 'I told you so' again. You've said it enough. I can hear you thinking it every half-hour. I *know*, okay?" He abruptly stopped complaining. "Have we gotten an answer yet?"

Allan followed his thought perfectly. "Only a complete denial from Marcol."

Carval's face changed: unpleasantly focused. "Right. We're upping the ante. I want everything nailed down to send in a process server. Bulletproof. *Lawyer* proof" –

"That's harder," Allan quipped.

"I'll *ruin* him. By the time we're done, he won't be able to get a job as a clean-up guy at the dog pound."

Allan stared at him. "Okay, what's happened this time?"

CHAPTER TWENTY FIVE

Carval, having had a night to think about it, had pondered O'Leary's gnomic utterances around Queens, Marcol, and Casey's father, and didn't like any of the conclusions he'd drawn. He regarded Allan bleakly.

"Casey's dad has a drink problem. He got arrested. The hearing was in Queens yesterday, and he got fined. She was there all the way for him, and then he told her he didn't want her and went straight to the nearest bar, where he got picked up and dumped in the tank again."

"Queens?"

"Queens is Marcol's patch."

Allan had never before seen Carval displaying his current expression, but it sent a shiver down his normally impervious spine.

"Anyway, even though he'd brushed her off, they called her and she went to get him."

Allan sucked in breath. "She did?" Carval nodded sharply. "That's…"

"Admirable? Brave? Crazy?"

"How often has she done it?"

Carval shrugged. "Isn't once enough? *Anyway*, Marcol will find out about it. That yellow-assed dickweasel'll have snitches all over the place, and then he'll smear Casey all over again, because *I* pissed him off. So I'll bury him first."

Allan watched agony and then fury slide through Carval's eyes, and wondered how he'd changed in such a short time from a care-for-nothing-and-nobody, outside of his photographs, to a man regretting acting on his impulses.

"Okay," Allan said. "I'll tie up all the loose ends, and establish a case that he can't defend. You worry about your Casey."

"Wish she was my Casey," Carval sub-vocalised.

"Go back to your shots. Anyway, the rest of her team still likes you, so maybe they'll help."

"She's not speaking to them much either."

"Oh."

Allan returned downstairs, and considered the value of another evening with Andy.

Carval, left to arrange his shots, mused over them. Something was missing, he felt, and it wasn't only Casey and Andy sparring. Inspiration struck. Holding. Allan had mentioned 'local cells', and the only local ones he could think of were the precinct holding cells. O-*kay*. He'd ask the desk sergeant to let him shoot there, which meant that he'd be in the precinct, which meant he'd have a chance to talk to Casey and patch this whole mess up. He hadn't missed that she hadn't answered his call the previous night, though that could be a result of anything from misery about her father to outright loathing of Carval himself.

He had another thought. He and the team had reached a convenient arrangement where he came and went as he pleased, and every week they confirmed that they were happy with that, so that they could truthfully tell Kent that he'd asked them. In the circumstances, he thought he'd better ask permission, in a way that he hadn't had to do since the very first case. He considered, and finally texted O'Leary, who'd played Cupid in the past and filled in the blanks last night.

***

O'Leary regarded the message from Carval with caution, and then began an affirmative text. Tyler and Andy weren't yet back, and Casey was talking to Fremont, who was giving her the correct answers – that was, he wasn't cowering under his desk. Yet. Even so, there was no point in poking the Casey-tiger. He added a suggestion that Carval avoid Casey by waiting for a couple of hours, till he was given the all-clear, and pressed Send.

"Fremont's finished with Caveman Bill. Nothing there." Casey made a face. "I'd have liked something, just because he's a chauvinistic waste of oxygen" –

"Stop hidin' what you really feel, Casey. It ain't good to bottle it up."

She snickered, and turned to scribble on the board. "It looks like he's out of the picture. We're coming down fast on the Washingtons, aren't we?"

"Seems so."

O'Leary looked at the board, where crosses had been drawn over Kayla, Steve, Roberts, Massapa, and Stanley. "What about the lawyer-folks?"

"Good point. We don't have anything on any of the people at Asher's firm – ambition isn't a crime."

"Naw, though for some people it oughta be. Politicians, mebbe. They shouldn't be allowed ambition."

"Rather them than me," Casey said dismissively. "I don't want to play God."

"Good." She glared at his cheerily impervious smile.

"So we've got the guys from Dorland & Andrews – Farman and O'Hagan – still to do. Did Larson find out about their gun ownership? What about ballistics on all the rifles? Do we have that yet?"

"Lemme speak to Larson. You better not – ev'ry time he sees you, he runs for the restroom. He can't hide from me in there. You c'n call Ballistics an' see if they got anythin'." He lumbered off towards an unnerved Larson, who'd spotted their glances at him.

Casey called Ballistics, and was briskly informed that the guns they had supplied were still being tested, seeing as she wasn't the only cop requiring their services.

"When will they be done?"

She could hear rustling and tapping. "You're next up. You'll have them by the end of the day."

"Okay."

She put the phone down just as Fremont skidded up to her and stopped an inch before he hit her desk.

"Detective Clement?"

"Yes?"

"That case. Varen & Dart. It settled this morning."

"How do you know?"

Fremont grinned. "I set up a press alert to watch for it, and it pinged a minute ago with Varen & Dart's SEC and press announcement. They've settled for an" – his fingers made air quotes – "undisclosed sum."

"Details?"

"Confidential. But it sounded like they were on the wrong end of it."

"Well, well." She wrinkled her nose, and then woffled it, just like a pet rabbit. Fremont tried not to laugh. "I don't think that takes Farman or O'Hagan out of it, though. Asher was shot ten days ago, and I bet they weren't in settlement negotiations then – not seriously, anyway. That would have come out of discovery, and the deadline for that was" – she consulted her file – "this past Monday – the 6th." Fremont's face fell. "It's still good information, and setting up the alert was good work. Even if it doesn't remove anyone, it's helpful." She smiled at him. "Well done. I'll give Schickoff & Schultz a call to see if they'll confirm it was something in the discovery. If so, we'll still be looking at the two juniors at Dorland & Andrews. We're not done with them yet."

Fremont left, at least two inches taller than he had been when he arrived. Casey thought for a moment, and then called Norman Dennison.

"Mr Dennison? It's Detective Clement here. I see your case has settled."

Dennison's grin shone through the phone line. "It sure did," he gloated.

"Our client was totally vindicated." He stopped. "What can I do for you?" he asked worriedly.

"I'd like to know – without you telling me anything confidential – if the settlement came as a consequence of something that came out in the discovery exchanges? I don't need to know what, just whether."

"Yes, it did," Dennison confirmed.

"Were there any settlement discussions before that?"

"Nothing serious. Nothing we would have advised our client to accept. They were just window-dressing."

"Okay. To be absolutely clear about timing, then, the discovery deadline was Monday, you reviewed the documents after that and found the smoking gun, and then serious settlement negotiations began, resulting in today's deal?"

"That's right."

"Excellent. Thank you."

Casey's next call was to Sue Tethers, to see what, if anything, Will Cornwall had reported. She was rapidly concluding that the Varen & Dart case was the only other possibility for Asher's death, though she was still firmly leaning to the theory that the murder was related to the Washington trust arrangements.

"Sue Tethers," an easy Southern drawl said.

"Ms Tethers, this is Detective Clement, NYPD."

There was a gasp. "Detective? What's happened? Is my family okay?"

"Yes. Don't worry, I'm not bringing bad news. I'm investigating a homicide, and you may have information relevant to our work."

"I'm" – it came out closer to Ah'm – "not sure how I can help you, but I'll surely try."

"Thanks. We're investigating Asher Washington's murder, and he was employed by your firm."

"I was so sorry to hear. God bless his soul."

"As part of our inquiries, we've been looking into the interactions between the Schickoff & Schultz attorneys and the Dorland & Andrews attorneys at the discovery hearing on January 27. We were informed that the opposition attorneys had improperly approached Asher, and he'd reported it to his boss. His boss then reported it to you?"

"That's right."

"What happened?"

There was a prolonged silence. Then, "I can't really tell you, but I don't think their career prospects are looking good."

"I get it," Casey said. "That's all I need to know. Thank you for your co-operation."

"Happy to help."

Casey contemplated her next move. Farman and O'Hagan should have known that their professional lives were on the line by trying to suborn Asher, and it had backfired. She had no sympathy. Ethics were important. *Shame Marcol doesn't have any* floated through her head. She shrugged it off. There wasn't time to worry about him. She decided on a subterfuge, and called Dorland & Andrews' main switchboard, asking for Farman, and then O'Hagan. Not at all amazingly, they didn't work there any more. Point to the firm.

O'Leary's heavy tread returned.

"Did Larson find any rifles around Farman or O'Hagan?"

"Nup. Nuthin' but what they admitted to."

Casey humphed. "They got fired," she said. "I'd hoped one of them would have a rifle."

"Naw. Alibis?"

Casey winced. She hadn't checked those. "We need to do that."

"You take one, I'll take the other, an' we'll be done in no time." He patted her shoulder. "We're gettin' closer. I c'n feel it. It'll be the Washin'tons, just like I said."

"You get *one* 'I called it' per week, and you already used it up ten times over. Hush up, and let's deal with these guys."

"*Hush up*?" O'Leary squawked.

"You can't hush down. You're too tall."

O'Leary groaned, vibrating the desk, and grumbled off to his own space, muttering "I got Farman," as he went.

While she was checking out O'Hagan's alibi, Casey's conscience was worrying at her with the insistent suggestion that she should get the team together and make sure everything was fixed. It hadn't *stopped* nagging at her since O'Leary had shown up at her apartment the previous day and simply been there for her, as the team always had been; and had only become louder – deafening – when that pompous ass of a shrink had suggested she needed *therapy*. She almost spat. She didn't need therapy, the team would do just *fine*. So…her move. Fix it, Casey Clement.

That settled, she got on with her work, until Tyler and Andy waltzed in, full of the joys of solid evidence.

"Write it up," Casey said, and while they did so, carried on with her alibi-checking.

When Tyler and Andy finished scrawling their findings on the board, Casey approached them. "I want to talk to all of you – *without* any of you calling Carval," she added rapidly.

"Sure," O'Leary said, without mentioning that Carval would shortly be buzzing around the precinct. "Abbey?"

"No." O'Leary drooped. "We're all coming back here afterwards to carry on. Starbucks."

"What about that little coffee place you like?"

"You won't fit."

"Won't fit through the door, more likely," Andy teased.

"Are you coming or not?" Casey asked impatiently.

Tyler nodded, and all three men followed Casey, wondering what the hell was going on. O'Leary surreptitiously texted Carval, which he easily justified as not a *call*.

Coffees, tea (Andy) and a lurid fruit drink that vaunted its health benefits (Tyler) in front of them, during the purchase of which not a word had been spoken between the team, Casey met each of their eyes in turn, and then dropped hers to the table.

"Okay," she mumbled. "I…I know it wasn't your fault that Carval went after Marcol? But why didn't you *tell* me?"

"Already done when we found out. Didn't want to interfere. Up to him to tell you. Said so. Said you wouldn't be happy."

"When did you know?"

"When that shithead" – Casey blinked at Tyler's vicious profanity – "showed up and hit on you, he accused us of sending the letter. Only one candidate."

"So we had a little chat," Andy said lightly. "Carval was really angry about Marcol stealing the photo. He must have said *stolen* ten times in five minutes. I don't think he likes his photos being stolen, you know. Just an impression I got."

"His problem, he got to decide to tell you. Just like you didn't tell him 'bout your dad till you had to. He likely thought you'd never know," O'Leary finished.

"I don't want to talk about Carval. So you guys knew nearly three months ago, but 'cause it was up to him to tell me, you didn't."

"Yup. An' while Marcol wasn't bein' a world-class pain in the ass – hey, I'm a poet! That rhymed" –

"Don't give up the day job," Andy snipped. Casey ignored the by-play.

"It wasn't important," O'Leary concluded.

"But you all told him he should tell me?"

"Yep."

Casey sipped her coffee. Eventually, she looked around them, meeting each of their eyes again. "Okay. We're good. You screwed up, but I get why. I'm over it. I" – she blushed violently – "well, the team's the thing."

"All for one and one for all?" Andy quoted.

Casey ignored that too. "His mess, he had to clear it up. It wasn't up to you." She sipped again. Everyone relaxed. They didn't need to talk any more: Casey didn't mess around with passive-aggressive comments or telling them things were good if they weren't. When the team had a problem, they were honest about it.

"C'n we go get a proper drink now?" O'Leary asked plaintively.

"No. We're going back to the precinct to finish up those alibis. Where's Pete?"

"Some audit in Milwaukee. Went off two weeks ago. Won't be back till Monday."

"So you're flying solo and you're bored."

"Yeah. An' it's your duty as pals to entertain me."

"Okay," Andy said. "I've got two tickets for the late-night show at La Mama tonight. You can come with me after we're done. I'll explain the set up over beer" –

"Naw."

"But it's entertainment."

"I was thinkin' of the football."

"If you're watching the football, Bigfoot, I'm out."

"Me too," Casey said. "I'm not that interested. Maybe Tyler'll go with you." She stood up. "Come on. Let's finish up."

***

Carval, having paid attention to O'Leary's text, showed up at the precinct shortly after the team had taken their Starbucks break, and made his way to the desk sergeant.

"Hey," he said, smiling. The sergeant just about returned it. "You know I'm shooting the precinct for my next exhibition?"

"Yeah," the man said, not obviously enthusiastic.

"Would I be able to shoot in Holding, if I blurred the faces?"

The sergeant pondered. "I dunno," he said. "You'll need to ask the Captain about that."

"Okay," Carval said. "Thanks." He hid his total disappointment. The person he second-least wanted to see right now was Kent, half an inch behind Casey. Correction: he'd love to see Casey, but only if they could mend matters. If not, he'd see Casey and less than three seconds later, that being the time it took to unsnap her holster and draw, he'd see a bullet. Still, he needed these photos, and he wasn't letting Casey, desk sergeants, or Kent stop him taking them.

When he reluctantly reached Kent's office, he knocked and waited.

"Come."

Carval sidled in. His nervousness was entirely justified by the ire on Kent's face as he raised his head from his busy desk.

"You." Carval nodded. Kent frowned blackly at him. "Shut the door."

Kent was surprised and displeased to see Carval, who he had been hoping to avoid. However, since the man had put his head in the lion's jaws, Kent would take full advantage. Carval had upset Clement, and Clement and her misfit team were the best detectives in his precinct. Having them upset was exceedingly undesirable and detrimental to the

222

precinct's excellent solve statistics. In addition, while Clement and her team had dealt with every issue that came their way, she shouldn't use his bullpen as a coping mechanism. Beneath his scowl, Kent had evolved a plan.

"You've upset Clement," he grated. Carval bristled, but stayed silent. "And that's upset the team. You have a week to fix it, or you don't come back." He scowled harder. "You said you don't lie down for blackmail: well, neither do I. Understand?"

"Yes," Carval bit, glaring back.

"Good. What are you doing here, anyway?" Kent's hostility didn't decrease.

"I want to shoot in Holding. Faces blurred."

Kent sighed irritably. "Yes. Now get out. I don't want to see you unless you fix it with Clement. Dismissed."

Carval barely managed not to say, "Yessir," as the detectives would, and left as fast as his feet would move.

Behind him, Kent harrumphed irritably, and scowled furiously at Carval's back to relieve his feelings. He'd been bluffing – his wife would kill him slowly if she didn't meet Carval as promised – but he was mad at Carval anyway. Dumb cluck, upsetting Clement, and Kent was the long-suffering guy who had to lay down the law. His face softened. Though he'd never let her know it, Clement's struggles with her father had tripped his limited sympathy, and he'd like to see everything fixed.

Come to think of it, the four of them were missing. Now that was very hopeful. He'd just see – actually, no. He poked his head out of his office, and saw Renfrew.

"Dr Renfrew," he said, when both of them were safely in his office, "did Clement's team go out together?"

"Indeed they did." Renfrew smiled thinly. "They appeared to be on good terms. Not quite as close as they could be, but you will be relieved to know that Detective Clement instigated the meeting."

"Yeah. That's good." Kent smiled. "Sounds like they're fixing themselves."

"Quite." Renfrew paused. "I confess to being worried about Detective Clement, but if the team is repaired, my concerns will be significantly lessened."

"Me too," Kent admitted. "Let's see what happens next."

CHAPTER TWENTY SIX

Carval marched back to the desk sergeant, at least as irked by Kent's dressing-down as pleased by the permission to shoot.

"Captain Kent said I could shoot, if I blur all the faces," he said.

"Okay, then. Let's get you down there." The sergeant gazed around and finally located a suitable escort. "Adamo? You take Carval here down to Holding and stay with him till he's finished snapping."

"Yessir," a small Italian-American type said smartly, and turned to Carval, who instantly whipped out his camera and took several shots of the lively face and dancing eyes. "Huh – er – sir?"

Carval gawped. He hadn't been 'sirred' by a single cop since the day he started.

"You don't need to call him sir," the desk sergeant pointed out. "He's taking pictures of us – he follows Clement's team around."

Adamo regarded Carval with a curious mixture of respect, astonishment, and a hint that Carval was suicidally stupid, which last comprised the majority of the desk sergeant's expression.

"Call me Carval," Carval said. "Everyone else does. Um..." – he remembered the rules – "do you mind if I take shots of you?"

"Nossir – Carval."

"Good."

"You won't notice after a few minutes, Adamo. He's always got that camera out. Ignore him." The words *we all do* were amazingly loud, for being unsaid. "Now, take him down to Holding and let the man work."

Carval followed Adamo's brisk steps – he was reminded of Allan – to Holding. It was grim. Miserable disbelief predominated, with a sub-harmonic of sullen anger, and, when Adamo and Carval were spotted, overt dislike. Carval, arrogantly sure of himself, simply wandered into the middle of Holding, camera out, looked around, announced, "I've got permission to shoot, as long as I blur all your faces. None of you will be identifiable," and began. His attitude shocked the detainees into astounded silence, lasting for quite some time, in which he happily shot everything from the gloomy corners of vacant cells, to the fluorescent light smeared on the cell bars, to the people incarcerated and their slumped postures. It all contrasted beautifully with Adamo's bright, shiny uniform – he must be a rookie, Carval decided – and alert face.

After at least an hour, Carval bounced out, perfectly happy with life, thanked Adamo, sent O'Leary a brief text to say that he was out of Holding, and betook himself to Casey's favourite coffee bar to waste some time. As he turned with his coffee, he saw the gang proceeding (O'Leary ambled, Casey was close to a jog) back towards the precinct, hoped that O'Leary might be arranging some kind of fix for Casey, and decided to stay put and await developments.

***

Casey and O'Leary couldn't find any information to break Farman or O'Hagan's alibis, and into the bargain Ballistics only produced a whole bunch of negatives.

"Okay. Barring illegal rifles, we've eliminated everyone except the trustees – Sella and Jarmyn – and Marlon." Casey sighed, and stretched.

"Okay. Sparring. You and Andy." She stared at Tyler. "None for two weeks. Unfit. Go get changed."

"C'mon. Time to sweat it out," O'Leary added.

"All of you should have a training session," Kent growled from behind them. "I won't have unfit teams." It carried the weight of an order. "You've done all you can for today." He waited. No-one moved. "Go!"

"Yessir," came from all four simultaneously, and they fled.

"What're you doing, Bigfoot?" Tyler asked, as Andy and Casey were changing.

O'Leary grinned widely. "Waal, Carval needs to take shots of them sparrin'…an' I'm pretty sure he's somewheres close by, 'cause he was shootin' in Holdin' earlier" –

"Told him we were out?"

"Sure did. An' I bet he didn't go far. Casey's li'l coffee place, I reckon." His phone pinged. "Yep. On his way now. Ain't that sweet?"

"Crazy. You're dead."

"Naw. Mebbe I'll get a li'l beat-up like, but nuthin' more."

Tyler's face betrayed scepticism; O'Leary's merely a happy smile.

"You ready? Five minute warm up with the bags, then mats."

Starting with the bags meant that neither Casey nor Andy could see the door, nor could they see Carval sneaking in and already shooting before he was fully inside.

"Okay. Mats."

Carval was half-hidden as the speed bag stopped swinging and Casey and Andy took their stances on the mats. In some mysterious fashion, Casey's back was still to the door and to Carval, and Andy didn't betray by a single blink that he'd noticed the addition.

They began slowly, but it didn't stay slow. Carval, shooting as fast as he could, thought that the two smaller cops were actually *faster* than O'Leary and Tyler – but then, they were also much lighter. They relied on speed and sneakiness – of which there was plenty – rather than brute force. They seemed pretty evenly matched, but Casey displayed an edge of focused rage that Andy didn't.

And then Casey saw Carval. Her face drained of colour, and refilled with cold ire. She deliberately turned her back on him, and went after Andy as if he were the Devil himself.

Casey couldn't stop herself. All the fury and resentment she bore: against Marcol, against Birkett, against Carval – but most of all against her drunken father; took over when she saw Carval taking shots as if he had a *right* when he'd been the one to start all this fuck-up all over again. Her attack was fuelled on blind rage: punches and kicks flying in; Andy defending, unable to reply without leaving himself open to another charge, Carval still shooting, transfixed, as Andy hit the mat for a third time and O'Leary stepped in over him. It didn't change Casey's full-out assault for a second. Carval didn't think she'd even noticed the swap as she hammered out her fury on O'Leary's enormous frame. She had as much impact on him as a gnat would, while Tyler brought Andy some water and they watched.

Finally, she ran down, exhausting herself against the O'Leary monolith, half-falling. At some unspoken signal, Tyler and Andy left, hauling Carval with them; leaving the other two alone.

"Waal, that was int'restin'," O'Leary drawled, steering Casey to a handy bench and sitting down with her, a bear-sized paw on her shoulder. "Guess you were a mite irritated?" He patted her gently. "Feelin' any better?"

She shook her head, staring at her bare feet, pulling the tie from her hair so that her face was hidden.

"We c'n go again, iffen you want to? You can't break me like you were tryin' to break Andy."

She didn't answer for a moment. "It won't solve anything."

"Mebbe not, but hittin' things c'n make you feel a whole bunch better."

"Not now." She sounded utterly defeated.

O'Leary patted her again. "Just sit here a spell, an' get your breath back."

"My dad's an alcoholic," she breathed out, and fell apart.

"I know," O'Leary sighed to her unhearing ears, all rustic drawl gone. "We knew. Probably long before you did."

***

226

Downstairs in the bullpen, Carval sat in Casey's chair, where Tyler and a cleaned-up Andy surrounded him. Andy dusted himself off, stretched, and groaned aggrievedly.

"What was she *doing?*" he wailed. "I thought we were fixed."

"*We* are. Carval isn't. Saw him."

"So it's my fault again?" Carval asked bitterly.

"No more than it was last week. It's all the same. Let Bigfoot deal with her for now. He's known her longest, and they..." Andy trailed off.

"Gets her," Tyler said.

"I thought you all..." Carval didn't finish his sentence either.

"Yeah, but...they were paired for three, four years before we joined them. Casey was still a rookie."

"Core."

Carval's question wrote itself across his face.

"Use your words, Tyler," Andy chided.

"They came first," Tyler explained, "then me, then Andy." He looked into a past only he could see. "First time I was comfortable." He straightened. "Not here. C'mon. Abbey, 'cause Bigfoot doesn't fit anyplace else."

"Yep," Andy agreed. "Text him, though, and *don't* forget to say Carval's with us." He turned to Carval. "If Casey comes, try not to start a fight."

"I wouldn't!" he said indignantly.

"She will," Andy pointed out mordantly.

"Might be a good thing," Tyler said, to consternation.

"What?"

"Why?" Andy asked.

"Punched it out just now. Fixed the team earlier. Fix you now. Maybe."

"Better than nothing," Carval agreed.

"Even if she fights, it's better than ignoring you and bottling the rest of it up," Andy pointed out.

"Should spar."

"You're kidding!" Carval exclaimed, starting for the stairs as Andy texted O'Leary. "She'd make mincemeat of me. I was *watching* that exhibition. I like being in one piece, and not in plaster."

Andy snickered. "You were shooting it. If you'd only been watching, we'd have pushed you on to the mat."

"Didn't want to pay breakages on that fancy camera." Tyler's mouth quirked.

Andy snickered again. "Nope. They don't pay us that much."

Carval managed a thin smile. "No. They don't." Both cops blinked.

"*That* much?"

"Yep."

Tyler shrugged. "Whatever. Andy spends fortunes on calligraphy pens."

"Brushes, Philistine!"

"Bar." Tyler let the insult slide off him as they strode out into the street, but he set a pace that Andy, much shorter, had to half-jog to keep up to.

"Slow up," he complained. "I'm not your height." Tyler grinned evilly, but slowed. "Philistines were giants. Goliath."

"You're not O'Leary. He's Goliath." Carval grinned down at Andy.

"Beer," said Tyler, which finished the squabbling. "Bigfoot texted back?"

Andy consulted his phone. "Yeah. He's cool."

"And Casey?" Carval asked.

Andy shrugged slim shoulders. "Not so much."

"What does that mean?"

"You were there same as us. You saw her. What do you think?"

"I think I need to drink this beer. And then another few," Carval said bleakly. "Maybe they'll be anaesthetic when she shoots me."

"We won't let her shoot you. Who'd make us famous if you're dead?"

"According to Allan, he's got enough for a posthumous exhibition. So you'll still be famous. Possibly in jail as accessories to my murder, but famous."

"That's okay, then," Andy smirked. "As long as we're famous."

Carval spluttered into his beer, and then grinned. "So good to know you have your priorities right."

They turned to light chat until O'Leary came in, trailing an emotionally-bedraggled Casey.

***

After a long period of silent companionship, in which he had received and answered Andy's text without Casey noticing or caring, O'Leary decided that it was time to move matters on. To his credit, he was solely concerned that Casey couldn't sit in the gym all night. For once, the prospect of the Abbey's beer didn't figure in his thinking.

"C'mon. Let's go get a drink. The others are already there an' you must need somethin' after all that."

"Whatever. Nothing I do will make any difference to Dad." She stayed slumped on the bench, head in hands, elbows on knees, staring at the scarred linoleum floor.

O'Leary pulled her up. "C'mon. We got you, an' you got us. You don't need to talk, just sit."

"Whatever," she said again, and allowed O'Leary to take her out of the precinct to the Abbey. Deferring to her state, he slowed his seven-league stride so that she walked at a comfortable pace. He allowed her to precede him into the bar, which conveniently meant that when she stopped, appalled, as she caught sight of Carval with the others, he could gently push her on.

"He don't bite," O'Leary encouraged, "an' you don't have to talk to him, nor anyone, iffen you don't want to. I'll get you a beer."

"Already getting it," Tyler noted.

To the private horror of everyone else around the table, Casey simply dropped down. She didn't lift her beer, nor take her dull, dead eyes from the smeared surface of the table: a small puddle of isolated misery in the midst of the group.

Three men looked at O'Leary, who looked back with a *your-turn* expression. They looked at each other, at Casey, at each other, at O'Leary, at Casey: around and around the group like hamsters on a wheel, almost as frantic. Finally, all their gazes landed on Carval, whose appalled face, pregnant with a horrifying idea, indicated that he expected to die shortly.

He took out his camera, raised it, and then whistled. Casey's head came up: she saw the camera and then the flash –

"What the *hell* do you think you're doing?" she exploded. Carval's next shot caught the relief on O'Leary's face as her temper fired and lassitude burned off in an instant. "You *dare* take more of your fucking *photos* when you started this whole disaster in the first place?" She lasered a furious gaze around the others, dismissed them, and returned her blazing eyes to Carval. "First you take that university photo and let some scumbag steal it and use it against me, and then when you find out you don't even *think* before going after him just so you can cosy up to me. Now that asshole Birkett" – Andy and Tyler drew in breath; O'Leary didn't – "knows about my dad and he'll be running off to tattle to that sonofabitch Marcol and it's all because *you* kicked the hornets' nest till it all came swarming out. It's not you who'll suffer, though. It's me. Us. You've screwed this team over and you haven't even the decency to apologise" –

"I *tried*! You wouldn't listen and you wouldn't let me explain! You told me you didn't want secrets and then you threw me out before I could say anything" –

"Why would I listen to your lies?" Casey shot back.

"I didn't lie to you."

"You sure didn't bother telling me the truth."

"It was *my* photo he stole. It doesn't matter if it was you or Allie or fucking *Yarland*, it was *my photo* and *nobody* gets to use it but me." Voices rose: point and counterpoint fired across the table.

"It's *my* life you ruined. Or doesn't that matter as long as you've got your photos?"

"I'm not responsible for someone else's actions. That's on them. You can't blame me for them being jealous of you. You're the one who says crimes are on the criminal, no-one else."

Casey's mouth opened to blast him, closed, then re-opened. "We're done. I'm going home."

"You don't have an answer for that, do you?" Carval hit back, his own temper lost long since. "If you did, you'd still be fighting. You just can't admit that I have a point because you'd have to admit that you're wrong."

"I am not!"

"Sure," he drawled disbelievingly. "First you wouldn't believe I had nothing to do with Marcol, then you wouldn't believe I was going after him because he *stole my photo*" – unseen, the other three rolled their eyes – "and then you wouldn't believe that I wouldn't shoot your dad, and now you won't believe that it *isn't about us!*"

Horrible silence descended as Carval sucked in furious breath.

"It's about Marcol," he bit. "And your dad. Not me, and not you. You're just taking it out on anyone around you because you can't bear to admit that your dad loves the bottle more than he loves you – owff!"

"Enough," O'Leary said, removing his elbow from Carval's ribs. "We know. No need to spell it out." He looked around the table, and his gaze snagged on Casey, blinking desperately but utterly unable to keep her eyes dry. "Now look where we are." His huge frame straightened up, and one arm landed around Casey. "Okay. We're fixin' this here an' now. I'm fed up, an' this is all gettin' silly. Casey, this ain't nearly as much Carval's fault as you're makin' it out to be. He got a right to stop people thievin' his photos, an' sure, it didn't hurt that it was you but that's not all of it. He ain't responsible for Marcol, or Birkett. He won't snap your dad, an' you know that too when you're thinkin' straight – or thinkin' at all," he added meditatively. "So give the man a break an' be nice."

She didn't react, staring at the table, hands still and lax in her lap.

"An' you," O'Leary carried on, "you were downright dumb not to tell Casey what you were doin', an' we all told you so. So iffen there's anythin' else, you oughta say so."

"I tried," Carval bit.

"Try harder. She's right here."

Carval turned to Casey, swallowed once, and opened his mouth.

"I don't care," she said.

"You're goin' to listen," O'Leary said sternly. "No secrets. That ain't this team. We don't keep secrets from each other. Nobody has to talk about 'em, but we don't keep 'em. It's already hurtin' us, an' I ain't lettin' it carry on. So you" – pointing at Carval – "spill, an' *you*" – tapping Casey – "listen. Or we stay here till you do."

Tyler and Andy stayed quiet while O'Leary laid down the law. Casey might lead the investigative team, but when O'Leary felt that the team needed fixing, not one of them would oppose him.

Casey shrugged, and didn't raise her eyes. Carval swallowed again. "You need to see the centrepiece photo. For the exhibition, I mean. Uh…it's of you. I took it in the alley where you found Belvez before I even knew who any of you were..." He ran down in the face of her complete lack of reaction.

"I'm tired," she said. "Tired of all of this. I'm going home. See you tomorrow." She stood up, wobbling a little. O'Leary gestured to Andy, who nodded.

"Come on, Casey, I'll walk you to the subway."

"I don't need a babysitter."

"Nope, but I don't want to watch Tyler and O'Leary showing off their muscles. It's not attractive."

"Whatever."

Andy walked alongside Casey for a good two hundred yards before he'd worked out what to say and how to say it without making matters worse.

"After you left, when Kent hauled us all in about the photo," Andy said, "Carval told Kent that the next step was a process server."

Casey gasped.

"Kent said what if he banned him, and Carval said he didn't care: Kent wasn't stopping him from asserting his rights. He said he didn't lie down for blackmail."

"What? Did Kent explode?" Sheer shock pushed Casey into a reaction.

"Just about. I thought he'd have a stroke right there." Andy waited expectantly.

"Spit it out. I'm not guessing."

"You're no fun. Whether it was because it's a photo of you or not, Carval faced down Kent about it being stolen. I don't think this is just about you, like he said and Bigfoot said. The reason he knows it's stolen is you, but I think he likely would do it for any stolen photo. Though it'll never get to court."

"Huh? Why not?"

"No financial loss. No damage to Carval."

"So why pursue it at all?"

"It sends a message." Andy left it at that. "See you tomorrow."

"Night," Casey said, and disappeared into the bowels of the subway.

Andy didn't follow her immediately. He tapped out a quick text to O'Leary: *made the process server point.*

In the bar, O'Leary and Tyler read the text, showed it to Carval, and exchanged satisfied smiles.

"There. Told you Andy could do it. Now mebbe we'll be done with all this fussin' an' frettin'. I don't like it."

"Getting fixed," Tyler stated, and changed the subject to sports.

CHAPTER TWENTY SEVEN

"Okay," Casey said, the next morning. "Let's get everything ready to bring in the Washingtons. We're all off tomorrow" –

"So we c'n all sing hymns in the choir," O'Leary suggested, to general disapproval.

"*So*, we can all be bright and fresh on Monday morning to get this case closed. Let's get to it."

Nobody mentioned the previous evening, nobody inquired into Casey's thoughts or feelings, and nobody remarked on Carval's absence, especially not O'Leary, who'd spotted him slipping back into Holding for another go-around with a different set of detainees.

The team divided up the various strands of the case, and then, just before lunchtime, reconvened to discuss.

"I've got the warrant for the Washingtons' financials ready to go," Andy said.

"Gave Ballistics a heads-up. Warrant for searching the Washingtons' house and removing guns ready."

"I want to interview Jarmyn first," Casey said. "Starting with why he didn't tell us he was a trustee. I'll ask if he has a gun. I know we didn't put him on the background runs, but let's set Larson searching. If he starts now he might finish by the end of the month."

"That's a bit unfair," Andy said. "Next week."

"I'll go talk to him," O'Leary offered. "Don't want to frighten him into fits."

"Okay. So let's go see Jarmyn today – you and me, Bigfoot, same as before. Andy, can you pick up the Cano Bank financials? See if you can make sense of what was going on with the money from the trust. They came through late yesterday and I didn't get to them. Tyler, can you go back to Asher's phone? See if you can trace those unknown numbers."

"Already begun. Waiting for the phone company. Follow up shortly."

"If you can't, can you and Andy find out how much the Washingtons' house cost – it was paid for out of the trust, so it should be in the audit somewhere – and what it's worth now. Most of that value had to go back into the trust."

"I know what you're thinkin'," O'Leary grinned. "You're thinkin' that it's all about the money."

"Yep. I'm thinking that the Washingtons didn't want to lose their cushy lifestyle and pretty home." She blinked. "Kayla said they tithed. That's a big drag on their income. They nagged Asher about tithing, too" –

"If he did, it didn't show up in his financials," Andy said.

"Mm. But they didn't have to pay anything for Asher, 'cause the trust did it all – though they implied that they did. So they had enough to tithe." She looked around. "But…maybe they thought Asher should have."

"Long shot."

"Yeah. I think they might have been skimming."

"Pastor Jarmyn didn't seem the type," O'Leary said.

"No. That's an issue. That's why I want to talk to him about his trusteeship." She smiled around the team. "We're off shift tomorrow, but let's be ready for Monday. And once we get the Washingtons in, we'll have a friendly chat with them." Her smile became distinctly unfriendly.

"Ranges," Tyler said.

"Do you want to unpack that?"

"Down to three, maybe four, people, yeah?" She nodded at Tyler, who continued. "Few enough we can ask ranges if they shoot there."

"You're still thinking one of them called, one fired?" Andy asked.

"Yeah. Good shot. Need practice to be that good." Tyler was definite, and nobody argued with Tyler about shooting.

"Okay, ranges. Maybe Fremont could help? He's done well so far."

"Yeah." Tyler agreed with Casey.

"Okay. You do that and the phones, Andy can do money, and we'll go talk to Jarmyn again. Let's go get 'em, boys." She grinned widely, the joy of the hunt splashed over her face, and the team closed around her, just as it always had. Tyler and O'Leary exchanged looks over Casey's head, and insensibly the team acknowledged its comfortable bonds.

From his desk, Dr Renfrew observed, and, as the team dispersed, considered. To his expert eye, the team had repaired itself. He wondered if they would now repair relationships with Mr Carval, whom he had spotted taking surreptitious shots of the team re-establishing itself.

***

"Okay, Bigfoot," Casey said between mouthfuls of sandwich, "let's go pursue this pastor."

O'Leary smiled. "Sure thing."

There wasn't much talking on the way out to Queens, but the quiet in the SUV was comfortable. They drew up at the Assembly of God church, and swiftly found Pastor Jarmyn's office.

"Hello?" he said, not looking up from what appeared to be a draft of a sermon.

"Pastor Jarmyn," Casey said, "could we please talk to you about Asher Washington's case?"

His head jerked up. "Detective? What – why are you here?"

O'Leary followed Casey inside and shut the door.

"You're a trustee of Asher Washington's trust fund," she began.

He stared at her. "Yes?"

"According to our information, you replaced Benjamin Stanley as trustee of Asher Washington's trust fund, four years ago." She let that lie between them. "The other trustee was Sella Washington, who had replaced Pastor Elijah Massapa."

"I did, yes. I don't remember exactly when." Pastor Jarmyn sat back in his chair and frowned in concentration. "Four years ago?"

"March 15th, 2013. Possibly within a couple of days either way."

"Let me look at my diary. I don't remember."

"Please do." Casey waited, the air still around her.

The pastor scrabbled through a drawer in his desk, and eventually emerged with a battered diary, which he thumbed through.

"March…fourteen, fifteen – oh, yes. Sella asked me to come to a meeting with her and Marlon, about Asher. I didn't remember the other man's name, but now you mention it, he would have been Mr Stanley. I didn't really understand the discussion, but everyone seemed to be quite happy."

"Were you asked to take on the trusteeship then?"

His brow furrowed. "Let me think." More creases appeared on his face. "It's so long ago…" He relapsed into concentration. The detectives waited. Jarmyn wasn't displaying any signs of panic, or guilt, merely incomprehension. Of course, that could all be an excellent act. "We talked about Asher, and how he was doing, and Sella suggested that it would make sense, since he was so busy – he was doing so well, but he never had much time – if all his affairs were here, and they discussed it for a while, and I think they all agreed." He smiled. "I was probably thinking about my flock. To be honest, at that point I wasn't sure why I was there."

"Mm?"

"But then they started to explain – it's coming back to me now." He blinked apologetically. "I'm not as young as I used to be, and my memory isn't always sharp. But the Lord will help me."

Casey didn't comment. O'Leary was trying his best to be invisible.

234

"We talked about what would be best for Asher, keeping him in good Christian ways. Mr Stanley explained that the trust covered all expenses, but Sella and Marlon – and I – thought that having too much money wouldn't be good for him. Mr Stanley agreed, I recall – he said that was how Asher's parents had thought of it. The love of money is the root of all evil. There had to be trustees, to ensure that no temptations fell in his way. But Mr Stanley was out in Connecticut, really too far away for urgent matters, and anyway Sella had replaced another pastor. We all felt that it was important that there was someone to give Godly guidance. Of course Sella and Marlon are very strong in their faith, but they are not ordained, and it does make a difference."

Casey nodded. She didn't necessarily agree – plenty of apparently Godly people had committed ungodly crimes – but Pastor Jarmyn was transparently sincere in his belief.

"So I agreed to take on the role."

"Why didn't you mention this when we first met?"

"I didn't think of it," he said simply. "I was shocked that Asher had died, and my first thought was to comfort Sella and Marlon. It didn't cross my mind."

"I see. How did you fulfil your duties?"

"For the first year, it was all fairly simple. We all met every month or so – separately from all our church matters, of course – and the audit was carried out just as it should be. But then Asher got busier: it was his final year of law school, and he was concentrating on his final exams and then the Bar exam, and then getting a job – he succeeded in all of those things, but it meant that he was barely here. All his comments came through Sella or Marlon, because once he'd moved out to Manhattan, we didn't see him often."

Ah-ha! Casey thought. *That's how it was done.*

"I thought he'd been back home and attending church with his aunt and uncle?" she queried.

"Oh, yes, but not often – busy, you know – and Sunday worship is not a time when I can devote all my attention to one person. My flock want to talk to me, and Sunday should be a day when work doesn't intrude on spiritual matters. If Asher had had a problem of faith, I would have spent all the time he needed with him, but he never mentioned anything. One Sunday he brought his girlfriend, who was another call on his time."

"What did you think of her?"

"I didn't really have much of a chance to talk to her, but she seemed nice. Quite shy, and didn't push herself forward." He smiled sweetly. "She was happy to let Sella and Marlon have time with Asher."

Casey compared Jarmyn's words with Kayla's view of her visit, and decided that Jarmyn saw the best in everyone, without considering that there might be less pleasant motives at play. She also thought, from the description of Pastor Massapa, that he would have been far more assiduous in ensuring he spoke directly to Asher. She didn't need to look at O'Leary to know that he was already considering the next steps.

"All the audits were still done, weren't they?"

"Oh, yes. Of course. Sella insisted. We used a local firm – from our congregation. It was so much cheaper than the firm that Mr Stanley had employed, and Sella was very insistent that the fund shouldn't overpay. It would have wasted Asher's inheritance."

"What did the trust spend money on?"

"Oh, I don't know the details, but it supplemented his pay-check, so that he could rent an apartment closer to his work, and of course he tithed."

"Tithed?" asked Casey, who knew perfectly well what it meant.

"He gave ten percent of the trust income to the church, just as Sella and Marlon did. He had so much, and he wanted to give back. We used it to support disadvantaged children, who didn't have the close family that he had had. God worked through him, and us, to help them."

What? Absolutely *nothing* Casey had heard, read, seen or found indicated that Asher had tithed – quite the reverse, in fact, if she believed Kayla.

"Very generous," O'Leary rumbled approvingly. Casey knew it to be put on.

"Yes. Such a good boy. Tragic."

"Thank you very much for your time, Pastor. That's been very helpful." She paused. "Asher's death means that the trust will be terminated. A final audit has to be arranged, by a law firm – Marswell & Eglinton. May I give them your details so that they can contact you?"

"Of course. Everything should be properly done." He handed Casey a card. "Please give this to the appropriate people, and tell them I'm happy to hear from them."

"Thank you."

"Go with God," the pastor said. "I hope you find Asher's murderer."

"We're working very hard to find them."

"I shall continue to pray for your success."

"Thank you, sir," O'Leary said, echoed by Casey.

They left, quietly.

***

"Tithing?" Casey spat. "Asher wasn't *tithing* – that was all Sella and Marlon. They were skimming, and that's how they did it. According to Kayla, Asher wasn't tithing and they were guilt-tripping him about it. Looks like they decided to do it anyway. The end of the trust was coming up, so they would be found out, one way or another. Let's get back so Tyler and

Andy can tell me if they've found out if Sella or Marlon are members at any rifle ranges."

O'Leary gunned the engine, and they were back at the precinct faster than traffic regulations allowed. He loved using the lights and sirens, and Casey hardly ever allowed him to. Today, she'd encouraged it.

"Tyler, Andy, on me," Casey called, as soon as she was through the door. "The Washingtons did it. We just have to prove it."

"Huh?"

"We talked to the pastor again, and all the instructions that were supposedly from Asher came through Sella or Marlon. They were skimming. Had to be. It would all come out as soon as he got married or turned thirty – and both of those were coming up. They did it."

"I called it," O'Leary said smugly.

Casey groaned. "Shut up, Bigfoot." She turned to the others. "We need to look specifically for them at the ranges. Who's doing it?"

"Fremont."

"Good. Hurry him along. Andy!"

"The trust was paying out two monthly payments. One to Asher. One to the Washingtons."

"Got them. Okay. Finalise the warrant for their financials and file it – see if someone's on duty for urgent matters. I want that on the move before Monday, but no-one will act on it Sunday. Tyler, let's finalise the search warrant – specifically for Uncle Washington's rifle, but we'll search the whole house. We won't execute it till they're on their way to Interrogation."

"When're you hauling them in?"

"Not till we have their financials. That's what'll give us the opening. If we don't have those, all we have are theories. I don't want theories. I want evidence."

The others nodded.

From his discreet corner, Carval shot them: faces and builds so very different; expressions exactly the same. One team, one mission, one goal. One more success. If only he were a part of them…sure, the men were cool with him, but unless Casey allowed him back in, he'd only ever be on the outside, looking in. She was the heart of the team, and everyone knew it.

But – through grace of God and O'Leary – he hadn't broken them. He *hadn't*. And while the team was solid…he still had a chance. Maybe. If only she'd come and see the centrepiece, then he wouldn't be hiding anything.

Except how he felt, of course. There was that. But while she was so set on something easy, something casual – something at her own pace – he wouldn't push. Couldn't push. Suddenly, fiercely, he wanted to push; to crush her in and *insist* that she leaned on him, that she simply let him in. Let him help.

He turned away; the cops dispersing to their tasks and desks. No more shots to be taken, no more to see. Quietly, he left, almost unseen.

O'Leary noticed Carval go, as he'd noticed him shooting, and said nothing. He wouldn't get anything through Casey's concrete skull tonight, and likely not until the case was closed. No point in trying, he thought. She might do the right thing. He wouldn't bet on it, though: Casey only tried the right thing with relationships when everything else had failed.

***

Late in the afternoon, the team was done for the day. Everything that could be done, had been done. Every route had been exhausted; everything was ready: waiting for the financials.

"Okay, let's quit till Monday. We can't be any more ready."

"Sounds good to me," Andy said.

"Beer?" O'Leary asked hopefully.

"Could use one," Tyler agreed.

"Okay," Andy said.

Everyone looked at Casey, who looked coldly back, and then broke into an infectious, mischievous smile. "Sure. Let's go." Grins broke out around her as they followed her out and down to the Abbey.

Beers on the table – even for Andy – Casey grinned around the men. "Here's to a successful Monday," she toasted, and downed a slug.

"Team," Tyler added, and threw half of his down in one go.

"Team," the others echoed.

"You okay?" O'Leary directed at Casey.

She shrugged. "Dealing with it. Waiting for that asshole Marcol to pull another dirty trick." Her face tightened. "Guess I won't be going for dinner at Dad's tomorrow."

No-one spoke. Casey confiding was rare – as rare as for any of them.

"If he doesn't need me…" She swallowed. "He doesn't approve of me being a cop. But this…being a cop…the team – it's what I want. He doesn't get to change that." She swallowed again. "But…I've got to try and help him. I can't just leave him rotting in the tank. God knows what would happen to him. He couldn't deal with some of the stuff that goes down." She stared into the table. "He's all I've got left," she whispered.

"Iffen you need a bit of help, you got us."

"I sure don't need that arrogant ass of a profiler," Casey sparked.

"Huh?" Andy queried.

"Doc Renfrew suggested Casey could use some therapy," O'Leary said.

"He *what?*" Andy squeaked.

"I don't need any prissy-assed profiler," Casey bit. "We've got us. That'll do for me."

The last faint remnants of tension dissipated at Casey's flat, firm statement.

"Yeah," O'Leary agreed, "We c'n do therapy."

"Yep. Some high-class opera. That'll make you feel better."

"Only with earplugs to dull the noise," Casey flipped back.

"Culture's no use," Tyler disagreed. "Hard training. Weights, treadmill, spar. Cure anything."

"I do enough of that."

"Go see a show," O'Leary said, which was the best idea anyone had had. "Mebbe not the front row of Hamilton, 'less you've won the lottery an' not told us, but somethin' fun an' cheerful. That'll make you happy."

Andy made a face. "Uncultured mob."

"You could get returns. Go down to the ticket desk an' see."

"When we're done with the Washingtons."

"Promise?" O'Leary said.

"Promise. I'll even let you come along if you promise not to sing."

"Aw, you ain't no fun at all."

"Nope. But at least I don't sing."

"Can't," Andy put in.

Casey scowled impartially at them all, and slugged her single beer back. The bottle done, she yawned. "Time for me to go."

"Get some sleep," O'Leary said parentally, and patted her head. She humphed at him. "Can't catch killers on no sleep. You'll yawn them to death."

"Oh, *okay*. Mommy," she said with enough attitude for a whole high school's worth of teens. "I'm going home. See you all Monday, bright and early." Her smile turned sharp. "Ready to get them."

As she left the Abbey, Casey's stomach curdled. She hadn't said a word about it, but she had a different plan. She went back to the precinct to pick up her car, and shortly pulled up outside Carval's block.

She had to know the worst.

CHAPTER TWENTY EIGHT

Casey steeled her nerves, and buzzed Carval's entry-phone.

"Who is it?" an unfamiliar voice clipped, in snippy, unwelcoming tones.

Her hackles rose. "Detective Clement, NYPD."

"Jamie's Casey?" the voice said, utterly astounded. "Come in."

She was still getting her head around being referred to as *Jamie's Casey*, which she emphatically was *not*, when she was steered into a previously unseen office, a floor below Carval's studio, and examined by a slim, dapper man who precisely matched his tone.

"I'm Allan Penrith," he said. "You're Jamie's Casey."

"I'm Casey Clement," she corrected.

"I must say," he said, ignoring her correction, "I didn't expect to meet you. Certainly not here. You're not at all what I expected."

"Oh?" Casey said coldly.

"The way Jamie talks about you, you're ten feet tall and breathe fire. Of course I've seen the photos, but he makes you out to be the greatest hero since Superman." He inspected her. "You *really* aren't what I expected. You're small."

"I am not!"

"In Jamie's photos, somehow you look bigger. Even against that mountain O'Leary" –

"You've met the others?" Acid tinged Casey's icy tones.

"Yes. They come around, bully Jamie, harass me, and generally make fuss and noise and mess. I thought I got enough of that with Jamie, but no, he has to add more trouble."

Unwillingly, Casey's lips began to quirk upward. She couldn't see her team – except maybe Andy – getting along with this polished man.

"I like your Andy, though. He knows about culture." He half-turned. "Jamie, you have a visitor."

"Who is it? I don't wanna see anyone," grumbled down from the studio.
"Come down, Jamie."

There was a familiar and unhappy noise, followed by sluggish thuds on the stairs. "I don't want to – Casey?" His face lit up. "You're here." He took a step towards her, and then registered her chilly expression.

"I want to see the centrepiece," she stated.

"Sure," Carval said. "Come on up to the studio."

Allan followed them both upstairs. If nothing else, he could act as a witness in Jamie's murder. Jamie, he noticed with sardonic amusement, kept sneaking looks at his Casey-cop, who ignored him.

"There it is," Jamie said.

Casey gasped. Utter silence surrounded her. Allan noticed that Jamie had set up his corkboard as if it were the exhibition, even if he was short of shots. The picture of Casey was right in the centre. Even Allan would have admitted (if anyone had asked) that it was astounding. Show stopping. Jamie, though, was only watching his Casey, a desperate expression of hope in his eyes, clearly preventing himself asking what she thought. Her rigidity was equally frightening.

Finally, she wrenched her gaze from the board, and the central image. "I see," she said. It revealed nothing; and her face was blank. Allan, though, could see her hands, knotted behind her back, fingers twisting. He slid away. Whatever happened next – should stay between those two.

Casey didn't hear the click as the door shut behind Allan: forcibly stopping herself staring at the central image. Her face: fierce and focused; the slightly blurred forms of the others; hard blue sky above and the dark walls of the alley around her. It was brilliant.

It was terrifying.

She'd seen his panhandlers – but this was on a whole different level. This exhibition would eclipse the panhandlers – and she would be front and centre. Everybody would know her face. It didn't matter that the others would be equally well known; she only cared that *she* would be thrust into the public eye.

"Have the others seen this?"

"The centrepiece? Yes. Some of the other shots. Not this arrangement."

"I see," she said again, betraying nothing. She raised her eyes and looked him square in the face. He met her gaze.

"I'm not dropping it," he said. "This is the heart of my exhibition. *Everything* pivots on this photo." He stared her down. "You can see that. I know you can." He stopped, swallowed, restarted. "No matter what, it's not changing. If you walk away and never speak to me again, I'm still not changing it."

"Artistic integrity?" she said bitterly.

"Yes. And you've known that right from the start, so don't tell me it's a

241

surprise."

She sat down, suddenly, as if her knees had given way. "I never wanted to be photographed," she said brokenly. "I didn't want any of this. I just want to do my job and be a cop." She gulped, and sniffed hard. "You want to make me a celebrity, and Dad wanted me to be a lawyer. Why can't I just live my *own* life?"

Carval couldn't stand seeing her small and defeated; struggling not to weep, without trying to comfort her. He took the few steps to reach her, hesitated – he could see her gun on her hip, the badge gleaming beside it – and pulled her up into him. She didn't fight him, which was worse than anything else she could have done.

He didn't dare speak, or sit, or even turn her face up so he could see her eyes. He patted her back, not – though he wanted to – removing the clip from her curls, and waited. As suddenly as she had sat down, she slumped against him, which he took for permission to keep her close, a small lump of unhappiness in his arms.

"I don't want any of it," she whispered. "I never did."

"You don't have to go near the exhibition, though."

"It won't matter. Everyone'll know it's me." She took a breath, and sighed it out again. "Every cop who hated me already will use it as proof I couldn't do it on my own. I'm only there as good PR for the precinct and the NYPD."

"It's not true, though. Your team's stats" –

"Didn't the *first* photo tell you the truth doesn't matter?" She pulled away from him and started to pace the studio, never removing her gaze from the corkboard. "Have you forgotten already? You haven't shut down Marcol because scum like that never *stop*. He has an agenda, and this exhibition won't help. He knows about Dad, and he'll use that all over town to prove I'm dirty. Just watch."

"He won't. Kent'll make sure he doesn't."

"You can't stop gossip and rumours. They follow you around forever. It doesn't matter what Kent does, they're there." Her pacing halted before the corkboard. "I wish…"

"Wish what?" He couldn't bear it if the next words were 'I'd never met you'.

She turned to face him. "Why did you have to be a *photographer?*"

Carval had no answer to that. He just was. He couldn't stop photographing – he'd never been able to stop, from the day he had been given his first Kodak, age eight or so. He had no idea how to be anything else.

She stopped pacing, still staring at the arrangement. He watched her, trying to see it through her eyes.

Casey stopped staring at the corkboard and stared at Carval instead. "It's not real to you unless you shoot it. You really do only see things through a lens. Nothing else matters to you."

"You do," he blurted out.

"*What?*"

He managed to raise his gaze to hers; as shocked as she by his own words. "Uh…you matter." He summoned up his courage, presently residing in his toes. "I said we don't let anything pass. We don't. But if Marcol tries to fuck you over I'll *bury* him."

"And if I said not to?" she challenged.

"I'll still bury him. He doesn't deserve to be a cop – nor anyone else who helps him. But you know what? I won't get the chance, because Kent, Renfrew, your team, and likely even that agent, Bergen – they're all in line ahead of me."

Casey gaped at him.

"You don't get it, do you?" he said wearily. "You aren't on your own. Your team's there. Your captain's there. Even the goddamn FBI is there. Everyone who matters is on your side. Marcol doesn't have a chance in hell of surviving this, and everyone who helps him will go down too."

She boggled at him.

"But if they weren't – or if they won't – I'd still bury that cowardly prick," he grated.

"Even if I said not to?" There was an odd tone in her voice.

"Would you say the same to your team?"

"We agreed to ignore him a long time ago."

"And now? Have you asked them what Tyler said to Marcol when he came to fill you in on the Narcotics trail?"

"I don't need to. They won't do anything without talking to me. You're telling me you'd ignore what *I* want and just do what *you* want."

Carval stopped short, and actually looked properly at Casey's set face. Suddenly, he remembered her words. *I didn't need a hero.* He winced.

"You're right. If you say no, don't – I'll go after him about the first shot, because that's non-negotiable for copyright reasons – but I won't do anything else. The rest – it's up to you."

"Do what you have to about your photos. I'll…live with that," she conceded, and for the first time since the disastrous interview in Kent's office, she eased, fractionally. "Just don't try to manage *my*" – the emphasis was granite-hard – "life. I can do that just fine by myself."

"You don't have to be in the public eye," he offered. "Not if you don't want to be. Just 'cause the exhibition's in public, doesn't mean you have to be there."

"I wasn't going to be," she stated.

"I guessed," he said dryly. "But what I meant was that you don't even have to visit. I'll show it to you before it opens, if you want to see it, when no-one else is around. No newsies, no public, not even the rest of the team if you don't want them there."

"You'd be happy with that?"

"No, but…I can't make you." He half-smiled, sidelong. "You'd shoot me."

"Probably."

He took a step towards her. She didn't move to him – but she didn't move away. He took another step, and then a third. The fourth stride brought him within reach of her, and still she hadn't moved, only her sightline changing to stay focused on his face.

"I hate it," she said, switching her gaze to the corkboard. "Sure, it's brilliant. But I hate it."

"Not me, though?" He heard his own plea, falling into dead silence. The hush dragged on – but she wasn't disagreeing, and she wouldn't meet his eyes. "Not me," he said with certainty. "You can't tell me that. You don't mess around playing hard to get or with passive-aggressive crap; or expecting me to work out that you don't mean what you say." His hand extended, fell back to his side.

"It'll be huge," she whispered. "Everyone…I never wanted any of it."

He couldn't answer that, either. There was no answer. He had to shoot her, her team, and murder – he couldn't ignore it. If that meant he lost Casey…then he lost her. He wasn't sacrificing himself to be with her. He thought back to the evening after she'd closed the Telagon case, when they'd had almost the same conversation – but now she could *see* the shots; see what *front and centre* really meant, and….

And she was terrified, he realised. She hadn't known how exposed she would be. He'd opened up their souls for the world to see, and, faced with the reality of his talent, she was outright scared.

"I can't do this," she said. "I can't deal with it. *I never wanted this.*" She turned away from him, and dropped her head. A thin, cold silence stretched out, until Carval stepped around to be in front of her again.

"Casey," he tried. "C'mon. Look at me."

"So you can rip out more for your show?" Her voice cracked.

"No." He gave up on words, and simply tucked her in, feeling the quivers in her shoulders; knowing that she was barely holding on to control; a small, tight ball of tension. He petted, but she didn't react; rigid and unyielding. "Casey," he tried once more, "Casey. Don't shut me out again. Talk to me."

She stepped back from him. "There's nothing to say. You'll keep taking your shots. I don't get a say in that."

"That's not what I mean. Sure, now you've seen them, but you've known that for five months. This isn't about the exhibition. It's about what Marcol will do. About what your dad'll think when he sees it." She slumped, and he knew he was right. "You think he'll see it, and he won't approve."

"No."

"No?"

"He won't care. He'll just get drunk again, to forget I'm not the good little lawyer he wanted me to be. To forget what he and Mom hoped for. I wasn't supposed to be a cop, and they – *she* must have been disappointed in me too."

"You don't need him" –

"He needs *me*, though. He needs me to bail him out and find him a defence lawyer and make sure he goes to court and to pretend everything's all right every time I see him when he's killing himself and drowning me too!" She stopped. "I can't just let him die in a cell. He's my family. He's all I've got left." She paused again. "And don't tell me the team is my family. It's not the same and you know it."

Carval looked at his shots and, privately, thought that Casey had it totally right, for completely the wrong reason. The team weren't her family – the four of them were far closer than that, and every shot showed it.

"Let's get some dinner," he diverted, mentally crossing his fingers. "Did you have lunch? You look hungry and tired."

"I'm not hungry."

"I am. C'mon. If you're not hungry, have a coffee."

"I" –

He didn't let her finish. "Look, I get why you're mad with me. I've said I won't do anything more and I meant it. I want to fix it. I'm sorry. I – please, Casey? You" – he gulped – "you matter." Words began to tumble out. "I – yes, there's the copyright and we'd go after that whatever but I did the rest because you matter, just like O'Leary reported Marcol's machinations to Kent because the team really matters. It's…you don't need me to protect you but I didn't think of that because it never happened before." He ran down under her astounded expression.

"*What* never happened before?"

"Uh…nobody ever tried to use my photos like that."

"Or you never found out," she said cynically. "Would you have cared?"

"Probably not," he admitted, after a long, uncomfortable pause. "Not enough to go hunting like this."

"Oh."

Casey, unwillingly, had to respect Carval's honesty, even if she didn't appreciate his actions. She was still mad at him, but he'd apologised – more than once, she remembered – and…. And she just wanted to be curled up beside him and be comforted and then to sleep properly with everything fixed.

"If you do anything more than go after your copyright, we're done," she said, after a long gap to collect her thoughts. "So you'd better tell Allan that."

Carval opened the studio door and simply hollered down the stairs, "Allan, Allan, come here."

Short, brisk footsteps followed. "You haven't been shot, then?" Allan inquired. "I'm amazed."

"Far too much paperwork," Casey quipped, "and I wouldn't like Bedford Hills. No coffee."

Carval muttered. Allan laughed. "Don't be a child, Jamie. Now, why do you want me? I was just about to go home. I should have gone hours ago."

"Going after Marcol," Carval said. "We stick strictly to the copyright point. And we nail him to the wall for it – but Casey doesn't want me to go after him for anything else, so we won't."

Allan goggled at them both. "Wow," he eventually managed, and switched his gaze to Casey alone. "How did you convince Jamie to follow a path of sense and reason?"

"I have a gun," Casey said, ignoring Carval's insulted squawking in the background.

"Maybe I should try that," Allan mused. "God knows, I've tried nearly everything else."

"Hey!" Carval squeaked indignantly. "Who pays your salary?"

"Who pays all your bills, keeps the lights on, and makes sure you can shoot anywhere the fancy takes you?" Allan riposted, which silenced Carval. Casey's lips quirked. "Anyway, yes. We can easily stick to the copyright point." Allan smiled. "Nice to meet you, Casey. Night, Jamie."

He tip-tapped off.

"Dinner?" Carval asked.

"Okay."

"Are we? Okay, that is."

"Maybe?" She became extremely interested in her linked hands. "I don't know. Don't push."

"Let's get dinner. What do you want?"

"Pizza," Casey decided. It was easy and comforting, and right now she didn't think she could handle chopsticks without dropping all of her food in her lap.

"Okay. Here, or upstairs?"

She deliberated. If she went upstairs, it was a statement that they were – probably, or until the next time they fought – okay. If they stayed here, it was halfway to a rejection.

"Upstairs." She couldn't stay mad at him forever, no matter how she might want to. O'Leary's words came back to her: *better to have someone who'll hug you.* Much as she hated to admit it, O'Leary had been right. The team didn't go in for hugs, except O'Leary, in private, and there had been enough of that. O'Leary gave good comfort, but...it wasn't the same. Oh God, what was she *thinking?*

Carval didn't touch her as they waited for the pizza, which was mildly disconcerting, nor when they'd finished. As she registered that he'd sneaked peeks at her every other second, it finally occurred to Casey's tired mind that he was waiting for her to let him know it was okay, which was a whole different ball game from his usual approach. She shifted towards his corner of the couch, which produced an arm around her. She was perfectly happy with that: too tired for anything more.

Carval regarded the top of Casey's head, and relaxed. She'd seen the centrepiece, and he wasn't dead. More, they'd had a fight, and survived that too, and since she had accepted an arm around her, they were probably okay. He tucked her in a little more closely, dropped a tiny kiss on the top of the dark curls, and left it at that.

It took him some moments to notice that Casey wasn't eating anything more, and another minute after that to realise that she was asleep, or nearly so. He pulled gently at a stray curl, and received only a mutter.

"You're falling asleep."

"Urgh," she yawned, and forced her eyes to open. "I should go home."

"You don't have to," he said without really thinking about it.

"Uh?"

"Stay. You can sleep here just as well as at home." He thought. "Unless you're on shift tomorrow?"

"No." She yawned, and nestled back in. She'd go home in a minute. Staying...wouldn't be smart. Not when they were so fragile. In a minute, she'd go.

Carval watched Casey drift back into slumber, settled himself comfortably, and lost himself in thoughts of his shots and their potential arrangements. Casey made a funny little noise, and curled herself up within his arm, deeply asleep. Close up, he could see the darkness under her eyes, the pallor beneath her skin; the evidence of bone-deep tiredness. Ridiculously, he felt guilty.

Anyway, he thought, with smug satisfaction, she was sleeping now. The feeling of guilt disappeared. He carefully propped her against the back of the couch, made himself a coffee, and picked up a book: on photography, naturally. Fiction didn't interest him: he had his cops for crime stories; but he was always keen to expand his knowledge of the technical aspects to match his on-the-fly instinct for the perfect shot. He stretched out, and began to study.

An hour later, he picked up his coffee mug, tried to drink, found only cold dregs, and realised both how much time had passed and that Casey was still sound asleep, curled into the corner of the couch. He undid her clip, admired the fall of dark curls against her still-pale face, and considered his options. He'd *like* to put her in his bed. He *ought* to wake her so that she could go home.

He split the difference, tugging a curl until her eyes winched themselves open. "It's late."

"Huh?" She woke up a little more. "What?"

"It's nearly eleven. Bedtime" – his conscience kicked in – "or home time."

Casey scrubbed at her eyes, and acquired a modicum of intelligence. She hadn't meant to fall asleep at all, still less for hours.

"I need to go home," she said.

Carval's disappointment spread over his face, but he didn't argue. "Before you go…" –

"You could come by tomorrow afternoon," she said.

"Yes," he gasped. He hadn't expected that. "Okay, I will. But before that – can I kiss you?"

She stretched up to him, and he wrapped her in and kissed her deeply. It tasted of forgiveness.

CHAPTER TWENTY NINE

Casey woke late. It took her a few seconds to remember the previous night, and a few more to realise that she'd slept less brokenly, for the first time since...since Carval had stayed, before they'd fought. She dragged herself out of bed, through a shower, and into simple, comfortable clothes. She'd change later – oh. She wouldn't be changing, because she wouldn't be seeing her father for dinner. He hadn't contacted her at all since Thursday, and she hadn't called him.

She sniffed, and faced the fact that her father really didn't care. Even so, he might have abandoned her, but for the sake of her own conscience, she couldn't abandon him. She knew too much about what could happen in a cell.

She'd have to go to her father's sometime. He had another desk appearance ticket, with which she'd have to deal; and then she'd have to have another painful discussion with Carla Jankel; another excruciating interview with Kent: explaining the situation, and asking for another day's leave. This would be her life, she thought acidly: cleaning up after her father; bailing him out until a court put him away on the spot; pretending she didn't know he didn't care.

Pretending they were still a family.

She drank her coffee, and stared her future down, dry-eyed. There were no good options: her dad would keep drinking, keep getting picked up, acquire a record that any ill-intentioned person could search. The whole photographic fuck-up would pale beside the damage that a drunken, criminal father would cause her.

It would all come out when the exhibition opened. Some hack stringer would research all of them, and plaster it over the papers. *Secrets of the Misfit Cops*, no doubt: *that* would be a great headline. Tyler's history, O'Leary's sexuality, Andy's past, and her father. They'd be made out to be a disaster, if the media were minded to go that way, and Casey's natural cynicism was pretty sure that they would. Another disaster with which the team would need to deal.

She desultorily made herself some lunch, unenthusiastically ate most of it, and settled down to try to read. She was jerked out of her miserable morass by a knock on the door, whereupon she remembered that she'd told Carval he could visit this afternoon. She supposed, dully, that it was better than dripping into her book.

"What's wrong?" were the first words out of his mouth. He hadn't even unbuttoned his coat.

"Same as yesterday. Dad…and what the exhibition will do to us. All of us. They'll put everything out there. All the history, all the issues. The whole team'll be ripped open and our guts displayed in every tabloid rag."

"It didn't happen to the panhandlers."

"No. You know why? Because a journalist would never find the right panhandler. They move around, they're all interchangeable until you've known them for a while, they don't like talking to others and they're scared of well-dressed people because they've been hurt by them too often. But we're all instantly identifiable – and like I said, there are plenty of other cops who'll rat us out."

Carval thought, unwinding his navy scarf, taking off the heavy coat that had replaced his leather jacket. "We can head it off."

"How?"

"Get your story out there first. Kent'll do that for you: he wants *good* PR and he'll do a hell of a lot to make sure of it. Academy prize-winners, top solve rate, overcoming challenges, decorated veteran, gay rights, women's equality, ethnic mix…. The team's got it all, if it's spun right. You can shape the narrative. Everything else'll look like sour grapes after that, especially against your solve rate."

"You think?" she queried.

"Yeah. Allan could help, too. He's pretty good at fending off annoying newsies and gossip hounds."

"I'll think about it." She wandered in the direction of the kitchen, shutting down the conversation. "Coffee?"

"Please." He followed her, and when she'd switched the kettle on, wrapped her in. "It'll be okay," he said. "Don't think about it now."

"I'm not," she said, but the hunch of her shoulders and tension in her neck betrayed the lie as she measured coffee into her Gaggia, taking particular care with the settings.

Coffee provided, Carval succumbed to his instincts and tucked Casey back into his arm, where she fit just nicely. He didn't like this caution, the need to check himself before each move, but he liked it less when Casey was absent from his comfortable world. Somehow, without her, it became uncomfortable, and when he was uncomfortable, his shots changed: shifting with his moods.

He turned to a different subject. "Do you have a clear suspect yet?"

Just as he'd hoped, Casey flicked out of her miserable mood into full-on hunting mode. "Yeah. The Washingtons did it. We just have to prove it. They were skimming, and using the money to tithe."

"Tithe? Stealing to *tithe*? I thought the Eighth Commandment was 'Thou shalt not steal'."

Casey stared at him, wide-eyed. "*You* can quote the Commandments by number?"

"King James Version," Carval stated smugly, and then grinned at her shock. "I went to an old-fashioned Sunday School for a while – my parents thought I should be well-schooled in underlying cultural assumptions – and the teacher believed in the beauty of the language, even if some of it is a bit, um, mis-translated."

"I'd never have guessed," Casey marvelled, and then went back to her case. "Yeah. It doesn't seem right, but it looks like that's what they were doing. We need the financials to prove it, but with luck they'll come through tomorrow. And then I'll tie them all up in a nice bright ribbon and put them away forever."

"Is it always about money?"

"Huh?"

"The three big cases that I've shot have all been about money. Fraud, porn and money, and money. Is it always money?"

"Not always. Sometimes it's love – or they call it that, anyway. Sometimes it's anger. Sometimes it's money. Why?"

"It changes the story if it's nothing but money. It's a different backdrop." He regarded her seriously. "You don't *look* like bean-counters."

Casey choked on her coffee. "Us? Bean-counters? You...you..." She dissolved in an incoherent swirl of irritated indignation. "You *snapshotter*!"

Carval was laughing too hard to be indignant in his turn. "Got you good," he chortled. "You should see your face."

"You *rat*!"

Casey didn't get any further, because Carval took full advantage of her straightening up to plant a kiss full on her lips.

"And now you're back to normal, spitfire," he smirked. "So how about I – mmmffff!"

Casey wasn't inclined to let Carval keep the initiative, and effectively shut him up by kissing him back. Her advantage lasted barely a moment, but it was enough. She lost herself in the instant arousal: obliterating thought, regrets, and misery in one explosive clash of lips. He wasn't taking any prisoners – but then, neither was she.

Her phone rang, shattering the mood.

"Clement?"

"Catkin?"

Oh, *hell*. It was her father. She couldn't deal –

She had to deal with him. She pulled on cool composure like a coat. "Dad? What's up?" she said, determinedly breezy.

"I thought we'd been to court and it was all done," he wavered, "but I've still got the pink ticket. What do I do with it? Can I just throw it in the trash?"

Casey's crashing hopes didn't make it to her voice. "Dad, that's a new citation. After the hearing, you went to a bar." She didn't mention any of his hurtful words. "You got picked up again, and because you'd had one violation, they handed you another ticket. You have to go back to court for the new one."

Carval watched, not Casey's face, which was white and strained, but her free hand, which had knotted into the ribbing at the bottom of her soft blue sweater, worrying and rubbing. Her voice, horribly, remained absolutely calm: *we can solve this so don't you worry*. She was about to – yep.

"Look, Dad, it's Sunday. I'll be over for dinner as usual. Should I bring something?"

"Yes, please. One of those nice pies – peach, for a change?"

"Okay. I'll see you around six. We'll deal with it then. Bye."

"Bye."

Casey delicately put the phone down, and stared at it, unseeing. "He doesn't remember. That was three days ago, and he doesn't remember because he got blackout drunk right after the hearing. Now I have to do it all over again." She glanced at her watch. "It's already nearly four. I need to go out and get a pie, and probably something we can eat. The last meal was inedible." Her face was set. Her words wobbled.

"I'll come with you, if you want," Carval said, and then watched in utter disbelief as her eyes welled up. His arms were around her a second later as she sobbed hopelessly into his sweater. "What did I say?"

"Nothing," eventually dribbled out of the mess of tears. Casey straightened up, detached herself, and scrubbed her eyes. "Sorry." She wouldn't meet his gaze. "You don't have to come shopping with me." She forced a rictus that wasn't even a cousin to a smile. "I didn't think you did domestic. You only ever seem to eat takeout."

"I don't do domestic. But I do pies. I love pie. I can manage to heat it up. Maybe they'll have apple, or cherry, or peach. Anyway, I'm coming with you. You never know, there might be something to shoot, or you might fall over a corpse."

"It's my day off. If I fall over a corpse I'll call it in and someone else can have it. This isn't my patch anyway."

"Shame."

"Don't wish people dead," Casey said sharply. "Enough of them get dead already."

"I guess so. Pies, then. Nobody'll ask you to investigate the death of a pound of apples."

"It sounds like all I'd have to do is ask McDonald to pump your stomach."

"Ugh," Carval said, as they left.

Pies purchased, Carval began to follow Casey back to her apartment.

"Aren't you taking the pie home?"

"Sure, but I'm taking you home first."

"I think I can find my own way to my apartment. I've only lived in Manhattan my whole life."

"I wanna," Carval said stubbornly. "Besides, I can't kiss you goodbye in the street."

Casey quirked an eyebrow over a still-red eye. "Who said you could kiss me goodbye anywhere?"

He smirked smugly. "You were quite happy to kiss me earlier, so I'm returning the favour. Anyway, I've had an arm around you all the time we've been out, so unless there's been a major change in the definitions, I guess you're quite happy with me."

"Uh?" Casey said inelegantly. Had she not even *noticed*? Clearly not, since now that she *did* notice, his hand was planted on her waist, holding her in. "Oh. Uh…"

"And you're home," he pointed out.

"Oh." She mechanically opened the door.

"So now I can kiss you goodbye. If that's what you want, of course. I wouldn't kiss you if you didn't want to be kissed."

Casey was, briefly, tempted to remove the smug smirk from his face by saying that she didn't want to be kissed. The only problem with that was that it would be a blatant lie, although she wanted to be hugged considerably more than she wanted to be kissed. She removed the issue by stretching up and planting a peck on his cheek, which resulted in a considerably more enthusiastic kiss being planted on her lips. A hug also arrived, which helped.

She pulled away.

"Huh?"

"I need to get ready to go to Dad's." Her brief wince didn't go unnoticed. "No point in borrowing more trouble. I might as well look like the smart corporate lawyer he wanted."

Carval, sensibly, didn't comment. "Okay," he said. "See you tomorrow in the precinct?"

"Yeah. If we're lucky, we'll have financials. If not, I'm sure you can amuse yourself."

Carval watched Casey withdraw behind a cool façade, and bit back words that wouldn't help. It was clear that she was preparing to deal with her father.

"I don't want to do this," she whispered.

He hugged her again. "If…" he ventured. "If you need to, come by after." He left it at that, dropped a final, futile peck on her curls, and departed.

***

Casey pulled up at her father's apartment, but sat in the car for several moments before she could force her face to compliant calm and her roiling tension down to a level that would allow her to eat. She would rather have walked into a gang gunfight unarmed than deal with her father tonight, but she steeled herself. He was, after all, her only family.

"Hey, Dad," she greeted him, and presented him with the pie. "Peach."

"Looks delicious. I'll put it on the counter."

"What are we having first?"

"Southern chicken tenderloins."

They'd had that last time. "And?"

"I got potato wedges and some peas."

"Sounds nice. Can I do something?"

Her father swung his gaze to her, revealing bloodshot eyes, the whites yellowed. "Uh, maybe you could cook the potatoes and peas?"

"Sure, Dad. Give me a little room to work. The potatoes'll take longer than everything else." And she could, unobtrusively, make the whole of dinner. "Actually, go sit down. You'll hover, and then I'll misread the package."

Her father wandered to his armchair, and…oh. Oh, shit. Picked up his glass, half full of pale amber liquid, and sipped. She didn't comment, but turned away, and surreptitiously wiped her eyes as she bent down to find a tray for the wedges. She'd put the tenders on with them, after a few minutes.

By the time the wedges were in the oven, she'd blanked her face. They'd take twenty-five minutes, but she'd break that up by putting on the chicken, and then the peas. Maybe she could defer the difficult discussion until she'd eaten.

She could. Her father didn't refer to the pink ticket once, confining his conversation to irrelevant stories of his professional days; of construction and architecture, and the constant arguments between architect, site surveyors, clients and constructors. It would have been amusing, once, when he could tell a story without the ghastly, gaping pauses; the disconnections and the shift from one client to another mid-sentence.

Finally the meal was done. The pie, at least, had been good.

254

"Dad," Casey opened, "you called me about the pink ticket. Do you have it there?"

He startled, and then looked guilty. "Uh, yes." He fumbled through papers on the coffee table, and found it: held it out, crumpled and soiled. She rapidly read down it.

"Okay. We'll need to get Carla Jankel back. Likely this time they'll give the judgement straight away – she said it was unusual to have to wait."

"Okay. I...I don't remember it, Catkin. Why don't I remember?"

"I don't know." She couldn't say *because you're drowning in whiskey and it's starting to tell.* "But, Dad, they won't go easy on you. Violations like this add up, and you don't want that. They get tougher if they see you more." She wanted to add *lay off the booze*, but that wouldn't achieve anything. Even being arrested again hadn't achieved anything.

"Will you call her? Please?" He sounded like a small boy, pleading for help.

"Of course. I'll do it first thing tomorrow." What else could she say?

As soon as she could, she left, but she didn't start the engine until she was sure that she could see clearly. Morning, and her team, and her investigation, couldn't come soon enough. She sent Carval a brief text, simply telling him that she wouldn't come by, and didn't question why she felt the need to contact him at all. His reply came almost immediately: *OK. Tomorrow.*

Carval regarded Casey's text with astonishment. She'd actually contacted him – actually told him what she'd do: albeit that she wouldn't come by. Compared with any time since he'd met her, that was a major change for the better. Even if there were no explanations, it was an improvement, and anyway he knew why she wasn't coming around: it was because she wouldn't let him see her cry again; couldn't or wouldn't explain her father again; couldn't bear the truth.

A problem shared, for his Casey, was merely a short route to a problem doubled. Nothing like experience to teach her that, he supposed. He resigned himself to seeing her tomorrow in the precinct, but fell asleep more hopeful than for some time about their relationship.

***

Once more, Casey hit the precinct far too early, taking out her pain on the speed bag, but by the time – also earlier than usual – that the others joined her, she had showered and changed, leaving no evidence except slightly reddened knuckles. She knew that O'Leary had noticed, but he didn't comment.

"I want those financials," she complained.

"It's not even nine o'clock. They probably haven't even opened the e-mail yet. Then it has to go through their processes. You won't see them before lunchtime. You *know* that, Casey," Andy pointed out.

"I can't *do* anything till we get those financials. I want those Washingtons wrapped up like a package and then I'll grill them till they're ashes."

"Mixed metaphors," Andy smirked.

"Go be cultural somewhere else," Casey humphed. "Or speed up those financials."

When lunchtime rolled around, Andy had called the bank twice (to prevent Casey calling, which wouldn't help anyone, especially the bank clerk) and Casey had tidied up the paperwork to such an extent that not even a comma was misplaced. She'd also called Carla Jankel, but she didn't mention that. Her morning hadn't been improved by her discussion with Jankel, whose surprise at being retained again so soon had been palpable even through the phone.

O'Leary was hunched protectively around his chaotic desk, since Casey, having polished hers into pristine, perfect emptiness, was eyeing up his as a target for her fretful fingers.

"Lunch," O'Leary said firmly. "An' don't even *think* about touchin' my desk. I know where ev'rythin' is, an' you'll mess up my system."

"System? That's a *system*?"

"Looks like a stratum to me," Andy quipped. "No diamonds, though, just coal."

"Lunch," Tyler suggested. "Food. Don't need coal."

"I don't got no coal," O'Leary mourned, "an' there's a draught around my toes."

"Lunch, or are you having whine?"

"Food, I guess, since sympathy ain't on offer."

"Nope. And if anyone's getting sympathy, it's me, 'cause I haven't got those financials and *that* means I can't have a nice interrogation."

"Better get you coffee, then."

"Raw meat, more like," muttered O'Leary, with an evil grin. "An' here it comes."

Carval was ambling up, having noticed the team standing and shrugging into coats, hats and scarves. "Hey," he smiled.

"Lunchtime," Casey said. "Wanna tag along?"

Three men gasped, and then O'Leary smiled sweetly. "Aww. You've patched it up. Ain't that lovely?"

"Lunch," Andy said sardonically. "Before Bigfoot gets sappy and we all drown in maple syrup." Tyler was already halfway to the stairs, Andy and Casey following.

O'Leary held Carval back for a second, and winked at him. "Nice goin'," he murmured. "Now, don't you pair screw it up again. All this fuss makes my fur spiky, an' that's no good for anyone."

Carval merely grinned back at him, and then loped after Casey. O'Leary clumped after all of them.

CHAPTER THIRTY

In Popeyes, Carval sat next to Casey. Magically, none of the other men got in his way. Much more magically, at least to the three cops, Casey looked...well...happy. An air of relief descended, swirled around, and dissipated before Casey noticed. Carval kept both hands firmly on the table, but managed to press his knee against Casey's for the whole of the short lunchbreak. As ever, nobody said anything about it, though the cynically amused glances told their own tale.

"Time to get back," Casey decided. "Can we give the bank another call?"

"They'll refuse to talk to me. Leave them alone. They won't work any faster if you hassle them."

Casey subsided into another pit of grumbling, which made lunchtime no different from the morning so far.

"Why does it take so long?" Carval asked.

"The bank has to check the warrant, and only then pull the records. So if one of those is slow – usually the first one – we have to wait." Andy shrugged.

"How long?"

"Depends. It's a big bank, and it's murder, so...not too long."

"I want it now," Casey muttered.

"Let's go back and find out. You'll only fret till we do."

Back in the bullpen, the e-mail was obdurately empty of the Washingtons' financial records, and Casey and the team were reduced to cold cases and more waiting. Carval prowled around, taking photos of frustration and fretful fidgeting, and then resorted to shots of hands. He wanted to go and ask Kent for permission to take his photo, but didn't think it would go down well, though he was almost bored enough to try.

Finally, well into the afternoon, Casey yelped happily. "We got them!" The team crowded around her. "Okay. Andy – you follow where the payments *from* their accounts went – especially to the church. Tyler, see if you can find anything to do with phones – and then try and match it up to those unknown calls into Asher's phone. O'Leary, you see what went *into* their accounts – everything but the trust. I'll match the amounts from the trust to it coming in." She bared her teeth. "Let's go get them, guys."

Carval shot the answering predatory smiles, and considered calling the sequence *Stalking the Prey*. Not one of the team noticed him: absorbed in their work. He finished, and slipped out, leaving Casey a short note shoved under her almost-oblivious nose; receiving only a tiny wiggle of fingers in return.

Two hours later, the team gathered in a conference room, and spread their work out on the table.

"What do we have?"

"Inwards," O'Leary began, "we got two salaries, 'bout what you'd expect, an' nothin' else reg'lar except what I guess is the trust fund. And there's some one-off type big numbers, that I think musta come from the trust. Checked up on the salaries, an' they're comin' from the right places. I hafta say, they couldn't have afforded that there house on 'em."

"Yeah, but we know they didn't have to. The trust paid."

"Yeah. So anyways, that's it."

"Okay. The amount that goes in from what you think is the trust fund all matches up, pretty exactly. Out of the fund and into their account."

"Now here's the fun thing," Andy said with cheerful malice. "Not all of that amount is reaching the church."

"You don't say!" O'Leary gasped with utter insincerity. "Waaallll, I'll be."

"Colour me not surprised," Casey said flatly. "Go on?"

"A lot of it's going churchwards – I didn't check every time, but it looks like Pastor Jarmyn's had around two years of monthly tithes that he shouldn't have had" –

"Not that he knew it" –

"No – totalling," Andy paused for dramatic effect, "quarter of a million dollars, near enough."

"The *fuck*?" Tyler ejaculated.

"Wow. Okay, so the trust could afford it, but Asher would've been sure to notice that." Casey's eyes narrowed.

"Yeah. So would the final audit, faster."

"What wasn't going to the church?" she asked.

"About another half," Andy said.

"*What!*" came from the other three.

"Yep. Supplementary income of almost five thousand a month."

"What about those one-off amounts?" O'Leary asked.

"It's not clear."

"Credit cards?" Tyler suggested. "Debts?"

"Marlon had a bit of a chequered past," Casey mused. "Borrowed money from his brother, and didn't pay it back. Did we ever find out why?"

"Don't recall as we did," O'Leary thought aloud. "You thinkin' gamblin', mebbe?"

"Maybe. Who told us about it?"

"Pastor Massapa," Tyler filled in. "Could ask him if he knew more."

"An' that lawyer – Chigthorne. He'd know more – he was good pals with Asher's pa."

"Okay. As soon as we're done with this, check with them. Anything else?" She looked around the men.

"Usual expenses, but those big one-off receipts tend to go with big one-off payments. One or two are vacations, or furniture stores, but the rest aren't really clear. Checks, so there's no easy way to know."

"Tyler – phones?"

"Monthly payment to Verizon – single payment to AT&T."

"Two?" she asked.

"Yeah. Verizon's the known phones. Don't know about AT&T. Put a request in."

"Mm," Casey hummed. "We don't need that to haul the Washingtons in. Do we have the range information? Who was doing it?"

"Fremont. I'll check," Tyler replied.

"Okay. That'd be nice to know." She looked around. "I'll hole up in here and think about interrogation tactics. Let me know if we get anything else."

"Sure," came back in three-part harmony. The others departed, and Casey began to put her thoughts and evidence in order.

An hour of concentrated thought later, with no further information from Massapa, Chigthorne or Fremont, Casey had a plan. She'd *prefer* to know why Marlon had needed to borrow money from his brother, and she *really* wanted to know whether the Washingtons were members of a range, but she had enough to tear into them already, and if they got flustered and scared, they'd likely admit far more than they wanted to.

"Got a call from Pastor Massapa," Tyler said almost before she'd come into the bullpen. "Didn't *know*, but suspected Marlon liked the horses."

In the background, O'Leary completed a call and ambled over to join them. "That was Chigthorne," he grinned. "Marlon liked sports. An' he liked bettin' on sports, too. Shame he weren't no good at it. Pa Washin'ton bailed him out from some not so nice guys. He'd owed a lot. Pa was pretty loud about it, then, but it only happened but once, so it was all patched up an' friends again."

"Once that Chigthorne knew about," Casey said cynically. "Probably why he only got a hundred thousand – it would all be lost to betting. What're the chances he's gambling again?"

"Pretty high," O'Leary said.

"All I need now are the ranges," Casey mused. "How's Fremont doing?"

"Finishin' up. Likely tomorrow, though."

"Perfect. That's our jam, but we got the doughnut here already." She smiled nastily. "Got them."

Satisfaction swirled around her, which promptly shattered at the sight of Kent emerging from his office, scowling at the team.

"It's well after shift end, Detectives. Why are you here?"

"Planning the interrogation of the Washingtons, sir," Casey said. "We'll bring them in tomorrow. Their financials make it clear that they were skimming."

Kent harrumphed. "Okay. Be out of here in the next half hour."

"Sir."

Kent took his own advice, and left. The team tidied up, and, after a brief plea for beer by O'Leary, roundly rejected by everyone else, dispersed.

Casey considered Carval's short note, now tucked into her pocket, and decided that his place seemed good to her. She'd put her father and the call to Jankel out of her mind, but now that she'd finished work, they had returned. She went up to Carval's apartment less cheerful than she had been.

"Hey," he said, surprised. "I didn't expect you this late."

"Kent kicked us out, and I'd gotten far enough." She made a face. "I'd *like* one more bit of information, but I can grill the Washingtons without it."

"When?"

"Get them in mid-morning, most likely. Uniforms'll pick them up before they go to work."

"So mid-morning *actually* means around nine a.m.?"

"Yep."

"Ugh."

"You don't have to be there," Casey provoked, sitting down.

"Of course I do," Carval blurted. "Every interrogation's crucial to the story. Even with blurred faces the atmosphere and emotion comes through. I have to be there" – he clocked her smirk, and the strain beneath it. "That's mean. You're yanking my chain." He dropped down beside her. "If you're going to rag me, I won't give you any coffee."

"No coffee, no stay," she flipped back.

Carval waved his hands in a concessionary gesture. "Coffee, then." Before he rose, he hugged her, and felt the stress in her spine.

Coffee brewed, Carval provided another friendly hug, expecting nothing much in return. Casey turned into him, and buried her face in his sweater.

"I had to call Dad's lawyer again," she forced out, determinedly not crying. "Explain…. I'll have to go see her, soon. I can't take Dad. He…he'll drink because he can't face the truth and that won't help anything." She choked back emotion. "If Birkett hadn't been there then I wouldn't have had to say out loud that they had to treat him like anyone else and maybe he'd have been…maybe they wouldn't have given him the ticket but I had to say it. I can't ask for favours, but Dad's taking the pain because of it…"

"No," Carval disagreed bluntly. "You did the right thing. If your dad hadn't gone to a bar, he wouldn't have been picked up. You couldn't have done anything else. It's not – well, okay, maybe this Birkett – who is he?"

"Marcol's technoweasel sidekick," Casey said bitterly.

"Oh. Okay. Well, anyway, maybe he can try and make trouble, but I thought O'Leary had scotched that with Kent?"

"Yeah, so he says." Casey sounded entirely unconvinced.

"The *point* is, none of it would've happened if your dad hadn't gone to the bar. And there's no way you would let anyone do you favours like that, and the results aren't on you. It's integrity. You wouldn't do it. You just wouldn't. It shows – it shines through all my shots. All four of you, not just you." He became aware that Casey wasn't listening, probably because her whole attention was focused on not crying. Words became inadequate. He petted, and reflected that though he'd wanted Casey to let him in, he'd much rather she were letting him in to happiness, not the disaster of her father's alcoholism.

She pulled herself together far too quickly for Carval's peace of mind, and sat up. "Sorry. It's not your problem. It'll be fine."

He raised his eyebrows, deeply sceptical.

"It has to be. Carla can get him a fine, not jail time. He hasn't done anything except get drunk. They won't put him inside for that." She didn't sound convinced.

They will the next time, Carval thought, *if not this time.*

"Anyway, I need to think about the Washingtons."

"Or try not thinking at all." He tipped her woebegone face up and kissed her. "No need to think." He kissed her again. "Just feel." He pulled her in. "It'll be okay," he asserted, and kissed her deeply enough that she responded. Her hands slid around his neck to hold him to her, exploring deeply and beginning to go further, and though he was sure that she was seeking oblivion, he'd invited that; and he'd much rather have her than not.

He stroked down her back, loosening the silky t-shirt: a steel-blue shade that shouldn't suit her dark hair and eyes, but did; his hands slipping up on to the skin of her back, smooth and warm. She made a pleased little noise, and pressed closer.

"Take me to bed," she murmured, and whispered, "Something good."

Carval kissed her hard, and then stood up, tugged her up after him, and took her to the bedroom. Her t-shirt slithered over her head; her pants slid down and puddled at her feet, joined by his sweater, shirt and then jeans; and then he sat on the edge of the bed and drew her down, lying back and leaving her atop him where his hands could roam.

Fingers moved, mouths met, Casey sighed and Carval gasped as he moved within her and tipped her over the edge with him; and then he gathered her close and simply held her; her head on his chest, legs tangled; breathing slowing. He'd go clean up in just a minute, after he'd cuddled her in....

Casey woke, disoriented, weighed down and wrapped in, before she remembered that she was in Carval's apartment, and therefore the weight had to be Carval's arm, keeping her next to him. She snuggled back down – and then woke up fully. She had to go. Not because she wanted to – she didn't – but because she had no clean clothes here. She peered at her watch. Five a.m. How was it five a.m.? They'd fallen into bed before nine, surely, and, oh, who cared? She'd *slept*. She nudged Carval, and when he neither woke nor indeed moved, elbowed him harder.

"Owwffff," he wheezed. "'s not morning." His eyes didn't open.

"I have to get home," Casey said.

"No." He curled around her, intelligence not in evidence. "No go."

"I have to get clothes and go to work." She had an idea. "Interrogation photos," she rapped into his ear.

"What? Where? Now?" His feet were out of the bed before he remembered to open his eyes.

"This morning. I've got to get home and change."

"Urgh. You have to go?"

"Yeah." It wasn't her first choice of action. "I'll see you in the precinct. Don't be late. We'll be starting interrogations at nine." She decamped hastily.

It wasn't until Carval was almost asleep again that he realised that Casey had actually woken him to tell him she had to go, rather than sneaking out. He fell back to sleep smiling.

***

"Uniforms have gone to bring the Washingtons in," Casey told the team. "O'Leary, with me. We're taking Marlon. Andy and Tyler, I want you to take Sella."

"Split them?"

"Yeah. I'm leaning to Tyler's theory that one called Asher and one shot him. But 'cause he didn't have his phone, he didn't stop to take a call. So I wanna split them and go in hard on Marlon about the gambling and the rifle, and you two can take Sella about the trust and the money – what is it, Fremont?"

Fremont stopped his dash to Casey's desk and gathered himself. "Detective, both Sella and Marlon Washington are members of the same range. I called the range, and they said they're both pretty good. The range master said they do a bit of hunting."

Casey's eyes lit. "Guess we've got a second string now. Change of plan.

We'll keep them together. Tyler, you and Andy get over there and execute the search warrant – it authorises entry without notice, but we know their house will be empty. Get an officer to stay there till you get there so we don't need to break the door down. Let's get that rifle into Ballistics with *urgent* stamped all over it, and we'll have that moving while they're on their way to Interrogation."

"Sure." Tyler and Andy hurried to the door, and Casey looked up at O'Leary.

"Are we good to go?"

"Yep."

"Then let's *do* this."

"Coffee first," O'Leary drawled, "otherwise you'll be even meaner than you usually are. They won't be here for another hour, anyways."

Casey glared at his guffaw, but she took her espresso from him anyway, and went out to review her strategy and evidence. She fretted fruitlessly: wanting to be in two places at once: the Washingtons' house and here, interrogating.

"Hey," Carval said. It sounded like it wasn't the first time.

"Hey." Her fingers tapped on the desk, clicking impatiently. "They're on their way."

Carval took a couple of quick shots of her restless fingers, and didn't comment. Casey put her head back down and studied her strategy until, finally, an officer told her that the Washingtons were in Interrogation.

"O'Leary?" she called. "Showtime."

Carval dashed to Observation. Casey and O'Leary didn't hurry themselves to Interrogation, agreeing with two glances that the Washingtons would be better for a little stewing, before Casey cooked them.

Menacing formality pulled on, Casey and O'Leary marched into the interrogation room. Sella was perfectly calm. Marlon already had a fine dew across his forehead.

"Do you have some news for us?" Sella asked.

"Not yet. We'd like to ask you about the trust arrangements that Asher's parents set up. First, just to keep everything regular, we'd better read you your rights." She read the Miranda warning, and they confirmed they understood. Sella didn't flinch. Marlon's forehead beaded.

"Now, can you tell us about the trust?"

"Sure," Sella said, and related almost the exact history that the cops already knew – except for the need for a final audit.

"You haven't mentioned that there has to be a final audit, instructed and supervised by Marswell & Eglinton, and conducted by an accounting firm who's never been involved with the trust."

"There is?" Sella said. "I guess that makes sense. Who should I contact to arrange it?"

"It's already in progress," Casey noted casually, and watched Sella's hands drop out of sight. Marlon hadn't been as smart. His fingers were locked tightly.

"That's good."

"The auditors will be looking into the withdrawals from the trust – and the authorisations." Casey opened her file at a bank statement, but left it upside down. Sella flicked a glance at it. Marlon openly tried to read it. "There were a number of payments which don't seem to have any proper purpose. For example, you were receiving five thousand dollars a month."

"Asher wanted us to live comfortably," Sella said smoothly. "He was a kind and loving boy, and he held to the Commandments. Honour thy father and mother. Even though we weren't his parents, he treated us as though we were."

"And the ten thousand a month going to the church?"

"Tithing. Asher believed in our mission to help others, and he was glad to do it."

"Interesting," Casey said, and let her disbelief shine. "I would have thought that Pastor Jarmyn would want to talk to Asher – thank him for his contributions, at least, as befits a man of God."

"Once Asher moved into his own home, he worshipped elsewhere."

"Strange," O'Leary rumbled, "that he didn't tithe to his own church, then. Where did you say that was?"

There was a tiny, uncomfortable pause.

"He supported Pastor Jarmyn's youth outreach work," Sella said, but everyone knew she'd evaded the question.

"Do you have Asher's agreement to the payments?" Casey asked. "They're big sums."

"We were family. We didn't need it written down." Marlon finally spoke.

"It's not written down?" Casey let her incredulity hang in the air. "So how will you prove to the auditors it's all above board?"

"Asher agreed." Sella took back control. The cops weren't sure that she hadn't kicked Marlon to shut him up.

"Did he agree to the one-off payments too? How will you show that?" Casey smiled nastily. "What were those for?"

Another pregnant pause occurred. Marlon was sweating profusely. "I…. Asher was helping me out. I…I was gambling. I've tried to get help, but…I was foolish and listened to temptation. He saved me."

"I'm guessing there's no evidence for that either?"

"He agreed. It's all in the family, anyway. Even if we can't show the auditors a paper trail, it's all in the family."

"Is it?" Casey asked.

"What do you mean?" Sella asked sharply. "We're Asher's next of kin." Marlon's mouth hung open.

"Mm," Casey hummed. "Didn't you know that Asher had made a new

will?"
Both Washingtons gasped, faces drained of colour. "What?"
"Asher had made a new will. You are not the beneficiaries."

CHAPTER THIRTY ONE

Absolute silence fell. Frantic calculations ran across Sella's face, Marlon merely gaped, flicking glances from Sella to Casey to O'Leary's imperturbable mass.

"You really didn't know," O'Leary marvelled. "Now, ain't that a thin'. Iffen you didn't know that, mebbe you didn't know that Asher was gettin' engaged. Bought the ring an' everythin'."

Neither Washington spoke.

"I'm thinking that you didn't know Asher all that well. If you didn't know that, how did you know what he wanted about tithing and helping you? He'd have been starting to cleave to his own family – his fiancée – and maybe they'd have different views." Casey waited, in vain. "Everything we've found out about Asher says that he didn't want to tithe. I don't think he knew about it. I don't think he knew about the money you were stealing from him. Because if he'd known, he'd have discussed it with his fiancée."

"Asher agreed," Sella asserted.

"But you can't prove it. Looks like you were skimming, and oh, how dreadful," Casey bit sarcastically, "just about the point the trust ended – even if you didn't know about his engagement it would end when he was thirty, so pretty soon – he turns up dead, and you thought you'd inherit everything."

"Tithing isn't skimming!" Marlon disagreed. "Render unto God that which is God's."

"You stole from Asher to pay it to the church. Thou shalt not steal."

"Giving to God is not stealing," Marlon cried. "Asher should have" – Sella elbowed him, too late.

"So Asher didn't know. Stealing is stealing, whether the money is used for a good purpose or not." Casey made a note. "When the auditors have worked out the full amount of the theft, we'll know how much you should repay. You won't be needing the house or the money in prison. Tell me," she added conversationally, "did you kill Asher because you knew he'd have you prosecuted, or because being found out would ruin your good Christian reputation?"

"We didn't!"

"Your home is" – Casey blatantly checked her watch – "being searched under a warrant right now. You, Marlon, own a rifle. It's on its way to ballistics testing. You're both members of a gun range, and the range master says you're pretty hot stuff with a rifle."

"None of that proves anything."

"Not on its own. But it's enough to hold you till the search is completed, though the amount you've skimmed would do that. Don't worry, we'll give you a receipt for everything. We don't steal."

Even Sella winced at that shot.

Casey stood, and summoned two officers. "Take them down to Holding and get them processed. Thanks." She watched impassively as they were walked away, and then turned to O'Leary. "How long d'you think Ballistics will be?"

"Quick, iffen they know you're after them," he grinned.

"Let's give Tyler and Andy a call: find out what they've got." Her phone rang before she could dial. "That's them now. They must have something."

"Casey," Andy's light tones bounced through the speaker. "Guess what we found!"

"Just tell me."

"No fun. We found the rifle – it's already gone to Ballistics," he added, before she could ask, "but we also found a GoPro, so it's gone for DNA testing, *and* we found three cell phones. Can you tell us the Washingtons' cell numbers and that burner number?"

"You want to call them to see if one of them matches up to any of the numbers that called Asher's phone just before he was shot? Surely they wouldn't be so dumb as to keep a burner phone?"

"Worth a try. Criminals can be stupid."

"Yeah, but *that* stupid? I mean, sure, two of them'll be their ordinary cell phone numbers. I'll dial from here. You watch the phones."

"Beers on me iffen it works," O'Leary drawled, "'cause ain't nobody that dumb."

Casey read out the numbers, and dialled as she read. "Marlon's cell," she said, and clearly heard the ringtone – it sounded like *The Lord is my Shepherd*. "Sella's." Another ring – an upbeat gospel tune.

"*Oh Happy Days*," O'Leary identified. "Don't seem too appropriate right now."

"No," Andy agreed. "Okay, let's go with the unidentified numbers – we figured the ones that called between five and five-forty-five?"

"Yeah." Casey started dialling them from the phone records.

The first four numbers didn't ring the unidentified third phone. The fifth number connected, and the third phone sounded: a tinny electronic toll of judgement.

"They really were that dumb!" O'Leary squawked. "How do they remember to breathe without someone helpin' them?"

"I bet Marlon was supposed to throw it in the trash, and didn't. We can split them on that, next go-around, or we can wrap it up in a hurry."

"C'n we get it wound up by five?"

"Why?" Casey asked O'Leary.

"'Cause it's Valentine's Day, an' I got plans with Pete." He smirked evilly at the phone. "An' I reckon Tyler's got plans that don't involve the gym mats but do involve that Allie-girl of his, don't you?"

Tyler said nothing. Andy wasn't as restrained. "That looks like a blush to me," he gibed. "Oooohhhh."

A certain quality to the silence indicated that Tyler was unimpressed.

"You got plans, Casey?"

"Nope."

"Yes, you do," Carval said, appearing out of nowhere. "Well, I have a plan."

"Aww," O'Leary began, swiftly cut off when Casey glared at him.

"We have a case to close," she said briskly. "That comes first. All your romantic plans will have to wait."

O'Leary pouted, like a giant toddler. Carval merely grinned. "They'll wait," he said. "When are you interrogating again?"

"We could start now, but I'd like Ballistics, just to tie it all up in a neat bow."

"The rifle went off about an hour ago – we searched for it first, and it wasn't difficult to find. It's probably only just gotten there. Give them an hour, and then call, if they haven't called you first," Andy suggested.

"Put a rush on it," Tyler added. "Should be priority one."

"I don't want to wait," Casey grumbled, "but I guess I have to give them a little time."

"We'll be back soon," Andy said. "Leave CSU to it."

"Found the right things," Tyler added.

"Okay. If you start back now, you'll be here in time for the final act."

"Don't raise the curtain without us."

"Hurry back, then. If you're late, we won't wait."

"On the way."

"Better get a coffee, then, iffen we ain't goin' terrorisin' suspects for another hour or more. You'll explode without one." O'Leary turned her to the break room.

"Mean."

"Naw, that's you. Small and mean."

"Overgrown bully," Casey sulked.

"C'mon," Carval stopped the bickering. "Coffee. I'm thirsty."

Supplied with their favourite forms of caffeine, the three perched in the break room. O'Leary acquired an evilly mischievous grin, and looked from Casey to Carval and back again.

"Valentine plans?" he queried. "An' surprises. Aww. Ain't that sweet."

"Butt out, Bigfoot," Casey snapped.

"Don't be like that. Someone's doin' somethin' nice for you. You oughta appreciate it."

"That someone isn't you, so I don't need to appreciate you."

"Unkind," he grumped. "I'm just lookin' out for you."

"Look out from a lighthouse. There's one by the South Street Seaport."

O'Leary chortled. "I don't need a lighthouse. I'll just stretch up on my tippy-toes."

"Don't do it in here, you'll be billed for breaking the ceiling."

"Guess so," he said amiably. "So mebbe I should just leave you two to discuss these plans you don't know about?"

"Yep," Carval said, before Casey could comment.

O'Leary waggled his eyebrows, and then smiled fondly. "Don't let me stand in the way of romance," he beamed, and exited, leaving Casey fulminating behind him.

"Oversized Cupid," she growled. "All he needs are wings and a quiver of little golden arrows. Big sap."

"Don't you want to know what the plan is?"

"You *meant* it?" Casey squeaked. "I thought you were just pulling my leg."

"That could be arranged," Carval oozed. Casey glared. "You're cute when you're mad," he improved the shining moment. The glare intensified. "Okay, okay. Yes, I meant that there are plans."

"What plans?"

"Flexible plans," Carval teased. The twin lasers of Casey's eyes burned into his skull. "Can't I surprise you?"

"I don't like surprises," she admitted. "They're not usually good." Carval waited. "Mom...Dad...photos...Marcol showing up on cases..."

"Oh. Okay, um, well...I made a reservation for dinner."

"Yeah? Why are you worried about that? We've had dinner before."

"Yeah. In fast food joints and burger bars. This...um...isn't."

270

"I promise not to eat the peas off my knife," Casey said dryly, "or lick the plate where anyone can see."

"I didn't mean that, and anyway if I took you to Jean-Georges or Balthazar we'd be interrupted every two minutes."

"So what did you mean?"

"Well, there's a little Italian restaurant not too far from my apartment, and the food's fabulous and they're really nice."

Casey scrutinised Carval's face. He almost seemed...*shy*? Carval didn't do *shy*. Arrogance, pushiness, cheekiness...shyness was definitely new. She looked again. Not shyness, nervousness. "Okay," she said. "But don't you have to give them a time? I don't know when we'll be done – it depends on CSU."

"Er..." Casey's eyebrows conducted an interrogation all on their own. "They'll keep the table." The eyebrows inquired further. "They always do."

"Why? You're not George Clooney."

Carval actually blushed. "My parents...we used to go there when I was a kid, okay? I've been going there forever."

It took Casey a moment. "You...you want to take me to somewhere they actually *know* you? Know Jamie, not reality photographer playboy Carval?" She drew a few fast, shallow breaths.

"You already agreed," he said. "You can't back out now."

"This" – she stopped her sentence short. Carval's eyes held something that she didn't want to damage. "Yes. Okay. When we're done tonight, we'll go."

His eyes lit up, but all he said was, "Great!"

"More coffee," Casey decided, wondering exactly what she'd signed up for, but not willing to ask questions to which she didn't necessarily want answers. This dinner felt meaningful, but she had a case to solve, and that came first. She looked up at Carval, lounging against the counter in the break room, watching her through those penetrating blue eyes, alert for the next shot, and briefly laid her hand on his, gone almost as soon as it landed. He blinked, but before he could form words Casey had gone, back to her desk and her strategy, with her refuelling container of caffeine.

***

One hour to the second after Andy's call, Casey rang Ballistics.

"Clement," she said. "Do you have results on that rifle from the Washington case yet?"

"Casey, why do you do this to me?" the tech asked plaintively. "You're not the only cop in New York, and we're supposed to deal with all of you."

"C'mon, Evan. I've got my perps waiting in Holding. I just need this to send them down for Murder One. You know you love it when we close cases fast."

"Only because it means you don't call me every hour on the hour," Evan muttered.

"Mean."

"But fair."

"C'mon. Do you have something for me?" she wheedled.

"Yeah. Your boys said it was urgent, so we squeezed you in, and…"

"Tell me already."

"It's a match."

Casey emitted a long whistle, and grinned at the phone. "Thanks, Evan. I owe you."

"Sure do. I'll add it to the rest of your IOUs, and you can buy me champagne all night when you *finally* cough up."

Casey laughed. "Thanks," she said again, and cut the call.

"Guys!" she called. "We got it."

Tyler and Andy, barely in the door, and O'Leary, hurried over. Carval stayed back, taking shots: capturing the team's elation at their success.

"Ballistics matches. That's all we need. Fremont!" she rapped. "Get the Washingtons back into Interrogation."

"Yes'm," Fremont said, and dashed off.

"Let's go really spoil their day."

"You goin' to tell 'em who the beneficiary really is?"

"Oh, I think so. Should go down well." They exchanged evilly satisfied looks.

"They're in Interrogation, Detectives," Fremont confirmed.

"Shall we?" Casey said.

"Let's," O'Leary replied, and gestured theatrically for her to precede him. Behind them, the others scuttled for Observation, dragging Fremont along with them.

"Your rifle, Mr Washington, was the rifle used to shoot Asher," Casey announced.

Sella's jaw dropped.

"Are you surprised that it was your husband, or surprised that he didn't dispose of the gun like you told him to?"

"How" – Sella began, and clamped her lips shut.

"Which of you actually took the shot? My bet is it was you, Sella, and when we find your fingerprints we'll have proved it."

"You won't find any fingerprints because I didn't do it, and nor did my husband."

"So how come we found Asher's GoPro in your house too? And the phone used to call him while he was out running – except that didn't work because he didn't have his phone. Good shot, to hit a running man in semi-dark."

"Asher's GoPro?"

"It's gone for DNA testing."

"Why would we have his GoPro?"

"Oh, I dunno," O'Leary drawled. "Mebbe because you took it off him when you held him down in the snow to suffocate?"

"There's no way you could prove it's Asher's."

"Wrong again. He'd linked it to his laptop to post updates. So when we charge it up and switch it on, it'll go live." She paused. "Sella and Marlon Washington, you are under arrest for the murder of Asher Washington. One of you called, one of you shot. It doesn't matter which way around it was, because that's conspiracy to commit murder, and the charge and sentence are the same for everyone involved."

"I want a lawyer," Sella said.

"Certainly. You can wait for one in the cells." She paused. "Oh. Didn't you want to know who Asher's beneficiary is?"

"No," Sella said.

"Yes," Marlon blurted, over the top of her.

"His fiancée. Kayla Burton. The woman you hoped wasn't important to him."

Sella lost it. "That conniving, ungodly, little *slut*. Living in sin and corrupting Asher away from the Church and righteousness" –

"Kayla wasn't – yet – living with Asher. And she knew nothing about his trust fund – in fact, she doesn't even know she's the beneficiary."

Sella continued to pour out bile and venom until Fremont appeared, to take them back to Holding and allow their call to a lawyer.

"Waaaallll," O'Leary stretched out, as long as the Mississippi but far slower, "I guess we're done for the day?"

"Yeah. They're all tied up, ready for the prosecutor."

"Evening's free, then."

"Is it?" Kent inquired, from behind them. "Are you sure of that?"

"Sir?" Casey said blankly.

"I might require you to report to me on both the case and your team dynamics," he said, straight-faced. "I might also require you to assist Dr Renfrew in completing his research into the team."

"Sir."

Unusually, Kent smiled. "But I won't." The team breathed a sigh of relief. "Good work. Take the evening, and come back fresh tomorrow." His face turned stern. "And there will be no more team spats, or matters that require me to intervene."

"Sir," they said in chorus.

"Now, git!"

They didn't linger. Kent in a good mood and actively encouraging them to have a relaxing evening was sufficiently rare that they didn't test it. Amazingly, Tyler was first out of the door, swiftly followed by O'Leary's mass. Andy sauntered off without comments on his evening, which left only Casey and Carval.

"Do I need to go home and change?" she asked.

"Only if you want to. It's not formal – though I'd love to see you in an actual dress, not just pants or a skirt." His eyes gleamed, imagination running wild. "But you don't have to."

"I think I want a shower. Sella made my skin crawl."

"Okay. I'll pick you up" – Carval consulted his watch – "at seven? That gives you a couple of hours, and I'll let Mario know we'll be there around seven-thirty."

"Okay. See you then." Casey started for the door.

***

Captain Kent regarded the space where his team had been with satisfaction. They'd fixed themselves, and it looked like Clement had forgiven Carval. He sighed with relief, which was only partly to do with the preservation of the excellent solve stats of his precinct. He cared about their well-being. Secretly, of course. It would ruin his hard-ass reputation if anyone thought he actually had *feelings*.

His face twisted as he thought about Marcol's behaviour, and Birkett's. He had feelings about them, oh yes: all of them angry. Cops shouldn't behave like that. Still, he knew the situation now, and *that* meant that he would be on top of anything, hm, *untoward*. Renfrew might be the worst stick-up-his-ass guy that Kent had dealt with, but Agent Bergen did good tech work. Kent already knew that Bergen had acquired a clean copy of the existing records, checked them for alterations, and preserved them safely.

He everted his lips in a vicious not-smile. If anyone tried to meddle with the records, they'd quickly find out that they'd made a career-ending mistake.

***

Casey considered her clothing options while in her shower, briskly washing her hair and the taint of murderers from her skin. They weren't extensive. She had no reason to have elegant dresses or designer outfits, so she didn't. She had two dresses, but one of them was a classic, demure, little black number and the other, um, wasn't. It was crimson, a little lower cut, a little shorter, and emphasised her cleavage in a way that would undoubtedly knock Carval's socks off, followed later by the rest of whatever they were both wearing.

It was also a clear statement that she was more into this than she'd previously admitted. She chewed her lip, and then a fingernail. So far, Carval had chased her: tonight, in this dress, she'd be making it clear that she wanted to attract him.

She nodded her head decisively, and pulled on the red dress. She even put on a fraction more make-up than her normal minimal efforts: a second coat of mascara, some eyeshadow and eyeliner, and even lip gloss, and finally found a pair of higher heels, though, since tottering was not attractive, they still didn't qualify as *high*. She looked at herself in the mirror, mainly to check that she hadn't mascara'd her nose by accident, and then waited.

She didn't wait long. Carval was dead on time, which was a little surprising, since punctuality was only a feature of his when photography was involved. So far, times had generally been vague on both sides, firmed up by a last-minute call or text. She let him in, and turned to collect her coat.

He turned her back, hands on her shoulders, and simply...stared.

"Wow," he breathed. "You look fabulous." His hand went to his pocket, half-pulling out his camera, and then slid it away again. "Could I" – he hesitated, then went for it – "Could I shoot you? In that dress? Now?"

Casey boggled. "You what? Photo? Me? Why?"

"Because that is the sexiest fucking thing I've seen in *years*," Carval blurted out.

"So why do you want a photo? To kiss goodnight?"

"I'd rather have the real Casey."

"So why?"

"It's...look, it's just a great photo, that's all. I can't *not* want to take great photos: that's what I *do*."

Casey boggled some more, and gulped. "Uh...okay."

Carval's camera went into overdrive. It left his pocket faster than an Old West gunslinger's draw, firing off far more shots, faster. She hadn't blinked twice before he was prowling around the room, shooting from every angle.

"That's enough," she said, wondering whether he'd teased out another piece of her soul and transferred it to film.

He stopped.

"No more," she said. "I don't want you to take any more photos." She swallowed, and straightened up, meeting Carval's concerned expression.

"You okay?" he asked, came back and hugged her close. "They're not for anyone else to see. Except you, if you want to."

She dropped her eyes, turned away, buying time to think. "I just wanna have a nice dinner with you."

"I think we can manage that," he murmured, and kissed her deeply,

275

removing all of her carefully applied lip gloss.

"Let's go," she said, and took his hand. "You can show me the shots later."

Fin.

ABOUT THE AUTHOR

SR Garrae grew up in Scotland and then worked in international finance in London until her retirement. She lives in the UK with her family, who are somewhat bemused by but supportive of her complete change of career.

She always loved books, but didn't start to write original fiction until after she retired. She now balances writing with travel, reluctant but very necessary gym visits, and designing her own book covers.

Printed in Great Britain
by Amazon

79248940R00164